D0421915

LAST ACT

By the same author

A Piece of Resistance
Last Post for a Partisan
The Judas Mandate
Seven Days to a Killing
The October Plot
Skirmish
State Visit
The Mills Bomb
Backfire
The Winter Touch
A Falcon for the Hawks
The Russian Enigma
A Conflict of Interests
Troika
A Different Drummer
Picture of the Year
Death of a Sahib
Missing from the Record
In the Red

LAST ACT

CLIVE EGLETON

St. Martin's Press
New York

This book is for Maria Rejt and Ania Corless
and all my Polish friends.

LAST ACT. Copyright © 1991 by Clive Egleton. All rights reserved. Printed
in the United States of America. No part of this book may be used or
reproduced in any manner whatsoever without written permission except
in the case of brief quotations embodied in critical articles or reviews. For
information, address St. Martin's Press, 175 Fifth Avenue, New York,
N.Y. 10010.

Library of Congress Cataloging-in-Publication Data

Egleton, Clive.
    Last act / Clive Egleton.
        p.   cm.
    ISBN 0-312-05887-X
    1. World War, 1939-1945—Fiction.   I. Title.
PR6055.G55L37   1991
823′.914—dc20   90-27506
                                                                        CIP

First published in Great Britain by Hodder and Stoughton Limited.

First U.S. Edition: July 1991
10 9 8 7 6 5 4 3 2 1

LAST ACT

Chapter 1

Granger left the fairground in Battersea Park, crossed Albert Road and started looking for a car in Salamanca Avenue. Triumph Mayflower, Morris Oxford, Zephyr, Mini, Ford Prefect or Austin Westminster; the make didn't matter, nor was he after the latest model. His choice was governed by the strip of plastic bonding tape in his jacket pocket.

He walked on, the music from the carousel's steam organ gradually fading away to nothing in the still night air. All he needed was the right sort of car in the right place and he would be up and away in no time. The pale blue Zephyr convertible which eventually caught his eye was parked in the shadow of a horse-chestnut tree, a good twenty yards from the nearest street light. Although the elderly SS Jaguar directly behind it was almost touching the rear bumper, Granger reckoned there was enough space between the convertible and the Hillman Minx in front for him to pull straight out from the kerb. Furthermore, the terrace houses on either side of the road in the immediate vicinity were in darkness, which suggested that the occupants had retired for the night.

Some people he knew would have cut a hole in the canvas roof and reached inside to open the door, but Granger was an artist and deplored such crudeness. Using the bonding tape, he eased it past the weather-proofing and the central pillar, then hooked the looped end over the protruding door catch and raised it up to release the lock. After that, it took Granger just over two minutes to hotwire the ignition and start the engine. There were no late-night pedestrians about when he drove off and no lights came on in any of the houses.

Martin was waiting for him at the entrance to the fairground, a redhead on one arm, a blonde on the other. The redhead was Terri Watts, a twenty-eight-year-old grass widow whose husband was a steward on a cruise liner, or so she had told Granger soon after he had picked her up. They'd met on the dodgems when he and Martin had deliberately bumped the car she was driving with her blonde cousin, Lena. Two well-stacked tarts out for a good time, two randy stags with money to burn; Granger thought a professional dating agency could not have made a better match. Not only that, everyone had known exactly where they stood the moment he and Martin had started to put their hands in their respective pockets. Now, some four hours and approximately fifteen quid later, the time had come for both Terri and Lena to repay some of their joint hospitality.

"Don't tell me this is your car?" Terri said as she got in beside him.

"'Course it isn't, I just nicked it, didn't I?" Granger said and laughed uproariously.

"Idiot."

Terri pinched his thigh, then moved her hand upwards until it was almost resting in his crotch. She was wearing a blue satin blouse with a plunging neckline and the short, tight black skirt was riding high enough to give him a glimpse of a pink suspender. The proximity of her hand and the display of the goods on offer were a little too much for Granger and he began to erect.

"Down, Fido," Terri said, playfully tapping the bulge.

Granger reared back, inadvertently stabbed his foot on the accelerator and lost control of the Zephyr convertible. The car swerved across the centre line which put it on a collision course with a Wolseley saloon parked on the opposite side of the road. In the back seat, Lena disentangled herself from Martin's sweaty embrace and shrieked loud enough to wake the dead. Reacting instinctively, Granger yanked the wheel hard over to the left and missed the other vehicle by a cat's whisker.

"Watch what you're doing," he shouted. "I damn nearly had an accident back there."

"Well, we certainly can't have that, can we?" Terri said, giggling.

Granger took a deep breath and slowly exhaled. Presently, his pulse beat returned to something like normal. "Let's see," he said, "you live in Vauxhall, right?"

"No, Southampton. Got a nice semi-detached in Highfield."

"But you said . . ."

"I only said I came from Vauxhall, meaning I was born there. Matter of fact, our house was just round the corner from Lena's mum and dad. They invited me to spend a few days with them because they know how lonely it can be when Roy's away at sea."

Granger continued on Battersea Park Road into Nine Elms Lane angry that he had allowed himself to be taken in by a red-headed prick tease from the sticks. All the readies he'd spent on Terri was money down the drain. She wasn't going to come across; when they

2

arrived at her aunty's place, it would be a quick peck on the cheek, thank you and good night. Martin was trying to do a number with Lena in the back seat but a quick feel was about all he was going to get.

"So where does your aunty live?" he growled.

"Bonnington Square."

"How about giving me some directions then?"

"You want to go on to the roundabout beyond Vauxhall Underground Station and turn into South Lambeth Road."

Granger heard a faint tapping noise in the rear, wondered if it was coming from the transmission tunnel, then Lena moaned softly and he realised that in her mounting excitement, she was drumming her high heels on the floor.

"I'm glad someone's having a good time," he muttered.

A police car appeared in the rear view, its blue and white sign on the roof rapidly filling the whole mirror as the driver closed on the stolen Zephyr. The police were still there, sticking to his tail as he approached the roundabout. The temptation to put his foot down in an effort to shake them off was almost irresistible but somehow Granger managed to stay cool. No one could have driven more carefully or paid greater attention to the highway code; trafficator winking to show that he was turning right, Granger edged his way into the flow. The police car drew abreast and for a brief moment or so they were motoring side by side, then it veered away towards the Albert Embankment.

"I bet that shook you," Terri said.

"What?"

"Those rozzers, they seemed very interested in this car. Are you sure it belongs to you?"

"Don't be daft, of course it does."

They were on South Lambeth Road now, the railway embankment carrying the main and suburban lines out of Waterloo on their right.

"Do we keep straight on?" Granger asked.

Terri shook her head. "Next left."

A few minutes later, she told him to take the second turning on the right which led to a housing estate.

Four multi-storey blocks, each named after a Labour politician, were positioned haphazardly around a grass-covered communal area which in turn was broken into segments by the access road and numerous footpaths. On the east side of the estate, there was a play area for the children consisting of a seesaw, four swings, a climbing frame and a slide. Terri directed him to the south-facing

3

Morrison House and suggested he should park the Zephyr round the back.

"I wasn't about to stop outside the front entrance," Granger told her.

He halted in the shadow cast by the block of flats and applied the handbrake, then, with the gear still engaged, he let the clutch out and deliberately stalled the engine.

"Lost the ignition key, have we?" Terri asked and smiled knowingly.

"Yeah, I suddenly discovered I'd got this hole in my pocket." Granger twisted round. "I expect you want to stretch your legs, don't you, Martin?" he said.

Whoever nicked the car enjoyed certain privileges. It was an unwritten agreement they had between them and he didn't have to press the point. Without a murmur of protest, Martin got out of the convertible, dragging a complaining Lena with him.

"Got it all worked out, haven't you?"

"So have you; this isn't Bonnington Square."

"Well, we don't want to shock Aunty, do we?" Terri said, then opened the door and got into the back.

Granger followed her, gratified to find that she wasn't a prick tease after all. He closed the door behind him and almost fell on top of her in his eagerness.

"Take it easy," she murmured. "What's the hurry?"

But Terri was just as impatient; her open mouth fastened over his and she began to undo his flies the moment he shoved a hand up her skirt. At the crucial moment, she raised her hips off the seat, making it easier for him to remove her nylon briefs. Then he slid into her and began to thrust.

The man who came through the roof of the Zephyr convertible had stepped off the parapet eight storeys above. He was carrying a certain amount of ballast which increased his all up weight to approximately twelve stone. Consequently, he slammed into Granger with the force of a piledriver and broke his spine. Pinned beneath their combined weight and splattered with blood from both men, Terri found it difficult to breathe. Her chest felt as though it was slowly being crushed in a giant press and she couldn't slide out from under because Granger was wedged between her thighs. She opened her mouth to scream for help but nothing came of it except an animal-like grunt and she could feel herself slipping into unconsciousness.

The jumper was Stefan Zagorski. A former officer in the Polish Home Army, he had arrived in London via Warsaw, Colditz and

Paris. Still alive when the ambulance men arrived on the scene, he was rushed to Lambeth General where, following an emergency trepanning operation to relieve the pressure on the brain, he was put on a life support machine. Inside the breast pocket of the jacket he had been wearing, the police found a wallet containing his naturalisation papers, three one-pound notes and a letter addressed to a Mr Michael Kimber MC, CG of 'Roselands', Cathedral Close, Salisbury, Wilts. On the franked envelope, someone had written in a shaky hand, 'Not known at this address, return to sender'.

1944
WARSAW

Tuesday 1 August
to
Monday 2 October

CHAPTER 2

Safety razor, a much-depleted stick of shaving soap, a brush that had lost most of its bristles and a square of white towelling that served as a face flannel: Michael Kimber checked the contents of the drawstring washbag to make sure he hadn't overlooked anything, then tucked it into the small haversack containing his few personal belongings which would be handed over to his host for safe keeping. He looked round the subterranean room which had been his refuge for the last hundred and forty-eight days and nights and wished he didn't have to leave. It was hardly the Ritz; poorly lit by a sixty-watt bulb and lacking every facility apart from a camp bed, a metal wash bowl and a foul-smelling earth closet in one corner, the bolt-hole was cold in winter, oppressively warm in summer. But he had felt safe here in the improvised cellar of this house situated on the outskirts of the Wola District of Warsaw and it was highly unlikely that the next place would be anywhere near as secure.

Kimber undid the top two buttons of his shirt and pulled out his dog tags. Number, rank, name and blood group; the two metal discs were the best protection a man in his position could hope for. They proved he was a British soldier, not a partisan, and should make the Wehrmacht think twice before they stood him up against a wall or put a noose around his neck. So what if he had been a prisoner of war? It was a soldier's duty to escape and the Germans wouldn't hold it against him because he'd swapped places with an NCO so that he could join a work party outside the wire from which he had then quietly slipped away. But it was the Polish Underground who had taken him under their wing and that could alter their whole attitude. The Poles were regarded as Untermenschen who were marked down for special treatment and in the eyes of the Gestapo, there was such a thing as guilt by association.

He looked at his reflection in the cracked mirror his host had provided and saw a gaunt face that should have belonged to someone much older than twenty-four. And with his thinner features, the

9

jagged scar high up on the right cheekbone, which he'd acquired in childhood when he'd blundered into a trailing bramble and damn nearly put his eye out, now seemed much broader and longer than it used to be. Few Poles had his coppery hair, so they had blackened his with some kind of home-made vegetable dye which irritated the scalp.

But it was his pallor that people would notice. For close on five months now he hadn't been outside the house in daylight and it showed. Halina, the guide he was waiting for, had said she would pass him off as a consumptive if anyone asked, and conceivably they might get away with it. He had lost twenty pounds since he was taken prisoner at Salerno in September '43 and his weight was down from twelve stone to ten eight. Although hardly a walking skeleton, he was only a half inch under six feet and the clothes provided by the Resistance had once belonged to a much fatter man and therefore swamped him.

Kimber heard footsteps on the cinder path above his head, then the man of the house raised the trapdoor which was disguised as a cold frame and for the first time in months he felt the sun on his face. A home-made ladder was lowered down to him; quickly positioning it at an angle against the wall, he picked up the small haversack containing his belongings and climbed out of the hole to find Halina waiting to embrace him.

"This is the day Poland begins to live again," she said dramatically and threw her arms around his neck.

"I'm happy for you," Kimber said, "for everyone. It's been a long time."

She nodded. "Five years – but we have them on the run now."

A Soviet tank division was reported to have captured Wolomin, ten miles north-east of the capital, and for days now the population of Warsaw had watched the demoralised units of the 9th German Army heading west across the three principal road bridges over the Vistula. All the German civilians had left and even the Governor of Warsaw had fled the city, though only briefly. It was 1918 all over again, or so the Poles maintained. Kimber had witnessed none of these events for himself but the man of the house had been full of it and had spoken slowly so that he should understand him.

Halina led him into the house, inspected his appearance with a critical eye and gave the threadbare jacket a quick once-over with a clothes brush.

"You have your work permit and identity papers?"

"In my breast pocket."

"Your name and address?"

"Josef Maly, Poznan Street 44, Wola."

"In Polish," Halina snapped.

"Sorry." Kimber answered the question again, haltingly in the smattering of Polish he'd acquired while on the run.

"Try to sound breathless and don't forget to cough. You're supposed to be suffering from TB. It will also be helpful should anyone ask you something you don't understand or if you can't think of the appropriate expression in Polish."

Kimber smiled. "Don't you worry, if things get tricky, I'll cough my head off."

"Are you ready?"

"Yes."

"Then we should go."

Kimber embraced both the man and the woman of the house, said goodbye to their children and left with Halina. The ground had been covered with snow that winter's afternoon in February when the guide had brought him to the house, now it was the height of summer and the dirt road had been baked hard as a rock. Halina took his arm and they walked on down the street past identical-looking timber frame houses, each boxed in behind a low wooden fence and surrounded by sunflowers. At the end of the street, she turned left into a paved road, then took the second one on the right which led to the last tram stop on the city centre line.

They would leave the streetcar before it reached the Saxon Gardens in the centre of town and make their way on foot to the flat above Kuba's Café on Jasna Street near Napoleon Square, roughly half a mile south-east of the tram stop. The flat was to be the headquarters of the 5th battalion of the Home Army commanded by Stefan Zagorski. Kimber had never met him, but there was nothing unusual about that. All over the city, small groups of men and women, who had never come together before, were moving to pre-arranged assembly points to form platoons, companies and battalions. They were the Home Army, the Armja Krajowa, commonly referred to as the AK; but whatever their title, they were essentially a guerrilla force organised on a cell system. For such a force to suddenly change its tactics and fight a conventional battle would, in normal circumstances, be tantamount to committing suicide. Circumstances, however, were anything but normal because, as everyone kept repeating, the once mighty Wehrmacht was now a demoralised rabble.

Kimber wanted to believe it. What troubled him was the sight of ten JU 87 Stuka dive bombers from the airstrip at Bielany heading east towards the Russian lines. They did not support the contention that the Germans were finished; nor did the hard-eyed men of a reconnaissance patrol who passed them in their half-track as they waited at the tram stop.

Stefan Zagorski raised his binoculars and for the umpteenth time studied the two main objectives assigned to his battalion. According to Intelligence sources, the main post office in Napoleon Square was guarded by two NCOs and six riflemen; unfortunately, part of the building was occupied by a field post office and courier unit and estimates concerning the strength of this unit varied from an officer and nine to one and twenty-four. Even though most of the soldiers were either too old for combat duties or medically unfit, Zagorski thought it only prudent to assume they would give a good account of themselves when the chips were down.

The complex housing the headquarters of the Occupation Police and the SS Internal Security troops was in the next street, slightly to the left and rear of the main post office. This was the other objective he had been given and was likely to prove an even tougher nut to crack. At any one time, there would be a minimum of fifty well-armed men in and around the area. From a purely numerical standpoint, his battalion outnumbered the combined enemy force by almost six to one but that advantage was more than cancelled out by a lack of real fire power. The assault companies would be armed with a variety of automatic pistols and Sten guns, weapons which could be broken down into their component parts and were therefore that much easier to smuggle into the city centre. However, compared with the Mauser rifles, Spandau machine guns and Schmeisser machine pistols the Germans had, they were inaccurate, had a much shorter range and lacked stopping power. To make matters worse, the Home Army was short of hand grenades.

"If we seize the Prudential Insurance building, we'll dominate the whole area."

Zagorski glanced at the younger man crouching beside him at the window. He had never worked with Jan before and had only met him for the first time a little over an hour ago, but he knew his reputation. An electrician by trade, Jan was said to be shrewd but argumentative, courageous but foolhardy. He was also a natural born leader and blessed with more than his fair share of arrogance which was a pretty dangerous combination. When the attack went in, Jan would be commanding the company on the right flank.

"There are no Germans in the Prudential."

"All the more reason for taking it," said Jan.

The Prudential Insurance building was sixteen storeys high and the only skyscraper in Warsaw. From the rooftop, an observer had a panoramic view of the city from the Citadel in the north to the inland harbour in the south and eastwards from the suburb of Praga on the right bank of the Vistula to the working class district of Wola beyond the old Jewish cemetery and the fire-blackened ruins of the ghetto in the west.

"And what do we do to the Fascists after we've captured the skyscraper? Make faces at them? Most of the weapons your men are armed with have a maximum range of one hundred yards. They couldn't even hit the post office from the Prudential building, never mind the guards."

"What's your problem? The rifles and machine guns will arrive with the second wave," Jan told him airily. "That's when we start to pick off the Germans."

"And what's to stop them picking your company off first? There's a lot of open ground out there."

"We launch the first phase of the attack under cover of darkness."

"Brilliant." Zagorski snorted derisively. "Everyone else is ready to go at 1700 hours except the 5th battalion." He took a deep breath, then said, "No more arguments, the attack goes in as planned."

Zagorski left the window and returned to the table and chair which served as a desk in the centre of the room. He had enough problems to contend with without Jan, the boy General, wanting to change everything at the last minute. The battalion was under strength, poorly armed and short of ammunition for what few weapons they did possess. There were no radios, and to communicate with his company commanders and Area Headquarters, once it was established in the Victoria Hotel, he would have to use one of the runners waiting in the next-door flat across the landing.

Runners. Zagorski scowled. Young women and boy scouts; who could say how they would behave when they came under fire? And to cap it all, Headquarters had wished this Englishman on him who was about as fluent in Polish as he, Zagorski, was in English. But never mind, some genius of a professional staff officer at Area had overcome that little difficulty by detailing a woman called Halina to act as an interpreter.

And what was this Englishman going to do? Why, he was supposed to interrogate the prisoners of war captured by the 5th battalion, a task he was well qualified to undertake since his mother was an Austrian. Well, he had news for him; the 5th battalion weren't about to take any prisoners, they were strictly in the business of killing Germans.

*   *   *

13

The eight AK men who had been detailed to collect the small arms from the secret cache in Wilson Square, north of the Citadel in the Zoliborz District, went about their task as if the Wehrmacht had long since withdrawn from the city. Every man wore an armband in the colours of the Polish national flag and made no attempt whatever to conceal the rifles being carried up from the basement of the apartment house to the waiting horse-drawn cart. Furthermore, the NCO in charge of the work party had posted two sentries, one armed with a shotgun, the other with a Schmeisser 9mm MP38 machine pistol which had been stolen from a German Army supply depot in the early days of the war.

In one respect, Warsaw was no different from any other occupied city in Europe and there were the usual number of collaborators amongst the civilian population. Having been tipped off, a mobile patrol consisting of four uniformed police officers from the German Field Gendarmerie arrived on the scene in a Kübelwagen while the AK men were still loading the horse-drawn cart. The sentry armed with a shotgun opened fire before the Kübelwagen was within effective range and the spread of shot merely peppered the windscreen. Even so, the driver decided to get the hell out of Wilson Square and, skidding to a halt, he started to make a three point turn.

The police vehicle was broadside on across the road when the man with the Schmeisser emptied the entire magazine in one long burst, riddling the bodywork of the car from the nearside front mudwing to the rear fender. Both police officers on that side of the vehicle were killed instantly, the one in the rear falling out to lie face down in the road while the lower half of his body remained inside the car. The driver, who had been hit in the right leg, hip and shoulder, crawled out of the Kübelwagen and tried unsuccessfully to draw the Walther PPK automatic from the pistol holster with his left hand. The fourth officer survived the initial burst of fire only to be shot in the face at point blank range by the sentry with the shotgun when he tried to surrender. The driver died a few minutes later, clubbed to death by the other members of the work detail.

There was one other casualty, a little six-year-old girl playing with her doll's pram outside one of the apartment blocks on the other side of the square. She was hit in the stomach by a ricochet, but none of the AK men noticed her when they made off in the horse and cart.

Kimber did not witness the incident, nor did he hear the gunfire, but he and Halina were caught up in the aftermath when they encountered a checkpoint in the neighbourhood of the Saxon Gardens some ten minutes after they had started walking from the tram stop. The soldiers conducting the snap check were in SS uniform but there was nothing Aryan about their features and it was obvious they had only seen the Third Reich as prisoners of war.

"Azerbaijanis," Halina whispered.

Kimber nodded. The ranks of the SS were full of former Red Army men, Balts, Ukrainians, Georgians, Crimean Tartars, Uzbeks, Azerbaijanis – representatives of every racial minority in the Soviet Union who'd become turncoats for a variety of reasons, not least the promise of pay, regular food and better living conditions.

There was no way of avoiding the checkpoint. To retrace their footsteps would only arouse suspicion and although they hadn't passed a sentry as far as Kimber was aware, he was sure the German Scharführer in charge of the Azerbaijanis would have put out a cut-off to intercept anyone who attempted to backtrack.

The young man who proved his theory had followed them into the street and was some ten to fifteen yards to their rear when he suddenly lost his nerve and wheeled about. The Scharführer whipped the butt of his assault rifle into the shoulder and ordered him to halt; when he failed to do so, the NCO opened fire. Simultaneously, the cut-off started blazing away from a second-floor window of an apartment house a good twenty yards away. The copper-jacketed rounds struck the cobbled road and ricocheted, buzzing like angry bees around them. Kimber pulled Halina down and made her hug the ground as one of the Azerbaijanis pointed his rifle in their direction and began to squeeze off one shot after another.

"Nicht schiessen," Kimber bellowed. "Nicht schiessen."

He stood up slowly, raised his hands and repeated Nicht schiessen until the Scharführer ordered his men to cease firing. By then, the Polish youth was lying flat on his back, a ribbon of blood oozing from beneath his body to find a meandering route around the cobblestones towards the gutter.

The Scharführer removed his left hand from the assault rifle, crooked a finger at Kimber and pointed to the row of civilians lined up on the sidewalk outside a block of flats.

"Schnell."

Kimber stooped down, helped Halina to her feet and held on to her arm as they walked forward to join the other Poles. Her pallor matched his; there were beads of perspiration on her forehead and she was trembling as though gripped by a fever. As well as being the only woman to be caught up in the snap check, Halina was

15

young, tall and slender. Nature had given her large, beautiful green eyes and high cheekbones in a striking face that both men and women looked at twice and remembered. Worse still, despite the drab, loose-fitting dress, her equally attractive figure was going to be noticed by the stormtroopers and Kimber could guess what they would do to her. So could Halina; she closed her eyes and braced herself for the inevitable mauling.

One of the Azerbaijanis went through Kimber's pockets, turned them inside out and handed the forged work permit and identity card to a German official in civilian clothes before starting a body search. The stormtrooper knew how to inflict pain and tugged the hairs under both arms and around the groin. To Kimber's relief, he did not feel his chest; had the Azerbaijani done so, he would have discovered the dog tags and that would have meant certain death for Halina.

"Your name?" the German official shouted in his ear.

Gestapo. No one had to tell Kimber who the German was. The former Ministry of Religion and Education in what had now been renamed the Strasse der Polizei was crawling with the bastards. "Josef Maly," he said huskily.

"Address?"

"Poznan Street 44, Wola District."

The stormtrooper had moved on to Halina. Out of the corner of his right eye, Kimber could see him feeling her breasts, tweaking the nipples between thumb and index finger. Eventually, the Azerbaijani sought fresh pastures, squeezing her ribs, stomach and flanks before travelling up the inside of her legs from the ankles to the buttocks.

"You're a bank clerk?"

Kimber nodded. The work permit showed that he was employed by the National Savings Trust and he had been warned not to give any further information unless he had to. To disclose the fact that he knew more than a smattering of German would be equally dangerous. Silence and feigned ignorance were his best defence.

"Why are you absent from your place of work?"

"Please?" The question presumed a fluency in German few Poles were likely to possess and he played it accordingly.

"Why aren't you at work?"

The Gestapo agent repeated the question slowly in simple terms, cuffing Kimber about the head to give special emphasis to each word.

"I have been ill, sir."

"What with?"

"Tuberculosis."

Somewhere in the middle of the line-up a man started shouting in Polish with the odd word of German thrown in.

Then the Scharführer laughed and said, "Seems we've caught a Yid for you, Herr Neurath."

Kimber turned his head and looked to the right. The Jew was no more than fourteen years old, under-sized, under-nourished, his large round eyes bulging with terror in a pinched, heart-shaped face. The NCO was holding the boy by his right ear, lifting him up so that he was forced to stand on tiptoe. The Pole who had betrayed him continued to babble away.

"What's he saying now?" Neurath demanded impatiently.

"Apparently, the man we shot a few minutes ago is the Jew's older brother." The Scharführer laughed again but there was no mirth in it. "You want me to despatch this little bastard as well?" he asked.

"No, I'll take him in for questioning. If there are any other Yids still alive in this city, he may know where they're hiding." Neurath rubbed his chin. "Tell you what though, you can shut that babbling Pole up."

"My pleasure." The NCO told one of the Azerbaijanis to hold the boy, then walked up to the man who had betrayed him and casually pressed the barrel of the semi-automatic rifle against the back of his head. "Auf Wiedersehen."

Kimber averted his gaze and stared at the block of flats to his front. Even though he knew what was coming, the ear-splitting crack of the high-velocity round still made him flinch.

"What do you want me to do with the rest of this riff-raff, Herr Neurath?"

"Whatever you like, Scharführer."

"I hear these scum are murdering our boys in Zoliborz."

"You know what to do then," Neurath said.

"You bet I do."

He's going to kill us, Kimber thought. And what are you going to do about it? Stand there passively waiting for a bullet in the brain like some dumb ox in a slaughterhouse? A voice inside his head told him to cut and run but his legs refused to respond. One of the flies that had already been attracted by the smell of the warm blood on the pavement settled on his sweating forehead and slowly walked down his nose; very soon now, it would be feeding on his blood. The Scharführer would execute them one by one; the only issue in doubt was whether he would start on the left or the right flank. Listening intently, Kimber heard him move away and knew that he and Halina had been given a brief respite. Then a Kübel-wagen spluttered into life and ran unevenly.

"Not staying to see the fun, Herr Neurath?" the Scharführer shouted above the noise.

"No, I'll get all the amusement I want from my little Jew boy."

The SS NCO waited until the Gestapo officer had driven off, then slowly retraced his steps, deliberately crashing the steel-tipped heels of his jackboots on the cobblestones to intimidate the Untermenschen, as if they weren't terrified enough already. Halina closed her eyes and moved her lips, praying silently. Standing next to her, a small man with a monk's fringe of greying hair suddenly burst into tears as he involuntarily urinated into his trousers.

"Ein."

A shot rang out and a man in dark blue overalls on the extreme right went down.

"Zwei."

Another shot, another victim dead on the sidewalk, the Scharführer singing out the numbers like the notes of a well-known folk song.

"Ein, Zwei, Zufer . . ."

Jesus Christ, the bastard really was doing just that. He was murdering the prisoners in time to the chorus of the Munich Beer Drinking Song.

"Scharführer – telefon bitte."

One of the Azerbaijanis telling him he was wanted on the telephone? Or did he mean the radio? The SS had obviously arrived in the truck which was parked farther down the road and they were bound to have some means of communicating with their headquarters. Kimber listened to the receding footsteps, strained his ears to hear what was being said, but the lorry was too far away.

A few moments later, a whistle shrilled and the stormtroopers closed on the truck at the double. Someone raised the tailgate after the last man had scrambled aboard and the driver started the engine; then the Scharführer pounded on the roof of the cab and ordered him to move off. But why did he tell him to go slowly? The answer came to Kimber a split second before a Schmeisser opened up, and throwing himself sideways, he brought Halina down in a flying tackle.

As the truck went past them, the driver put his foot down. For some time after the vehicle had departed, they continued to lie there, hardly daring to breathe. When finally they did get to their feet, it was all too evident that they were the only survivors.

CHAPTER 3

Kimber was not the only Allied prisoner of war hiding out in Warsaw. For the past four months, Staff Sergeant Leon Jarrell from Chicago, Illinois, had been living in the attic of a tenement overlooking Lublin Union Square and Lazienki Park in the Mokotow District. Technically speaking, Jarrell was an evader rather than an escaper. A twenty-two-year-old waist gunner in a B24 Liberator, his plane had been shot down over Romania in August 1943 when the 376th Bombardment Group had attacked the Romana Americana oil refinery at Ploesti.

He had been able to avoid capture for two reasons. First and foremost was the fact that although he himself had been born in America, his parents hailed from Cracow and he had learned to speak Polish fluently from a very early age. And secondly, despite his lack of inches and his unremarkable features, the vast majority of women found him irresistible.

Jarrell also possessed a highly developed instinct for survival. His plane had run into a wall of flak shortly after dropping their delayed-action bombs on the oil refinery from an altitude of two hundred feet, and had come out of it with both starboard engines on fire and the wing engulfed in flames. The pilot had climbed, desperately seeking height so that they could bail out before the B24 blew up. Without a static line to open the 'chute, anyone who jumped under a thousand feet was courting death or serious injury. Jarrell had survived because he hadn't waited for the pilot to reach a safe height, nor had he counted up to ten before pulling the ripcord. Tossed about in the slipstream, he hadn't seen or heard anything, but when the canopy had finally opened, the Liberator had vanished.

He had landed in a field miles from anywhere and had started walking north, looking for a hiding place where he could lie up until it was dark. His thinking had been extremely simple; Romania was on the side of the Axis; Poland was an ally and lay to the north. His plan of action had been pretty much on the same unsophisticated level – move by night, live off the land and avoid all human contact until he was over the border.

Barely five days later, Jarrell had been forced to change his plan. The weather had turned nasty, there was no food to be had and he'd gone down with pneumonia. Weak with hunger and delirious, he had staggered into a hamlet with the express intention of giving himself up and had been taken in by a middle-aged widow who'd had other ideas. There had been other benefactors, humble people who'd provided food and shelter and guided him through the Carpathian Mountains into Poland where he had eventually made contact with the Resistance. Jarrell had figured that if they could get him to Gdansk, there was a good chance that he could sneak aboard a freighter bound for neutral Sweden. That idea had gone by the board when he'd made the acquaintance of Maria Bolek soon after arriving in Warsaw.

Maria Bolek was the only daughter and youngest child of a distinguished professor of medicine at the University of Warsaw. Of her two brothers, Konstantin, who was also a doctor, had not been heard of since he had been interned by the Red Army in 1939, while Karol, the younger of the two, was believed to be a pilot in RAF Bomber Command. The man to whom she had been engaged had been sent to Hamburg to work in the shipyards where, according to the Germans, he had been killed in an air raid in September 1943. It was therefore hardly surprising that Maria should have hated the Russians almost as much as she did the Germans.

Maria Bolek had trained to be a teacher and had been employed as such until the Governor of Warsaw had decided that Polish children did not need to be educated and had closed the school down. Jobs had not been easy to come by in 1942 unless you were prepared to work for the Nazis, and she had done just that, carving out a niche for herself as a clerk in the Civil Affairs Bureau in Krasinski Square. To the neighbours, Maria was a collaborator; to the AK, she was an agent in place who was able to supply the Home Army with false identity papers, work permits and a hundred and one other documents used by the Occupation authorities. And because the Germans trusted her, the attic flat where she lived on Josef Pilsudski Street made an ideal safe house.

Leon Jarrell had been sent to the flat the day after he had arrived in Warsaw from Radom. Originally it had been intended that he should stay there for two or three weeks while arrangements were made to move him on to Gdansk, but he and Maria had fallen in love and he had persuaded the AK that he could be of use to them. Before Pearl Harbor, Jarrell had been a typesetter for a jobbing printer on Chicago's North Side but the Poles weren't to know he hadn't worked for the *Tribune* as he'd claimed. They were running an underground press and needed people like him. Besides, he was bilingual and could listen to the BBC, translating the bulletins for inclusion in their own newspaper.

In another hour and a bit, he would be setting the greatest headline of the war – 'Liberation Day – Home Army Seizes Warsaw In Surprise Attack'. In another forty minutes, he and Maria would leave the tenement and make their way to the corner shop in Lublin Union Square where the printing press was concealed.

"You think we're going to surprise the Krauts?" he asked, breaking a lengthy silence.

"Of course we will," Maria said.

Jarrell looked doubtful. "I don't know. For the past two days there have been more troops about than usual. You told me so yourself."

"Only down by the river, Leon, and they were engineers preparing the bridges for demolition."

Jarrell was an airman, not a foot soldier, but it was obvious to him that you didn't leave a bridge unguarded once you had laid the charges to blow it up. It was also a fact that the 9th German Army was going to need the Citadel, Kierbedzia and Poniatowski road bridges and the railway bridge until they were forced to withdraw behind the Vistula. Conversely, if the Wehrmacht held the bridges, the AK would be cut off from their units in the suburb of Praga.

"What's the matter, Leon?"

"Nothing."

"Something is worrying you, I can tell."

"Not on this occasion," he said, lying cheerfully. But the smile on his face faded very quickly when someone pounded on the door and called to Maria in German.

"Go into the kitchen," Maria told him sharply.

"No dice, I'm not leaving you to face the music alone."

"Don't argue with me, just do as I say. I can handle the Fascist scum."

While Jarrell hesitated, the German thumped the door a second time; then Maria pummelled his chest with her clenched fists and he finally got the message.

The kitchen was a small alcove off the bed-sitting-room. In addition to the sink and tiny gas stove, there was just enough space for a broom cupboard which also served as their larder. Kneeling down, Jarrell removed the wooden panel below the bottom shelf and crawled through the false wall into the bolt-hole behind the cupboard.

The walls were less than two feet apart. With some difficulty he stood up and turned round, then lay down on his right side to reach through the hole and replace the panel. As he started to drag it across the entrance, he heard Maria invite the German into their bed-sitting-room and immediately stopped what he was doing.

Although fluent in German, Maria lapsed into Polish every now and then as if the appropriate phrase had momentarily escaped her. Even so, Jarrell only caught the drift of their conversation, but it was enough. The German, who wanted to know why Maria hadn't been into the office, seemed to be satisfied when she told him that she had been threatened by the Resistance and had been too frightened to venture outdoors. Then, from what Jarrell could gather, he offered to escort her to the Civil Affairs Bureau in Krasinski Square and refused to take no for an answer.

It didn't make sense; in another seventy minutes, the offices, shops and factories would close and the rush hour would begin, which was precisely why the Home Army had decided the uprising should start at 1700 hours. Jarrell heard the front door slam behind them with a finality that convinced him that he would never see Maria again. Sick at heart, he crawled out of the hiding place and wandered aimlessly about their bed-sitting-room, an unlighted cigarette glued to the mucus on his bottom lip.

The popping sound in the distance reached him faintly and he froze, his pulse suddenly racing. Another reprisal? There was always one after every act of sabotage. In July alone, more than two thousand men and women had been executed in batches of fifty on street corners throughout the city. But this was different; the firing was sporadic and accompanied by a clanking noise which was steadily drawing nearer.

Tanks? Jarrell ran to the garret window and looked out. Two PzKw IVs with the long-barrel 75mm gun were advancing up Josef Pilsudski Street; he recognised their silhouettes from the illustrations in the training manuals he'd printed for the Home Army. From the rooftop of an apartment house a hundred yards down the road, half a dozen bottles sailed through the air to burst on and around the leading panzer. Each Molotov cocktail contained a deadly mixture of petrol, diesel oil and sulphuric acid which was ignited by a small amount of calcium chloride taped to the outside of the bottle. Within seconds, the armoured vehicle was engulfed in liquid flames which seeped through the ventilation slits and observation vizors. Their overalls on fire, the crew commander, gunner, loader/wireless operator, driver and hull gunner came out fast and were shot down before they had covered more than a few yards. Then the second tank scuttled away like some giant armadillo seeking refuge in its burrow.

The time was seventeen minutes past four. In Mokotow, as in Zoliborz to the north, the uprising had started prematurely.

Kimber unfolded the map and placed it on the floor. Nearly five hours after the massacre, he still had the shakes and needed to do something to occupy his mind. He also wanted to forget the reception he and Halina had received from Stefan Zagorski when they'd reported to the headquarters of the 5th battalion above Kuba's Café on Jasna Street. A slim, austere man in his mid-thirties, the Pole had looked Kimber over from head to toe and had then calmly informed him that he had no use for an interrogator. He had also made it brutally clear that the same applied to interpreters, especially one who obviously had the wind up and was determined to spread alarm and despondency. Consequently, the street map was by way of being an olive branch after Halina had given him a piece of her mind. The gesture, however, had failed to have the desired effect.

"Zagorski is a fool," she said contemptuously. "Of course people have been rounded up and shot out of hand before, but what we saw this morning was different. Those Azerbaijanis who searched us were looking for small arms, hand grenades and ammunition. The element of surprise has been lost, the Germans are ready and waiting for us to attack. Why can't he see that?"

"Zagorski probably does," Kimber told her, "but he knows there is nothing he can do about it. Things have gone too far now for anyone to call a halt."

"He could at least send the children home."

After they had reported in, Zagorski had directed them to the flat across the landing from his tactical headquarters where the battalion runners were assembling. Sharing the back room with Kimber and Halina were four young women and seven boy scouts who were barely into their teens.

"Maybe he could, but I don't think they would take any notice of him."

Kimber orientated the map with the ground, then studied it closely. The battalion objectives were marked in blue, so were the left and right boundaries. As was the practice in the British Army, enemy dispositions were shown in red together with an estimate of strength which, more often than not, was accompanied by a question

23

mark. The main thrust of the Home Army was directed against the rail and road bridges over the Vistula but a mass of arrows indicated that the AK concept of operations was on a far bigger and much more ambitious scale. As well as every ammunition, petrol and supply depot, they were going for the Citadel barracks, the main power station on Good Street down by the river embankment, Gestapo headquarters, the Eastern and Wilno main railway stations in Praga, Danzig and Central stations on the west side, the main telephone exchange, the Bielany airstrip and the Wehrmacht Garrison Headquarters in the Palais Brühl in Theatre Square.

"I hope we've got enough troops," Kimber muttered to himself.

"What did you say?" Halina asked.

"Nothing important."

But it was. Concentration of Force was one of the basic principles of war, yet the Home Army was preparing to dissipate its strength on a dozen or more side shows. Not that anyone would take any notice of his opinion even if he were tactless enough to voice it. The uprising had been planned by professional staff officers and what did his military experience amount to? Nine months in the Officers Training Corps before the war when he was up at Brasenose College, Oxford, reading English, followed by four years in the Army culminating in the landing at Salerno and a prisoner of war camp in Silesia.

"Then why the frown, Michael?"

"I'm trying to think of some way to make myself useful."

Another lie, but Halina was rattled enough already and he didn't want to share his disquiet with her about the map. There were too many arrows on it giving information about the objectives of other AK units which Zagorski did not need to know. Kimber wondered how many copies were in circulation. Only one had to fall into the wrong hands and the Wehrmacht would be able to crush the uprising before it really got underway. The element of surprise had already been lost after what had happened in Wilson Square; now it looked as if the security of the operation had been blown as well.

"It's beginning," Halina said in a brittle voice.

Kimber folded the map away, got up from the floor and walked over to the window. Several of the buildings on the opposite side of Jasna Street had either been destroyed or reduced to fire-blackened shells during the battle for Warsaw in 1939. Through one of the gaps, Kimber could see a group of armed civilians forming up in the back yard of the neighbouring house which was still intact. According to his wristwatch, it was four fifty-one which meant that H hour was still nine minutes away. Only someone with a referee's whistle got tired of waiting and all it took to get them moving was one shrill blast. Like children let out of school at the end of the day, they left by the back gate on the double, whooping eagerly. A few seconds later, a Spandau machine gun opened fire.

Kimber experienced the old, familiar sinking feeling in the pit of his stomach and his legs seemed to be made of cotton wool. It had happened to him at Mareth in Tunisia, at Salerno just before he was taken prisoner, and again that morning when the Scharführer had murdered eighteen Poles in cold blood. There was more firing over to the right in the direction of Poniatowski bridge where a 20mm flak cannon was obviously being used in an anti-personnel role. And why not, there were no Stormovik ground attack planes in the sky.

A young man wearing a red and white armband on the left sleeve of his jacket walked into the room, called for two volunteers and was practically trampled under foot in the headlong rush. Passing up the boy scouts, he chose the two prettiest girls and nearly caused a riot in the process.

"What was all that about?" Kimber asked.

"Zagorski is going forward to see what's happening," Halina told him.

"Maybe I'd better tag along. I'm not doing any good here."

"You'll need an armband."

It took Kimber a good ten minutes to persuade one of the boy scouts to part with his. By then, Zagorski and his team had already left the building. Undeterred, he went downstairs to the café and nipped out the back way through the kitchen, then sprinted across the road to enter the burned-out shell of the tenement across the street from Kuba's through one of the gaping windows on the ground floor.

The floors above his head had collapsed and most of the slates on the roof were missing, leaving the building open to the elements. Scrambling over the compacted rubble, he made his way through the tenement, drawn on by the sound of Polish voices to what had once been an enclosed courtyard. The tall, wrought-iron gates had gone, so had most of the outside wall, which meant that Zagorski and the rest of his tactical headquarters could see the whole of Napoleon Square.

The main post office was on the far side of the square, a good hundred and fifty yards from Zagorski's HQ in the courtyard. A few survivors from the first wave crouched behind the lime and plane trees, hoping the trunks were broad enough to stop a high-velocity bullet. The dead were everywhere, thick upon the ground in tangled, bleeding heaps. Of the seventy or so bodies within Kimber's field of vision, not one man had got to within grenade-throwing distance of the objective before he was cut down. The machine gun had ceased firing but from the rooftop and upper floor of the post office, snipers zeroed in on anyone who attempted to break cover.

Men from one of Zagorski's reserve companies, who were in the second wave and were armed with rifles, began to arrive in numbers and Kimber began to fear that there was too much bunching in the courtyard. Sooner, rather than later, the enemy was going to call for artillery fire and then what was left of the AK battalion would be decimated. A rifleman on his right adopted a kneeling position only to keel over before he could take aim.

Kimber felt a hand on his back, looked over his shoulder and saw Halina.

"What the hell are you doing here?" He reached out and pulled her down. "Are you trying to get yourself killed?"

"Look, Michael, look over there."

Halina raised herself up on one elbow and pointed to the Prudential Insurance building. Glancing to his left, Kimber saw that someone had nailed the Polish flag to the mast on the roof of the sixteenth floor. The skyscraper was about a hundred yards from the main post office but to get there, he would have to move sideways to the T-junction at the top of Jasna Street and approach the building along the parallel road on the north side of the square.

Kimber retrieved the obsolete 1898 model rifle from the dead AK soldier and collected the spare clips of 7.92mm from the leather pouch attached to his belt, then crawled over to Zagorski to tell the Pole what he had in mind. Getting through to him wasn't easy; apart from the language barrier, Zagorski had seen a third of his battalion mown down and was in a state of shock. He was also being harangued on all sides by his subordinates and seemed incapable of providing the kind of leadership they were looking for.

"We should attack the post office from the direction of the Prudential building," Kimber said fiercely. "We take out the snipers from above, then rush the west side of the building while you put down covering fire from here. Give me fifty men from the reserve company and the post office is yours."

"Impossible."

"What do you mean, impossible?"

"I'm saying it can't be done."

Kimber signalled Halina to join them and got her to repeat everything he had just said in Polish, but still Zagorski refused to budge. Unfolding a street map, he traced the left and right boundaries to make the point that although the skyscraper lay within their area, they would have to move through the neighbouring battalion in order to reach it if they adopted Kimber's plan.

"They may think you are the enemy and open fire."

"We have to take that chance," Kimber told him.

"No."

"We don't have any choice."

Zagorski continued to shake his head. Halina tried to reason with him but he wouldn't listen to her. One of the company officers came to her support and ranted away at machine gun speed seemingly to little effect. Unable to follow what he was saying, Kimber looked to Halina for an explanation.

"His name is Jan," she informed him. "Those are his men lying out there in the square and he is telling Zagorski that if he had listened to him, most of them would still be alive. He also thinks we should seize the Prudential building."

"Then tell him to follow me with the surviving members of his company."

Kimber crawled back into the hallway of the gutted tenement where the two messenger girls who had accompanied Zagorski were sheltering, waited for Jan to round up his men and then led them out into Jasna Street. For the most part, they moved in single file, hugging the buildings which were still intact. Whenever they came to a gap where the original tenement had been destroyed in the autumn of '39, Kimber marshalled them into line abreast and crossed the open space at a gallop. In all, it took them just over half an hour to reach the skyscraper; by that time, Napoleon Square was under artillery fire and several buildings in the Polish-held area were burning fiercely.

Kimber did a quick head count in the lobby and found he had thirty-seven men and Halina.

"I'm a soldier too," she informed him before he had a chance to ask what the hell she thought she was doing. "Besides, your Polish is not good enough and you need me to translate your orders."

"All right, tell Jan I'm taking six of his men up to the eighth floor to engage the snipers on the roof of the post office. He is not, repeat not, to storm the building until we bring effective fire to bear on the enemy."

There were no protests, suggestions or debates; Jan accepted everything Halina said without demur. There were, however, two minor snags; a power cut in the Central District meant the lifts were out of action and there was a distinct possibility that the AK men who had raised the Polish flag and were still there somewhere inside the building would mistake them for the enemy.

Kimber led the way up the staircase, seeking what protection he could from the walls of the lift shaft. At the top of each flight of steps, he paused for Halina to call out that they belonged to the 5th battalion. Her message drew no response until they reached the sixth floor when a harsh voice somewhere above them demanded to know the password. Halina didn't know it, neither did anyone else in their party. For a few bad moments, it looked as though a firefight between two friendly groups was on the cards, but then Halina threw off Kimber's restraining hand, told the men on the landing above that she was unarmed and went on up to meet them. After that, the situation became much more amicable.

Once they'd reached the eighth floor, Kimber assigned two men to each office on the east side of the building and instructed them to select their own targets and fire at will. A sniper who was using one of the chimneys for cover caught his eye and taking a deliberate aim with the rifle, he held his breath at the critical moment, gently squeezed the trigger, and blasted a hole in the window.

Through a spider's web of cracked glass he saw the bullet hit the German below the right ear and knock the field service cap off his head. The soldier dropped his rifle, clapped a hand to his face as if to ease the pain, then began to slide inexorably down the slate roof. His feet missed the gutter and he went over the edge, his weight above the hips automatically taking him through a backward somersault as he plummeted towards the ground.

A few hours ago, Kimber would have gladly killed the Scharführer and the odious Herr Neurath, but somehow this was different. Numbed by the sight of a wounded man tumbling to his death, he sought to exorcise his horror on the window by knocking out the pane of glass with the butt of his rifle. In his determination to remove every last fragment, he was still chipping away when Jan and the others stormed and captured the post office.

CHAPTER 4

There was a loud rushing noise as another salvo from the battery across the river in Praga passed over the Civil Affairs Bureau before exploding in Napoleon Square. Although they were some twelve hundred yards from the impact area, the blast rattled all the windows on the west side of the building. Maria Bolek thought she should have become used to the din by now considering the bombardment had started more than half an hour ago, but she still flinched every time an incoming salvo erupted.

"No need to be frightened, Fräulein. Those are our guns you can hear so you won't get any shells dropping short. Isn't that right, Herr Doktor Witzleben?"

"Yes indeed, Herr Neurath."

Witzleben, a plump, grey-haired civil servant, gazed at her thoughtfully from behind a large mahogany desk that had been looted from some Polish household. Walther Neurath, from Gestapo headquarters, was seated on his right. Neither man had invited Maria to take a chair and she remained standing in front of the desk looking at the blackout curtains that had been drawn across the window. A signed photograph of Adolf Hitler occupied pride of place on the wall behind her.

"That's a relief." Maria smiled weakly. "I just hope they're giving those bandits hell."

The only Poles employed by the Civil Affairs Bureau were collaborators; as one exception to the rule, it was essential she kept her personal feelings well under control.

"Where do you live, Fräulein?"

"In Mokotow."

"And the address?"

"Josef Pilsudski Street number seventy-two."

Neurath looked up from his notebook. "Good. Now what's all this nonsense you've been telling the Herr Doktor about the terrorists? Lots of other Poles work for the Occupation authorities; why did they go out of their way to frighten you?"

"I don't know."

Another salvo screamed overhead to burst somewhere in Napoleon Square. Neurath waited until the noise from the multiple explosions died away to nothing, then said, "Perhaps you have been telling Herr Doktor Witzleben a pack of lies; perhaps you are a member of the so-called Home Army and knew that today was the day set for the insurrection?"

Don't clench your hands, don't bite your lip, just let your jaw drop and stare at Neurath as though astounded. Maria tried to follow her own advice, but it wasn't easy. She couldn't think who had betrayed her but at least one question had been answered. If nothing else, she now knew why Witzleben had sent his deputy together with an armed escort to bring her into the office, and why she had been told to stay on when the rest of the staff left.

"It would seem the Fräulein has lost her voice," Neurath observed acidly.

"It's not true," Maria said huskily.

"What isn't?"

"That I'm a member of the AK; you would know that if you saw the way the neighbours treat me. So far as they are concerned, I do not exist. No one looks at me, no one speaks to me, and the only letters I receive are full of hate."

She could say it with total conviction because it happened to be true. The Germans had made sure her neighbours knew she worked for them. It was a means of securing her loyalty through a sense of isolation, or so they believed.

"You are regarded as a traitor by the residents of your apartment house and a potential Fifth Columnist by the Home Army. Is that what you're implying?"

"I'm not implying anything," Maria lied. "It happens to be a fact. If, by some chance, the Third Reich should lose this war, they'll hang me from the nearest lamp-post."

"Any more of your evasive tactics and we may just do the same."

Maria felt her skin crawl. How much did the Gestapo know, how much were they guessing? And why the cat and mouse act? Usually, anyone who was suspected of being a member of the Home Army was either taken straight to the Gestapo headquarters on Szucha Avenue or to the Pawiak Prison in the centre of what used to be the Jewish ghetto, where they were then systematically tortured. And perhaps the worst part was the knowledge that the odds of leaving either place alive were a thousand to one against.

"Evasive? Oh, I assure you I'm not the least bit evasive, Herr Neurath. Like most other educated Poles, I know that only the

Wehrmacht stands between us and the Bolshevik hordes. The German Army is our shield and defender."

"Deeds speak louder than words, Fräulein. I'd like to have some tangible proof that you are pro-German."

"How can I do that?"

"By identifying the people who have been threatening you." Neurath leaned to the right, picked up a small, leather attaché-case and placed it on the desk in front of him. Opening it up, he took out a brown envelope and extracted a batch of photographs. "I want you to look at these prints very carefully and tell me if you recognise anyone. Take your time, there's no hurry."

Neurath shuffled the prints like a pack of cards and then began to lay them down, face uppermost. The first exposure was a long-range shot from a concealed camera which had not been properly focussed so that the definition was poor. It showed a man in shirt-sleeves alighting from a tramcar, the trees on the sidewalk in full leaf providing further proof that the photo had been taken at the height of summer.

Maria shook her head and the next one appeared for her inspection. This time it was Lazienki Park and there was a light covering of snow on the ground. A young woman in a winter coat was hanging on to the arm of a frail-looking man whose bent figure suggested he was old enough to be her grandfather. The upper part of her face was obscured by the brim of her felt hat but she had a well-shaped mouth and a strong jaw. The old man had protected himself against the cold with a scarf which he had wound around his mouth before crossing it over his chest and tucking the loose ends inside his sports jacket; he had also pulled his black beret forward, leaving only his nose visible.

"They do not seem familiar to you, Fräulein?"

"Their faces are hidden."

"Quite so."

Neurath produced another photograph of the same young woman taken outside Kuba's Café, her face in full view of the camera. She had the most beautiful eyes Maria Bolek had ever seen but she remained a stranger.

"I still don't recognise her, Herr Neurath."

"No matter."

Yet one more print but glossier than any of the others. The subject looked a very much younger edition of the grandfather and, although unable to place him, Maria had a feeling that she had seen him somewhere before.

"You know him?"

31

"No."

"Liar," Neurath shouted and threw the photographs in her face.

For a big man he could move surprisingly fast. Before Maria could think how she might defend herself, Neurath moved round the desk and punched her nose. The pain made her eyes water, then the blood fountained from both nostrils and damned nearly choked her when she tried to breathe through her mouth.

"Polish bitch, pox-ridden whore." Neurath grabbed a fistful of hair and dragged her out of the room, along the corridor and on down the ornate spiral staircase. He booted her down the last half dozen steps and she landed heavily on her hands and knees. He kicked her again, this time in the ribs; then seizing one ear, he hauled Maria to her feet. A wave of pain engulfed her and the hall lights began to revolve, fading into the distance as they did so.

The night air partially revived her. How she came to be in the garden was something of a mystery to Maria but there was the statue of the Grecian lady which she could see from her office on the second floor.

"On your knees."

Maria knelt down, knew that death was coming to her with a bullet in the head delivered by a butcher with a cast in his left eye even before she heard him cock the automatic pistol. She raised her eyes and looked up at the clouds, pink as candy floss from the dozens of fires that were raging out of control in various parts of the city.

Neurath shifted his aim just enough to miss her head by a few millimetres, then squeezed the trigger and thought it hilarious when she passed out. It was, however, the last joke he was destined to enjoy. As he stood there shaking with laughter, a home-made mortar bomb landed in the garden. It weighed approximately seven pounds and was filled with ball-bearings which virtually churned Neurath into a bloody pulp from the stomach up. Supine as she was, not one pellet struck Maria Bolek.

The Feldwebel was short, overweight, myopic and out of condition. Eighteen months ago the Army would not have spared him a second glance but astronomical casualties coupled with Doctor Goebbels' rabble-rousing demand for total war had persuaded the military authorities to find a suitable niche for the former Bundespost worker in the Warsaw detachment of the 385th Postal and Courier Unit. His name was Gottfried Exler and he had seen twelve of his comrades shot down in the vicious hand-to-hand fighting that had taken place when the AK had attacked the Army's sorting office in

Napoleon Square. He had also witnessed the terrifying death throes of a further two soldiers who had been butchered in cold blood after they had surrendered. It had therefore been comparatively easy for Kimber to convince the sergeant that it was entirely due to his intervention that he had been spared.

As a source of information, Exler exceeded Kimber's wildest expectations. In his anxiety to please him, the sergeant produced a list of the field post offices which served the various formations they supported so that within minutes he knew the complete Order of Battle of the 9th German Army. Exler also gave him the composition of the Warsaw garrison and the location of individual units.

"The Army has only one combat unit in the whole city?" Kimber shook his head. "I find that hard to believe."

"It's true, Herr Hauptmann; there is just the 654th Engineer Battalion."

"We ran into some SS troops this morning – Azerbaijanis."

"They belong to a special anti-partisan group," Exler said eagerly.

"Are they part of the garrison?"

"Yes."

"Who else?"

"Elements of the 896th Quartermaster Battalion, the staff of the railway transport office, a signals company, 9th Army Convalescent Depot, factory guards and the civil police, but of course they're not very reliable." Worried in case Halina and Zagorski heard him, Exler lowered his voice to a conspiratorial whisper. "Polish collaborators, you understand."

"Who is manning the 20mm flak guns at the bridges?"

"Luftwaffe personnel, probably from the Bielany airstrip on the northern outskirts of Warsaw. They're nothing to do with the Army."

"So what's the strength of the garrison including the auxiliaries?"

"I don't know, Herr Hauptmann."

"Well, give me an informed guess."

"Five, perhaps as many as eight thousand." Exler shrugged. "But don't quote me, I'm only a postman."

Kimber rubbed his jaw. Whatever their numbers, the Germans were too strong for the Polish Home Army. Fire power would be the deciding factor and the Wehrmacht had already demonstrated that they outgunned the AK. The number of casualties inflicted on the 5th battalion by the section of fifteen men defending the post office was proof of this. So was the fact that a slightly larger detachment of the SS had stopped Zagorski's men in their tracks when they'd attempted to storm the police headquarters in the adjoining street. There was one other crucial difference between the opposing forces; the German High Command would take urgent steps to reinforce the garrison whereas the Poles were ultimately dependent on the Red Army, and it was questionable whether they could expect much help from that quarter.

"Is the German talking?" Zagorski demanded.

"Yes, very freely."

"So what has he been telling you?"

Kimber's command of Polish was good enough to answer the first question but not the second. He looked round for Halina, spotted her amongst the surviving runners in the near left-hand corner of the sorting office and beckoned her to join him. With her assistance he was able to give Zagorski all the information he had gleaned from the Feldwebel.

"I could have wished for better news," Kimber told him. "There are five armoured divisions between the Red Army and Warsaw – 3rd SS Panzer Division Totenkopf, 4th Panzer, 5th SS Viking, 19th Panzer and the Hermann Goering Division. There is also the 73rd Infantry Division; it's probably their artillery which is bombarding the city right now."

"Anything else?" Zagorski demanded.

"That's all there is so far."

"So far?"

"I propose to go through the mailbags awaiting collection and delivery, especially the pouches which are being handled by the special despatch service."

"Then you and Halina had better get on with it," Zagorski growled.

The courier mail was held in a strong room located in the basement. Each sack awaiting despatch was tagged with a seal and secured with a padlock, the key to which was carried by the courier and had to be signed for by the receiving officer. Incoming mail was still being sorted when the post office was attacked and although some letters had been pigeon-holed, the vast majority were lying in a heap on the table.

"Where does the Herr Hauptmann wish to start?" Exler inquired politely.

"With the outgoing stuff."

Kimber's assumption that mail addressed to the Oberkommando des Heeres, the Supreme Headquarters of the Army, were likely to be of more immediate interest to the AK than the incoming mail was not borne out. Much of the correspondence was concerned with logistics and various disciplinary matters, including the transcript of a Field General Court Martial convened for the purpose of trying four soldiers of the 73rd Infantry Division for desertion in the face of the enemy, all of whom had been sentenced to death and executed by a firing squad.

"May I say something, Herr Hauptmann?"

"By all means."

"That particular court martial was a little unusual. Although the death sentence is mandatory in such cases, convicted deserters are invariably sent to a penal battalion. It's hardly a reprieve; penal battalions are always in the thick of it and get all the really dirty jobs. But sometimes a man will survive three or four suicide missions and he is then rehabilitated and returned to normal duty."

"So what's odd about this particular case?" Kimber asked.

"The four infantrymen in question were sent out on a reconnaissance patrol behind the Russian lines. They completed the task they'd been given and reported back on time. So how can they be guilty of desertion in the face of the enemy?"

"Maybe they just sat out there in the middle of No Man's Land and put in a fictitious report when they returned."

"The only prosecution witness was an officer in the Gestapo."

"Seems to me you've been poking your nose into things that don't concern you, Exler."

The Feldwebel avoided Kimber's gaze. His neck began to turn a delicate shade of pink. "Not so, Herr Hauptmann." Exler cleared his throat. "The transcript is classified Secret, which means it should have been double-enveloped for despatch. The clerk at Garrison headquarters omitted to do this, so I was obliged to correct his error. Naturally, I had to open the envelope to make sure the contents tallied with the description on the docket."

Kimber had met soldiers like the Feldwebel before and didn't believe a word he said. Every army had its Exlers, smart alecs who had to know everything there was to know and were ready with a plausible excuse whenever they were caught nosing into files which were none of their business.

"Let's have a look at the incoming stuff," said Kimber. "I'm not interested in disciplinary matters."

The official mail awaiting collection seemed just as uninteresting. Among other dross in the various pigeon-holes there was a Special Order of the Day from the Führer forbidding any withdrawal from the Vistula line on pain of death, and an impressive list of train schedules for the movements staff. Kimber had to wait until the Feldwebel tipped the contents of a previously unopened bag on to

35

the floor before he found anything to make him sit up and take notice.

The envelope was marked TOP SECRET, Personal for the Chief of Staff Headquarters Warsaw Garrison. A smaller stamp in the bottom left-hand corner indicated that the document was from the Fremde Heere Ost, the army department responsible for evaluating War Intelligence in the east. Consisting of seven closely typewritten pages, it was signed by Major General Reinhard Gehlen and was a blueprint for the destruction of the AK.

"Who are the People's Army, Halina?"

"The Communist equivalent of the Home Army. They used to call themselves the People's Guard."

"This document says they are Stalin's Army, not Poland's."

"We've always known that."

"They have three aims; the destruction of the AK, the liberation of Poland and the creation of a Communist state. Since the last two are dependent on the first, they've set out to suborn the AK High Command through an agent known as 'Phoenix'."

"How very apt," Halina said dryly. "Out of the ashes of the Home Army the Communist Party will arise."

"I think your Commanding General should see this document."

"Unfortunately, I don't know who he is or where to find him."

"Someone at Group Headquarters will and the Victoria Hotel is no distance from here."

"You'd better speak to Zagorski first."

"I was planning to," said Kimber.

He could imagine what the Pole was going to say. The Gehlen letter was a piece of black propaganda, a trick to undermine the morale of the Resistance. There was, however, one major flaw in that premise; for such a ruse to be successful, the perpetrators had to ensure the material ended up in the right hands and Gehlen had had no way of knowing that the post office in Napoleon Square would be seen as a major objective by the AK.

But Zagorski did not react in the way Kimber had expected. Instead of dismissing the document as a ruse de guerre, he accepted his evaluation and agreed it should be shown to the Commanding General or his deputy. He regretted he was unable to provide Kimber with an escort but Halina could accompany him as his interpreter.

"You can also have this automatic for your personal protection."

The automatic was a Mauser 7.65mm pistol which had been taken from the body of the officer commanding the postal and courier detachment. Checking the weapon, Kimber found there was one round in the breech plus three more in the magazine.

"Do you have a spare magazine lying around?" he asked.

"No."

"How about a few loose rounds?"

"I regret we don't have any 7.65mm ammunition."

"Just thought I'd ask." Kimber hesitated, then said, "Look after my German; he's been quite useful and I wouldn't like anything to happen to him while I'm away."

"He'll have to take his chances like the rest of us."

The battery across the river in Praga had ceased firing on Napoleon Square and was now bombarding a target somewhere in the Mokotow District. Light rain was falling, but it had no effect on the dozens of fires raging in the Central District.

Leon Jarrell crouched in the doorway of the corner shop bakery while he tried to make up his mind whether to go left, right or continue straight on. Left was dark, so was right; up front, the sky glowed from a dozen or more fires which indicated the natives in that area were friendly. Any location that had been or was being shelled had to be Home Army territory. He had learned this truism for himself when the German artillery had zeroed in on Mokotow and Josef Pilsudski Street in particular. On this basis, the way ahead was the obvious choice; the only thing that held him back was the fact that the scene of the fire was some distance away and just who controlled the intervening real estate was a matter of conjecture.

Lazienki Park over to his right was certainly held by the Germans; he had come under heavy machine gun fire from that direction shortly after he'd left the apartment to look for Maria. Taking evasive action, he had veered off in the opposite direction and now wasn't too sure of his present whereabouts. Without a firearm, Jarrell felt naked and vulnerable. He wished he had equipped himself with something more effective than a kitchen knife, but that would have meant spending a lot of precious time looking for a dead German who hadn't already been stripped clean by the AK. And when it came to finding Maria, time was the one thing he couldn't afford to waste.

Then it occurred to Jarrell that he was doing exactly that. Hesitating no longer, he launched himself from the doorway like a sprinter in a hundred-metre dash. Chest expanded, head thrown back, he raced across the intersection and went to ground in another hallway farther up the street. While regaining his breath, his eyes searched the buildings on the opposite side of the road for snipers lurking in the upper floors or on the rooftops, but saw nothing suspicious. Nevertheless, when he broke cover again, Jarrell thought it prudent to zigzag in case he had failed to spot the enemy.

He continued to move forward in short bounds of thirty to forty yards and always towards the scene of the fire which he surmised was raging in the city centre. The Civil Affairs Bureau lay in that direction and unless the Germans had detained her, Jarrell figured Maria Bolek would have linked up with whatever Home Army unit happened to be closest to her place of work. As he drew nearer, ash from the conflagration fell like snow from a leaden sky and the acrid smoke attacked his lungs. Then a slight breeze stirred the billowing clouds just long enough for him to catch a glimpse of the Prudential building in Napoleon Square and he was able to orientate himself.

Not much farther now, he thought. Krasinski Square, where the Civil Affairs Bureau was located within the Old Town, was roughly three quarters of a mile due north of the Prudential building. Allowing for diversions along the way, it would take him about an hour to reach it. A few minutes later, Jarrell came to a Y-junction and forked right to bring himself on course for Napoleon Square. Shortly thereafter, an over-enthusiastic sentry took a pot shot at him and very nearly drilled a hole through his head. The challenge delivered in Polish was very much an afterthought.

"Don't shoot," Jarrell shouted at the top of his voice. "I'm on your side, for God's sake."

The sentry opened up again, getting off four rounds in rapid succession with a bolt-operated rifle. Hugging the cobblestones, Jarrell wondered what it was the man didn't like about his Polish accent. He tried to make the soldier understand that he wasn't a German and threw in a few choice epithets for good measure. It seemed to have the desired effect inasmuch as the firing stopped and they started to communicate, though he had no idea what the word 'tempest' was supposed to convey.

"You mind repeating that?"

"Tempest." The sentry, who had a high-pitched voice, cleared his throat, then said, "If you are a friend, tell me what goes with 'tempest'."

It was the old password system. Someone challenged you with 'mice' and you were supposed to say 'blind', except that that was a little too obvious and the correct answer was probably 'cheese'. For 'tempest', the appropriate response might be 'whirlwind', 'tornado' or 'hurricane', but Jarrell wasn't inclined to make a guess because if he happened to get it wrong, there was no surer way of getting himself killed.

"I don't know what the password is, nobody told me." Jarrell removed the kitchen knife from the waistband of his slacks and laid it aside. "But I am a friend and I'm going to stand up now with my hands raised. Okay?"

His declaration of friendship was received in total silence, if not disbelief. Very slowly he got to his feet.

"Over here."

The voice came from a pile of rubble that had once been a house some twenty yards or more to his left.

"I'm coming."

Jarrell turned to face the sentry and walked towards the pile of masonry, horribly conscious of being silhouetted against the glare from a blazing gas main directly behind him.

The outpost was manned by three AK soldiers none of whom looked much above sixteen. They were in a highly excitable state and it took Jarrell some time to calm them down. There was one bad moment when the sentry was all for shooting him out of hand on the grounds that he was probably a Ukrainian, but he managed to persuade them to leave that decision to their company commander.

The Lieutenant in charge of their outfit could recognise a tricky problem when he was faced with one and proceeded to pass Jarrell on up the chain of command. Battalion headquarters was located in the main post office on the far side of Napoleon Square; the commanding officer was Stefan Zagorski, a slim austere man in his mid-thirties who was not exactly overjoyed to make his acquaintance.

"I'm an American." Jarrell unbuttoned his shirt and produced his dog tags to prove it. "591468 Staff Sergeant Leon Jarrell, United States Army Air Force. I've been hiding out in Warsaw since my plane was shot down over Ploesti."

"You're not another German speaker, are you?" Zagorski asked.

"Absolutely not. I can't speak a word of the language."

"Good. I've just got rid of my last interpreter, an Englishman called Kimber who has also been hiding from the Germans. Perhaps you have heard of him?"

"No. Will I get to meet him?"

"I doubt it," said Zagorski. "He's probably dead by now."

CHAPTER 5

The ghetto was said to be something the Devil had created and God had overlooked. Sandwiched between the working-class district of Wola and the Old Town, it had been the final stop-over on the one-way journey to the gas ovens at Treblinka. At times, more than half a million Jews had been crammed into the thousand-acre compound with as many as nine men, women and children sharing one room. A veritable hell on earth, this city within a city had been administered by the Jewish Council, a committee of well-meaning elders who had sincerely believed that by co-operating with the German authorities, they could somehow make things more bearable for the vast majority. It had also been policed by men who were not averse to cracking the skulls of their fellow Jews in return for better rations.

Every adult inmate of the ghetto had known that the day would inevitably come when they too would be marched to the railway yards near Danzig station and packed like sardines into a freight car for that last train journey to oblivion. In April 1943, some of the younger and more militant inhabitants had decided that enough was enough. Armed with a pitiful number of home-made grenades and automatic pistols which they had purchased from the Polish Resistance, they had fought back. Under the personal direction of Gruppenführer Josef Stroop, two training battalions of the SS, supported by demolition teams, flame-throwers, mortars, tanks and artillery employed in the direct fire role, had burned, blasted and smoked them out of every room, every cellar and every sewer in the ghetto. Five weeks later, when every man, woman and child had been accounted for to Stroop's personal satisfaction, those few buildings which had not been destroyed in the fighting had then been razed to the ground. Only the ten-foot-high wall enclosing the Quarter and the dreaded Pawiak Prison, which the Gestapo used as an interrogation centre, had been left intact.

. If Kimber had sometimes found it hard to believe that the war was a crusade against evil, his uncertainty was resolved the moment he entered the ruins of the ghetto. General 'Bor' Komorowski, Commander-in-Chief of the Home Army, had established his headquarters in Kamler's tobacco factory which was located at the bottom end of a cul-de-sac in the Wola District; crossing the ghetto was the quickest way to reach it. The Intelligence officer at Group Headquarters who had briefed Kimber after he and Halina had arrived at the Victoria Hotel, had also assured him that this was also the safest route. Apart from the prison itself, the entire area was allegedly in the hands of the AK; the guide who had been detailed to accompany them was coming along merely to ensure that they didn't lose their way.

The codename of their guide was 'Jerzy'. A short, elderly man with a thin, hooked nose, he had been a tramcar driver all his working life and claimed to know every road, every boulevard and every building of any importance in Warsaw. There were quicker ways of reaching the tobacco factory than the route he had chosen but using only those areas which were known to be held by the AK was the surest means of getting there in one piece. On leaving the Victoria Hotel, 'Jerzy' had made a wide detour to avoid the Saxon Gardens where the Wehrmacht was still entrenched, and had then cut back to the ghetto.

To consolidate their gains, the Poles had barricaded the major roads with streetcars, trucks and hand carts, filling in the gaps with cobblestones and paving slabs which they had prised from the sidewalks with picks. The Home Army fighters who were manning the barricades were armed with every conceivable type of weapon ranging from a .22 target pistol to Sten guns that had been manufactured in secret factories dotted all over the city. Their uniforms were equally diverse and were sometimes only distinguishable from the Waffen SS by the red and white armbands they were wearing on their right sleeves. There was, however, one thing which they all had in common, the tense, expectant faces of men who expected the Germans to launch a counter attack at any moment.

Kimber felt the same kind of tension as they moved through the ghetto in single file with 'Jerzy' in the lead and Halina bringing up the rear. The roads still existed, pot-holed and uneven with tufts of grass and weeds sprouting through the cracks in the surface, but the tenements had been reduced to mounds of rubble. Yet it was the wall topped with barbed wire and the empty watchtowers which disturbed him most. In his mind's eye, he saw it the way it used to be, the guards looking down on the crowded streets, laughing and joking amongst themselves while the ghetto's own Jewish police

41

force assembled the next trainload of men, women and children destined for Treblinka.

He saw 'Jerzy' stumble, then heard the crack of a rifle. Still rooted in the nightmare that had been the ghetto, he did not associate the two events until Halina yelled at him to get down. Responding to her urgent warning, Kimber threw himself sideways and took cover behind a large slab of masonry. He counted off the seconds – one minute, two, three – all quiet. Kimber crawled to his left to look round the slab rather than raise his head above it. 'Jerzy' was lying flat on his stomach, his head over on one side, his rifle several feet away in the gutter. He was very still.

"What's happening?" Halina whispered urgently. She was directly to his rear and near enough for him to hear her breathing.

"I think our guide has just bought it. You stay where you are while I take a closer look." He reached inside his jacket and took out the envelope containing the Top Secret Intelligence summary prepared by Major General Reinhard Gehlen and placed it on the ground. "I'm leaving the document here. If anything happens to me, pick it up and try to make your way to Army headquarters."

Kimber crawled forward, wriggling like a snake. As he had feared, the puddle he'd spotted next to 'Jerzy' was not rainwater and it was evident that the Pole had died the instant he had been hit. Inching his way past the corpse, he reached out for the rifle and drew it towards him, then turned about and crawled back to his former position where Halina was waiting for him. From his jacket pocket, he took out the Mauser 7.65mm automatic and gave it to her. He didn't have to explain anything; the rifle told the whole story and the way she bobbed her head told him that the inference had not been lost on her.

"Shall I hold on to the papers?" Halina asked softly, patting the small leather bag she was carrying bandolier-fashion across her chest.

"I think they would be a lot safer if you did."

"I think so too." She frowned, then said, "Which way do we go now?"

The ghetto was supposed to have been cleared, so the sniper who'd shot 'Jerzy' was probably a straggler who had seized the opportunity to make a quick kill. Isolated and cut off from his parent unit, he probably hadn't fired on Kimber because he wasn't sure how many other AK men were in the immediate vicinity. Although the facts tended to support the theory, Kimber wasn't prepared to risk his neck a second time.

"We'll pull back a bit, then move round to the right. We should be okay provided we don't go anywhere near Pawiak Prison."

"We'll know soon enough if you're wrong," Halina told him wryly.

"That we will. I'll lead, you follow and keep your head down."

Kimber about-faced and, staying low, moved back some thirty yards before turning left to reach the parallel east–west axis. There was a certain orderliness about the destruction of the ghetto which was typically Germanic. When the burnt-out tenements had been bulldozed, every road and pavement had subsequently been cleared of rubble to leave clear lanes of fire. 'Jerzy' had made the mistake of staying on the footpath and had paid the penalty; Kimber had no intention of repeating his error and picked a route across the pyramids of demolished buildings.

The going was difficult and treacherous; cellars were often concealed beneath an apparently solid pile of bricks which were in fact only supported by the shattered remains of the original floorboards. He learned early on that with every stride it was necessary to test the ground under his feet before putting his full weight on it. The way ahead was painfully slow and progress was never measured in a straight line. He stopped frequently to peer into the darkness while straining to catch the slightest sound of movement and had his heart in his mouth whenever he heard the squeak and pattering feet of a rat. Then, just to make things worse, it began to rain again.

From east to west, the ghetto was exactly a mile wide. In terms of time and space, Kimber reckoned it had taken them more than an hour to cover approximately half the distance. A few minutes later, his calculation would have ceased to have any relevance had the shot been an inch or so to the right. The bullet came from behind him, clipped the rubble on his immediate left at head height and ricocheted; simultaneously, Halina slipped and fell while trying to maintain her balance on the greasy surface of a slate roof that had collapsed to form a sloping bridge over a cellar.

"Oh, my God, I almost killed you." Halina picked herself up and hurled the offending automatic pistol into the night.

"I'm okay," Kimber assured her.

"It was an accident. I must have forgotten to apply the safety catch and the gun went off when I slipped."

"These things happen," he said.

And they did too. Many of the casualties his battalion had suffered at Salerno had been inflicted by friendly forces. A salvo from the artillery supporting regiment falling short, a jumpy sentry firing on an incoming patrol which he'd been warned about, a mortar bomb exploding prematurely as it left the tube – such things were an everyday occurrence in war.

But there was no comforting Halina; over and over again she blamed herself for being careless. She was in fact still apologising when they reached Kamler's tobacco factory a few minutes after midnight.

The shrubbery towards the bottom of the garden made a good hiding place but it offered no protection against the rain and was anything but a safe refuge when the area was being mortared. Cold and wet, hungry and frightened, Maria Bolek hugged the earth and prayed she wouldn't be killed. The time to have escaped was immediately after she had regained consciousness but the discovery that she was still alive had numbed her brain and she had been unable to think clearly. Now it was too late; the Civil Affairs Bureau had been turned into a strongpoint and if she attempted to climb over the wall, the machine gunner up on the second floor of the building would cut her to pieces.

A loud explosion rocked the wall behind the statue of the Grecian lady, a second explosion followed before the echo of the first had died away. The noise deafened Maria and made her ears ring and while she escaped the worst effects of the double blast, the hurricane-force wind buffeted her about the body. Fragments of concrete whipped above her head and when she opened her eyes again, a thick cloud of dust hung in the air like an impenetrable mist. There was a momentary and unnatural lull, then three or four light automatics opened up and what sounded like a crowd of drunken revellers started screaming and yelling.

They came through the mist, firing as they ran towards the Civil Affairs Bureau, ghostly figures in a variety of uniforms. One man paused to put a bullet into the corpse of Walther Neurath which was still lying on the lawn. Another soldier threw his rifle away and clawed at his throat before he sank down on to his knees and toppled forward, his body twitching spastically in its final death throes. Rifle and machine gun fire, a stab of flame milliseconds before the thump of a hand grenade, the sound of glass shattering, the hollow whoosh of a Molotov cocktail; Maria clapped her hands over both ears in a vain attempt to shut out the cacophony. Another explosion, this time close to the building and the fog of brick dust thickening just as it was beginning to disperse. She could taste it on her lips, a gritty flour-like substance that made her want to vomit.

The gunfire became intermittent, dying away to the occasional shot one moment, then suddenly flaring up again the next. The firefight was taking place inside the building now, room by room, floor by floor, the enemy slowly being driven towards the attic as they were flushed out of their defensive positions. Finally, the noise of battle gradually died away to nothing and a kind of peace returned. When the dust eventually settled, Maria saw that the wall at the bottom of the garden had collapsed in two places, while, of the statue, only the plinth and one leg remained. She was also aware that her body was trembling as though gripped by malaria and just getting to her feet required a tremendous effort of willpower. On November the fifteenth, she would be twenty-eight, but as of that moment she felt twice as old. Like an old woman crippled with arthritis, she shuffled towards the nearest gap in the wall.

"Where do you think you're going, mother?"

The AK soldier was carrying a box of ammunition on his right shoulder and a small sack of home-made grenades in his free hand. Maria did not see what business it was of his where she was going, but there was no way past him. Every time she tried to go round him, he side-stepped to block her path.

"Wait a minute, you're not as old as you look." He peered into her face, eyes narrowing suspiciously. "Where have you come from?"

"Over there," Maria said vaguely.

"And where exactly is that?"

"The big house behind me."

The soldier gave a low whistle, then said, "Hey, Corporal, I think I've got me a collaborator."

The corporal was in his early thirties, had fair hair and blue-grey eyes which studied Maria thoughtfully from behind a pair of thick glasses. After some deliberation, he said, "Let her go, she looks harmless enough to me."

"The hell with that, this bitch worked for the Germans."

"Because I was ordered to by the Resistance."

"Have you ever heard anything like it, Corporal? The Resistance told her to lie on her back and open her legs to the Nazis. I ask you, what does this whore think we are? A couple of prize idiots? Let's shoot the cow and have done with it."

"Oh, yes, you do that," Maria cried hysterically. "Finish the job for Neurath."

"Who's he?" the corporal asked.

"A Gestapo agent. That's his body over there by the statue."

"Don't listen to her, just take out your revolver and use it."

"No." The corporal shook his head. "No, we'll take this woman to 'Wolf' and let him decide what's to be done with her."

45

The corporal turned Maria about and shoved her towards the house. A Molotov cocktail had set one of the rooms on the ground floor on fire and a dozen or so AK men were tackling the blaze with stirrup pumps, fire extinguishers and buckets of sand which they'd found at various points throughout the house.

The back door was hanging askew off its hinges and, wherever they went, the floor was covered with broken glass. Empty cartridge cases in the hall marked the course of the battle but there were surprisingly few casualties in evidence. A dead stormtrooper was sitting bolt upright, his back resting against the wall at the top of the spiral staircase, his legs stretched out in front of him. Another SS man lay face down in the corridor, his head and shoulders wedged inside the men's lavatory. Both Germans were covered in a fine white dust from the ceiling and bizarrely looked as though they were a couple of badly-made-up clowns from a travelling circus.

The smoke from the fire was everywhere, dense in some places, sparse in others, but always pungent enough to have a crippling effect on Maria Bolek whose ribs felt as though they had been splintered by the kicking Neurath had given her. Unable to breathe through her nose and nursing her injured side, she was hustled from room to room on the upper floor until they finally located the officer whose codename was 'Wolf'.

'Wolf' was a professional soldier. A Battery Commander when the war had started on the first of September 1939, his unit had formed part of the Modlin Army facing East Prussia. It was entirely due to his leadership that the battery had not been encircled when the 4th German Army had smashed its way across the Polish Corridor from Pomerania to link up with the 3rd Army driving south from East Prussia. Constantly harassed by Stuka dive bombers, he had fought a series of rearguard actions after withdrawing behind the Narew river and then the River Bug. By the time the horse-drawn battery had reached the outskirts of Praga, only one 75mm field gun had been serviceable and his unit had fought on as infantry. When Warsaw had surrendered on Wednesday the twenty-seventh of September, 'Wolf' and most of his senior NCOs had taken off their uniforms, changed their names and gone underground. In five years of guerrilla warfare, he had come to hate all collaborators as much as he did the Nazis, a fact which Maria Bolek rapidly discovered for herself.

"I never realised we had so many volunteers in the Home Army," 'Wolf' said acidly. "When did you enlist – ten minutes after the uprising began?"

"I've told you the truth."

"You know what I find hard to believe about your story? That a minor cog like you should have known the exact time of zero hour. Shall I tell you when my battalion was notified? Five minutes after three o'clock yesterday afternoon, less than two hours before the kick-off. But Maria Bolek, she is so important that the Commander-in-Chief personally sees to it that she is notified a full day in advance."

"It wasn't like that," Maria shouted, and winced in pain.

"No, you got it from Doctor Karl Heinz Witzleben; that's why you stayed at home. You guessed the Civil Affairs Bureau in Krasinski Square would be one of our objectives and you didn't want to be around when we attacked it. Only your German masters weren't having that, so they detailed one of their minions to fetch you."

"I was brought in for questioning."

"By the Gestapo." 'Wolf' snapped his fingers. "What did you say his name was? Neurath? Yes, Neurath. Strange we don't have his name on our wanted list. Perhaps he only exists in your imagination?"

"His body is lying out there in the garden."

"Unfortunately, there are no papers on the corpse to prove that he was one of Himmler's own. The corporal here made a thorough search and found nothing."

"He showed me some photographs and asked if I recognised anyone . . ."

"Where did this happen?"

"I've already told you, in the Director's office." Maria clenched her hands. By taking her over and over the same ground, 'Wolf' was endeavouring to trip her up. She told herself that she had nothing to hide and therefore nothing to fear. Sound advice, but it wasn't easy to follow it when there wasn't a shred of evidence to support her story.

"No photographs and no Karl Heinz Witzleben, but of course he fled the building in the nick of time. You should have done the same."

"What about my broken nose? Who do you suppose gave me that?" Both nostrils were blocked with congealed blood and she had to breathe through her mouth.

'Wolf' shrugged his shoulders. "Perhaps you fell down the staircase and knocked yourself out. Frankly, I'm not really interested, I have more important matters to attend to."

He was going to hand her over to the corporal and his bloodthirsty

47

henchman and they would take her out into the garden and execute her. At the most, she had only a few precious seconds to make him change his mind and she couldn't think of a thing to help establish her innocence. Then all at once she began to talk about Leon Jarrell and couldn't think why she hadn't told 'Wolf' about the American before.

"How long have you been hiding this man?" he asked.

"Four months. The Resistance was planning to move him on to Danzig where it was hoped he could sneak on board a neutral ship bound for Sweden. However, Jarrell can speak Polish and was a printer before he enlisted, so when he volunteered to stay on and help run the underground press, our people jumped at the offer."

"What's the name of this newspaper?"

"*The Ramparts.*"

"And where is it printed?"

"In the cellar of the hardware store at 38 Lublin Union Square."

'Wolf' gazed at her sombrely, apparently unable to make up his mind. A runner from the fire-fighting squad on the ground floor briefly interrupted his train of thought to report that the blaze had been extinguished, but it seemed an interminably long time after that before he finally came to a decision.

"Get our medical orderly to see what he can do for Miss Bolek," he told the corporal, "then put her under guard in the cellar. As soon as it gets light, we'll escort her to Group Headquarters at the Victoria Hotel and they can verify her story."

"Thank you," Maria said huskily.

Somehow she managed to keep her composure in 'Wolf's presence, but after she left him, the tears of relief welled over and ran down her blood-stained cheeks.

The wall surrounding the Jewish ghetto had turned Pawiak Street into a cul-de-sac. Kamler's tobacco factory was situated at the bottom of the dead-end road opposite a stores sub-depot which was guarded by troops drawn from the Warsaw garrison. The AK had established their headquarters in the tobacco factory because, so far as command, control and communications were concerned, its central position meant that the staff were well placed to deal with any threat which developed from the east or west. On the other hand, it left a lot to be desired tactically and the headquarters defence platoon had had to eliminate the guard detail across the street and beat off a strong local counter attack mounted from within the ghetto by the SS Security Police before the factory was secured. When Kimber and Halina arrived at the plant, the sentries guarding the headquarters were still in a mood to shoot first and ask later. Only Halina's calm, reassuring voice persuaded them to hold their fire.

The defence platoon and communications section occupied the shop floor; the operations, Intelligence and logistic staffs had taken over the works' offices on the gallery above. To the right of the factory entrance, four signallers were embroiled in a heated argument over a transmitter they were trying to assemble. Although Kimber understood only every other word, it was evident that certain essential components were missing. Halina said something to the sentry who had escorted them into the factory, then told Kimber to stay where he was while she introduced herself to the Chief of Staff.

Five minutes became ten and moved on to twenty. Finally, just when he was beginning to think that she had been detained for some reason, an orderly appeared and led him up to the Accounts Department to see the Commanding General.

General Tadeusz Komorowski was a thin, balding man whose most notable features were a small clipped moustache and a permanently melancholy expression. A cavalry officer, he had made a name for himself in the international show jumping arena before the war, at which time he was reputed to have had no political or military ambitions. In keeping with the social status attached to a minor sprig of the Polish nobility, he was happy to farm his estate, ride his horses and attend the Army's autumn manoeuvres. After the surrender in October 1939, he had decided, in common with thousands of other Poles, to join General Sikorski in France. However, friends in Cracow had persuaded him that it was his duty to remain in Poland and help organise the Resistance. In furtherance of this, he had changed his name to Wolanski and obtained employment in a newsagent's which had enabled him to meet key members of the Home Army without arousing suspicion. To the rank and file he was known only by his codename of 'Bor'. That much Kimber had learned from Halina before they left the Victoria Hotel; now meeting the General face to face, he was impressed by his air of quiet determination.

"Halina tells me you are a British officer," Komorowski said, then waited for her to translate.

Kimber nodded. "I escaped from a POW camp in Silesia and made my way to Warsaw."

"And you speak German?"

"Yes." Kimber was about to add that he had learned the language from his Austrian mother but thought better of it.

"Good, we can use you as an interrogator. But first you must talk to London on the radio and tell your Mr Churchill what we need."

What the General wanted was for the 1st Polish Parachute Brigade in England to be dropped over Warsaw, the Allies to bomb all the German air bases within range of the capital, and for the Home Army to be resupplied by air. The document signed by Major General Reinhard Gehlen, Chief of War Intelligence on the Eastern Front, was of no consequence.

"I am not saying that it is a fake," Komorowski told him. "The Russians have always been our enemy, but these allegations are irrelevant. I've no doubt there is nothing they would like better than for the Fascists to destroy the AK, but we shall force the Red Army to come to our aid. And do you know why? Because Stalin dare not allow us to liberate Warsaw. It would be the end of his political ambitions in Western Europe."

The political analysis was way above Kimber's head, but he could read and understand the military symbols on the war map in front of the General and it seemed to him that the AK High Command was looking at life through rose-coloured spectacles.

CHAPTER 6

Half a mile due south of the Kamler tobacco factory, four yellow-nosed Messerschmitt Bf109s came in at rooftop height to strafe Chlodna Street and Elektoralna Avenue, the main thoroughfare from Wola to the Saxon Gardens in the city centre. Above the din of cannon and machine gun fire, Kimber thought he could hear the clatter of tracked vehicles. Five days after the uprising had begun, the long-awaited counter attack from the west had started.

Spearheading the advance to the Vistula was Brigadeführer Oskar Dirlewanger's Anti-Partisan Brigade. Composed of hardened criminals and former SS men who had been courtmartialled and imprisoned for a variety of offences ranging from petty theft to rape and murder, they were regarded with disdain by the Wehrmacht. Their reputation for brutality had preceded them long before they had left Danzig to detrain on the outskirts of Wola. Raised in 1941 to crush Resistance groups in Poland and White Russia, their barbarous activities had led more than one enraged army commander to demand their withdrawal from his operational area.

Yesterday morning, the first battalion of Dirlewanger's Brigade had gone into action in the Wola District some considerable distance from the forward defended localities of the AK. Supported by quadruple 20mm flak cannons and a mixed bag of Panther tanks and self-propelled assault guns from the Hermann Goering Division, they had rounded up and executed every man, woman and child in their sector, then burned the timber-frame houses to the ground. If ever Kimber felt inclined to doubt the horror stories of those few survivors of the massacre who had staggered into the headquarters, the heavy pall of smoke rising from the suburb supported what they said.

The Bf109s made a second pass and dropped a cluster of 30-kilogram delayed-action fragmentation bombs. Seconds later, Chlodna Street as far as the crossroads before Elektoralna Avenue was rocked by a series of explosions. Shattered timbers, masonry, the roof of what looked to be a tramcar and several bodies fountained into the air as the flimsy street barricades were ripped apart.

Kimber trained his binoculars in the direction of Ochta. If Dirlewanger's thugs smashed their way through to the Saxon Gardens, they would link up with the Germans still holding out in the Brühl Palace, Parliament Square and the Kierbedzia bridge. They would also split the AK forces on the west bank in two, and it didn't end there. Coming up from the south-west was another column which would divide General Komorowski's army yet again. Fortunately, there was no sign of activity in that suburb, which didn't altogether surprise Kimber; leading the advance through Ochta was the Russkaya Oswoboditeljnaja Narodnaja Armya, more commonly known as the RONA Brigade.

The so-called Russian Liberation Army consisted of Ukrainian peasant farmers and Cossacks who, in return for complete autonomy, had voluntarily banded together to hunt down Soviet partisans operating behind the German lines. At their peak strength they had numbered around twenty thousand and had been able to put five infantry regiments and a battalion of T34 tanks into the field. When the tide of war had turned against their German masters, they and their families had been evacuated to Silesia. Now they were back in action, this time fighting as a conventional military unit even though they were nothing more than an armed rabble. Lacking any kind of discipline, they were more interested in looting than engaging the AK.

Kimber felt a hand on his back and glancing over his shoulder, he found Halina had joined him.

"The Chief of Intelligence would like to see you, Michael," she said before he had a chance to ask her what she was doing up on the factory roof.

"Any idea what it's about?"

"Major Jacob's group on Jerusalem Avenue have just brought in a prisoner; he wants you to interrogate him."

"Okay, you go ahead, I'll follow."

Kimber waited until she was clear, then backed down the sloping roof and entered the factory through the open skylight where there was an extending ladder to the gallery above the shop floor. The AK Intelligence section occupied what had been the foreman's office.

The German was still blindfolded, his hands tied behind his back. What little that could be seen of his face was pale and drawn and he had a bad case of the shakes which amused the four members of the Intelligence section and the rifleman who was guarding him.

The shock of combat and the fear of what the Poles might do to him had unnerved the Gefreiter and when the strip of cloth covering his eyes was removed, Kimber fancied he could see why the NCO lacked resilience. The best combat infantrymen were in their late teens to early twenties; the Gefreiter had to be knocking on forty and had the delicate features more associated with poets than with hardened soldiers.

"Number, rank and name," Kimber demanded harshly.

The NCO snapped to attention. "S 6015478 Gefreiter Heinricci Georg Thomas."

"And your unit?"

Heinricci swallowed. "You know I can't tell you that, sir," he said nervously. "Under the Geneva Conventions . . ."

"You can forget the Geneva Conventions," Kimber told him icily. "Your side hasn't observed them once since the uprising started and these Polish soldiers know it. One word from me and they'll happily slit your throat from ear to ear. Of course, it won't come to that if you co-operate. You understand what I am saying?"

"Yes, sir."

"Do you want me to repeat the question?"

"That won't be necessary, sir. I'm with the 4th East Prussian Infantry Regiment."

Heinricci closed his eyes as though appalled by the enormity of the military offence he had just committed, then realising that it was already too late for regrets, he held nothing back. Much of his information was low-level stuff but from it, Kimber was able to fix the left and right boundaries of the Regiment. When plotted on a map with a chinagraph pencil, it amounted to a couple of tramlines either side of a broad arrow denoting the main thrust line of the 4th East Prussian Infantry Regiment. The question mark above the arrow indicated that this was unconfirmed. There was, however, no disputing the fact that 4th Infantry were in a very unenviable position.

"With any luck, they could end up fighting each other," Kimber said, thinking aloud.

Halina frowned. "Who are we talking about?"

"Heinricci's lot and the Russian Liberation Army. They've got Dirlewanger's convicts for neighbours on their left and the RONA Brigade is coming up on their right from the south-west. They're on a collision course with the East Prussians and anything could happen when they meet up."

And then maybe, just maybe, the AK would be able to hold out until the Red Army was ready to resume its offensive. Yesterday, a Captain Konstantin Kalugin, a liaison officer from Marshal Rokossovsky's First White Russian Front, had arrived at Komorowski's headquarters eager to arrange all kinds of material help. Until his arrival, it had begun to look as though there might be some substance to the Gehlen document which alleged that the Soviets would sit back and allow the Wehrmacht to destroy the Home Army.

"Is that what you want me to tell the Chief of Staff?" Halina asked.

Kimber shook his head. "Just give him the bald facts; he can draw his own conclusions."

"Right. I assume you have finished with this piece of filth?"

Heinricci was a conscripted soldier but as far as Halina was concerned, he was tarred with the same brush as the Gestapo.

"Yes, you can send him back to the POW cage with the other soldiers."

"Is that what he is – a soldier?" Halina said scornfully. She turned to the rifleman and spoke to him in a tone of voice that did not augur well for the German.

"He's a prisoner of war," Kimber reminded her.

"You English and your gentlemanly rules. Sometimes you make me sick." She said it again in Polish for the benefit of the Intelligence section.

Komorowski had appealed to London for help; perhaps some of his demands had been unrealistic, but it was hard for the Poles to understand why Eisenhower's forces should continue to receive a hundred per cent of all available resources when they were fighting for their lives.

The night before last, two RAF Halifax bombers had dropped a total of twenty-four containers of small arms and ammunition over Warsaw. Each plane had come in at an altitude of four hundred feet, trapped in a cone of searchlights and a prime target for every anti-aircraft gun within a radius of fifty miles. With their flaps down and at a speed close to stalling, they had flown through a wall of flak to plant the containers in the old Jewish cemetery north of the ghetto, the drop zone selected by the Home Army. Twelve other planes had set out from their base in Southern Italy, but they had been intercepted and five of their number had been shot down before they reached the DZ.

There had been no further flights since then. According to the messages they'd received from the Polish Government in London, the RAF were reluctant to repeat the operation for one very sound reason. The planes had come from a squadron of 334 Wing which

54

specialised in long-haul supply drops over enemy territory and they were unable to sustain the losses they'd already suffered. To the Poles in Warsaw, however, it looked as though the British had abandoned them.

Nobody had said as much to Kimber, but it was clear enough how they felt. The AK would hang on to their present positions come what may because they hoped Churchill would order the RAF to keep them supplied, no matter what the cost. There could be no retreat because every inch of territory they gave up reduced the size and number of dropping zones at their disposal. But with the sound of battle in Chlodna Street drawing ever nearer, Kimber wondered just how much longer General Komorowski's headquarters could remain in the tobacco factory.

High above the centre of Warsaw, a JU 87 hovered momentarily like a sparrowhawk before the pilot put the aircraft into a steep, almost vertical dive. The banshee wail of its air-activated sirens mounted on the spats of the fixed undercarriage obliterated the roar of the 1200-horsepower Junkers Jumo engine until it too finally succumbed to the even-higher-pitched screech of a 500-kilogram general-purpose HE bomb, which the pilot released a split second before he hauled the stick back and pulled out of the dive. The resultant explosion demolished the greater part of a city block and made a crater twenty feet deep in the road. The blast wave travelled outwards, rocking buildings up to half a mile away like an earthquake.

In the cellar of the Victoria Hotel, Leon Jarrell held Maria Bolek's hand while they waited for the next one. Late on Thursday morning, a runner from the hotel had fetched him from Zagorski's headquarters in the post office to identify a suspected collaborator. Maria had been the last person Jarrell had expected to see and at first he hadn't recognised the dirty, unkempt figure who had been paraded for his inspection. To be honest, she didn't look an awful lot better even now. The right side of her face was still swollen and disfigured by a dark bruise the colour of an over-ripe banana. She also had on the same skirt and blouse she had been wearing the afternoon Witzleben had summoned her to the Civil Affairs Bureau. Since then, she had been interrogated by the Gestapo, survived a mock execution, had damned nearly been shot as a traitor by the AK and had been locked up for forty-eight hours until a man called 'Wolf' had judged it safe to move her out of Krasinski Square.

Jarrell could prove he was an American airman and had testified that Maria had sheltered him from the German military authorities and the Gestapo. On the strength of his evidence, the local AK group commander had given her a clean bill of health and she was no longer under suspicion. But the memory of Neurath's interrogation was still fresh in her mind and Maria wouldn't let it rest until she had discovered the reason behind it. She had talked of little else since they had been reunited, and she returned to the subject again now in the middle of an air raid.

"I've seen that woman somewhere before, Leon."

"The one in the photographs," Jarrell prompted dutifully even though he knew exactly who she meant.

"Quite tall, very attractive, high cheekbones, blonde hair, about my age . . ."

"And a touch of class about her," Jarrell added.

"Yes."

Another heavy, general-purpose bomb exploded in the city centre and rocked the cellar.

"Neurath believed I knew her."

"Nah, he was just bluffing. Hell, the Resistance wouldn't have lasted five minutes if everybody had known everybody else."

"Perhaps the woman had nothing to do with the AK?" Maria took her tentative suggestion a stage farther. "What if she were a secret collaborator? A sort of agent for the Germans who had friends inside the Home Army?"

"And the Gestapo kept her under observation the whole time and photographed the people she met?"

"Yes."

"So why didn't they arrest them?"

"How do you know they didn't?" Maria countered.

"Because if they had lifted everyone she fingered, the AK would have gotten wise to her long ago. I'll tell you something else that doesn't make sense; why would Neurath go to the trouble of getting Witzleben to haul you into the office so that he could question you? No, like all the other Nazis in the city, he'd heard rumours of an uprising and your absence from work had been reported, so he dropped by the office to find out what you knew."

"I wonder . . ."

"You'd better believe it, otherwise you'll drive yourself nuts trying to put a name to a face that looks vaguely familiar."

Jarrell broke off, suddenly conscious that the bombing had stopped and the other inmates of the cellar could hear what he was saying. One of the girls who had been eavesdropping busied herself with the switchboard, but this was more out of hope than expectation. Although the AK had captured the telephone exchange on Thursday, bombing and heavy shellfire had destroyed most of the civil network, leaving the Poles still dependent on the messenger service.

A runner appeared via the mousehole that had been knocked through the wall to the adjoining cellar and handed a note to Second Lieutenant Tatar, the assistant signals officer at Headquarters 2 Group. Observing the way his expression darkened, Jarrell figured the messenger hadn't been the harbinger of good news. Then Tatar crumpled the note into a tight ball and hurled it across the room and it was no longer a matter of conjecture.

"I want ten volunteers," he shouted. "The Germans advancing along Elektoralna Avenue have broken through to the Saxon Gardens and we've got to hit them in the flank."

Jarrell got to his feet. Zagorski had relieved him of the Mauser rifle he'd acquired from a dead German on the grounds that he wouldn't need it at Group Headquarters, but the fact that he was unarmed did not stop him volunteering. Apart from the Second Lieutenant, he was the only one of military age in the cellar; the others were boy scouts, young women and old men.

"I'm going too," Maria told him.

"The hell you are . . ."

"The hell I am," she said.

They moved out in single file, the runner leading the way, followed by Second Lieutenant Tatar, a retired electrical engineer, three men from the sanitation department, a lawyer, Jarrell, Maria Bolek, a messenger and two fifteen-year-old boy scouts. Between them they had four rifles, two Sten guns and a revolver. By using the passageway the Home Army engineers had tunnelled through the cellars, they were able to stay below ground as far as the top of Jasna Street.

They surfaced into a mist of brick dust that blotted out the sunlight and made winter of a summer's afternoon. Everywhere Jarrell looked, the city was burning. In Zoliborz, north of the ghetto and the Old Town, four dense columns of black smoke rose vertically in the still air like the pillars of a Grecian temple. Jasna Street itself was under sporadic mortar fire and they crossed it one at a time on the double before heading due west along another subterranean route hacked out by the AK.

Like the rest of the squad, Jarrell depended on the runner knowing where he was taking them. Approximately three quarters of an hour after they had set out from the Victoria Hotel, they reached an ammunition supply point which had been established in the basement of a chemist shop. As they filed past a large trestle table, the owner handed a postbag to anyone who wasn't carrying a gun.

57

Every haversack contained four assorted bottles separated by wads of old newspapers.

"Careful how you go with that," the chemist told each recipient mournfully, "I don't want to see you light up like a torch."

They surfaced a second time and headed north once more, guided by the staccato rattle of machine gun fire as much as by the street map which Tatar and the runner consulted periodically. Somewhere up front a tank opened fire with its main armament, the gunner pumping off round after round as fast as the loader could shove them into the breech. Still in single file, Tatar led them through a tree-lined square and into a narrow street where a rescue squad was digging for survivors under a house that had been demolished in the Stuka raid. Then suddenly a tank appeared at the T-junction directly ahead and they were caught up in the battle.

Jarrell saw no point in waiting for orders; the moment the turret began to traverse in their direction, he grabbed Maria by the hand and ran for cover. A hail of machine gun fire swept the street and cut down the rescue workers before they could scatter. Without a backward glance, Jarrell dived into the hallway of a tenement that was just about standing and ran up the stairs.

The tank made a ninety degree turn, the turret rotating to the twelve o'clock position; then, at a walking pace, it advanced towards the tree-lined square, the hull gunner hosing one side of the street while the crew commander directed the coaxially-mounted Spandau to put down suppressive fire on the other side of the road. Behind the Panzer Mark IV, a double file of infantrymen scanned the rooftops and upper floors.

Their presence did not deter Jarrell; as the tank crawled past, he lobbed a Molotov cocktail through the open window. The bottle struck the engine deck and shattered; a split second later, the sulphuric acid combined with the calcium chloride to ignite the diesel oil and several liquid tongues of flame oozed their way into the turret. Moving to the left side of the window for maximum protection against the small arms fire coming his way, he hurled bomb after bomb at the infantrymen.

The Mark IV continued to trundle forward but the ready ammunition inside the turret was already beginning to cook up. The first 75mm shell exploded before it had covered thirty yards, then the remainder went up and blew the tank apart. Slowly but inexorably, the infantrymen were forced to retire and the line held.

Kimber stripped off to the waist. For the past six days he had been unable to wash or shave and the dirt had become ingrained like an extra layer of skin. The half bucket of water he'd been given had come from a standpipe which the AK had tapped into one of the few mains in the Wola District that hadn't been closed off by the Germans who still controlled all the waterworks in the city. This source of supply, however, was contaminated and unfit for drinking purposes, which meant they were still dependent on the bottle of beer per head per day they commandeered from the local brewery.

The small bar of household soap belonged to the Intelligence sergeant as did the cut-throat razor. Although the soap refused to lather and the razor needed honing, he felt better for having washed and shaved. Discarding a pair of woollen socks that were stiff with dirt and sweat, he soaked his feet and cleaned them as best he could, the water gradually turning from grey to a muddy brown.

The blouse, trousers and black leather boots had come from a supply depot near Danzig station which the AK had captured. The Germans would shoot him out of hand if he was caught in SS uniform but they would probably do that anyway. Dirlewanger's convicts weren't taking any prisoners and they were unlikely to pay much attention to the identity discs he continued to wear around his neck. And ironically, the only thing which would save him from being executed by his own side was the armband in the Polish national colours on his left sleeve.

"It suits you, Michael," Halina said, then closed the door to the storeroom behind her.

Kimber turned about. Her voice had sounded mocking and inferred that he would not feel out of place in the ranks of the SS. He suspected her antagonism stemmed from the fact that she believed the RAF had let the Home Army down, and he just happened to be a convenient whipping boy. She was also aware that his mother was an Austrian which didn't help.

"You're looking pretty smart yourself," he said evenly.

It was not an idle compliment. On one occasion after delivering a message to the AK commander in Zoliborz, she had stopped off at her home to pick up a change of clothing.

"I ought to be in deepest black."

"Why, what's up?" Kimber asked.

"We're pulling back to the Old Town."

"When?"

"This evening, as soon as it's dark. The Chief of Staff will be holding an orders group ten minutes from now."

"Well, we could hardly stay here much longer."

"Wars are not won by retreating," Halina said bitterly.

59

Maybe not, but the Kamler tobacco factory had been under sporadic machine gun fire since mid-afternoon when Dirlewanger's Anti-Partisan Brigade had started to widen the salient they had punched through to the Saxon Gardens. The way things were going in Wola, General Komorowski and his staff could find themselves in the front line by nightfall. The Old Town would be much easier to defend; it was sixty feet above the rest of the city and the Panzers would be vulnerable to ambush in the narrow streets.

There were other tactical considerations. Although the uprising in Praga had been crushed, the whole of the west bank, with the exception of the German enclaves at the bridges and the Brühl Palace, was in Polish hands. The rail links across the Vistula from the Central and Danzig stations were still blocked, which meant the Wehrmacht was finding it increasingly difficult to keep the 9th Army supplied. But most important of all, the AK would provide a valuable springboard when Marshal Rokossovsky's First White Russian Front went over to the offensive again.

The Chief of Staff said much the same thing at his briefing, possibly in a bid to lift the spirits of the assembled troops before he told them how the withdrawal was to be conducted. The plan was simplicity itself; at 1945 hours, the headquarters would move out in single file through the Zoska battalion defending the ghetto and the old Jewish cemetery. This well-trained and well-equipped unit would also furnish a platoon for their close protection until they reached their new location in Barakowa Street in the heart of the Old Town. The emphasis was on speed and silence and there would be no stopping for stragglers. There was no mention of what would happen to anyone who was wounded on the way back but the absence of stretcher bearers suggested to Kimber that they had better be capable of walking.

The withdrawal started on time and for a while it looked as though they had stolen a march on the SS and were going to make a clean break. Kimber could hear the sounds of battle somewhere to the south of Elektoralna Avenue but except for the usual harassing fire directed against the tobacco factory by a solitary machine gun, their own sector was quiet. But the hollow cough of a mortar and the para illuminating flare which bathed the column in an eerie white light soon changed all that. From the church tower inside Pawiak Prison, the angry fireflies of tracer bullets arched across the night sky to strike at the pathfinders up front. Almost simultaneously, the artillery opened up and started ranging on the column, a forward observer concealed in the ruins of the ghetto correcting the fall of shot until he achieved a perfect bracket.

"Scatter." Kimber couldn't think of the Polish equivalent and repeated "Scatter" at the top of his voice.

The column reacted like a disturbed ants' nest and broke in every direction. As they did so, the artillery began to fire for effect, putting down a heavy concentration of 105mm HE shells over an area of five thousand square yards. Dragging Halina with him, Kimber took cover in the rubble and waited for the storm to pass.

When the barrage lifted momentarily, he doubled forward, only to go to ground again as a loud whooshing noise heralded the imminent arrival of the next incoming salvo. Up, run, down. Up, run, down. Up, run, down. Kimber repeated the sequence as the barrage leapfrogged forward, sideways, and back. Up, run, down. Up, run, down. He maintained the pattern until Halina and the AK men who had fastened on to him reached the far side of the killing zone.

Somewhere to his left and rear, a soldier moaned in agony and pleaded feebly for his mother to come and help him. There were no stretcher bearers, no medics and no plan for the evacuation of casualties; they had also been warned that there would be no halting for stragglers but it was hard to leave one of your own to a lingering death. Kimber turned back to look for the wounded man and found him ten yards in from the road behind a pile of rubble.

The Intelligence sergeant was in a bad way; his left arm had been severed just below the shoulder, the left foot was hanging by a tendon and he was losing blood at a horrendous rate. The Polish national colours made one effective tourniquet, a bootlace the other. Racing against time, Kimber closed off the severed arteries and pulled the sergeant across his shoulders in a fireman's lift. The Pole screamed just the once before he passed out.

Kimber started running. Every instinct told him the shelling would start again at any minute and it was vital to distance himself from the last impact area. Halina was calling to him to get a move on as if, for some ludicrous reason, he was deliberately holding back. He heard the rushing noise of an express train and tried to run even faster in a futile attempt to escape the incoming salvo. The shells crumped into the rubble and suddenly the air was full of lethal metal. A violent blow behind the right ear made him stagger like a man the worse for drink and then he felt himself being sucked into a black hole.

61

Chapter 7

Witzleben folded his handkerchief into a triangular bandage to cover the blisters on the right palm and holding one end between his teeth, contrived to knot it behind his wrist. Yesterday, the Poles had put him to work digging a well, today it was half a dozen graves in the courtyard of a block of flats on Barakowa Street. A fortnight ago, he had been a complete stranger to manual labour and if he hadn't stayed on at the Civil Affairs Bureau while Neurath questioned the Bolek woman, he would have remained one.

He should have left with the other German officials, but he had wanted to know how big a threat Maria Bolek posed to him and by the time Neurath had got the answer, the uprising had already started. In view of this, Witzleben had planned to take refuge in the Brühl Palace for the night, but the AK had intercepted his Volkswagen on the way there. Looking back, he considered himself fortunate that he had not been shot out of hand like his Polish driver whom a Field General Court Martial had tried and condemned to death for treason. Had he been one of the Ukrainian prisoners, the Poles would have stripped him to the waist, painted a large black 'U' on his back and detailed him to build a barbed wire fence in the so-called neutral territory between the opposing forces where he would have been caught in the crossfire. As it was, they had taken his civilian clothes away and issued him with a pair of dungarees with a swastika emblem on the back and front.

The AK Intelligence officer who had interrogated Witzleben soon after his capture had taken a great delight in humiliating him. To hear the Pole, you would have thought he was the only man on either side who carried a set of pornographic photographs in his wallet. Every combat soldier he had talked to had told him the battlefield was littered with dirty pictures. There was nothing perverted about it, a soldier needed something to keep his mind off the war and he was just as much a soldier of the Third Reich as any man in uniform. But the Intelligence officer had scoffed at the idea.

"Family snapshots, Herr Doktor?" The AK Lieutenant had shown him a well-thumbed picture of a blonde in stockings and shoes whose hooded eyes gave the impression that she was enjoying an orgasm as she played with her breasts. "Would I be right in thinking this is Frau Witzleben?"

There had been many other impertinent questions no less insulting which of course had been intended to destroy his self-respect before the real interrogation began. But knowing this hadn't made him any the less vulnerable. He had a lot to hide and would be a dead man if the Poles ever learned the truth concerning Maria Bolek, especially if they knew why he had turned her over to Neurath for rigorous interrogation and termination should this prove necessary. So he had told the AK Lieutenant where to find the list of Polish workers employed by the Reich administration and how to interpret the symbols on the card index which graded their political reliability.

"Arbeit schnell, nicht langsam."

The Pole who had been assigned to guard the cemetery detail had only a very limited vocabulary but he knew how to get what he wanted out of his prisoners. Work swiftly, not slowly; Witzleben stopped leaning on his shovel and started digging. A few minutes later, the guard spoke to him again.

"Sie haben ein kameraden."

"Bitte?"

Witzleben wondered whether or not he had been asked a question and looked up into the chubby face of a decidedly overweight Feldwebel with myopic eyesight.

"I am Sergeant Exler," the newcomer said, introducing himself. "I think I am required to help you dig this grave, Herr . . . ?"

"Herr Doktor Witzleben."

"My apologies." Exler straightened up and stood to attention. "I did not recognise you, Herr Doktor."

"Do I know you?"

"I am with the Warsaw detachment of the 385th Postal and Courier Unit. I used to deliver classified mail to the Civil Affairs Bureau."

"Arbeit, nicht sprechen," the guard shouted and pushed Exler into the shallow grave.

Witzleben moved as far away from the Feldwebel as he could. What little water there was on tap was strictly for drinking purposes and everyone was beginning to smell to some extent, but Exler's body odour was overpowering.

"Take a pick and look busy, Sergeant," Witzleben said in a low voice. "We don't want that Polish Untermensch breathing down our necks the whole time."

"Yes, Herr Doktor."

Exler reached for the pick, took a firm grip of the shaft and swung. A shock wave travelled up both arms.

"The ground is rock hard, Sergeant."

"Yes, sir." Exler took another swing and managed to loosen a clod of earth about the size of a tennis ball.

"Where were you captured?"

"At the post office in Napoleon Square."

Witzleben frowned. Army units attacking from the west had linked up with the troops defending the Brühl Palace, effectively splitting the insurgent forces in two. As a result, every road leading from the city centre to the Old Town was now controlled by the Wehrmacht.

"How did you get here, Sergeant?"

"Through the sewers, Herr Doktor."

"I should have guessed."

"Sir?"

"Nothing, Sergeant; I was merely reflecting that I had overlooked the obvious."

There were two main sewage tunnels both running in a north–south direction with the outflow into the Vistula not far from the Bielany airstrip in the north. Witzleben thought it likely that the AK were using the one which ran from where the Bolek woman lived in central Mokotow beneath the city centre and Old Town to Zoliborz in the north. In addition to this main artery, the Poles could also use the drainage systems, a labyrinth of underground ducts which fed into the main sewage tunnels. However, there were serious risks involved; the diameter of these feeder conduits varied from two to seven feet and a sudden downpour or persistent rain would turn most of them into death traps.

"What do you think the Poles will do to us, Herr Doktor?"

"Nothing. Any day now they will be forced to surrender and they know what will happen to them if they harm us."

"Do you really believe it will soon be over?"

"Only a fool would believe otherwise, Sergeant," Witzleben said coldly.

He could not see how the insurgents could last more than another day or two at the most. Attacking from the west and north-west, the SS, together with units of the Wehrmacht, had cleared the old Jewish cemetery and the ghetto and reduced the AK to isolated pockets of resistance.

"I think it all depends on how many men like Zagorski they have," Exler said gloomily.

"Who's Zagorski?"

"The commanding officer of the battalion that captured Napoleon Square. He's a real fanatic; I can't see him giving up without a hell of a fight."

"It will take more than a few fanatics to stop the Wehrmacht. You, of all people, should know that, Sergeant."

The German Army and the SS were better trained, better led, better equipped. The Luftwaffe enjoyed complete supremacy in the sky above Warsaw and the Red Air Force was conspicuous by its absence. The Poles might have captured the main power station facing Good Street on the Vistula embankment but they were short of water and they were having to bury their dead in the streets. They had nothing heavier than a light mortar and ammunition was like gold dust; the Russians had abandoned them and there was nothing the war-mongering Churchill or Roosevelt could do to help them. The end was a foregone conclusion, so was the fact that he would be a very rich man when the shooting stopped.

"Look out, Herr Doktor."

Exler grabbed hold of his dungarees and pulled him down into the grave. He was vaguely aware of a peculiar rushing noise like the whirr of a spinning top; then the earth trembled and his senses were deadened by an ear-shattering explosion.

"My God, what was that?" Witzleben asked in a voice that sounded far away.

The explosion was louder and more terrifying than anything Kimber had experienced thus far in the siege of Warsaw. The Stuka could deliver an eleven-hundred-pound bomb but this sounded much heavier and in any case, there wasn't a plane in the sky. Neither could it have been the armoured train which the Germans were operating on the loop line between the Central and Danzig stations; that mounted nothing heavier than a 105mm.

Kimber looked at Halina and thought how pale and ill she looked; not that he was exactly the picture of health. The medics had practically scalped the right side of his head and a large first-aid field-dressing covered the ugly wound behind his ear. Ninety-nine per cent of the wounds inflicted by artillery fire were caused by shell splinters; he was one of the ironic exceptions and had been hit by a half brick thrown up by a 105mm round. It had, however, been almost as lethal and the impact had fractured his skull and left him concussed for several days. Even so, Kimber had been more fortunate than the Intelligence sergeant whom he had tried to rescue; the AK NCO had been wounded a second time and had died on the operating table.

"Are you okay?" he asked Halina.

"Perfectly."

"Shall we go then?"

"Why not? They do say lightning doesn't strike twice in the same place, at least, according to you English it doesn't." She smiled lopsidedly. "Besides, Zagorski won't like it if we keep him waiting."

"I think I'd be jumping up and down in his shoes; a weapon is no good to you unless you know how to handle it."

The night before last, two Halifax bombers had made a supply drop over the Old Town. The second plane had just been approaching the DZ when it had been hit by flak. Taking violent evasive action, the pilot had overshot and jettisoned his supply containers over the city centre before crashing somewhere in Praga. Five of the eleven containers had fallen in the region of Napoleon Square; the rest had ended up in German hands. Of those recovered by Zagorski's men, two had contained British anti-armour weapons of a type the Poles hadn't seen before. It was going to be Kimber's job to show them how to use the Projector Infantry Anti-Tank, known to the British as the PIAT. It was Halina's job to get him to Napoleon Square via the sewers.

Dressed for the part in thigh-length waders, protective clothing, helmet and flashlight provided by the City Sanitation Department, she looked twice her normal size and moved awkwardly. Kimber followed her out of the school on Barakowa Street where Komorowski had established his headquarters and turned right. At the top of the road, she raised a manhole cover and climbed down the iron rungs set into the wall. The drainage conduit was about three feet in diameter; with some difficulty, she managed to kneel down and crawl inside the horizontal tube. Kimber waited until only her ankles were visible before he climbed down and replaced the manhole cover.

The air below ground was fetid and warm and if it hadn't been for Halina's flashlight, he wouldn't have been able to see a hand in front of his face. The conduit snaked this way and that and sloped downward steep enough to make it difficult to retain a grip on the slimy surface of the tube.

After they had been crawling for approximately twenty minutes they reached the first of several feeder pipes, each marginally smaller in diameter than their conduit. No rain had fallen in the last week and the flow had been reduced to a mere trickle; a sudden cloudburst and the situation would change dramatically. Within minutes, the feeder pipes would create a raging torrent in the main conduit and their chances of survival would be minimal.

"Holera, do dupy ztym."

Halina slipped and cursed as she inadvertently let go of the flashlight. The beam of light began to recede into the darkness as it gathered momentum and eluded her grasp. She scrabbled after the flashlight, but the gradient rapidly became much steeper, her hands slipped on the greasy surface and she measured her length. Lying flat on her stomach as though on a toboggan, Halina sledged the rest of the way to the bottom and just managed to grab the guardrail before she was swept across the walkway into the main sewer. When Kimber caught up with her, she was on her knees sobbing uncontrollably. The flashlight was lying on the bottom of the sewage tunnel, its beam dimmed to a faint, blurry orb by the murky waters.

"We . . . we . . . we're . . ." Halina gulped, hiccuped, then tried again. "We're lost . . . I've got to have a light . . ." A note of panic crept into her voice. "Otherwise, how will I know where we're going? And where are we?"

"We'll be all right, I promise you." Kimber gently squeezed her shoulder. "We'll be out of here before you can say Jack Robinson."

"Who's he?"

"God knows."

The tunnel was wide enough to take a train; gauging the depth of the water below the level of the walkway was a much more difficult piece of guesswork. Not that it made a great deal of difference whether there was four, seven or ten feet of water; to reach the flashlight, he would have to submerge beneath the raw, untreated effluent.

Kimber climbed over the guardrail, stood on the edge of the walkway, took a deep breath and gradually lowered himself into the channel. The water level reached his chest, then his chin, finally rose above his head. He kept his eyes open, his mouth closed and his mind a blank because that was the only way to stop himself throwing up. Homing in on the flashlight, he grabbed hold of the shaft and surfaced a whole lot faster than he had submerged. Kimber passed the torch to Halina, reached for the bottom slat of the guardrail and hauled himself up on to the walkway.

"Shit – pure, unadulterated shit." Kimber retched. "I think I'm going to be sick."

His stomach heaved and there was a terrible gagging sensation as the bile rose in his mouth. Then the vomit spewed out and he crouched there coughing and spluttering, fur on his tongue and sweat on his brow.

"Oh, Michael, Michael." Halina went through the pockets of her coverall, found a piece of cloth, then knelt beside him and wiped his face clean. "I'm so sorry, it's all my fault."

She had never spoken to him so fondly nor shown such concern and he was touched by her tenderness. It would, he thought, be very easy to fall in love with this Polish girl even though he didn't know a damned thing about her, not even her surname.

"It was nobody's fault, just the bloody war." Kimber struggled to his feet. "What say we move on?"

"Do you feel up to it?"

"You bet I do. I don't want to stay down here a minute longer than I have to."

They continued on the walkway, Halina using the flashlight to check the conduits leading into the tunnel on either side. She had been told which landmarks to look out for by the engineer from the Sanitation Department who had accompanied her the first time she had delivered a message to Zagorski. Having gone solo on two further occasions since then, she claimed to know the route backwards.

"I think we're under the German positions in the Saxon Gardens," Halina told him.

Kimber instinctively looked upwards. He hoped the enemy wouldn't suddenly take it into their heads to flush the sewer with smoke and tear gas. As a professional, it also occurred to him that flame-throwers supplemented by hand grenades would be a particularly effective way of clearing the smaller conduits. Once he heard a dull roar coming from one of the tributaries and wondered if the Germans hadn't already cottoned on to this idea but, on reflection, he realised that the explosion had happened above ground.

Some ten or fifteen minutes later, they crossed the main channel by a small footbridge and entered the drainage conduit under Napoleon Square. The glimmer of daylight ahead of them was the most welcome sight Kimber had seen in a very long time.

Elektoralna Avenue had been Jarrell's passport to acceptance. Before the battle, Zagorski had treated him with suspicion bordering on hostility; after the battle, he was practically a national hero. Kimber had yet to be elevated to that status and on the basis of what Zagorski had told him, he had expected the Englishman to be soft-centred and effete. But the guy in SS uniform who had just walked into the post office was anything but a dandy. He was roughly six feet tall, lean as a rail and looked about as pliable as a steel ingot. One side of his head had been shaved, giving him a quasi Sioux hairstyle and there was a grubby-looking first-aid dressing in place behind the right ear which covered half the scalp.

Zagorski did not seem best pleased to see Kimber; the way the Englishman poked him in the chest with a finger suggested the feeling was mutual. Although Jarrell couldn't hear what she was saying, the girl at Kimber's side appeared to be angry with both men, rounding first on Zagorski before giving her companion a piece of her mind. Then she calmed down a bit, pointed to the field-dressing on Kimber's head and indicated she wanted someone to have a look at the wound.

"Look at them," Tatar growled. "I wish to God they would bury their hatchets in the Germans instead of each other."

Of the blocking force Tatar had commanded in the battle of Elektoralna Avenue, only Jarrell, Maria Bolek and two AK riflemen had survived. A single-minded soldier, Tatar believed that every ounce of energy, anger and hatred should be channelled towards destroying the enemy instead of being dissipated in petty squabbles amongst themselves.

"Relax," Jarrell told him in Polish. "They'll soon get over it."

"They're wasting valuable time."

When Jarrell looked their way again, Kimber had stripped off his soiled camouflaged smock and was changing into a field grey jacket taken from one of the dead while Maria was busy changing the field-dressing for a clean one. As Kimber walked towards them, Jarrell went forward and introduced himself; then, in his usual direct manner, he asked the Englishman what Zagorski had gotten so steamed up about.

"I wanted to know what had happened to a POW called Exler. Zagorski claimed that, in accordance with the instructions he'd received, all civilian internees and captured Wehrmacht personnel had been sent into the Old Town to help prepare the defences."

"Well, he happens to be right." Jarrell grinned. "I guess he resents you checking up on him."

"We never hit it off from the first day we met," Kimber told him. "His battalion was stopped cold when they attempted to storm this place. I suggested we should sneak up on the post office by taking the Prudential building first. Zagorski didn't think much of the idea but one of his subordinates, a man called Jan, was all for it."

"Jan was killed a couple of days ago; he got his in a Stuka attack."

"I'm sorry to hear that. Anyway, Jan gathered what was left

of his company together and we went ahead without Zagorski's permission. Consequently, he blames me for undermining his authority." Kimber looked past the American at the group of AK men hunkered down to the right of the entrance. "I presume that lot are waiting for me?"

"Yeah, they're the class of '44. I don't know how good your Polish is, but I could translate any questions they may have which you don't understand."

"Thanks." Kimber smiled. "I have a feeling you're going to be a very busy man."

The PIAT resembled a metal cylinder balanced on a monopod with a trough shaped like a half moon at one end and a vertical shoulder pad at the other. The firing mechanism consisted of a pistol grip, guard, and an outsize trigger to accommodate the index and two middle fingers. Housed inside the cylinder was a foot-long steel spigot and a return spring. A web sling attached to swivel clips just in front of the shoulder pad and forward of the trigger guard enabled the user to carry the weapon over one shoulder like a rifle or bandolier-fashion across the back.

"All right," said Kimber, "keep your eyes on me and I'll show you how to load one of these gadgets."

He picked up the nearest PIAT, unclipped the retaining catch which locked the cylinder in position, then placed the weapon upright on the floor and stood on the shoulder pad. Bending over the PIAT, Kimber took a firm grip on the trigger guard, wrapped the sling around the other hand and unlocked the cylinder from the shoulder pad by giving it a quarter turn to the right. Then he straightened up, compressing the return spring until it locked in with a loud click and the spigot was cocked. He returned the cylinder to its normal position and clipped it into the shoulder pad.

"Now we come to the tricky part," he told Jarrell.

"Yeah, why so?"

"There are no drill rounds, we've got to use live ammunition."

Kimber opened a metal container and took out a hollow charge anti-tank projectile which resembled a mortar bomb with a circular fin. He showed the assembled AK men how to fit a graze fuse on to the nose cone and a ballistite cartridge in the tail sleeve. Before Jarrell had finished translating, they had already guessed that the armed projectile was then placed in the trough with the fin towards the spigot. The trigger released the return spring which slammed the spigot into the ballistite cartridge. The resultant explosion sent the projectile on its way and automatically re-cocked the weapon.

"What's the maximum range?" Jarrell asked.

"Seventy-five yards. The hollow charge will stop a Tiger tank in its tracks."

"Seeing's believing."

"We can't afford to waste a single round. Where's the nearest tank?"

"Corner of Elektoralna and Rymarska up by the Saxon Gardens."

"All right, let's get out of here before the storm breaks."

"What storm?"

"Halina, the blonde girl who came with me," said Kimber, "she has a letter from the commander of the Old Town ordering Zagorski to hand over twenty-four PIAT rounds."

"He sure as hell won't like that."

"He'll like it even less when he learns he's got to provide the carrying party," Kimber said grimly.

Maria Bolek had thought she recognised the girl who had arrived with the Englishman the moment she'd walked into the post office. As soon as she removed the protective helmet and shook out her blonde hair, Maria knew she hadn't been mistaken. The Englishman had told her that she called herself Halina and had shrugged his shoulders when Maria had asked him if he knew her family name. Although her background was therefore something of a mystery, it was evident that Halina was used to commanding respect and was not impressed by men like Stefan Zagorski. Nor did she show much interest when Maria Bolek introduced herself.

"Have we met before?" she asked with genuine indifference.

"I think so. Your face is very familiar and I've certainly seen photographs of you."

"Not in any glossy magazine," Halina said with a laugh.

"No, the ones I saw were produced by the Gestapo."

"Wh . . . a . . . t?"

"They were snapshots taken without your knowledge. In one of them you were holding the arm of a frail and elderly-looking gentleman while walking through Lazienki Park. The other showed you outside Kuba's Café . . ."

"Never mind all that." The blonde girl reached for the fleshy part of Maria's left arm and dug her fingernails into the muscle. "I'm not interested in the trivial details, I want to know where and when you saw these photographs."

The colour had drained from Halina's face and although this was due in some measure to her anger, Maria thought she was also very frightened.

71

"Let go of my arm," she said loudly, "you're hurting me."

Halina glanced about her, realised that their raised voices could be heard by some of the Home Army men who were resting in the post office, and immediately let go of Maria's arm.

"I'm sorry." She smiled hesitantly. "My nerves are overstretched, I guess."

"It happens to us all."

"Yes. About the pictures . . . ?"

"Yours were just two of many I was shown when I was called into Doktor Witzleben's office for questioning by a Gestapo agent called Neurath."

"Neurath?" Halina's voice rose in surprise.

"Yes. Do you know him?"

"Not personally, but he was present when the Englishman and I walked into a road block manned by the SS. He left moments before the Scharführer began to execute the civilians his men had rounded up." She broke off and stared at Maria, her eyes narrowing. "You worked for the German administration in their Civil Affairs Bureau," she said accusingly.

"Yes. I supplied the Home Army with false papers."

"Every collaborator I've ever met has told me a similar story."

"In my case, it happens to be the truth," Maria told her with quiet dignity. "I'm lucky to be alive. Neurath would have killed me if a mortar bomb hadn't got him first."

"When was this?"

"A few hours after the uprising began. Neurath knew I'd recognised you in one of the snapshots and when I denied it, he dragged me out into the garden . . ."

"It wasn't my photograph you saw," Halina said, interrupting her. "It might have been someone who looked very similar, but it definitely wasn't me."

"But I know it was . . ."

"Don't be stupid, Maria. Neurath saw me at the road block that very same morning. If I was on his wanted list, why didn't he arrest me then? Answer me that if you can."

Maria couldn't. She just wondered why the blonde girl should be so triumphant about it.

Chapter 8

To the gun crew, the artillery piece was affectionately known as 'Thor', for the simple reason that the twenty-four-inch mortar was the heaviest and largest weapon in the world. The God of War weighed a hundred and thirty-two tons and could throw a four-thousand-eight-hundred-and-fifty-pound shell over a distance of eight thousand yards. The warhead could penetrate eight feet of reinforced concrete or seventeen and a half inches of armour plate and had previously been used in action in 1942 against the forts protecting Sebastopol in the Crimea. Manned by a gun crew consisting of three officers and a hundred and ten enlisted men, 'Thor's' maximum rate of fire was four rounds in an hour. For the past eight days, the mortar had been used to bombard the Old Town from a position north-west of Danzig station.

The other surprise weapon was known as 'Goliath'. A remote-controlled miniature tank, it was still very much in the development stage, but there could not have been a better proving ground for the robot than the battleground of Warsaw. There were two variations of 'Goliath'; one was powered by a small petrol engine and was guided by a trailing wire, the other was driven by an electric motor and controlled by radio. Both models carried a two-hundred-pound warhead over a maximum range of two thousand feet. Slow moving and cumbersome, the tracked vehicle looked like a reptile from a prehistoric age but there was no more terrifying sight than a 'Goliath' suddenly appearing round a street corner and lumbering remorselessly towards its intended target. As a means of destroying key Home Army strongpoints, it was proving horribly effective.

Kimber had seen for himself the destructive power of both weapons as the medieval buildings of the Old Town were systematically pounded into dust. The AK had failed to capture a single bridge over the Vistula; they did, however, control most of the west bank from Zoliborz in the north to the inland harbour three quarters of a mile below the southernmost bridge. In places, the depth of this extended bridgehead was less than three hundred yards but so long as Komorowski's men held out, the Red Army would not be faced with an assault river crossing when they eventually seized the suburb of Praga.

No one appreciated this better than the German High Command. Nor was the tactical importance of the Old Town lost upon them; situated at the narrowest point of the river, it dominated the whole city from an elevation of sixty feet. By committing the bulk of their forces to this sector, the Germans aimed to eliminate what they regarded as the most dangerous bridgehead while at the same time dividing the AK into isolated pockets of resistance which could then be dealt with piecemeal.

The AK had roughly two thousand armed men in the Old Town. The heaviest weapon in their armoury was the PIAT of which they had three, with eight rounds for each projector, plus a further twelve as a central reserve. With such a chronic shortage of anti-tank ammunition, it was essential that not a single missile was wasted. Kimber was one of three detachment commanders who decided what target should be engaged and when.

His team had been assigned to a strongpoint in the south-west section of the Old Town near the junction of Dluga and Miodowa Streets where their arc of fire ranged from Krasinski Square on the left to the heap of rubble which had once been Franciszkanska Road to their front. The suburb of Zoliborz lay directly to the north with the Wehrmacht strongly entrenched in between. If the AK could drive the Germans out of their salient and establish a secure corridor, they could draw on the Zoliborz contingent for reinforcements. General 'Bor' Komorowski would also gain a tenuous link with the partisan forces operating in Kampinos Forest farther north who had been the main beneficiaries of the supplies dropped by the RAF, the South African Air Force and the Polish Special Duties Flight.

It had been a very big 'if'. Kimber had lost count of the number of attacks that had been launched under cover of darkness against the German salient from both Zoliborz and the Old Town. Every one had ended in total failure with the Home Army cut to ribbons by the superior firepower of the enemy. Now, all they could do was hang on and hope for the best, thirsty, half-starved and bleary-eyed from lack of sleep.

"Michael." An unwelcome hand on his shoulder roused him just as he was about to nod off.

"Wake up, Michael." Maria Bolek exhausted her few words of English and switched to German. "Aufwachen, bitte, aufwachen."

After teaching Zagorski's men how to load and fire the PIAT, Kimber had returned to the Old Town. Jarrell and Maria Bolek had gone with him to help carry the twenty-four anti-tank missiles which the Polish battalion commander had been ordered to surrender. Both had subsequently been retained at Home Army headquarters, Jarrell as a fire controller in charge of a tank-hunting team, Maria as a liaison officer.

"The General and his staff are pulling out of the Old Town, Michael." There was no mistaking the anguish and despair in her voice.

"When?" Kimber asked dully.

"Tonight; they're moving to the city centre. Three of our four wireless transmitters are buried under the rubble; now something is wrong with the remaining one and General Komorowski is cut off from the outside world. The signals officer told me there are spare sets with Group Headquarters in the Victoria Hotel which are still working."

It was vital that the General should be able to communicate with the Polish Government in Exile. If the Red Army was too exhausted to resume the offensive against Warsaw, the Russians could at least keep the AK supplied with small arms and ammunition but, to date, they had done absolutely nothing, despite the arrival of a liaison officer from Marshal Rokossovsky's First White Russian Front. And the Luftwaffe was ranging free in the skies above the city because the Red Air Force was conspicuous by its absence. Not only that, the Soviet High Command had made all kinds of excuses for not allowing the United States Army Air Force and the RAF to land and refuel at their forward airfields. The only way to bring pressure to bear on Stalin was through London and it would be impossible for the Polish Government to brief Churchill about the latest situation in Warsaw unless the Home Army remained in contact with them.

"The General wants us to hold out to the last," Maria said quietly.

"I bet he does."

The longer the Germans committed the bulk of their forces against the Old Town, the more chance there was for the other Districts to continue the struggle until Soviet help arrived. It was all very well in theory, but the defenders were exhausted and in the southern area around the Town Hall, the Treasury Printing building and the Cathedral of St John, the battle had raged non-stop for a week.

"What day is it?" Kimber asked.

"Sunday," Maria told him. "Sunday the twenty-seventh of August."

"Have you seen Halina recently?"

"I talked to her briefly on Friday; she's with the Kanalarki now."

As well as carrying orders through the network of sewers, the Kanalarki were also responsible for traffic control, signposting and reconnoitering alternative routes. It was doubtful if there was a more dangerous or unpleasant job in the whole of the AK.

"How long have you known her, Michael?"

"Just about a month; we met the day before the uprising began."

"Did Halina ever mention a man called Nowotko? Count Ladislaw Nowotko?"

"No, who's he?"

"A very rich, rather frail, but very nasty old man. When I was being interrogated by the Gestapo, I was shown a photograph of Halina walking arm-in-arm with him in Lazienki Park on a winter's afternoon. It must have been a bitterly cold day because the Count had a scarf wrapped around his mouth and nose. Only his eyes were visible and I didn't realise who he was then. In fact, his name only came to me this morning."

"Really?"

"I'm curious to know where and how Halina met him."

"You'll have to ask her," Kimber said.

"I mean to."

One of the sentries watching the heap of rubble which marked Franciszkanska shouted a warning. Moving to one of the loopholes they had drilled through the wall on the ground floor of the police station, Kimber saw a 'Goliath' trundling slowly towards them.

"You'd better get out of here," he told Maria.

"But . . ."

"No buts, just do as I say."

Two hundred pounds of high explosive through the front door was the quickest and most economical way for the Germans to reduce the strongpoint which had delayed their advance for so long. And they weren't taking any chances with a wire-guided job which could get snarled up in the debris; this particular 'Goliath' was radio-controlled and powered by an electric motor.

"Let's go."

Kimber snapped his fingers at the PIAT team and ducked through the sand-bagged entrance into the trench that captured enemy personnel had dug along the sidewalk fronting the police station. Thirty plus yards and closing at five miles an hour; it was going to be touch and go. The tank-hunting team jumped into the trench beside him, a burst of machine gun fire enhancing their sense of urgency.

No orders were necessary; both Poles could see the target clearly and knew that it would be on top of them if they didn't get a move on. The Number One flipped up the back sight and leaned into the shoulder pad while his Number Two placed a missile in the loading tray. When he squeezed the trigger and released the spigot, the 'Goliath' was less than twenty yards from the trench. The hollow charge round struck the miniature tank head on; a millisecond after it detonated, the tracked vehicle blew up and a hurricane force wind buffeted the police station.

No bombs or shells had fallen in the quiet, tree-lined avenue in Zoliborz where Ladislaw Nowotko lived, which those who knew him best would have said was a classic case of the devil looking after his own. Nowotko was tall, frail and was frequently mistaken for a man in his mid-seventies although he was only fifty-nine. A voracious sexual appetite and pulmonary tuberculosis had contributed to his ravaged appearance, but the primary cause was his addiction to alcohol.

The Nowotkos were minor nobility who could trace their lineage back to the Tartar invasion of 1241 when one of their ancestors had fought alongside the Teutonic Knights and Henry the Pious at the battle of Legnica forty miles west of Wroclaw, which the Germans now called Breslau. They had become wealthy landowners by a series of judicious marriages down through the ages. Ladislaw's grandfather, who had inherited money, had increased the family fortune through his alliance with Sophie Louise Tresckow, only daughter of Otto Tresckow, a prosperous mine owner and steel baron. Inter-marriage between Poles and Germans was not uncommon in the border area with Silesia and this once-removed Aryan connection had done the family no harm in two world wars.

Ladislaw Nowotko had taken a well-endowed Catholic of good Polish stock for his wife and had been unfaithful to her for the first time while they were on their honeymoon in Paris. Following the birth of their only son in 1912, they had lived separate lives to all intents and purposes.

Halina was the latest in a long line of mistresses Ladislaw Nowotko had kept. He had met her in 1938 through his son, Adam, a lecturer at the University of Warsaw. She had been reading English and their relationship had been much deeper than the usual tutor and student. Taking her away from Adam had gratified him

77

almost as much as had her sexual prowess both in and out of bed. Born in Praga within a stone's throw of Wilno station, Halina was the only child of an impecunious music teacher and a dressmaker. From a very early age, she had been determined that life would be kinder to her than it had been to her parents. A worker's flat in a tenement was not for Halina, she wanted an apartment in the fashionable part of town and a villa in the country. She had brains, beauty and enormous willpower but, as Halina was quick to realise, these attributes alone were not sufficient to enable her to fulfil her ambitions. She had no hope of earning enough to buy what she wanted, nor, in view of her humble background, could she expect to marry well. Girls like Halina could only obtain the luxuries of life by being nice to men like Count Ladislaw Nowotko.

Halina had come to him comparatively inexperienced; under his tuition, she had learned every trick practised by the whores working the back streets around the Gare St Lazare, his favourite stamping ground in Paris. There was, however, one big difference between Halina and the harlots; you could take her into the Adlon in Berlin or the Alcron in Prague knowing there would be no raised eyebrows. Not surprisingly, her services were a good deal more expensive than those of her professional sisters.

Nowotko poured himself another vodka and walked out into the neglected and overgrown garden. Another hot summer's day, the Vistula a broad ribbon of blue, not a cloud in the sky to the north but a dense pall of smoke rising from the Old Town three miles south of Zoliborz. Yet, apart from the distant crump of a heavy artillery piece, the sounds of battle were virtually non-existent.

"Ladislaw."

A familiar voice that was at once seductive and commanding. He turned about slowly, not wanting to appear too excited at the prospect of seeing Halina again. The stained overalls and the foul odour of the sewers made him genuinely disdainful.

"You stink," he said brutally. "Get yourself cleaned up before you come anywhere near me."

"Is there any water in the house?"

"I filled all the baths while the mains were still working."

"How clever of you to follow my advice, Ladislaw."

"Water is becoming precious," he said coldly. "Don't waste any; just fill a wash basin and make do with that."

He had wanted to provoke her and was disappointed when Halina turned about and went back inside the house without saying another word. When, after a few minutes' interval, he followed her into the drawing room, she had already stripped off the overalls and rolled

78

them into a ball. As he stepped across the threshold, the soiled bundle of clothing struck him in the face.

"Don't you ever ever talk to me like that again, you drunken sot."

Her anger made him feel apprehensive instead of ecstatic because this time she wasn't play-acting and this wasn't one of their little sex games where she abused and dominated him before their roles were reversed. Times were changing and he fancied he knew the reason.

"You wouldn't dare treat me like this were I still a wealthy man."

"When did you become poor?"

"The day I met you," Nowotko told her. "I bought you this villa, paid for the clothes on your back, showered you with expensive gifts and supported your worthless parents. Had the Germans not invaded Poland, you would probably have tried to persuade me to sign over to you the title deeds of the estate. As it is, Reichsmarschall Goering's removal men will have looted Kepno of all its treasures."

"There was nothing left for them to steal; I made sure of that."

"So you say."

"You make me sick." Halina turned her back on him and walked away. "Try doing something useful for once," she called from the hall. "Fix me a drink and look out some clean clothes while I have my bath."

"Where did you bury the Monet?"

"At Wolomin with the other paintings." Her voice floated down, mocking him from the landing above. "But of course it's no longer there, nothing is."

Nowotko poured himself another vodka, the sixth that morning, then slumped into an armchair. The bitch had sold the Monet as well as everything else she had removed from the estate at Kepno immediately before the outbreak of war in 1939. When the Army had begun to mobilise on the thirtieth of August, Zofia, his wife, had left the manor house and fled to her parents in Lodz, abandoning amongst other items, a valuable collection of paintings which alone were worth some three million dollars. And he had been powerless to do anything about it. As a reserve officer, he had been ordered to join the 14th Infantry Division at Piater, sixty miles to the west of Warsaw. Adam, too, had been called up and there had been no one else he could turn to other than Halina. She had procured a car from somewhere and, accompanied by her shiftless father, had driven to Kepno some twenty odd miles from the German border.

In the space of two hours, they had cut two Renoirs, the Monet, a Rembrandt, Tissot's 'The Garden Bench' and a Holbein from their frames. They then filled the boot of the Ford V8 with silver candlesticks, knives, forks, spoons, vases and a centrepiece that was only good for melting down. They had gone through the house again and packed every gold trinket they could find into a suitcase, after which, Halina had driven the hundred and fifty miles back to Warsaw. She had stopped off at the villa in Zoliborz long enough to collect a garden spade before crossing the Vistula and going on to the small country residence near Wolomin that had belonged to his family for generations. There, in the middle of the night, Halina and her father had buried a small fortune.

At least, that was what Halina had led him to believe, but with the passage of time, he had become less and less inclined to take her word for it. He had never seen the hiding place for himself, nor had she told him exactly where in the grounds he should look for it. If that wasn't damning enough, he'd also caught the whore out in a whole catalogue of lies. The Nowotko gold and silver had never been interred at Wolomin; it was stashed somewhere in that festering tenement where her parents lived.

Every once in a while, the scheming bitch sold the odd trinket to buy him a case of vodka. He enjoyed a drink; what man didn't? But she had made him dependent on alcohol until he had difficulty in remembering which day of the week it was. Furthermore, a lot of the stuff she was pouring down his gullet was pure wood alcohol, the kind of poison which could cost him his sight or even his life. Nowotko sat up; that was it, the cheating bitch was trying to kill him. The war was coming to an end and it was the only way she could hang on to what was left of his fortune. Tears of self-pity filled his eyes and he struggled to his feet. The glass of vodka slipped through his fingers and the room began to revolve faster and faster like a runaway carousel; then suddenly it grew pitch dark and he felt himself falling into a bottomless chasm.

Nowotko was still lying flat on his stomach, his nose pressed into the Persian carpet, when Halina came downstairs. It was not the first time she had found Ladislaw in a drunken stupor and she had no sympathy for him. The days when Halina would have done her level best to sober him up were long gone; now she merely turned him over to his right side and placed a cushion under his head. She then emptied the rest of the vodka bottle down the kitchen sink.

Roughly half an hour after Halina had left the villa to return to the Old Town, Nowotko died in his own vomit, having been violently sick into the cushion.

*　　*　　*

The earth trembled as though there had been a volcanic eruption and a fine trickle of dirt from the parapet of the trench fell into the mess tin of potato soup and horsemeat which Kimber was endeavouring to eat. In the most Teutonic of ways, the air raids had become highly repetitive. Every hour on the hour, four Stukas appeared in the sky a thousand feet above and dived one by one on the Old Town to release a cluster of one-hundred-and-ten-pound bombs into the ever-shrinking Home Army perimeter. The Luftwaffe were so regular that he could have set his watch by them; the same, however, could not be said for the Quartermasters of the AK. Their feeding arrangements were so haphazard that you simply ate what you could, when you could, air raid or no air raid.

Kimber froze, the spoon halfway to his open mouth as the last of the JU 87s went into a steep dive, the sirens on its fixed undercarriage activated and powered by the slipstream. A feeling that the pilot was aiming for the police station was reinforced by an ear-piercing whistle as the bomb load fell to earth. Kimber dropped the spoon and mess tin and instinctively raised both arms to protect his head.

The cluster exploded directly behind the police station and demolished what was left of the building. Part of a tie-beam fell into the trench and caught him a glancing blow on the left arm, bruising the bone. Wedged diagonally across the trench above him, the baulk formed a sloping roof ahead of the avalanche of debris which buried him alive. The sunlight vanished with the speed of a camera shutter and he heard someone scream and wondered if it was him. Then there was this terrible weight on his chest and he couldn't breathe.

CHAPTER 9

A low murmur of voices reached Kimber and he tried to call out, hoping to attract their attention, but the weight bearing down on his chest was too great and he couldn't draw a deep enough breath. Dirt clogged his nose, mouth and ears, clung to both lids and made his eyes water. A chink of light appeared near his head and grew larger; the pressure on his chest eased and suddenly he could move his legs, then his arms. A dozen willing hands reached down into the trench and lifted him out, but he could not stand up unaided and had to be supported on either side.

He coughed, spluttered, spat the dirt out of his mouth and blew down his nose. A girl with a grubby handkerchief carefully removed the grit from both his eyes. All around him people were burrowing into the rubble like moles, scattering the spoil behind them. A man gave a triumphant yell and raised an arm he had uncovered. Two other men and a boy barely in his teens abandoned the spot where they had been digging and joined him. The head and shoulders appeared, then realising the soldier was dead, they hauled the body out of the rubble and dumped it on the ground with about as much regard as they would a sack of coal.

The Number Two of the tank-hunting team had also been killed, his skull compressed as though it had been squeezed between the jaws of a giant vice. They went on digging until they found the PIAT and the metal box containing three hollow charge anti-tank rounds. The anti-tank projector had been dented, the tube encasing the spigot and return spring bent into a deep V which effectively damaged the weapon beyond repair. The metal container had fared little better and at least one of the precious missiles was no longer usable.

Four women stretcher bearers arrived with a stout wooden door that had been converted into a makeshift litter. Deaf to Kimber's protests, they insisted on carrying him back to the nearest First Aid Post. It turned out to be a rough, bone-shaking journey. Whole streets no longer existed as such and it was impossible to tell just where the road itself had been, so that a town map was hardly worth the paper it was printed on. Relying on certain familiar landmarks that were still standing to guide them, the stretcher bearers worked on the principle that the shortest distance between two given points was a straight line.

Undeterred by sporadic mortar fire, they carried Kimber through derelict buildings and on across a wasteland of pulverised bricks and mortar littered with pieces of household furniture, an iron bedstead, a dining table with only one leg, a matching chair without a seat and a tallboy minus all its drawers. Items of clothing hung from lamp-posts and shattered trees like yesteryear's tired bunting – a pink camisole, the bottom half of a pair of men's pyjamas, a fur coat. In what had been a small plaza, he saw the carcass of a horse, the skeleton so gleaming it looked as though every scrap of flesh and sinew had been picked clean by carrion.

The underground hospital on Miodowa Street was roughly five hundred yards from the police station; by the time the stretcher bearers reached it, Kimber was prepared to believe that it was located on the far side of the moon. There were no beds, just mattresses side by side on the floor. If there was an operating theatre, it wasn't in the cellar Kimber had been taken to. The youth in the stained white coat whose badge of office was a stethoscope didn't look old enough to be a doctor.

"I've not been wounded," Kimber told him in halting Polish.

"There are different kinds of wounds, you are in a state of shock."

"No."

He felt cold and he couldn't stop shaking, but that was understandable; he'd been lying in a cramped position and had a bad case of the old-fashioned pins and needles. This medical student, intern, or whatever, had got it wrong. He wasn't in shock, his circulation hadn't been fully restored yet, that was all it was.

"You've been buried for over eighteen hours."

Eighteen hours? Now he knew this lunatic in a white coat was barmy. The Stukas appeared on the hour every hour, and the sun had still been well above the horizon when the midday meal had come up, so it couldn't have been much later than four o'clock when the police station had been demolished. Kimber sat up, grabbed hold of the doctor's left hand and pulled it towards himself to look at his wristwatch. Five minutes past eleven? The bloody thing was going on wheels.

"What's today?" he asked in English.

"Excuse please?"

Kimber repeated the question in bastardised Polish, then added, "Today is Sunday, isn't it?"

"No, it's Monday."

Monday! Kimber sank back on the mattress and lay there supine while a nurse wrapped a blanket round him. Monday! It didn't seem possible. He heard the pulsating throb of aero-engines and concentrated his gaze on the ceiling as though he had X-ray eyes and could see the images in the sky; then the banshees started wailing and the cellar trembled. What was it now? Ten minutes after eleven? So much for German efficiency.

"What's the matter with you bastards?" he roared. "Don't you know what time it is?"

Kimber started laughing and went on laughing until the nurse slapped his face.

Adam Nowotko walked down the tree-lined avenue towards the villa where his father had installed his mistress, Halina Sosna, shortly before the war had started. He was a fairly tall man with dark wavy hair and the kind of distinguished looks which, in the days when he had been a university lecturer, had reminded some of his more impressionable female students of Ronald Colman, the film actor.

In keeping with this Hollywood image, his style of dress was also somewhat theatrical at times. On this particular morning, he was wearing a pair of black riding boots, jodhpurs and a check shirt under a fireman's tunic. The leather belt around his waist had a silver buckle and the inscription 'Gott Mit Uns'. On his head he wore a coalscuttle steel helmet with the Death Head heraldic shield of the 3rd SS Panzer Division 'Totenkopf' emblazoned on the right side. There was, however, nothing theatrical about the 7.62mm PPSh sub-machine gun he carried and which he had used and would continue to use to good effect.

Adam Nowotko was a member of the People's Army which had previously been known as the People's Guard when it had been formed in 1942. Adam was not a Communist but he had joined this underground army because, by the middle of 1943, they had seemed to be the only people keen to fight the Hitlerite forces. This impression had been created because the political aims of the two Resistance organisations had been diametrically opposed. The Communists wanted to intensify operations so as to assist the Red Army which was then in headlong retreat, while the AK were under orders from London to conserve their strength for a large-scale uprising when the tide of war had turned decisively against the

Germans. The Home Army had not ceased operations but the efficient propaganda machine of the Communist Party had convinced many people that this was indeed the case, and a large number of men and women had left the AK to join the People's Army. Adam Nowotko had been one such recruit.

Nowotko opened the front gate, walked round the villa and found that the French windows to the drawing room were open. The familiar sickly smell which he had come to associate with the dead hit him the moment he crossed the threshold. His eyes took in the body on the carpet but the sight of his father lying there, his face in a mess of dried vomit, had no effect on him whatsoever. As a boy, Adam had seen very little of his father and had ceased to have anything to do with him after he had stolen Halina. A malignant loathing had displaced any filial affection he might have had and the passage of time had not assuaged it one little bit.

Adam had had to wait until the summer of '42 before he had been able to repay his father in kind. After four years of pandering to his father's perverted tastes, Halina had come to despise him almost as much as Adam did and had been looking for someone who would treat her with a little tenderness and affection. And of course he had done just that, except that the tenderness and affection he had shown Halina had simply been a means of luring her back into his bed. Each time he had fornicated with her, it had been a sublime act of revenge; that invariably it had also been sexually gratifying had been a distinct bonus. He was here now during this temporary lull in the fighting around Zoliborz because he was hungry for Halina, as well as for food. Unfortunately, it seemed he was going to be disappointed.

Nowotko walked round the body, inspecting it dispassionately. His father had obviously been drunk again and Halina had placed a cushion under his head before she had walked out and left him to sober up. Only she hadn't positioned him correctly and he had drowned in his own vomit. There was something funny about his eyes, though. Adam crouched down, took a closer look and saw that the pupils were dilated. It wasn't just the drink that had killed him; he'd pepped himself up with morphine or perhaps opium. But what did it matter how one old, unpleasant man had died when thousands of innocent people were being killed every day? The best thing he could do was bury the body before it became a source of infection.

Without any feelings of pity or regret, Adam Nowotko went down into the cellar to look for a shovel.

*   *   *

85

The feeder pipe was roughly three feet in diameter which meant that anyone using it as a passageway had to bend themselves into a human question mark. Her back fouling the slimy roof of the conduit, Halina inched her way forward, knee deep in sewage, a flashlight in her left hand. Slung diagonally across her chest was an MP40. 9mm machine pistol, more commonly known as a Schmeisser. Before entering the sewer in Napoleon Square, she had folded the stock forward to reduce the overall length of the sub-machine gun and make it easier for her to grab the pistol grip if she was jumped and had to use the weapon in a hurry.

The drainage system was fast becoming her natural habitat, a subterranean existence which she shared with colonies of sewer rats. Yesterday she had been to Zoliborz and back, then helped to guide General Komorowski and his staff from the Old Town to the city centre where he had set up his new headquarters in Marszalkowska Street west of Napoleon Square. With diversions, the mile-long journey had nearly doubled and had taken over four hours; now, hungry, exhausted and alone, she was retracing her steps.

Halina reached the main Zoliborz–Mokotow sewer running north to south under the city and straightened up. The lack of oxygen had made her heart beat faster and the obnoxious fumes in the feeder conduit had dried out her mouth and nasal passages making her eyes water and burn. Things weren't much better in the main channel but at least she no longer had to contend with backache.

Ignoring the small footbridge over the main channel, Halina turned left and headed north along the catwalk. The Germans had discovered that the sewers were being used by the AK and had established listening posts above every manhole in the areas they controlled. In order to further restrict the Home Army's freedom of movement below ground, they had also sealed off many of the subsidiary conduits with barbed wire. For 'Kanalarki' like Halina, who often worked in pairs or on their own, there was the added danger of running into an ambush. Every step she took, every breath she drew was magnified tenfold in what was a vast echo chamber; stealth was therefore absolutely vital.

She walked cautiously on, sweeping the ground a few feet in front of her with the flashlight. The noise of battle above ground was an intermittent rumble that reached her through the feeder drains. Some distance up ahead, she could hear the waterfall that had been created when a five-hundred-kilo bomb had breached one of the wells beneath the Old Town and penetrated the main sewer without exploding. The bomb had embedded itself in the tunnel floor in an upright position, its tail fin askew and protruding above the level of the water. This new addition to a number of landmarks Halina had committed to memory was only a few yards away when she stopped dead and cried out in alarm.

The soldier was sitting in the sludge, his back resting against the guardrail, his feet pointing towards the wall. His lips were stretched in a ghastly caricature of a smile and the sewer rats had already feasted on his eyes. Forcing herself to take a closer look at the body, Halina saw that the soldier had been carrying a 12-volt battery in the haversacks strung bandolier-fashion from his shoulders. The dead man had probably fallen behind the rest of the column and had lacked the willpower to get up again after taking a rest.

She heard the patter of feet coming towards her from the left and hurriedly swung the flashlight in that direction. The beam picked out a sewer rat about the size of a large Abyssinian cat. Unintimidated by the light, the rodent stood its ground and coiled itself, ready to spring at her face if she came any nearer. Halina stamped her feet, then hissed at the rat making a noise like a locomotive blowing off a head of steam. The rodent squeaked, turned about and fled. Somewhere in the darkness beyond the beam of light it was joined by other sewer rats.

Halina wiped the sweat from her forehead and moved on again. A few minutes later she could just make out the waterfall which cascaded across the catwalk on the opposite side of the tunnel. It was then that some instinct prompted her to switch off the flashlight. She remained stock-still, ears attuned to catch the slightest sound of movement while her eyes adapted to the dark. There was a large feeder pipe up ahead which could be entered from a manhole outside the Saxon Gardens, roughly fifty yards from the Brühl Palace. Although she had no reason to suppose that anything was amiss, she had an itchy feeling that someone was hiding in the conduit ready to ambush the first person who came past. Tucking the flashlight into the belt around her waist, Halina closed her right hand around the pistol grip, pushed the safety off, then held the magazine with the other hand and eased the Schmeisser into a position where it could be fired from the hip.

She took a pace forward, then another; five yards became ten before making a quantum leap to twenty. A tickle developed in her throat and she tried everything she knew to contain it, but to no avail. When eventually she coughed, it was like the roar of a lioness.

The stick grenade rolled out of the conduit and fell on to the catwalk close enough in front of Halina for her to see the wisp of smoke coming from the four-second-delay fuse. For a couple of heart-stopping moments the grenade teetered on the edge before it toppled over and exploded below the surface. The explosion deafened Halina and created a water spout of sludge which drenched her from head to foot. As the echoes from the detonation reverberated through the sewer, she side-stepped up to the conduit and opened fire, emptying the thirty-two-round magazine in four long bursts. Another grenade rolled out onto the catwalk; bending down, she grabbed it left-handed and tossed it back, then side-stepped again and pressed herself against the wall a split second before the grenade went off. In the silence which followed the last echo, a man groaned in agony.

Halina turned and ran. The diversion from the main sewer was marked on the wall with a Polish cross in luminous paint and she went into the side channel like a rabbit into a burrow. Scrabbling along on hands and knees, the Schmeisser on her hip bounced off the wall and repeatedly bruised her right thigh.

Sweet Mary mother of Jesus, help me through this day. Hail Mary mother of Jesus. The flashlight! Dear God, where was it? She stopped, felt the belt around her waist, found that the flashlight was now above her left buttock and sobbed with relief. On, on, a right turn followed by another, second conduit on the left, one more right turn and then back into the main sewer and wading neck-deep to reach the opposite catwalk. Coughing and spluttering, Halina finally reached the entrance to the sewer. Determined that no one should see that she had been crying, Halina waited at the bottom of the shaft until she had regained her composure. Then she climbed the steps and emerged from the manhole in Dluga Street behind Krasinski Square.

Kimber responded to the hand on his shoulder and reluctantly opened his eyes. The medical orderly bending over him was dressed in field grey and according to the chevrons on his sleeve was a Feldwebel. There was, he thought, only one possible conclusion to be drawn from that.

"We've surrendered."

"Bitte?"

Kimber threw the blanket aside, unbuttoned his shirt and showed the NCO his dog tags. "I am a British officer," he said in German.

"I already know that, Herr Hauptmann."

There was something vaguely familiar about the unshaven, chubby face and the myopic eyes blinking at him from behind a pair of glasses with a missing lens. The nervous smile also made Kimber wonder just who, in this particular situation, was the prisoner of war.

"Exler?" he said doubtfully. "Sergeant Exler?"

"Yes, sir."

"What are you doing here?"

"Helping to look after the wounded, Herr Hauptmann. At first they had me digging graves and trenches but then Herr Doktor Witzleben was . . ."

"Who's Witzleben?" Kimber interrupted.

"A government official, Herr Hauptmann. He was in charge of the Civil Affairs Bureau in Krasinski Square. I understand the Herr Doktor practised law in Iserlohn before he became a civil servant. Anyway, he was injured in an air raid last Friday and I brought him here in a wheelbarrow so that his broken leg could be set. The surgeon in charge of the hospital told me to stay because he was short of ward orderlies, so here I am."

"Lucky old you," Kimber said dryly.

"Some of us are not so sure about that, Herr Hauptmann."

"Us?"

"Herr Doktor Witzleben and I are not the only Germans in the hospital." Exler glanced left and right, then lowered his voice. "And some of the soldiers are worried that the Poles will shoot them if things go badly for their Home Army. One hears that the SS have committed all sorts of terrible atrocities since the uprising began . . ."

"You heard correctly, Sergeant, but I don't think you or any of the other Wehrmacht personnel will be victims of any reprisals."

"That's a great relief."

"Provided you've had no dealings with either the Gestapo or the SS."

But was that necessarily true? What about Corporal Heinricci of the 4th East Prussian Infantry Regiment? Kimber hadn't seen the NCO since the night General 'Bor' Komorowski and his staff had withdrawn from Kamler's tobacco factory in Wola. But what the hell did that prove? He hadn't run across Konstantin Kalugin, the liaison officer from Marshal Rokossovsky's First White Russian Front since then either.

"Herr Doktor Witzleben is terrified the Polish woman will denounce him."

"What Polish woman?"

"The one who was here yesterday – a young woman, twenty-seven or eight, dark curly hair, turned-up nose. I don't know her name but she used to work in the Civil Affairs Bureau."

Maria Bolek; it had to be her, it was too much of a coincidence for it to be anyone else.

"Why should she denounce Witzleben?"

"Because the Herr Doktor was present when she was questioned by Neurath."

"Neurath!"

"You remember him," Exler said eagerly.

Kimber nodded; he was unlikely to forget that bastard in a hurry. Neurath had been present when he and Halina had walked into the SS road block near the Saxon Gardens the day the uprising had begun. It was he who had practically invited the Scharführer commanding the Azerbaijanis to execute all the Poles his stormtroopers had detained. What was it the Scharführer had said? "Not staying to see the fun, Herr Neurath?" And the Gestapo officer had replied, "No, I'll get all the amusement I want from my little Jew boy."

"Neurath was the only witness for the prosecution when those four soldiers from the 73rd Infantry Division were tried for desertion in the face of the enemy."

"What are you talking about?" Kimber asked.

"The transcript of the Field General Court Martial you saw, the one that was in the mailbag for the Oberkommando des Heeres."

"I didn't pay much attention to it, Sergeant."

It had been the Top Secret document addressed to the Chief of Staff Warsaw Garrison which had interested him at the time; it had been prepared by the Fremde Heere Ost, the Army Intelligence department responsible for the Eastern Front and had been signed by Major General Reinhard Gehlen.

"You'd better refresh my memory," Kimber told him.

"They had been sent out on a reconnaissance patrol to Wolomin ten miles north-east of Warsaw. This was on the twenty-third of July, the day the Ivans were reported to have pushed one of their tank divisions into the area. Two days later, the four infantrymen were picked up at the Central Station as they were about to board a train for Berlin. All four were in uniform and had been granted ten days' furlough; unfortunately for them, the leave passes in their possession were forgeries. They were tried the next day and convicted on Neurath's evidence. He was investigating some kind of Black Market racket the Poles were running and interviewed the soldiers after they'd been arrested by the military police. He claimed that in their statements they had admitted buying the leave passes from a Polish forger and had intended to disappear once they arrived in Berlin."

"And the court believed him?"

"Well, they would, wouldn't they, Herr Hauptmann? In July,

the 73rd Infantry Division in Praga was the only combat formation between the Ivans and Warsaw. The Hermann Goering Division was still the wrong side of the Vistula and the other Panzer divisions were re-forming. In those circumstances, what Divisional Commander would have granted leave to any of his soldiers?"

CHAPTER 10

A fly landed on Jarrell's forehead and dipped its proboscis into the beads of perspiration. Still half asleep, he raised his left hand and brushed it away; a few moments later the bluebottle was back again. This time it moved down his cheek; lifting his hand slowly, Jarrell waited until the fly was under his palm, then struck. The bluebottle however was a lot quicker.

"Fuck you."

"That's what I call a real friendly welcome."

Jarrell rolled over on to his back, opened his eyes and saw Kimber standing over him. A hard wooden floor didn't make the most comfortable of beds and it was with some difficulty that he pushed himself up into a sitting position.

"What are you doing here, Mike?" he asked, yawning. "Maria told me you were in hospital."

"I was, then this lieutenant paid the ward a visit and said the AK needed every man at the barricades who could hold a rifle, and I decided I'd been malingering long enough."

"I don't buy that, you're no goldbricker. The way Maria tells it, that police station you were defending was knocked flatter than a board."

"There wasn't much of it left after the Stukas had finished with us."

"You're lucky to be in one piece."

"Yes, someone up above must be looking out for me." Kimber squatted down beside the American. "Everyone else bought it; apart from a bruised left arm, there wasn't a mark on my body. The stretcher bearers insisted on taking me to the hospital on Miodowa Street because they could see I had the wind up."

"Cut it out," Jarrell told him. "Battle fatigue is battle fatigue and no one could say you were faking it."

"Okay, have it your way, I'm a hero." Kimber smiled. "We're all heroes."

"I can't afford to be one, I'm a married man."

"Since when?"

"Yesterday afternoon."

"You married Maria?"

"I haven't been going with anyone else."

"Well, congratulations."

"Thanks."

Jarrell went through his pockets, found a crumpled packet of cigarettes that had been looted from a bombed-out tobacconist's and gave one to Kimber, then struck a match and held it out so that the Englishman could light up before he did.

"When you're in a bad situation, you tend to see things very clearly, and it suddenly occurred to me that I couldn't think of anyone else I'd sooner spend the rest of my life with than Maria." He drew the smoke down on to his lungs and exhaled slowly. "Which is some joke, huh? I mean, I'm here looking out on Krasinski Square and she's back at the command post. Anyway, we heard about this priest at the Church of Our Lady who was dispensing with the usual formalities and got permission to look him up. We both made a solemn declaration that we knew of no impediment to our marriage and that was more or less it. Maria's commanding officer gave her away and one of the platoon leaders from my outfit stood up for me."

"I'm happy for you both."

"Yeah, well, we haven't made too many plans for the future."

Kimber nodded. Who had? Most people were living one day at a time in the knowledge that the defenders of the Old Town would soon be overwhelmed. What happened then was anybody's guess.

"Have you still got your identity tags, Leon?"

"For what they're worth."

"They might come in handy," Kimber said carefully.

"Yeah, I heard the Krauts weren't taking too many prisoners."

That was something of an understatement; Dirlewanger's murderous gang of poachers and ex-convicts had carried out wholesale massacres in Wola after the AK had been driven out of the suburb.

"See, the trouble is I was never taken prisoner; as far as the Army Air Force is concerned, I'm missing presumed killed in action. It's different for you, Mike; both the International Red Cross and your Government are aware that you're still alive and the Krauts know they'll have to answer a lot of awkward questions if you don't show up when the war is over." Jarrell sighed. "Besides, there's Maria . . ."

The rest was left unsaid but Kimber knew what he meant. Maria

93

Bolek was not protected by the Geneva Convention and would be shot as a Franc Tireur.

"If the worst comes to the worst, our best hope is to find some way of reaching the city centre."

The route through the sewers was no longer considered viable, at least not for a large body of men and women. Alerted by their listening posts, specialist engineers of the Wehrmacht were now pumping an explosive gas into the sewers which produced a chain reaction akin to fire-damp explosions in a coal mine. Last night, the AK forces in the Old Town had made a determined effort to link up with the main body in the city centre. Attacking from the Bank of Poland towards the Saxon Gardens, they had attempted to smash a corridor through the German positions to reach the comparative safety of Napoleon Square six hundred yards away. Home Army troops from the city centre had been ordered to assist them by hitting the Wehrmacht units from the rear, but the Poles had failed to synchronise the operation and had been easily repulsed.

"I hear tell the AK have got enough men in the city centre to hold out until hell freezes over. And the Red Army ought to be in Warsaw before then."

And with them would come the NKVD, a distinctly unpleasant probability which Kimber thought was best kept to himself. There was no point in broadcasting the fact that Halina had said more than once that she feared the Soviet secret police as much as she did the Gestapo. And with good reason. In April 1943 the Germans had uncovered the graves of four thousand five hundred Polish officers in the woods around Katyn. Representatives of the Swiss Red Cross had visited the scene and were of the opinion that the victims had been executed some twelve to fifteen months before the Germans had invaded the Soviet Union.

"Look alive, they're coming."

The warning was shouted by a sentry on the landing above and no one had to ask who he meant. Kimber stubbed out his cigarette and rolled over on to his stomach to peer through the loophole that had been chiselled through the dividing wall between one of the salons on the ground floor of the Krasinski Palace and the ballroom where he and Jarrell were stationed. There was a corresponding loophole in the outer wall fronting the square through which he could see a group of infantrymen moving purposefully towards them from the direction of the ghetto.

Kimber unbuttoned the top pocket of his tunic, took out four clips of 7.92mm ammunition and placed them within easy reach. The 1898 carbine he'd been issued with was a cross between the

94

German Mauser and the Russian Mosin Nagant and looked as though it belonged in a museum. It was however perfectly serviceable, or so the battalion's quartermaster had assured him.

He heard a peculiar swishing noise which got progressively louder, then in rapid succession a dozen smoke bombs landed in front of the palace. It was a still, hot morning without a breath of wind and the smoke rose in separate plumes so that the intended screen never materialised and the advancing infantrymen remained in full view. Riflemen, sub-machine gunners and combat engineers armed with satchel charges and flame-throwers; Kimber noted the composition of each assault section and selected a target while their platoon leader went from room to room shouting last-minute instructions.

"Did you get all that?" Jarrell asked him.

"No. You want to repeat it?"

"The Lieutenant said not to open fire until the leading section is halfway across the square. He wants every round to count."

So do I, Kimber thought, so do I. He eased the safety to fire, pulled the butt into his shoulder, then picked out a combat engineer armed with a flame-thrower and keeping the blade foresight in the centre of the V backsight, aimed at his chest. He took up the slack on the trigger, held his breath and squeezed one off. The soldier went down, so did the rest of the section in a hail of fire from the palace. Ejecting the spent cartridge, Kimber fed another round into the breech and selected a fresh target.

The man was totally bald, in his late sixties, and had a large wart on his left eyelid. He lived round the corner from the post office in Napoleon Square and had refused to give his name when he had walked into Zagorski's headquarters. When asked to state his business, he had said that fifty pounds of TNT would do him nicely, thank you, then added that before retiring, he had worked for the telephone company as a lineman.

The lineman had not been idle since the uprising had begun a month ago. From the basement of the block of flats on Panska Street where he lived with his married daughter, he had dug a tunnel under the road to reach the trench which carried the lines from the telephone exchange south-west of the Saxon Gardens to the government buildings in Pilsudski Square. Once he'd broken into the trunking, the lineman had enlarged the underground trench, picking out the bricks and stacking them the other side of the entry point. When that task had been completed, he had dug through the north wall to make a sap leading to the nearest government building.

He had laboured eighteen hours a day for exactly four weeks, a large part of which had been spent directly beneath the German positions. In all, the crawlway was approximately two hundred and eighty yards long and stretched as far as the Museum of Fine Arts on the corner of Pilsudski Square.

On Monday, Zagorski's 5th battalion had been ordered to attack the German positions in the Saxon Gardens to support the breakout by the garrison of the Old Town. Shortly after crossing the start line, the leading company had come under heavy fire from the Museum of Fine Arts and had been forced to withdraw after suffering fifty per cent casualties. Now, less than forty-eight hours later, he had been presented with a golden opportunity to make the enemy pay dearly for that costly defeat.

"What do you think?" he asked Tatar.

Tatar studied the diagram of the tunnel which the lineman had brought with him. There had been a time not long ago when Zagorski wouldn't have bothered to ask for his opinion but the casualties had been such that, in a few short weeks, he had been elevated from a humble second lieutenant and assistant signals officer at 2 Group Headquarters to second in command of the 5th battalion. Although the fighting strength of the unit had been maintained by an influx of enthusiastic volunteers, few had any previous military experience, so that platoon and company commanders had to be found amongst the survivors of the original cadre.

"You know my feelings, Stefan, the only good German soldier is a dead one. But where are we going to find fifty pounds of TNT?"

"We don't even bother to look," Zagorski told him. "Nor do we go cap in hand to Group Headquarters to beg for it. One of those containers the RAF dropped into Napoleon Square was full of plastic explosive. We helped ourselves to some of it before turning the rest over to superior headquarters. There's only five or six pounds of it left now but that should be enough to blow our way into the museum. You pop up through the floor while I lead a frontal assault above ground. That ought to catch them with their trousers down."

Tatar looked at the diagram again. "How accurate is this?" he asked the lineman.

"There's a scale at the bottom of the page."

"I can see that. But does this S-bend in the trunking exist or did your pencil slip?"

"Of course it didn't slip," the lineman said indignantly. "What do you take me for – the town drunk?"

"You know we don't," Zagorski said hastily, "and I'm sorry if we gave you that impression. We certainly didn't mean to belittle your remarkable achievement. Isn't that right, Tatar?"

"Yes, please do accept my sincere apologies."

"Well, all right . . ."

"So tell us about this S-bend in the trunking," Tatar said.

"It's roughly thirty feet from the museum. I don't know why there should be a jink unless they were trying to avoid a water main or a gas pipe, but you can take it from me that it exists."

Tatar scratched the stubble on his chin. The S-bend was far enough back to protect the assault team from the blast yet close enough for him to reach it in time after he'd lit the safety fuse.

"I can do it, Stefan. Give me fifteen to twenty men armed with sub-machine guns, hand grenades and Molotov cocktails and the museum is yours."

"I'll give you the flame-thrower just to make sure," Zagorski told him.

"I'll need an hour to get into position."

"We'd better synchronise our watches then."

"Aren't you going to ask permission from Group Headquarters first?"

"What the hell for?" Zagorski demanded. "They'd only come up with a dozen good reasons why we should not launch the attack without first obtaining the approval of General Komorowski himself. Meantime, our comrades in the Old Town are dying in their thousands. It's our duty to do everything we can to relieve the pressure on them."

Tatar nodded. It was difficult to dispute the argument when you could hear the non-stop bombardment of the Old Town. Besides, Stefan was the battalion commander and that made him next to God so far as the officers and men were concerned.

"When do we start?"

Zagorski looked at his watch. "The time now is 1217. We'll cross the start line five minutes before you blow the charge at 1330 hours."

"Right."

"Choose only the most experienced men and take them from the same sub-unit."

Tatar had to look no farther than the survivors of the company which Jan had commanded before he was killed in an air raid. They had seen more action than the other sub-units in the battalion and were used to working as a team. He selected eighteen men in all, of whom only half were armed with a variety of Russian, German and

British sub-machine guns. Except for the man with the flame-thrower, the remainder had pistols, hand grenades and petrol bombs.

The block of flats in Panska Street was less than a hundred and fifty yards from the post office but there was precious little cover and they had to cross the open ground on the double. By the time they reached the basement where the tunnel began, the lineman was purple in the face and looked as though he was going to have a heart attack at any moment.

Contrary to what was shown in the diagram, the first section was anything but straight; it was, however, high and wide enough to crawl on all fours. Tatar led the way, probing the darkness with the fading light of a bicycle lamp. The lineman's tunnel seemed much longer than he'd calculated and he began to doubt the accuracy of the drawing, but a glance at the luminous face of his wristwatch showed they hadn't been going long enough to reach the junction. Four minutes later, the beam illuminated the entrance hole in the brick trunking and the telephone cables beyond.

He turned right, found the trunking was much lower and had to worm forward on his stomach. The heat was oppressive and the lack of oxygen combined with the physical exertion made his heart pound. Sweat oozed from every pore, made his eyes smart and turned the shirt on his back into a damp rag. He thought about the lineman and marvelled that a man in his sixties who was not particularly fit could have worked in such a confined space eighteen hours a day, week in, week out. It was his example more than anything else which kept him going; then, almost before Tatar knew it, he reached the S-bend in the trunking.

Tatar ordered his men to halt, but the command sounded like the muffled grunt of a pig rooting for truffles. He took a deep breath and tried again. This time he got a brief acknowledgement from the man behind him.

"Pass the word back that I'm going to lay the charge."

Tatar crawled on round the S-bend and over the telephone cables into the sap which led to a small chamber the lineman had dug directly under the Museum of Fine Arts. He shone the bicycle lamp up at the roof and found that the lineman had even scraped the earth away to expose the concrete foundations of the building.

From the small haversack he'd carried on his back, Tatar took out the plastic explosive and moulded it in a circular sausage on the concrete slab above his head. Then he cut off two feet from the reel of safety fuse, pushed one end into the hollow sleeve of the fulminate of mercury detonator and crimped it in place. Although the fulminate of mercury would be sufficient to initiate the plastic, Tatar wasn't taking any chances. Easing the detonator into a gun-cotton primer to make doubly sure, he plugged the whole assembly into the explosive and lit the safety fuse with a match.

There was no room to turn round in the tunnel itself and he was forced to back out of the chamber and along the sap. His feet struck the heavy-duty cable encasing the telephone lines and precious seconds were lost as he negotiated the obstacle. In his mind's eye he could see the fuse spluttering, getting nearer and nearer to the detonator and gun-cotton primer and wondered if he had allowed himself enough time.

The charge went up moments after he had reached the first part of the S-bend. The blast hit him like a physical blow and he thought his eardrums were going to burst under the pressure. He could taste the obnoxious fumes on his lips and almost vomited. Swallowing the bile, he shouted for the others to follow him and crawled back to the firing chamber, frantic to break into the museum before the enemy had a chance to recover.

The hole in the concrete slab was almost three feet in diameter and Tatar could see daylight above. He took a British-made 36 grenade out of his jacket pocket, withdrew the pin and allowed the safety lever to fly off. The four-second fuse started burning and he counted up to three before lobbing the grenade into the room above. The first sub-machine gunner had already joined him in the chamber when it went off. No orders were necessary; knowing what he had to do, the soldier climbed out of the chamber and opened fire with his Sten gun. It was the beginning of a pattern that was to continue until they had bombed, burned and shot their way room by room, floor by floor, to secure the building.

The irregular line of the dead from the first assault wave marked the high tide of the German advance into Krasinski Square from the direction of the ghetto. Every other attack had run out of momentum long before the halfway point and the casualties stretched all the way back to the start line on the fringe of the old Jewish Quarter roughly five hundred yards from the palace. By comparison, the slaughter of Zagorski's battalion in Napoleon Square on the first day of the uprising paled into insignificance. In the lull that had followed the last attack at 1430 hours, the cries of the wounded were clearly audible to the defenders of the Krasinski Palace.

Kimber stared through the loophole, thought he detected signs of movement near the enemy's start line and reached for the carbine at his side. The twenty-five rounds he'd originally been issued with had been expended some time ago; since then, a messenger girl had been round doling out loose rounds from a belt of 7.62mm ammunition that had been recovered from the body of a German machine gunner. Although the same calibre, the Spandau rounds were fractionally longer and fatter than those manufactured for the Polish army in 1939 and were therefore harder to feed into and extract from the breech.

Two men were advancing side by side, one an officer judging by the side arm in the leather holster on his hip, the other seemingly unarmed. He would take out the officer because a commissioned rank was always the first priority of a sniper and, in any event, he would only get the one chance. If he missed, the two Germans would hear the crack made by the bullet passing overhead as well as the thump from the carbine and would go to ground before he had time to reload, aim and fire.

Kimber waited patiently and allowed them to draw nearer, confident that no one would steal a march on him. To conserve ammunition, Ignace Orska, the company commander, had nominated him as one of three snipers who were permitted to fire at will, and the two Germans were clearly within his designated arc of fire. Not much farther now and the military career of this unknown German officer would come to an abrupt end. A bead of perspiration trickled into his right eye and made him blink at just the wrong time so that the opportunity to increase his personal score was denied him.

"Well, what do you know," Jarrell said quietly, "they're carrying a white flag."

"You'd better tell Orska."

"Right."

Kimber waited until the American had crawled into the next room, then brought the carbine up into his shoulder, right cheek pressed into the butt, left eye closed, left hand gripping the weapon at the point of balance. It would be so easy to drop the officer and for a moment he was tempted to do just that; then sanity returned and he put the rifle down. He had fought at Mareth in Tunisia and Salerno in Italy, neither of which had exactly been a picnic, but he had never felt as murderous as he had a few seconds ago. That was what the battle of Warsaw had done for him, numbing his senses to the point where there was very little to choose between himself and one of Himmler's sub-humans.

The two Germans reached the entrance to Krasinski Square and started shouting. Although they were still too far away for anyone to hear exactly what they were saying, it was pretty evident what sort of message they were trying to convey.

"Are they still friendly?" Jarrell asked as he crawled towards him.

"I don't think the white flag is a ruse to catch us off guard."

"Let's hope you're right because Orska doesn't speak a word of German and he wants you and me to be his interpreters."

"Terrific."

"I knew you would be pleased."

"Have you a white singlet or something like that which we can wave at them?"

"How about the dust cover over the grand piano?"

"Why not, we can always use it for a shroud."

"You know something, I just love your British sense of humour."

The dust cover, an old bed sheet, was paper thin and easy to tear. Jarrell tied a strip to the barrel of his rifle, then led Kimber out the back way and round the left side of the building where they were joined by Orska. There followed a rapid exchange in Polish, most of which was lost on Kimber.

"Do you mind telling me what all that was about?" he asked.

"Ignace would like you to go forward and tell the Germans to halt." Jarrell swapped rifles with him. "Here, you'd better have the one with the bunting."

"Thanks a lot."

"You're welcome," the American said solemnly.

No one fired at Kimber when he moved out into the open. Holding the rifle aloft so that they could see the white flag tied on the barrel, he called out and asked the two emissaries from the German lines what they wanted.

"My name is Fellgiebel," the officer told him, "Major Klaus Fellgiebel. I wish to parley with your commander."

"What about?"

"To arrange a truce."

"On whose authority?"

"Gruppenführer Erich von Bach-Zelewski, the Commanding General. We wish to evacuate our wounded and bury our dead. I imagine you will want to do the same."

Kimber told him to wait, then glanced over his shoulder at Jarrell and repeated everything that had passed between him and Fellgiebel.

"For what it's worth, you can tell Orska that I don't think we'll lose out by negotiating with them."

The negotiations were conducted in the middle of Krasinski

Square where the German plenipotentiaries were surrounded by their own dead and wounded. The longer they continued, the more Kimber suspected that Orska could both understand and speak German and was merely using him and Jarrell as intermediaries in order to prolong the discussions. If so, his tactics were not unsuccessful. The terms and conditions of the truce weren't agreed until 1725 hours and then it allegedly took Orska a further three quarters of an hour to obtain the approval of higher authority. The ceasefire, which was to apply to the whole of the Old Town and not just Krasinski Square, finally came into effect at 2000 hours and was to remain in force until dawn.

CHAPTER 11

Exler found the prolonged silence intimidating. Like many others in the Old Town, he had become so accustomed to the bombardment that its sudden cessation had led him to believe that what they were now experiencing was merely the lull before the storm finally overwhelmed them. To add to the eerieness, the night had drawn in to cloak everything beyond the feeble pool of light from the oil lamp in a veil of darkness. The ward too was silent except for the occasional snore from Herr Doktor Witzleben and the even more infrequent moan from a bad stomach wound at the far end of the cellar.

Even though it was past nine o'clock, the atmosphere was oppressively warm enough to make Exler feel drowsy. His eyelids drooped and presently his head began to roll. Each time his chin met his chest, he reared back and came near to waking. It was, however, the blood-curdling scream of a man in agony which did that, sending a chill down his spine to rouse him more effectively than any alarm clock.

Thoroughly unnerved, he picked up the oil lamp and instinctively moved towards the serious stomach wound. Contrary to his expectation, the Polish soldier was sleeping fitfully, though his pallor suggested he was unlikely to live through the night. As he turned about to retrace his steps, Exler noticed that no one was occupying the adjoining mattress. The dead were of course removed from the ward and buried in the communal grave which other German prisoners of war had dug behind Miodowa Street, but the casualty who had been lying there had not been on the critical list. True, the shell splinter had made an ugly wound in his left thigh but there had been no sign of gangrene and he certainly couldn't have bled to death.

Two more empty spaces, one formerly occupied by a soldier who'd lost a hand, the other by an NCO who had gone down with dysentery after drinking contaminated water. Unless he'd also picked up some other bug which had suddenly caused unforeseen complications, there was absolutely no reason why he shouldn't have made a complete recovery. Exler walked past the inert form of Herr Doktor Witzleben and raising the blanket which screened the entrance to the adjoining ward, stepped through the hole in the dividing wall.

The last time he had ventured into the cellar next door, he had had to watch his step for fear of treading on the wounded; now the place was more than half empty. He heard a scuffling noise and moved towards the sound, holding the oil lamp aloft. Two prisoners appeared to be having a tug of war over a blanket that had been folded in half; drawing nearer, he saw a pair of feet protruding from one end and realised the two Germans belonged to the burial squad. There was no need for him to look any farther now for the man who had screamed. Some people died quietly, others with a protest.

"What do you want, Feldwebel?"

Exler jumped even though he recognised the voice of the young Polish doctor who'd put him to work as an orderly after he had delivered Witzleben to the hospital in a wheelbarrow.

"Nothing, sir," he said.

"Then go back to your own ward."

"I just wondered if I could be of any help?"

"There's nothing for you to do here, Feldwebel."

Exler took the hint and backed out of the cellar. Although he hadn't expected the doctor to be friendly, the young Polish intern was as arrogant as some of the Junkers he'd met. But there, all the Poles were arrogant, even Irena, the twenty-Zloty tart who haunted Danzig station and took her clients to a poky little room above Josef's Bar which was frequented by the railway workers. Half the bloody army must have climbed those stairs and allowed her to boss them around. No German was ever allowed to mount Irena, she was always the one who had to be on top, bouncing up and down on her tight little backside as though she was riding a horse.

Exler sat down on the camp stool facing Witzleben, placed the oil lamp on the floor and rolled himself a cigarette from the pouch of tobacco he had found on the body of a Gefreiter in the Hermann Goering Panzer Division. He had had a few good times with Irena himself and could remember every crack in the ceiling of that dingy little bedroom. 'Mein Hengst' she had called him in her broken German and had sometimes treated him like a stallion, laying a riding crop across his rump before she mounted him. Usually, he had lain there, eyes closed, savouring every moment while she brought him to a shattering climax. But, on what was to be his last visit, he had made the mistake of opening his eyes and had seen the look of utter contempt on her face, and that had been that.

Witzleben was snoring again, sighing heavily each time he breathed out. Then he started rambling in his sleep, holding a conversation with himself that was totally unintelligible to Exler except for the word 'bench'.

"The garden bench." Witzleben suddenly reared up. "The garden bench," he repeated loudly.

"What about it?" Exler asked sourly.

Witzleben opened his eyes and stared at him blankly, then slowly realised where he was. "What did you say, Feldwebel?"

Exler pinched out his cigarette and pocketed the stub. "You had something on your mind, Herr Doktor – a garden bench."

"I must have been dreaming about home. We have a wooden bench under a cherry tree in our garden." He laughed briefly and without mirth. "Though why I should dream about it is beyond me. I don't recall spending much time lounging about in the garden."

"We don't have a garden."

"You haven't missed anything," Witzleben assured him.

"Something very funny is going on," Exler said, changing the subject. "All the walking wounded have disappeared. What do you think it can mean, Herr Doktor?"

"The Poles probably need every man in the trenches who can hold a rifle."

"I think we must have agreed to a ceasefire; it's been some hours since anyone fired a shot."

"You're wrong, Feldwebel. The AK would have to surrender before we agreed to that."

"So why haven't we already been released, Herr Doktor?" Exler shook his head. "I reckon the AK have slipped away through the sewers."

"Then you'd better organise a reception committee to meet the SS," said Witzleben. "We don't want any unfortunate mistakes when they do liberate us."

Kimber stared into the darkness and tried to stay awake. He could not remember the last time he had really got his head down and the lack of sleep was beginning to catch up with him as it was with everyone else. It wasn't only the shelling which had stopped when the truce had come into effect at 2000 hours; the adrenalin had also ceased to flow and had been replaced by an unutterable weariness.

Exhaustion was currently their biggest enemy because now more than ever before they needed to be alert.

The truce was the only thing which was going to save the AK in the Old Town. As long as the ceasefire held up, the garrison could slip away through the sewers provided the withdrawal was carried out with the utmost stealth. In order to deceive the enemy, every position had to be held until the last possible moment, but the number of men assigned to each strongpoint could be reduced, with one notable exception. The Krasinski Palace was the last buffer between the enemy and the entrance to the sewer on Dluga Street. Since this was the only access in the Old Town which was still controlled by the AK, there could be no question of reducing Orska's command to skeleton strength.

The thinning out process had started one hour after the ceasefire had come into force. From the area of the police station in the north, Miodowa in the centre, and along the southern boundary facing the Brühl Palace, organised groups of AK soldiers and auxiliaries moved in single file towards the entrance to the sewers. Each group was led by a messenger girl as far as the main north-to-south drainage tunnel where another guide took over. The messenger girl then made her way to the next strongpoint on her list to collect another group. Although it was the only way to avoid a logjam, the operation was proving a time-consuming business, made even more so by the number of civilians who were tagging on to each group.

He heard Jarrell stir beside him, then give a low whistle. "Zero one two six hours. Is that what the time is?"

"You tell me," Kimber said. "You're the one with the timepiece."

"Something's wrong. We should have started to pull out half an hour ago. I hope to God nothing's happened to Maria."

He could understand Jarrell's anxiety. Maria was one of the messenger girls on whom the success of the withdrawal ultimately depended. She had been assigned to the southern sector but had come to a private arrangement with Halina that she would look after Orska's company when the time came for them to pull out. It was during this final phase of the operation that she would be most at risk.

"Nothing has," Kimber said firmly. "The ceasefire hasn't been violated and there are too many of the AK on the move for any infiltrator to make a nuisance of himself. Besides, he'd have to slip through our forward defences and he'd have a hard time doing that."

"Why? We're getting pretty thin on the ground."

"But the Germans don't know that, otherwise they would be swarming all over us. Right?"

"Makes sense," Jarrell said doubtfully.

"Of course it does; things are running a little late, that's all."

Kimber wished he could have sounded more convincing.

Maria was busy counting heads as the column filed past her in the sewer. She was supposed to have collected a hundred and eight fighting men from the southern end of Miodowa Street but the total already exceeded two hundred and forty and they were still coming. A considerable number of walking wounded had joined the column and there were also half a dozen stretcher cases who were holding things up. Behind them came the civilians, men, women and children of all ages, some little more than toddlers.

For the most part, the civilians were refugees from Wola who had fled to the Old Town in the early days of the uprising. Many of them had been lucky to escape the wholesale massacre of the civilian population which had been carried out by the SS after the Home Army had been driven out of the District, and were determined not to chance their luck a second time. Just how many would survive the two-mile journey through the sewers was anybody's guess, for death waited for them in so many guises. If they stumbled and fell, they could be trampled underfoot in the dark or drown in the sludge, or walk unsuspectingly into a lethal pocket of methane gas. Death might come to them in the form of a hand grenade down an open manhole as they passed under the German positions in Pilsudski Square or perhaps they would be killed in a fire-damp explosion which blew them to pieces. There were places off the main tunnel where, if you probed the darkness with a flashlight, you could see the pulverised remains of sewer rats glued to the roof and walls. But not tonight; tonight no one was allowed to use any sort of illumination.

Two ninety-nine, three hundred, three hundred and one; Maria decided it was pointless to go on counting. The whole idea of keeping a tally was to ensure that no infiltrators had tagged on to the column, but the presence of civilian refugees among the fighting men made it impossible to tell friend from enemy. In any event, the line had stopped moving and she could hear a quavering voice raised in anger which claimed her attention, and she went forward to investigate.

The hold-up had occurred some twenty yards along the catwalk where it was necessary to wade across the main sewage channel in order to reach the diversion which bypassed the unexploded bomb farther down the tunnel. The cause of the hold-up was a young mother who had a baby in one arm and was trying to hold on to a small boy with her free hand. The water was approximately four and a half feet deep and there was no way she could hold on to the safety line which had been rigged across the channel and carry both baby and her son. The quavering voice belonged to an old woman who wanted her to step aside so that she could go across.

"Shut up," Maria told her in a fierce whisper. "Do you want the Germans to hear you?"

"Don't speak to me in that tone of voice, young woman. Who do you think you are?"

"I'm sorry, but . . . ."

"You should have more respect for your elders."

Maria gritted her teeth. Old age did not automatically equate with being a nice person and, in her position, respect ought to be deserved, not demanded.

"I told you to shut up." Maria grabbed the old woman's arm and shook it. "Now hold your tongue or, so help me God, I'll hold your head under the water until you drown."

Her anger suddenly spent, Maria released the old woman, sat down on the catwalk and lowered herself into the murky waters, then turned about and reached for the child. She lifted the boy on to her shoulders and positioned him so that he was sitting astride her neck. Two small hands grabbed fistfuls of her hair and almost tore the roots from the scalp. Holding the safety line with her left hand, Maria waded across the channel, deposited her charge on the opposite catwalk and climbed out. Moments later, she was joined by mother and baby and the line started moving again.

The column shuffled on towards the diversion. The feeder drain was no more than three feet in diameter and she had no idea how the young mother was going to manage crawling on all fours. But she had done the best she could for the woman and it was no longer her problem. The AK had posted an NCO at the entrance to the diversion and he would have to sort it out.

Recognising the elderly man who had been the last person to pass her before she had abandoned the tally, Maria started counting again. The three hundred and forty-seventh and last was a Home Army straggler. She waited until his footsteps faded away before heading back to the entrance on Dluga Street. It was then that Maria thought she heard someone call her name.

Halina picked her way across the reverse slope of the manmade hill of rubble. There was no more dangerous corner of the Old Town than the south-east sector facing the Royal Palace, which, until it had finally been recaptured by the Wehrmacht, had dominated the approaches to the Kierbedzia bridge, the middle one of three road links spanning the Vistula. Mindful that the German positions were only a few yards away, she stayed well below the crest to avoid being silhouetted against the skyline.

Behind her, and moving in single file, were two officers and sixty-eight heavily armed men, the last combat unit in the southern sector. Shielding them from the enemy was a stay-behind party consisting of a dozen men with a light machine gun. When the last man from Orska's Company in the Krasinski Palace entered the sewers, they would get out as best they could.

Halina came down from the hillside and walked along the pavement. The heat from the sun and the innumerable fires that had raged in the Old Town had frequently melted the asphalt so that the footprints of those who had passed that way were preserved, if not for all time, at least for the foreseeable future. The mushroom-shaped entrance to the sewers on Dluga Street would never have featured in any guide book to Warsaw published before the war, but for the men of the AK it was, at that moment, the most beautiful structure in the whole city.

There were five men standing by the entrance; drawing nearer, Halina recognised the second-in-command of the garrison and assumed the others were runners from the stay-behind parties. The Garrison Commander and the rest of the staff were scheduled to pull out immediately before the southern area and the Krasinski Palace were abandoned. It was the second-in-command's job to establish a checkpoint to ensure this final phase of the operation had been completed before the stay-behind parties were authorised to disperse.

"You can scratch us off your list," Halina told the second-in-command.

"How many are there of you?"

"Two officers and sixty-eight."

"Have you seen Maria Bolek in your travels?"

"You mean Maria Jarrell."

"Jarrell, Bolek," the second-in-command said irritably, "what's the difference? Have you seen her?"

"Not since she left to collect a group from the southern end of Miodowa Street. That was almost two hours ago. My God," Halina bit her lip, "what about Orska's lot?"

"They're still holding the Krasinski Palace."

"Shall I tell them to pull out?"

"I think you'd better," the second-in-command told her. "Meantime, I'll send your lot on their way."

"Zero two fifty-eight hours."

Although it hadn't been intended for his ears, Kimber heard Jarrell murmur the time to himself and shared his concern. So in a less obvious way did Orska. He had left his observation post on the floor above to join them in the ballroom where he could watch Dluga Street from the back entrance.

"Something's happened to Maria, I know it."

"Nothing has happened to her . . ."

Kimber checked himself in time. Their conversation was already sounding like a repeat of the one they'd had an hour and a half ago, and it was no good telling Leon that the ceasefire was still holding. They should have withdrawn from the palace at 0100 hours and he needed to come up with a fresh and convincing reason which would explain why they hadn't seen Maria.

"All right, so we should have left a couple of hours ago, but that doesn't mean something bad has happened to Maria. If this operation was running to time, they would have sent one of the other messenger girls to pull us out. You think about that and then tell me if I'm wrong."

Jarrell was still mulling it over when Orska announced that a runner was coming their way, and suddenly what had started out as a comforting explanation became a prophetic nightmare. There was virtually no moon and the ballroom was in Stygian gloom but Kimber knew the girl was Halina before she even said a word. Jarrell too realised who she was and was at her side demanding to know where Maria was the moment she had finished briefing Orska.

"I don't know, Leon," she said quietly. "It's absolute chaos down there in the sewers. Most of the time you can hardly see a hand in front of you and there are people backed all the way up to the entrance. The last time I was down there, it was so bad that I had to crawl through a narrow feeder to get back up again. And I damned nearly surfaced in German-held territory."

"I'm not really interested in your problems," Jarrell said tersely. "I just want to know what's happened to my wife."

"Maria was okay when I saw her a couple of hours ago."

"Where was this?"

"The bottom end of Miodowa Street." Halina broke off, pointed to the AK soldiers who were assembling in the ballroom, then gently squeezed Jarrell's left arm. "I'm sorry, Leon, but we have to go now."

They moved out in single file, with the notable exception of Orska who marched side by side with Halina at the head of his company. Every man was aware that the need for silence was paramount and had wrapped strips of cloth around their boots to deaden the sound of their footsteps. The entrance they were making for was barely a hundred and fifty yards away; when the head of the column reached it, the tail was still back in the Krasinski Palace.

The bunching started below ground on the catwalk where the company from the Royal Palace area was still waiting to move off down the tunnel. No one really knew what had caused the hold-up but the air was thick with rumours. Some believed that the SS had broken into one section, others had heard that the diversion was blocked because a mother and child had drowned in one of the narrow feeder drains and no one could get past their bodies. Whatever the reason, all movement towards the city centre had stopped and time was running out for the AK.

"We'll have to turn everyone around and make for Zoliborz," Halina said.

Orska didn't like it, neither did Jarrell who said so loud and clear. Kimber could understand his objection, Orska's was less obvious but he gathered it had something to do with the Communists.

"I'm not overjoyed about it either," Halina told them, "but we don't have any choice. The ceasefire ends at dawn and that's less than two hours from now. The longer we stay here arguing about it, the more likely it is we'll be caught like rats in a trap."

"Okay, you go to Zoliborz, I'm going to look for Maria."

"That's your privilege."

Kimber grabbed the American and held on to him as he tried to move off down the tunnel. "Now, come on, Leon, where the hell do you think you're going?"

"You want to let go my arm before I break your jaw?"

"You are not a 'Kanalarki'; you'll only get yourself lost in the drainage system. If that happens, you will probably die in this stinking cesspit."

"Maria is somewhere down here," Jarrell said, and tried to shake him off.

"You're just guessing. For all you know she could be in the city centre by now." Kimber looked at Halina. "This group in Zoliborz, can they communicate with General Komorowski's headquarters?"

"They have a radio."

"Well, that's the answer, we'll ask them to run a check."

It would be asking a lot, but the staff at Komorowski's headquarters were bound to carry out a head count, otherwise they wouldn't know just how many fighting men they had at their disposal. Although Kimber had no idea how many women auxiliaries there had been among the troops defending the Old Town, he doubted if there had been more than a hundred. If his supposition was correct, it shouldn't be all that difficult for the AK to ascertain whether there was a girl called Maria Jarrell née Bolek amongst them.

Jarrell took a lot of convincing. Backing the American into a small nook on the catwalk, Kimber stood there, alternately cajoling, pleading and arguing with him while the column trooped past, heading north. When all these approaches failed, he endeavoured to reach a compromise.

"Listen, if the Home Army staff can't or won't help us, I'll help you look for Maria. Is it a deal?"

"Maria is not your concern."

"Do we have a deal?" Kimber insisted.

"Well, I don't see why you should get involved."

"Is that a 'yes'?"

"I guess it is."

"Then let's go."

Kimber eased Jarrell into the marching column and slipped in behind him.

Zoliborz was two and a half miles away; they had covered rather less than half the distance when the ceasefire ended and the first Stukas appeared over the Old Town. When the bombs began to fall, there were still two hundred AK soldiers waiting to enter the sewers in Dluga Street.

It was the umpteenth time that Exler had been under fire and for a while he thought it could well be the last. Shortly after the last Stuka had dropped its bomb load, the artillery and mortars opened up, putting down a curtain of fire that sounded like a continuous roll of thunder. He pressed both hands over his ears in a vain attempt to shut out the din, and he prayed as he had never prayed in his life before. The cellar trembled before his eyes and deep fissures appeared in the concrete. Dust rose from the floor and hung in the air like a thick sea mist. Then suddenly the bombardment stopped and he could hear tanks on the move.

"Well, don't just sit there," Witzleben snarled. "Go outside and meet our victorious troops."

And get myself killed in the process, Exler thought. He had heard enough stories in army canteens to know that most combat infantrymen were likely to shoot first and ask afterwards. The trouble was, he didn't have a lot of confidence in the white flag he'd made. Dirlewanger's convicts were unlikely to respect it and the Ukrainians of the RONA Brigade certainly wouldn't. Furthermore, the flag looked more grey than white.

"What are you waiting for, Feldwebel?"

"Nothing, Herr Doktor."

Exler picked up the flag he had tied to a piece of wood and reluctantly got to his feet. Taking his time, he walked to the far end of the ward where a flight of steps led to the hall above. The house was little more than a pile of rubble but the entrance had been cleared and he was able to make his way out on to the street.

He was not the only one to have surfaced from a hole in the ground. Wherever Exler looked, there were civilians climbing over the rubble, going forward to meet the soldiers with white flags. Grateful that they had saved him the job, he returned to the cellar.

"You were quick." Witzleben eyed him suspiciously. "I trust everything is in order?"

"I've never seen so many white flags."

"But do our soldiers know this is a hospital?"

"The Poles have put a big red cross above the main entrance."

A sudden burst of sub-machine gun fire in one of the cellars and the terrified screams of the wounded showed just how much notice the SS were taking of that. Without stopping to think, Exler charged through the cellars like an angry bull. He was a man who rarely swore, rarely raised his voice, but in the heat of that moment his vocabulary of four-letter words would have made a drill sergeant blanch. Elsewhere in the Old Town, the wounded were shot in their hundreds; thanks to Exler and a Luftwaffe NCO, only five men were killed in the Miodowa Street hospital.

Approximately four thousand men, women and children reached the city centre through the sewers. Included in this total were fifteen hundred combat troops and close on two thousand walking wounded. According to the Home Army, Maria Jarrell née Bolek was not among the survivors.

During the following week, Kimber and Jarrell made two attempts to find Maria. With Halina guiding them, they got as far as the waterfall on both occasions but could find no trace of her. Then, on the fifteenth of September, the day the Red Army entered Praga on the east bank, the badly decomposed body of a young woman was found in the barbed-wire entanglements blocking the sewers on the outskirts of Zoliborz. Bloated beyond recognition,

Jarrell identified his wife by the curtain ring he had placed on her finger when they were married.

The exact cause of death was not known but it was apparent that the deceased had received a severe blow on the left side of the head and was presumed to have been unconscious when she fell into the water.

1958

ENGLAND
and
WEST GERMANY

Wednesday 30 July
to
Saturday 30 August

Chapter 12

Kimber lifted his suitcase off the slow-moving carousel in the baggage hall, cleared it with Customs and walked on into the terminal building, a large prefabricated hut which had been erected during the war when Blackbush had been an RAF airfield. Of the dozen or so people waiting to meet the delayed Eagle Airways flight from Aden, Jean was the last person he had expected to see amongst the small crowd. In the eight years they had been married, she had never before met him at the airport and he wondered if his mother had been spreading dissension again. Then her face lit up with a fond smile and he knew everything was all right.

"This is a nice surprise, darling," he said, and kissed her warmly. "How did you manage to get a babysitter at such short notice?"

"I didn't," Jean told him. "Alison said we didn't need one."

Kimber nodded sagely. Alison was his fourteen-year-old stepdaughter who had been born three months after her father had been shot down over Munich in March 1944. Until quite recently, he had got on famously with Alison but puberty and the awareness that she was nearly a woman had changed all that. "You're not my real father," she had told him once when he had ticked her off for breaking a promise to be home by nine thirty after a party. "And I'm not a child any more."

"Well, I suppose at her age a babysitter is a bit of an insult."

Kimber held the swing door open for Jean, then followed her outside and fell in step as they walked towards the Triumph Mayflower in the car park.

"I said you would give her ten shillings if she put Richard to bed and read him a story."

"She'll have earned it; he's quite a handful for a six-year-old."

"Most six-year-olds are, Michael."

Kimber dumped his suitcase in the boot and walked round the nearside of the car. "You drive," he said.

"You must be tired!"

"It's a lousy time of the year to be in the Gulf. I didn't get a decent night's sleep the whole fortnight; wherever I went, the air-conditioning seemed to be on the blink."

"Poor old you."

Jean started the car, shifted into first and drove out of the car park. Turning left on the A30, she headed towards Camberley.

"All I want is a hot bath and an early night."

"You may not get the latter," Jean told him.

"Don't tell me we've got company?"

"In a manner of speaking. A Detective Inspector Viner phoned to ask if he could see you this evening. I gather it has something to do with your old friend Stefan Zagorski."

Kimber sighed. "What's he been up to now?"

"I don't know, Viner wasn't very forthcoming."

"Well, it doesn't matter anyway. I'm not seeing anyone tonight."

"I don't think Nigel Emmerson will be best pleased if you refuse to see Viner."

Emmerson was the head of the Arabian Department at the Foreign Office and, as such, was several rungs higher on the ladder than Kimber. A Balliol man, now in his mid-forties, he had joined the Diplomatic from Oxford and had spent the greater part of his service in the Middle East. By far and away the most outstanding entrant before the war, he was widely regarded as a future Permanent Under Secretary of State and Head of the Diplomatic Service. For the life of him, Kimber couldn't see why he should concern himself with a Polish immigrant and a junior officer of the Surrey Constabulary.

"Don't tell me Emmerson phoned you about Stefan?"

"Not exactly. He warned me to expect a call from Viner and said he would be grateful if you would see the Detective Inspector at your earliest convenience."

"Meaning tonight?"

"Yes."

"For a humble Detective Inspector, this man Viner appears to have friends in high places. I wonder what he's like?"

"You'll know soon enough, Michael."

And he would too. They had just passed the ornate gates at the entrance to the Royal Military Academy Sandhurst and the Staff College in the middle of Camberley and were approaching the traffic lights at the crossroads near Henley's Garage. Moving into the outside lane, Jean tripped the indicator to show that she was turning right into the High Street. 'Hillcrest', the large mock Tudor house which Jean had inherited in trust for her daughter from her former in-laws, was a quarter of a mile beyond the level crossing outside the railway station.

Alison was downstairs in the Snug watching television. Richard was upstairs supposedly in bed but fighting the Battle of Britain all over again with a Dinky toy Hawker Hurricane and his own unique brand of sound effects. Despite this, the girl who wasn't a child any more expected to be paid the ten shilling fee for baby-sitting.

Viner had left the number of the Camberley police station where he could be reached. Although the desk sergeant took the call, he was round at the house less than five minutes later, which made Kimber think he must have known the revised Estimated Time of Arrival for the delayed Eagle Airways flight and had been parked somewhere very close to Hillcrest.

The Detective Inspector was a slim, fair-haired man in his early thirties. Neat and dapper were two adjectives which readily sprang to mind and, in keeping with this image, he was wearing a double-breasted charcoal grey suit that hadn't been bought off the peg. His manner was brisk yet polite; his smile, though hardly spontaneous, was nevertheless generous enough to reveal teeth unstained by nicotine.

"I'm Detective Inspector Viner, sir," he said, introducing himself, and produced his warrant card for inspection. "MPSB."

"What?"

"Metropolitan Police Special Branch."

"Oh." Kimber raised his eyebrows. "My wife thought you were with the Surrey Constabulary."

Viner appeared to think it was a natural mistake but omitted to explain why this should be so. Some police officers professed not to drink on duty, but he had no such inhibitions and happily accepted a whisky and soda after Kimber had shown him into the study.

"I understand you want to see me about Stefan Zagorski?" Kimber smiled. "May one ask what he's been up to?"

"How well do you know him, sir?" Viner said, ignoring the question.

"I met Stefan in Warsaw at the beginning of August 1944 but I didn't really get to know him until we were both locked up in Colditz."

"The bad boys' prisoner of war camp."

"It's where they sent the persistent escapers."

Zagorski had shown almost suicidal bravery in escaping from Oflag VIIc at Laufen, north-east of Salzburg. The Home Army had won the right to be accorded combatant status because the Wehrmacht had been anxious to subdue the uprising before the Russians across the river in Praga were strong enough to force the Vistula. The German High Command had also been worried by the increasing number of casualties they were taking and were mindful of the threat Anthony Eden had made in the House of Commons when he had declared that the Allies would carry out reprisals against German POWs in England if the Poles were not treated in accordance with the Geneva Convention. The surrender terms had been negotiated with the 9th German Army because the AK had refused to deal with the SS. Zagorski had therefore been safe enough behind the wire at Laufen but in breaking out, he had run the risk of being recaptured by the SS who would have shot him on the spot.

"We had a few VIPs as well," Kimber continued. "Like Winant, the son of the US Ambassador to the Court of St James, and Lord Lascelles, one of the King's nephews. The Nazis were thinking of using them as bargaining counters."

"When did you last see Mr Zagorski?"

"Put it this way, when are you going to tell me what all this is about? Is Stefan in some kind of trouble?"

"He died a week ago, Mr Kimber. The inquest hasn't been held yet but there's a chance the coroner's jury may return an open verdict. You see, he had this half-hundredweight bag of cement lashed to his body when he fell off the roof of an eight-storey block of flats in South Lambeth. He landed on top of a courting couple who were having fun and games in the back of a Zephyr convertible. Killed the bloke outright, fractured the woman's pelvis and cracked four of her ribs. Your friend was in a coma for three days before he snuffed it." Viner reached inside his jacket, took out an envelope and tapped it against his thigh as though beating a slow cadence on à side drum. "But for that bag of cement, I think we would be looking at a suicide. I just wondered if you could throw any light on his state of mind? Was he worried or depressed about something?"

"I wouldn't know, it's over eight years since we last saw one another."

Viner glanced at the envelope once more before passing it to Kimber. "And you were then living in Salisbury?"

"Yes." The familiar spidery handwriting caught his eye – 'Not known at this address – return to sender.' Kimber shook his head. "My mother never did like Stefan. The feeling was mutual; she thought he was insufferably rude and arrogant while Stefan made it clear that he hated all Germans on principle. The fact that my mother was born in Austria was irrelevant as far as he was concerned." He looked inside the envelope. "What happened to the letter?"

"Someone had steamed open the envelope and read the contents before resealing it. Would your mother have done that?"

"Possibly." Kimber smiled. "Is this the way you've been trained to do things in the Special Branch? Answer a question with a question?"

"The letter is lodged in the case file."

"May I see it?"

"After the coroner's inquest." Viner paused, then said, "Are you fluent in Polish, Mr Kimber?"

"I picked up a smattering in Warsaw and expanded my vocabulary in Colditz. It helped to pass the time."

"Zagorski's landlady in Ealing told us that his command of English was very good but he chose to write to you in Polish. Naturally, we had the letter translated."

"Naturally," Kimber echoed dryly.

"He appeared to have a bee in his bonnet about the Warsaw uprising in 1944. He claimed to have incontrovertible proof that General Komorowski's Home Army was betrayed. Do you think there's any truth in the allegation?"

Kimber recalled the Gehlen document and wondered if it had been buried under the rubble of the Kamler tobacco factory when, on Himmler's orders, the SS had destroyed every building in Warsaw west of the Vistula.

"The Poles could make out a pretty good case against the Soviet Union. Moscow Radio repeatedly called on the citizens of Warsaw to rise; when they did, the Red Army appeared to give the Wehrmacht a free hand to crush the rebellion."

For a whole month, not a single Russian plane had challenged the Luftwaffe over Warsaw. Furthermore, the Soviet High Command had flatly refused to allow the RAF and the United States Army Air Force to land and refuel at their forward airfields.

"The battle for Warsaw was really lost when we had to withdraw from the Old Town. Ten days later, the Red Air Force were there in strength over the city. Finally, with the agreement of Moscow, a hundred and seven Flying Fortresses from the 8th Air Force made a supply drop on the eighteenth of September. They delivered almost thirteen hundred containers of arms, ammunition, medical supplies and food; unfortunately, fewer than one in four reached the Home Army. It wasn't the Americans' fault; by the time they got the go-ahead, we'd been squeezed into isolated pockets of resistance. In Polish eyes, Stalin was the real villain of the piece."

And it hadn't only been the Home Army that Stalin had seemed determined to destroy. After Praga had been liberated, the job of establishing a bridgehead on the west bank of the Vistula had been given to the 1st Polish (Communist) Army commanded by General Berling. Originally consisting of a single division raised from former prisoners of war captured by the Russians in 1939, its order of battle had been expanded by the forcible incorporation of AK units in the liberated areas of Poland. A very large number of these reluctant conscripts had subsequently been killed in the bloody attempts to force the Vistula.

"That isn't the way Zagorski tells it," Viner said. "According to him, the Home Army was betrayed from within by the Nowotkos and their cohorts."

"I knew an Adam Nowotko," Kimber said thoughtfully. "I was attached to his company in Zoliborz. This was after we had pulled out of the Old Town."

"Yes, so he mentioned in his letter. I believe you accompanied Nowotko when he took a reconnaissance patrol across the Vistula to liaise with the Russians?"

"That's correct. The Germans controlled most of the west bank by then and I was asked to go along in case the patrol was challenged."

It had been a dark night and the river had never seemed so wide or so intimidating. No one had challenged them on the way out but they had heard the Germans conversing in their foxholes and the patrol had had to move forward at a snail's pace. By the time they had paddled the inflatable across the Vistula, the first light of day had already begun to appear in the east.

"We went over one night, came back the next."

"The negotiations took that long?"

"What negotiations?"

"The ones you conducted with the Germans," Viner said calmly. "Zagorski alleges that you and your friends did rather well out of it."

"What?"

"I'm only repeating what he said in his letter. He mentions a whole catalogue of names like Witzleben, a Feldwebel called Exler, Ignace Orska . . ."

"Orska?" Kimber repeated incredulously.

"Maria Bolek . . ."

"She's dead, for God's sake . . ."

122

"Halina Sosna . . ."

"That's crazy, she was the best partisan in the whole damned AK."

Viner smiled in a way which suggested he thought he had been terribly clever. "Well, that would go a long way to ensure the coroner's court brings in a verdict of suicide." He swallowed the rest of his whisky and put the glass down on the desk. "The only thing that puzzles me is why Zagorski went all the way over to South Lambeth to do himself in when he lived in Ealing. Has he got any friends south of the river?"

"I wouldn't know."

"Yes, well maybe he couldn't find a tall enough building nearer home – you never know with a suicide." Viner got to his feet. "If I could trouble you for the envelope?" he said.

"Yes, of course."

Kimber escorted him to the front door and said good night. Viner walked towards his Vauxhall Velox, then suddenly turned about.

"I don't want to appear rude," he said, "but I wonder if you would satisfy my curiosity? I know MC is the abbreviation for the Military Cross but what does CG stand for?"

"Cross of Gallantry; it's a Polish decoration. They also gave one to an American called Leon Jarrell. I have a feeling Zagorski thought neither of us had earned it."

"Yes, he said as much in his letter."

Viner turned about again and got into the car. He started the engine, shifted into gear and, making a U-turn in the gravel drive, drove off into the night.

Nigel Emmerson gazed at the telephone willing it to ring. Kimber had his Reigate number and he couldn't think why he hadn't yet heard from him. The Eagle Airways flight from Aden had landed at six forty-five pm and he should have been indoors an hour and a half later, which would have allowed him plenty of time to clear Immigration, Customs and Excise and drive home from Blackbush to Camberley. Detective Inspector Viner would have been round at his house by eight thirty at the latest, but here it was after eleven o'clock and not a peep out of him.

He wondered if Jean Kimber had relayed his message to her husband. She was a nice enough woman but a little too independent to be the wife of a man who wanted to do well in the Diplomatic Service. If she had decided that Michael had had enough for one day, she might conveniently forget that he wanted Kimber to phone him the minute Viner left. Money, of course, accounted partly for her somewhat cavalier attitude. Jean's parents had settled a tidy old sum on her to avoid death duties and, by all accounts, she hadn't been left exactly destitute by her first husband either.

Kimber had met her on the ski slopes at Grindelwald in January 1950. He had booked himself into a modest pension across the road from the Bahnhof which had been all he could afford, while Jean naturally had been staying at the five star Regina Hotel. Stafford Cripps had been the Chancellor of the Exchequer in those days and in his determination to defend Sterling, twenty-five pounds had been the maximum any holidaymaker had been allowed to take abroad. However, it seemed this hard and fast rule had not applied to Jean whose parents were said to have assets in Switzerland. Small wonder then that Jean was used to getting her own way most of the time.

Tired of waiting for Kimber to call him, Emmerson lifted the receiver, dialled Trunks and asked the operator for Camberley 233. The number rang just twice before he got an answer which led him to believe the younger man must have been sitting by the telephone.

"I thought you were going to call me, Michael," he said testily.

"I was about to."

"Do you mean to say Viner has only just left?"

"No, he departed a few minutes after nine. I'm sorry if I've kept you waiting, Nigel, but there were certain things Viner told me which needed thinking about."

"Such as?"

"Well, first of all, I can't understand why Viner didn't give me a copy of Zagorski's letter. After all, it was addressed to me."

"Didn't he tell you what was in it?"

"Yes. It seems Halina Sosna, Ignace Orska, myself and several others sold out to the Russians. Or the Germans. Or possibly both. You could say Stefan was hedging his bets, except that, according to Viner, he has evidence to support the accusations. Obviously the police haven't found it yet."

"How do you know?"

"Because Viner was on a fishing expedition. All he's got is a letter and you can bet your shirt they have already been through Zagorski's digs in Ealing with a fine-tooth comb. Now they've no idea where to look."

"But perhaps you do, Michael?"

"What are you implying? That I'm privy to more than I'm letting on?"

Emmerson didn't care for his attitude and tone of voice but told himself that one had to make allowances. Kimber had spent an exhausting fourteen days in the Persian Gulf followed by a long and tedious journey home via Tobruk and Brindisi in a DC6. This on top of travelling by RAF Hastings from Bahrain to Aden to catch the connecting Eagle Airways flight. Then to cap it all, a Special Branch officer had descended on him shortly after he had walked into the house. In the circumstances it was small wonder that his temper was on a short fuse.

"That's the last thing I intended to convey, Michael. I was simply expressing a hope that you might still be in touch with members of the Polish community in this country who knew Zagorski in Warsaw. From what little I've heard about him, he seems to have been a very unstable person. It would be helpful if you could find someone to corroborate this."

"To ensure the coroner's jury arrives at an appropriate decision?" Kimber suggested coolly.

"Suicide while the balance of his mind was disturbed is infinitely preferable to one of murder by person or persons unknown," Emmerson said unruffled. "An open verdict would be equally undesirable."

"I met his second-in-command in Colditz, a man called Daniel Tatar. The last time I saw him was at his wedding in Blackpool when he married a Lancashire lass."

"When was this?"

"It must have been all of five years ago."

Emmerson frowned. 1953 – Coronation year – a lot of water had flowed under the bridge since then and Tatar could have moved on. But if he was still living in the UK, it would be easy enough to trace him through his National Health and Social Security number. The Security Department of the Foreign Office could help there; with their contacts in MI5 they were tailormade for the job.

"Do you have an address for him in Blackpool?" he asked.

"I did have, but I doubt if I could put my hand on it now."

"No matter, you can always check the electoral roll."

"You want me to go to Blackpool?"

"Yes, first thing tomorrow morning."

"Tomorrow?" Kimber fell silent, momentarily lost for words, then recovering, he asked the inevitable question. "But what about the on-the-spot assessment you wanted?"

"It can wait a day or two."

There was an even longer pause this time and he could visualise the puzzled frown on Kimber's face. A fortnight ago last Monday, King Faisal II, the Crown Prince of Iraq and General Nurias-Said had been murdered in a coup d'état by the Iraqi Army. In the wake of their assassinations, the Baghdad Pact which bound Turkey, Iraq, Iran and Pakistan in a military alliance to counter any Soviet invasion or incursion into the Middle East had ceased to exist to all intents and purposes. But unfortunately, it hadn't ended there; the five-month-old merger of the Kingdoms of Iraq and Jordan, formed in response to the Syrian alignment with the USSR, had also been destroyed. Finally, there was the little matter of the constitutional crisis in the Lebanon. With the whole of the Middle East in turmoil, Kimber had been despatched to the Persian Gulf to ascertain what measures were needed to protect the vital oil supplies.

"I don't get it," Kimber said. "Why should this Zagorski business take precedence?"

"Do I have to remind you how strained relations between the Foreign Office and the State Department are after the Suez invasion?"

"No, but . . ."

"Let me ask you another question. Despite the official request for assistance from King Hussein, would we have sent the 16th Parachute Brigade into Jordan without first obtaining the agreement of the Americans?"

"I don't see why not; after all, they put ten thousand Marines ashore at Beirut."

"At President Chamoun's request, who invoked the Eisenhower Doctrine."

"Well, I knew the US Treasury was in the habit of propping up the pound when it suited Washington, but I hadn't realised the people on 23rd Street were formulating the ground rules for us to follow in the Middle East."

"We can no longer afford to go it alone, Michael. We have to co-operate with the Americans."

"I know, I spent half my time conferring with them."

"Yes, the British Resident in Bahrain cabled me that you had succeeded in establishing a considerable rapport with the State Department officials and the Navy Intelligence people."

"They were easy to get on with."

"But they would rapidly distance themselves if you became contaminated . . ."

"By Zagorski," Kimber said, finishing the sentence for him.

"Exactly. He has implied that in 1944 you were pro-Russian and you can guess how the State Department would react if they suspected there might be some truth in the allegation."

"Thank you for telling me the score."

Emmerson ignored the irony in his voice. "Phone me as soon as you arrive in Blackpool," he said, and hung up.

CHAPTER 13

Daniel Tatar had joined the railway straight from school and had been trained as a signalman. From the beginning of October 1939 to the end of July '44, he had been assigned to the box controlling the marshalling yards near the Central Station in Warsaw, where he had worked under the close supervision of a German warrant officer. Kimber had met him at the post office in Napoleon Square when he had shown Jarrell and the other AK men how to use a PIAT. He had renewed their acquaintance in Colditz some two months after the Home Army had surrendered. In those days, Tatar had weighed less than nine stone which, since he was five feet eight, had made him look decidedly emaciated. By February 1953 when Kimber had attended his wedding, he had gained twenty-five pounds, his face had filled out and the dark shadows beneath his eyes had disappeared. Observing him standing there at the altar in a pale grey suit with a white carnation in the buttonhole, it had been easy to see why Eileen Martin had fallen for the dark-haired, good-looking Pole with the infectious smile.

Now, just over five years later, Tatar was beginning to run to seed even though he was only thirty-seven. The infectious smile was still there but the black hair had thinned out and receded from his forehead and a once-trim waistline had become a pot belly which strained against the buttons on his shirt. In the last five years he had changed jobs several times and was now a taxi driver, after having been a barman, a warehouseman and a self-employed glazier. He had also moved house and was now living in Hyde Road, halfway between the football stadium and the promenade. Kimber had found him by following Emmerson's advice and checking the copy of the electoral roll in the public library.

The terraced house in Hyde Road lay within easy walking distance of the Pleasure Beach on the South Shore, the Blackpool Tower and the amusement arcades near the Central Pier. During the summer, Eileen Tatar took in paying guests on half board. July and August were the busiest months, as the 'No Vacancies' sign in the bay window next to the porch indicated. They were also the busiest months for Daniel. Mornings he haunted Blackpool station from seven to three pm, then took a couple of hours off before plying for hire along the promenade and in the town centre until way past midnight.

"It's good to see you again, Michael," Tatar said, greeting him on the doorstep and pumping his hand enthusiastically. "Eileen tells me you're up here on business?"

"Yes. I dropped by at about one o'clock on the off-chance that you might be at home, and we had a chat."

"You should have stayed to lunch."

"I couldn't have done that, it would have been imposing on Eileen."

The offer had been there but Eileen wouldn't have thanked him if he had taken her up on it. The Tatars had two children under five and Eileen already had her hands full as it was with the guest house.

"Well, come on through."

Tatar led him into the front room where every bit of space was taken up by two sofas and three assorted easy chairs arranged in a semi-circle around the fireplace. On one side of the chimney breast, a twelve-inch TV set rested on a nest of occasional tables, while in the other nook, there was a low cupboard and matching half-size bookcase. The mantelpiece was crowded with ornamental souvenirs.

Crouching in front of the low cupboard, Tatar looked out a couple of glasses and poured two beers from a large bottle of Worthington.

"Your good health, Michael."

"And yours," Kimber said, raising his glass.

"So how are things with you? Are you still working for the Government?"

Tatar had come to England in 1947 understanding only a few words of the language and able to pronounce even fewer correctly; now he spoke it like a native Lancastrian with just a trace of a middle European accent.

"I haven't left the Diplomatic; the pay may not be marvellous but you've got to be totally incompetent to get the sack. How do you like being a taxi driver?"

"It's a living."

"I'm surprised you haven't applied for a job with British Rail."

"Trains lost their fascination for me during the war. I saw too many freight cars on their way to Auschwitz to ever want to be a railwayman again."

129

Kimber wondered how he could bring the conversation round to Zagorski in the absence of any cue from Daniel and decided there was no point being coy about it.

"You haven't heard the news about Stefan then?" he said.

"What news?"

"He died a week ago yesterday. It seems he fell from the roof of an eight-storey block of flats in South Lambeth."

"He fell?" Tatar went through his pockets, took out a packet of Gold Flake and offered Kimber a cigarette before lighting one for himself. He looked for an ashtray amongst the bric-a-brac on the mantelpiece above the fireplace and found one showing the illuminations on the Blackpool Tower. "What do you mean, he fell?"

"Well, it's not official yet, but he probably jumped."

"Stefan committed suicide?"

"The police have a letter he wrote which is pretty irrational. I haven't seen it myself but apparently he made all kinds of accusations against Maria Bolek, Halina Sosna, Ignace Orska, the Nowotkos and me. Apart from betraying the Home Army to both the Germans and the Russians, we are supposed to have made some kind of financial deal with Doktor Witzleben, the Head of the Civil Affairs Bureau." Kimber shook his head as though baffled. "You know something? He never once raised the subject with me the whole time we were in Colditz."

"He never said anything to me either. In those days, Stefan used to rave on about the Communists. He was always very political and ambitious with it. Before the war, he ran the Wola branch of the Socialist Party and saw himself as a future minister in a government of national unity. When he heard the London-based Government in Exile was returning to Poland in June 1945 to form such a coalition with the pro-Communist Committee of National Liberation, he wrote to Prime Minister Mikolajczyk from Paris offering his services. Fortunately, Mikolajczyk had the good sense to decline the offer. For a baker, he wasn't a bad café proprietor, but that was his limit."

"He owned a café in Warsaw?"

"Yes, Kuba's on Jasna Street. It was the perfect cover for a Resistance leader and the best possible place for Zagorski's battalion headquarters to assemble in secrecy the day the uprising began." Tatar stubbed out his cigarette even though he had smoked less than half of it. "But that's ancient history now."

"Then it's a pity Stefan couldn't let it rest," Kimber said. "He would probably still be alive today but for his obsession with the past. Hell, I know he didn't like me but what did he have against the others?"

"Search me; all I know is he didn't trust you, Michael. Before Exler and the other German prisoners were sent to the Old Town under guard, he got Maria Bolek to go through all the classified mail which was awaiting despatch when the battalion seized the post office in Napoleon Square."

"He was checking up on me. I had told him what the Home Army was up against and he wanted to know if I had exaggerated the number of divisions the Germans had in their order of battle."

"Something like that," Tatar agreed. "He also got very worked up over some German soldiers who were courtmartialled and shot for desertion. Couldn't see the sense of it myself. I mean, there we were locked in a life and death struggle for survival, and there he was worrying about some almighty cock-up by an enemy reconnaissance patrol."

Kimber recalled that Exler had been equally fascinated by the case and had seemed to think the four soldiers from the 73rd Infantry Division had been framed by the Gestapo.

"Is that when you began to think Stefan was a bit touched?"

"Hey, Michael, when did I ever say he wasn't right in the head? So it was hard to make Stefan see reason once he had made up his mind, but he was as sane as you or I. And he was one of the bravest men I have ever met. You wouldn't know because you never saw him in those final days, but I tell you he was a lion. He held the battalion together and inspired them to fight on when everyone else was talking of surrender."

"That was fourteen years ago," Kimber said. "Before he died, Stefan was claiming he had evidence in his possession which proved Maria Bolek and Halina Sosna had been guilty of treason. Maria was with you when the German tanks came rolling down Elektoralna Avenue, and the AK wouldn't have lasted a week if it hadn't been for women like Halina."

"He must have been crazy . . ."

It was what Kimber had come two hundred and fifty miles to hear. "Are you willing to get up in a coroner's court and say so?" he asked.

"Hey, I'm just a taxi driver. No one's going to listen to me. What do I know about mental illness? I'm not an expert like one of your . . ." Tatar snapped his fingers and groped for the right word. "Like one of your . . ." he repeated.

"Psychiatrists?" Kimber suggested.

"Yes, psychiatrist."

"But you don't need any special qualifications to know when someone is behaving strangely, Daniel."

"I never saw Stefan running around, foaming at the mouth . . ."

"He was obsessed . . ."

"Let me tell you something, Michael. I won't make a very good witness because it's almost three years since I had anything to do with him. The last time I saw Stefan was in November 1955. Eileen and I were up in London staying with her sister and I went round to his rooms in Ealing to see how he was getting on. I found him in bed with pneumonia; no one was looking after him and he hadn't sent for the doctor. None of his friends in London knew he was ill because he hadn't bothered to tell them, said he didn't want to worry them. And because he was self-employed and paid less National Insurance contributions than other workers, he didn't consider he was entitled to free medical treatment. 'You can't go on the dole if you are self-employed so why should the State look after you when you're sick.' I know it doesn't make sense but that was how Stefan saw it."

"Do you mind if I ask you a personal question?"

"Depends what it is," Tatar said and smiled.

"Why didn't you ask him to your wedding?"

"He didn't approve of Eileen." Tatar lowered his voice. His wife was in the kitchen busy preparing the evening meal for their paying guests and there wasn't the slightest chance that she would hear him but he wasn't taking any chances. "He said she was a tramp and tried to warn me off. We almost came to blows over it."

In addition to his uncanny knack for rubbing people up the wrong way, Zagorski was also a poor judge of character. Eileen might look a touch voluptuous in a sweater or the tight dresses she favoured and she certainly exuded an air of sexuality, but the first time Tatar had attempted to slide a hand up her skirt in the back stall of the Odeon, he had collected a black eye.

"Perhaps Ignace Orska can help you. He lived round the corner from Stefan in Ealing and used the same pub. He would be the man to know if Stefan was unstable."

"Where can I find him?"

"In the Oman; he's been a contract officer in the Sultan's army for the last nine months."

"What on earth made him do that?"

"Three reasons: it's the kind of job he is at home with, the money is good and it's tax free. In five years, Orska reckons to have saved enough to set himself up in business."

"Doing what?"

"He wants to buy a garage."

Kimber hoped he would live long enough to realise his ambition. There was a nasty little civil war going on in the Oman which owed a lot to the possibility of oil being found in the foothills of the Jebal al Akhdar. The rebels had the backing of the Saudis who were supplying them with arms and ammunition as well as anti-personnel and anti-tank mines which they in turn had originally acquired from the United States Army. The rebels also enjoyed the support of the local tribesmen living on the Jebal al Akhdar mountain and the inhabitants of Nizwa, a small village and the nominal capital of the province. The alienation of the local population was directly attributable to the Sultan himself, Said bin Taimur. There was no more feudal or despotic ruler in the whole of the Persian Gulf. Isolated in his palace on the coast at Muscat and tended by a retinue of slaves, he ruled by decree. At sundown, the gates of the walled city were locked and anyone leaving his abode at night was required to carry a lantern. More important, money raised in taxes on the people of Nizwa found its way into the royal treasury and was never spent on improving the interior.

"Stefan was a good baker," Tatar said, seemingly wandering off at a tangent, "he should have stuck to his trade. He had a nice thing going for him in Paris but of course he had to up sticks and move to London to join a small clique of Polish expatriates dedicated to overthrowing the Communist Government in Warsaw. At first, he was just a humble fund-raiser who had to support himself as best he could by taking odd jobs. Road sweeper, swimming pool attendant, commissionaire – you name it, Stefan did it. Finally, he made the grade and became the Deputy Assistant Minister of Information in Exile, which means he was a freelance journalist earning a pittance as a sub-editor with a Polish newspaper in London with a circulation of a few hundred."

"Do you know the name of this newspaper?"

"No, I never bothered to find out."

Kimber decided it wasn't important. Every newspaper had to be registered no matter how small its circulation might be, and it would be comparatively easy to obtain a list of those published in Polish together with the address of the head office.

"Have you got what you came for, Michael?"

"Yes, you've been very helpful." Kimber swallowed the rest of his beer and stood up. "It's been a great pleasure meeting you again after all these years."

"For me also," Tatar said, clapping him on the shoulder. "Let's not wait so long the next time."

Eileen said much the same thing when she left the kitchen to say goodbye to him in the hall and plant a wet kiss on his cheek. When he reached the top of the street, he looked back, but the Tatars were no longer standing there in the doorway and it was impossible to distinguish their house from the others in the terrace. He turned right, then right again on Lytham Road to make his way down to the promenade.

It was a fine summer day with hardly a cloud in the sky. The tide was out and it looked as though most of the population of Lancashire and the neighbouring counties were sunning themselves on the beach. Offshore, a de Havilland Tiger Moth puttered northwards at an altitude of two hundred feet towing a streamer advertising the 'Hylda Baker Show' at the Winter Gardens Pavilion.

From a phone box outside the post office in Dale Street, Kimber rang the Foreign Office in London and asked the switchboard operator for extension 892, then persuaded Emmerson's PA to put him through to her boss.

"This has got to be brief," Kimber told him, "because I've only got enough loose change for a three-minute call. The fact is we can't rely on Tatar; he is not prepared to go into the witness box and say that Zagorski was off his trolley."

"A bit of a wasted journey then."

"Tatar thinks we would have more luck with Orska who saw more of him latterly, but he's a contract officer with the Sultan of Muscat and Oman's army. He is probably serving with the Northern Frontier Regiment in Nizwa."

"We can't bring him back to the UK," Emmerson said crisply. "Too many tongues would start wagging."

"I do have one promising lead. Before he died, it seems Zagorski was working as a sub-editor on some Polish newspaper in London. If there is anything to his allegations, maybe that's where he buried the evidence."

"It shouldn't be too difficult to compile a list of publications."

"That's what I was thinking. And while we're at it, perhaps we can also discover the present whereabouts of a Doktor Karl Heinz Witzleben and a former Feldwebel called Gottfried Exler?"

"Why do we want to bother with those two?"

Kimber just had time to tell him before the pips started and he was cut off.

In nine months the sun had tanned Orska a deep mahogany so that only his heavier build distinguished him from his soldiers who were mostly Baluchis from Pakistan. Borehole number 1205, which he had visited with his recce patrol, was roughly forty miles west of Nizwa and consisted of two prefabricated, air-conditioned cabins, one serving as the living quarters for the eleven-strong drilling crew while the other was used as a recreation centre and mess hall. The camp also boasted an air strip big enough to take a Twin Pioneer, and a High Frequency wireless link to the support station in Muscat. The site had been established long before Orska had been recruited by the Crown Agents and thus far, the borehole was down to three and a half thousand feet with nothing to show for it.

Borehole number 1205 was a visible reminder of what the war was all about. Oil was power, oil revenues provided a cause. If the rig and others like it hadn't been there, the Omanis wouldn't have thought of secession and would have continued to pay their taxes while grumbling about it. The prospect of a gusher spawned mines on the track and mortars in the hills above the camp in Nizwa. Orska hadn't fathomed yet why the Saudis were happy to supply the rebels with the necessary hardware but he knew they were not doing it for altruistic reasons.

So far, the oil men had been left in peace which was only common sense. For the rebels to attack the British and American employees of Petroleum Concessions (Oman) Limited would be a bit like biting the hand they hoped would one day feed them. They were, however, known to mine all the tracks in the vicinity in order to discourage mobile patrols of the Northern Frontier Regiment from visiting the site every Thursday and Sunday. Orska had no doubt that a secondary aim of their tactics was to prod the oil company into doing something about the Sultan.

The mines were usually sown under cover of darkness and the outward leg from Nizwa to Borehole 1205 was always the slowest and riskiest phase of the patrol. Despite having to follow the same route back, the return journey was practically guaranteed to be trouble free provided it was completed before last light. Today, the chances of doing this were rapidly disappearing. The water pump on the second Land-Rover had packed up, the oil company didn't have a spare on the site for Orska to borrow and all attempts to effect a temporary repair had failed. If the vehicle was driven back to camp in its present condition, the engine would overheat and seize up; if he attempted to tow it back, the uneven terrain and the extra weight could well tear the guts out of the other Land-Rover. The only solution was to leave the broken-down vehicle and crew at the oil camp and return the following morning with a replacement pump.

Orska briefed the NCO in charge of the stranded crew, then

returned to his own vehicle and told the driver to move over. The Land-Rover had been specially modified for desert warfare. The windscreen and canvas canopy had been removed and external brackets had been welded to the body to hold extra jerricans of petrol and water. Balloon-type, low-pressure sand tyres had been fitted and, as an additional safeguard, two lengths of metal trackway were carried on the vehicle in case it bogged down in soft going. Conversely, the normal suspension had been replaced with heavy-duty springs to cope with the more usual bone-shaking terrain of the Oman. Sandbags had been placed on the floor to give the occupants some degree of protection should they be unlucky enough to run over a mine. Finally, the Land-Rover was equipped with a sun compass for navigational purposes.

Orska had seen more action than any other soldier in the Northern Frontier Regiment. Unwilling to return to a Poland under Soviet domination, he had joined the veterans of General Anders' Corps in England. Finding himself unable to settle after being demobilised in 1947, he had enlisted in the British Army for five years with the colours and seven on the Reserve. In 1950, he had been serving with the 1st Battalion of the Middlesex Regiment in Hong Kong when 27th Infantry Brigade had been sent to Korea. When his hopes of obtaining a commission had failed to materialise, he had taken his discharge, returned to London and found employment as a garage mechanic in Earls Court. Now, back in uniform again, this time as an officer in an Arab army, he counted on his experience to see him come through the next four and a quarter years un-scathed. Luck was not a factor which entered into his calculations because there was no accounting for it.

The sandbags could absorb the splinters from an M6 anti-personnel mine which came through the floor but they were never intended to cope with anything larger. Everyone was dreading the day the rebels acquired an M7; it was Orska's misfortune to encounter the first of a batch of anti-tank mines they had received from the Saudis. When the front nearside wheel ran over the pressure plate, the resultant explosion reduced the Land-Rover to scrap metal and hurled the mis-shapen wreckage into the air. The three Baluchis were killed instantly; Orska took longer to die.

CHAPTER 14

Like the weather, the atmosphere in Hillcrest was decidedly un-
settled. Stepdaughter Alison had gone off cornflakes and was sulking
because there were no Rice Krispies in the house, Richard didn't
want his boiled eggs because the yolks were hard, and Jean was
ominously silent.

Kimber had no need of a sixth sense to know what she was
thinking. Uppermost in her mind was the month-long summer
holiday in Brittany and the apartment she had rented in St Malo.
Tomorrow morning, Jean and the children were leaving on the ten
o'clock Southampton to Cherbourg car ferry; before the Iraq crisis
had thrown everything into the melting pot, he would have been
joining them for the last three weeks of the vacation. That plan was
now looking more and more doubtful every day, a fact which Jean
was extremely reluctant to face, let alone accept.

She had raised the issue on his return from the Persian Gulf, they
had argued about it again last night in bed and the bell for round
three would go the moment they had the kitchen to themselves. A
lingering hope that he would be out of the house before Alison and
Richard finished breakfast evaporated altogether when his son
announced that he had had enough and his stepdaughter said she
had some last-minute packing to do.

"Would you mind explaining something to me," Jean said as
soon as they were alone. "How is it that Nigel can send you off at
the drop of a hat to Bahrain one day, only to be in no hurry for you
to submit the report he so urgently wanted in the first place? What
is so important about your late friend, Stefan Zagorski, that his
suicide can take precedence over everything else?"

"We've been over this ground before."

"Well, I'd like to go over it again, Michael."

"All right. After that little difference of opinion we had with the
Americans over Suez, we devoted the whole of 1957 to kiss and
make up with Ike. This year the theme is mutual trust and united
we stand shoulder to shoulder in the Middle East. Unfortunately,

it looks as though Zagorski could undermine the mutual trust bit with his smears."

"Against you?"

"Amongst others."

"It doesn't matter what lies he has been spreading about you, Michael. The fact is you are not important enough to damage the accord with Washington."

"You don't have to be king of the castle; it's the amount of access you have which counts. It isn't only the Permanent Under Secretary of State who sees all the Top Secret documents; it's the humble paper-keepers who really have constant access, the clerks who have to account for every classified document in circulation. Take it from me, we're in trouble should the Americans begin to think I am a Soviet agent from way back."

"Well, if the evidence Zagorski claimed to have is so destructive, why are you the one who is running around trying to find it? Surely that's a job for professionals like Detective Inspector Viner?"

Jean could pose more awkward questions than a crusading journalist, and this one was particularly difficult to answer because he had asked himself the same thing and had been unable to think of a convincing reason.

"Most of the people he accused are his compatriots; I suppose Nigel Emmerson thought that in view of my special relationship with the Polish community, they were likely to be more forthcoming with me than they would with a police officer."

"What special relationship, Michael? The one you had with Halina?"

Telling Jean about the Polish girl had been a big mistake. His love affair with Halina had started in the cellar of a derelict house in Zoliborz a few days before the Home Army had surrendered and had ended in a small apartment on the Rue de Londres behind the Gare St Lazare in Paris one wet afternoon in July 1946. In between, there had been a long period of separation and the number of times they had actually made love could be counted on the fingers of both hands. With the benefit of hindsight, he could see it wouldn't have hurt Jean one bit if she had remained in ignorance of the affair but, at the time, he hadn't wanted any secrets to come between them.

"Let's get one thing straight," he said quietly. "I don't know where Halina is, nor do I care."

"Good. As long as she isn't involved, perhaps there's a chance you will be able to complete whatever it is you're doing in time to join us for at least a few days in St Malo?"

A lot was going to depend on what he learned from Mrs Irena Puzak, chairman and advertising director of *The Sentinel*, one of three Polish language newspapers published in London which appeared in the 106th Edition of *The Newspaper Press Directory*. It was, however, the only one which had employed Stefan Zagorski as an editor.

"I hope so."

"So do I, Michael, so do I."

Or else there will be trouble, he thought. Jean hadn't actually said it but it was certainly what her tone of voice had conveyed.

"Are you going up to town on the eight thirty-two?"

"That was the general idea," he said.

"You'd better get a move on then, it's twenty past eight."

Kimber checked his wristwatch against the clock on the wall above the gas stove. "Are you sure that's the right time?"

"If anything, it's two minutes slow."

"God, I am cutting it fine."

"I can run you to the station."

"No, you've got enough to do. Besides, the exercise will do me good."

Kimber gulped down the rest of his coffee, felt his jacket to make sure the photocopy of Zagorski's letter which he had collected from Emmerson on his return from Blackpool was in the breast pocket, then kissed Jean goodbye and told her he would be home by seven at the latest. Stepping out at a brisk pace, he reached the station with three minutes to spare. August was a popular month to go on holiday for those commuters with children of school age and many of the familiar faces were missing.

At Waterloo, he went down on to the Northern Line and caught a High Barnet train to Archway. The registered offices of *The Sentinel* were in Varley Mall off Junction Road, a bare five-minute walk from the Underground station. Newspapers like the *Mirror*, *Express* and *Telegraph* occupied a complete block in Fleet Street; *The Sentinel* got by with two rooms on the ground floor of a terraced house. Since the press were always being sued for libel, Kimber wondered if it was merely pure chance that Appleton, Crabtree and Forsythe, Solicitors and Commissioners for Oaths, were just across the hall from *The Sentinel*; and with an editor like Stefan Zagorski, having a finance company on the floor above could almost be essential. No reporters were in evidence and the staff in the front office appeared to consist of a clerk and an audio typist. Until his death, Zagorski had shared the room at the back of the house with the chairman.

Mrs Irena Puzak in the flesh was a very different person from the mental picture Kimber had formed. Emmerson, who had telephoned her to make an appointment on his behalf, had led him to believe she was much younger. Instead of the trim, thirty-year-old business executive he had imagined, Kimber found himself shaking hands with a tall, well-groomed woman in her late sixties. Within minutes he was to discover that she spoke English as though it had been her native tongue from birth.

"A voice on the telephone can be very deceptive, Mr Kimber," she said with a smile.

"I'm sorry – was I staring?"

"That's all right. For my part, I thought you would be quite plump."

Jean had often said that Nigel's voice reminded her of a man who regularly dined on pheasant and port wine. At the same time, Kimber made a mental note to ask Emmerson why he had been so coy about using his own name.

"Do sit down."

"Thank you."

The only spare chair in the room was a rickety ladderback which groaned in protest under his weight.

"You were a friend of poor Stefan's?"

"We met in Warsaw. I was attached to his battalion during the uprising."

"And you have stayed in touch ever since?"

Kimber sensed a loaded question. For all her twinkling eyes and friendly smile, Irena Puzak was as sharp as a needle and he thought it likely that Zagorski had told her about the letter he had written to him care of 'Roselands', Cathedral Close, Salisbury.

"No, I'm afraid I lost his address when I moved house some years ago. I only heard of his death through a mutual friend when I returned from the Persian Gulf the day before yesterday. He had seen the obituary in *The Sentinel*."

"Can you read Polish, Mr Kimber?"

"A little."

"You should become one of our subscribers. It would help you improve your knowledge of our language and you would be surprised to know how many long-lost friends we have reunited through the columns of *The Sentinel*."

"Was that part of Stefan's job as the editor?"

"No, he compiled the news, drawing on Reuters, Associated Press and the BBC Overseas Service and wrote the leader."

"And how many writs for libel did he collect?"

"No one has ever sued this newspaper, Mr Kimber. And I should know, it's my money that pays the bills and keeps the presses rolling."

He could believe it. The half-hoop of diamonds next to the gold band of her wedding ring was worth a good deal more than his annual salary as a First Secretary.

"I think you were about to collect your first writ." Kimber reached inside his jacket and took out the photocopy of Zagorski's letter. "You'd better read this; the original was found on Stefan when he was admitted to Lambeth General."

Irena Puzak took the letter from him, held it at arm's length and read it line by line, page by page. Her face remained expressionless even when she came to the final paragraph where Zagorski had said he intended to publish his evidence.

"Witzleben is wanted for war crimes, Mr Kimber. He surrendered to you British in May 1945 and was sent to a prison camp near Bremen from which he escaped and disappeared without trace some two months later. It's a matter of public record."

"In that case, no one will issue a writ for libel if you publish it – but what about his other accusations? Do you feel confident enough to print them?"

"Who said I was going to? Stefan never told me what he was up to and this is the first I've heard of his project."

"You haven't seen any of this so-called documentary evidence he refers to?"

"No."

"The police certainly didn't find anything when they searched his lodgings in Ealing." Kimber looked the room over. "Perhaps he concealed it somewhere in the office?" he said, gazing at the row of four-drawer filing cabinets against the dividing wall.

Irena Puzak placed the letter on one side and leaned forward, shoulders hunched, elbows on the desk. "What is this all about, Mr Kimber?"

"It's about how Stefan died. If only part of what he says in his letter is true, then it's possible he didn't jump off the roof. When you take a nose dive off an eight-storey building, your chances of survival are minimal; you don't have to lash a half-hundredweight bag of cement to your body to ensure you receive fatal injuries."

"Are you saying he was murdered?"

"A coroner's jury may well believe so, Mrs Puzak."

None of the residents in the block of flats had heard a disturbance, but the incident had happened late at night and most of them had been in bed at the time. Zagorski could have already been unconscious, doped out of his mind when he was thrown off the roof, though the killers could have made things a lot easier for themselves had they simply dumped him in the river instead. To drive an unconscious man all the way across London and then take him up to the top floor in a lift was asking for trouble. But if Zagorski had committed suicide, how had he transported a bag of cement from Ealing when the three-wheeler van he owned was still parked outside his lodgings?

"I'm quite happy for the police to go through my filing cabinets," Irena Puzak said quietly.

But not you; the inference was not lost on Kimber.

"Well, I expect they will be calling on you as soon as they learn that Stefan was a journalist. You see, his landlady told them he was an odd job man."

"Stefan was always a very private person."

"He certainly was. And secretive too." Kimber frowned. "Can you think of anywhere else the police should look? For instance, where is *The Sentinel* printed?"

"At Swanscombe in Kent. We use a small firm called Elliot Brothers. Each edition of two thousand copies comes up on the mail train to Charing Cross where it is collected and distributed to the newsagents."

"Thank you." Kimber hid his disappointment behind a smile. He had gone fishing hoping to catch a salmon and so far had only managed to hook a couple of sardines. Clearly, he had been using the wrong kind of bait. "I don't know whether you recall her name, but among the people accused of treachery by your former editor was a young woman called Maria Bolek. She worked for the Civil Affairs Bureau in Krasinski Square which apparently was enough to make her a collaborator in Stefan's eyes. The fact is that, at great risk to herself, she kept the Underground supplied with the means they needed to forge travel permits and false identity papers. I only mention this because she is no longer alive to defend her reputation. However, others are, and I think they should be forewarned because a lot of this mud Stefan was intent on throwing about is going to come out at the inquest."

"And what is it you want from me, Mr Kimber?"

"You told me earlier that I would be surprised how many long-lost friends your newspaper had reunited." Kimber pointed to the letter on her desk. "I'm hoping you can give me the addresses of some of the Poles Stefan has named."

Irena Puzak gazed at him, her brow furrowed in thought before she finally gave a slight nod. "I think we might do that," she said.

Erich Witzleben was the youngest of three brothers. The eldest, Manfred, had risen to the rank of Major General when he was killed in action at the battle of Kursk in July 1943 at the age of forty-six. The middle brother, Karl Heinz, a somewhat indifferent lawyer, had had the foresight to join the National Socialist Party in 1934, a move which had stood him in good stead when he had subsequently joined the legal department of the Foreign Ministry five months before the outbreak of war. Born in 1917 when his mother was approaching forty, Erich had been very much an afterthought. By choosing to be a dental surgeon, he had also succeeded in becoming a major disappointment to his father who had hoped he would qualify as an architect and join the partnership he had established with his brother-in-law and oldest friend, Georg Hanke.

In March 1940, shortly after he had qualified as a dentist, Erich Witzleben had gone some way to redeeming himself in his father's eyes by marrying Herta Ermsdorf, the only child of the largest property owner in Iserlohn. Although the Luftwaffe had claimed his services before he could set up his own practice, he had had a comfortable war as the dental officer on a night fighter station in Holland. Taken prisoner by the 1st Canadian Army in April 1945, he had been released in time to join his family for Christmas. He was also one of the very few servicemen to return to a town that had not been bombed.

A competent dentist, his highly successful practice was really founded on his charming manner which members of both sexes warmed to. Though a womaniser, he was the soul of discretion and made it a rule never to have an affair with any of his patients. He was also careful not to seduce any woman who moved in the same social circle. The only fly in the ointment was the fact that even now, fourteen years after the war had ended, the house in Goethestrasse which he and Herta had been given as a wedding present was still occupied by a British army officer and his family.

There were compensations however, the latest being his new receptionist and dental assistant, Katharina Voegel. An attractive twenty-four-year-old brunette, she was not the demure young wife of the elderly head cashier at the Ruhrland Savings Bank people took her for. As Erich Witzleben had been quick to discover, beneath her quiet almost placid exterior there lurked a very sexy lady who didn't get enough of what she wanted from her husband and was prepared to look elsewhere for it. Both Katharina and Erich had no desire to jeopardise what they already had and their amorous activities were therefore confined to the surgery during either the lunch break or after the last patient of the day had departed.

It was always Katharina who decided when they should have sex and while Witzleben normally preferred to make all the running, he found the way she signalled her availability a particularly erotic experience. This afternoon, for instance, she had managed to leave the fourth button from the top of her linen hospital coat undone and had made sure he noticed it before she did it up. This was shortly before Frau Arnim had arrived for her appointment and when he had begun to think that Katharina must have started her period.

Now he listened to Frau Arnim's heavy footsteps as she descended the staircase and waited for the low murmur of voices which would tell him that Katharina had presented the bill and was about to show her out. Presently a door opened and the noise from the passing traffic in the town centre increased slightly, then returned to its previous level. Not much longer now, he thought, and removed his coat. By the time Katharina walked into the surgery, he was practically naked.

Witzleben embraced her as she glided, feline as a cat, into his arms. He fastened on to her open mouth and savoured the pleasure to be gained from their darting tongues. Katharina rubbed herself against him, teasing the bulge in his Y-fronts. He dropped his arms and slipped both hands under the white housecoat to caress the backs of her thighs. Katharina never wore stockings in the height of summer but as his fingertips wandered delicately upwards to her buttocks, he found she wasn't wearing anything else either. They chasséd towards the dental chair, he steering her in the right direction while she drew him on. When her legs encountered the leather footrest, she gently pushed him away and shucked off the housecoat, then lowered herself into the chair and spread her legs.

The sultry smile on Katharina's face was all the invitation Witzleben needed to slide into her. There could not have been a worse moment for the telephone downstairs in reception to start burring.

"Ignore it," Katharina told him.

But he couldn't. For some unknown psychological reason, he had never been able to resist the intrusive summons of a telephone, especially when the caller seemed disinclined to hang up. Deaf to her entreaties, Witzleben scrambled to his feet and ran downstairs, worried now that it would stop ringing before he could answer it.

As he lifted the receiver and gave his subscriber's number, he heard the coins go down in the box.

"Herr Erich Witzleben?"

The voice was menacing enough to send a shiver down his spine.

"Yes, who's calling?" he asked nervously.

"My name is of no consequence. What is important is that you should pay attention to what I have to say."

"I'm going to hang up . . ."

"You do that and you will be in trouble, very serious trouble."

Witzleben discovered that his mouth had suddenly gone dry and tried to moisten his lips. "Now listen to me," he began.

"No, you listen to me. Some very nosy people in London have been asking after Karl Heinz. Naturally they have been told that we have no idea of his present whereabouts, but that may not satisfy them and it is possible that one of these Englanders may come over here to see you. If this should happen, you will tell him you have not seen or heard from your brother since he was posted to Warsaw in 1942. Do I make myself clear?"

"Very," Witzleben said huskily.

"Good."

The phone went down with a loud clunk that made him blink. For several minutes, Witzleben stood there holding the dead receiver in his right hand; then a plaintive voice called to him from the surgery and he slowly replaced it. Like a man in a trance, he went upstairs to find that in his absence, Katharina had swung the chair round to face the door so that he would see all of her as he walked into the room.

"Why, you're trembling, Erich," she said in a puzzled voice.

"Only with passion, mein Liebchen," Witzleben said and cackled nervously.

As befitted the head of the Arabian Department, Emmerson occupied a palatial corner office on the second floor of the Foreign Office building in King Charles Street. Situated at the west end of the building opposite the statue of Sir Robert Clive, the room overlooked Horse Guards Road and St James's Park. Because he did not wish to be distracted by the view, Emmerson had arranged the furniture so that his back was permanently to the window. In this position, the evening sun created the illusion of a halo above his head, adding substance to why the Arabian Department referred to him as the Messiah.

Emmerson did not work miracles; he was a pragmatist who, having digested all the facts, recommended a certain course of action to his Minister and awaited the latter's decision. That was something he could hardly do with a subordinate, but Kimber could tell he was finding the habit hard to break. It showed in the way he kept going over the same ground.

"No search warrant, no peeking inside her precious filing cabinets; Mrs Puzak is quite adamant about that, is she, Michael?"

"Absolutely. We might find the printers a bit more co-operative, but I wouldn't bank on it."

"Wretched woman! Why on earth does she have to be so coy?"

"Perhaps she is taking a leaf out of your book, Nigel."

"What do you mean?"

"She was under the impression that it was me who had phoned her at the office."

"She couldn't have been listening."

Kimber stole a glance at his wristwatch to confirm what he already suspected. A faint hope that Emmerson would get to the point in time for him to arrive home by seven was rapidly fading.

"We seem to be running into a blank wall at every turn," Emmerson complained.

"Surely Special Branch can get a search warrant?"

"I was referring to the inquiries our Embassy in Bonn has been making concerning the present whereabouts of Karl Heinz Witzleben. Apparently he hasn't been seen or heard of since he escaped from a prison camp in 1945 after being arrested for war crimes."

"So I gathered from Mrs Puzak."

"However, his brother, Erich, is a dentist in Iserlohn."

"Do you think he will tell us anything?" Kimber knew he was unlikely to get a straight answer and was not disappointed.

"Ex-Sergeant Gottfried Exler is living in Hamburg; he's a postmaster in the Altona District."

Another of Nigel's statements which invited a suggestion but for once, he was going to play the idiot boy. "I trust he's no longer in the habit of reading other people's letters."

"I'm beginning to think this whole thing is a complete waste of time," Emmerson said peevishly. "In my opinion, Zagorski was a madman and there never has been any evidence to support his ludicrous allegations."

"Maybe."

"What do you mean, maybe?"

"I got Orska's home address from Mrs Puzak . . ." Kimber paused, wished he could erase the vivid picture of the grief-stricken woman who had met him at the door when he'd called at the house.

146

The telegram informing her that her husband had been killed in the Oman was still on the hall table. "His wife's name is Ella . . ."

"So?"

"So she happens to be German. Furthermore, her father was stationed in Warsaw during the war." Kimber shook his head. "Doesn't it make you wonder if there might not be something in Zagorski's story after all?"

There was a long pause while Emmerson mulled it over. In the midst of his deliberations, he picked up his fountain pen and played with the cap. His face didn't give much away but Kimber could tell he didn't like the implications.

"I suppose we could always approach Gehlen and ask him if there was any truth in the Top Secret document I was shown soon after the Polish Home Army captured the post office in Napoleon Square."

"What?" Emmerson stopped playing with his fountain pen and looked up, a wary expression in his eyes.

"Gehlen alleged the Communists were aiming to suborn the AK High Command through an agent called 'Phoenix'."

"The Gehlen Bureau at Pullach is funded by the CIA. If we ask him to confirm the document, Washington will get to hear about it in five minutes flat, and we can't have that."

"It was just a thought," Kimber said and hid a smile.

"How soon can you let me have your report on the Persian Gulf?"

The sudden change of direction momentarily threw him. "I could work on it over the weekend."

"Good." Emmerson nodded emphatically. "Let me have it first thing on Monday, then you'd better take off for Germany and have a word with your friend, Exler."

"He's not my friend."

"Then you'd better cultivate him, Michael," Emmerson said almost cheerfully.

CHAPTER 15

Before Dresden and Hiroshima, there was Hamburg. On the night of the 27th/28th of July 1943, nearly eight hundred Lancasters, Stirlings, Halifaxes and Wellingtons had visited the city for the second time in forty-eight hours and had dropped over two thousand three hundred tons of high explosives and incendiaries in the space of forty-three minutes. Nine districts east of the Alster Lake and north of the River Elbe had been hit, with the greatest concentration falling on Borgfelde, Hammerbrook and Hamm. Major fires had rapidly become one huge conflagration covering four square miles with an estimated temperature of one thousand degrees Celsius at the centre. All the oxygen within the area had burned up and the rising gases had drawn in air from outside the immediate vicinity, creating hurricane force winds of a hundred and fifty miles an hour.

The firestorm had uprooted trees, overturned fire tenders and sucked their crews into the wall of flames. A total of forty-five thousand civilians had been killed and a large part of the city and dockland totally destroyed. Now, fifteen years after the event, only the odd scar from the bombing remained, or so it seemed to Kimber on the way into the city from the airport.

Although there was a British consulate in Hamburg, Emmerson had not informed them that Kimber would be visiting the city and consequently, no one had met him off the British European Airways flight from London. As if to discourage any contact with the Foreign Office representatives in Harvestehuder Weg on the west bank of the lake, the Arabian Department's chief administrative officer had booked him into the Fürst Bismarck near the Hauptbahnhof.

Soon after he had checked into the hotel, Kimber had looked up the number of the post office in Altona and called Exler. The switchboard operator had put him through to the sorting office from which entry point he had gradually worked his way up the chain. When he had finally been connected with the postmaster, a long silence had followed before recognition had dawned. From then on, there had been no holding the former Feldwebel and his unfeigned

148

delight had almost convinced Kimber that they had been close friends. An evening out on the town was not what he had had in mind when he'd phoned Exler but it was what he was going to get.

Exler picked him up from the lobby of the Fürst Bismarck at seven. The years had not been too unkind to him. When a sergeant with the 385th Postal and Courier Unit in Warsaw, he had been overweight, unfit and myopic; he was still all of these but didn't appear a day older. But even in a made-to-measure suit, he still didn't look any smarter than he had in uniform.

"This is a great pleasure, Herr Kimber," he said and gave a slight bow.

"I feel the same way."

"How did you know I was living in Hamburg?"

"I traced you through the Bundeswehr Office in Bonn," Kimber told him as they walked out on to the street.

"You traced me?" Exler froze in the act of opening the nearside door of the Opel Rekord. "I don't understand, why would you want to do that?"

"Because I've been commissioned to write a book about the Warsaw uprising."

"You are a distinguished author?"

"Well, I don't know about being distinguished, but I'm certainly a writer," Kimber said and got into the car.

He had a letter from the literary director of Hodder and Stoughton to prove it. Emmerson had produced it like a rabbit out of a conjuror's hat that morning when he had delivered his report on the Persian Gulf. "I think it will impress ex-Sergeant Exler," he'd said smiling, then added, "It will also allay his suspicions when you question him."

"Will this book also be published in Germany, Herr Kimber?"

"Please call me Michael – and yes, I hope it will be. The story will be written as it was seen through the eyes of the combatants on both sides."

"And you want to hear my story, Michael?" There was just a momentary hesitation before Exler used his Christian name.

"Yes, I also want to pick your brains."

"I'm flattered." Exler started the car, pulled away from the kerb and turning right at the top of Kirchenalle, headed towards the Rathaus. "Is being an author very profitable?" he asked.

"I'm being paid fifteen hundred pounds in advance of royalties – that's approximately eighteen thousand Deutschmarks in your money."

The fake offer was spelt out in the letter from the publisher. It had also been accompanied by a handwritten disclaimer from the literary director.

"You must be famous to command such a fee."

"I've got a brilliant agent," Kimber told him poker-faced.

They went on down through Rodings Markt, turned right again on the Ost-West Strasse and almost inevitably, made for the Reeperbahn.

"Are you married, Michael?"

"Yes, I have a wife and family."

"So have I," Exler said happily, "but this is a special occasion."

The Reeperbahn was not all brothels, bar girls, transvestites, striptease joints, erotic sex shows and blue movies. There was also a noisy Bavarian beer hall with an oom-pa-pa band and waitresses capable of carrying half a dozen litre-size tankards in each hand. Exler found a corner table far removed from the band and ordered two large beers, frankfurters and Sauerkraut.

"This is nice, yes?"

"Very atmospheric," Kimber agreed.

"So how can I help you?"

"Well, tell me what happened to you after I left the hospital on Miodowa Street."

"It was very bad." Exler avoided his gaze, looked down at the checkered tablecloth. "When Dirlewanger's criminals and their Ukrainian allies discovered that the Polish insurgents had escaped through the sewers, they began to shoot the wounded. There would have been a massacre if we hadn't stopped them."

"Who's we?"

"A Luftwaffe NCO, myself and some wounded Panzer Grenadiers from the Hermann Goering Division."

"But not Herr Doktor Karl Heinz Witzleben?"

"No, he refused to intervene. They say the Poles charged him with war crimes but I never saw him again after Warsaw surrendered."

Exler had been sent to a Reserve Army replacement depot on the outskirts of Dresden to await reassignment. With the chronic shortage of manpower, his one big fear was that he would be posted to one of the Volksgrenadier divisions composed of greybeards, the medically unfit and schoolboys, which Himmler, in his new capacity as an army commander, was hastily forming. The Anglo-American offensive had ground to a halt in Holland and the Ardennes and he could see himself back on the Eastern Front, this time as a rifleman.

"One had heard such terrible stories about the Ivans that I was terrified I'd fall into their hands." Exler reached for one of the tankards of beer a waitress had left on their table, wished Kimber good health, then drank almost half a litre in a few gulps and wiped the froth from his lips. "Fortunately, I secured a posting to Army Group 'B' commanded by Field Marshal Model."

Exler had continued to run a field post office all through the German offensive in the Ardennes. It was only in the final weeks of the war when the Army Group was trapped inside the so-called Ruhr Fortress that he had found himself in the front line as a rifleman.

"The Field Marshal blew his brains out for his beloved Führer; when an American patrol approached our position on the outskirts of Mulheim, I put my hands up for peace."

"Very sensible."

"That's what the Amis said."

Exler attacked his frankfurters with gusto. Up on the stage, the band broke into another hand-clapping, foot-stamping, beer-drinking song.

"Harping back to Warsaw," Kimber said gently, "do you remember a Polish girl called Maria Bolek?"

"Who?"

"Maria Bolek – young, dark hair, upturned nose, spoke German and worked for the Civil Affairs Bureau."

Exler snapped his fingers. "The girl I met at the post office in Napoleon Square."

"That's her."

"She was friendly with an American airman called Jarrell – I think it was Leon Jarrell."

"You have a very good memory, Gottfried."

"I like to think so." Exler wiped a piece of Sauerkraut from his lips. "Do you know what happened to them?" he asked.

"Jarrell survived and went home, Maria was drowned in the sewers."

"I'm sorry to hear that."

"You remember the Polish battalion commander at the post office?"

"Zagorski. I'm not likely to forget his name in a hurry, he really hated us Germans."

"I was talking to one of his officers the other day and he told me that Zagorski ordered you and Maria to sift through the mail again. Apparently he was particularly interested in the court martial proceedings of those four soldiers from the 73rd Infantry Division who were tried for desertion in the face of the enemy."

"That's correct."

"You want to tell me what you remember about the case?"

Kimber took out the small notebook he had purchased before setting off for Heathrow. "The names of the soldiers, where they came from, who defended them, the members of the court, any witnesses for the defence. I know the incident happened before the uprising started but it's the kind of thing to grab the reader's interest early on in the book."

According to his own reckoning, Exler had read the transcript on three occasions, the first time being when he had noticed that the classified document had not been double-enveloped in accordance with security regulations then in force. He had subsequently briefed Kimber and had then gone over the papers in considerable detail with Maria Bolek. Even so, most people fourteen years later would only retain the bare bones of the case, but not the former Feldwebel – he had almost total recall. The Prosecutor had been a Hauptsturmführer Rudolf Brack, a lawyer attached to the Gestapo Headquarters on Szucha Avenue from the Reich Main Security Office in Berlin. The accused had been denied legal representation and had been obliged to defend themselves advised by an Under Officer.

"The trial was rigged from the start and the Army allowed an SS officer to prosecute their soldiers. That's what I can't understand."

"What did this Under Officer say in his plea of mitigation, assuming he submitted one?"

"Oh, he observed the usual formalities, but he only just about knew the accused by sight, so there wasn't much he could do except draw the court's attention to their hitherto unblemished records. Anyway, the brass who were sitting in judgement wouldn't have paid any attention to him even if he had made an impassioned speech. The accused infantrymen were replacements; they had been in the 73rd Infantry Division exactly forty-eight hours when they were sent out on that patrol."

The four replacements had not joined the division straight from basic training. All of them had been in combat before and their length of service ranged from twenty months to four and a quarter years in the case of the senior rank, a Gefreiter called Wilhelm Freisler. Apart from a chestful of campaign medals, this soldier had been decorated with the Iron Cross Second Class for conspicuous bravery in September '41 and had been awarded a bar to the medal nine months later.

"I don't care what you say, Michael, a soldier like Freisler doesn't suddenly take it into his head to go over the hill. The more I think about it, and I have thought about it a lot over the years, the more I am convinced he genuinely believed he was being sent on leave as some sort of reward for what he and the other members of his patrol had done at Wolomin."

"Was Freisler in charge of the patrol?"

"According to the charge sheet he was." Exler reached for his tankard. "Drink up, Michael," he said jovially, "it's time we were moving on."

"Where to?"

"Somewhere a little more entertaining."

Somewhere more entertaining turned out to be the Club Erotisch which offered sport with a difference. Instead of a band, there was a master of ceremonies in a tuxedo and a boxing ring with a canvas floor six inches deep in liquid mud. By the time Kimber had paid the cover charge, ordered a bottle of Sekt and tipped the blonde hostess who served them, he had seen precious little change from a hundred-Deutschmark note.

The sport was all-in wrestling and the female contestants, some of whom came from the audience, were required to strip off to their bra and panties before they climbed through the ropes. Within a few minutes, both contestants could have been stark naked for all anyone knew and it was impossible to distinguish between a blonde, brunette or redhead. The referee wisely stayed out of the ring; Exler proved equally evasive when it came to holding his attention.

"We were talking about Wilhelm Freisler," Kimber reminded him.

"I thought we had finished with the Gefreiter."

"No, I'd like to know what task his patrol was given?"

"That was censored. Freisler started to tell the court but the Judge Advocate ordered the stenographer to strike it from the record. His amended testimony began with something like – 'We drove to the rendezvous . . .'"

"They were a mobile patrol?"

"Oh yes. In fact, there was more than one vehicle as I recall."

"What else?"

Exler didn't answer him. His whole attention was riveted on the ring where a tall, rather plump blonde was coming off a bad second best to a lithe, slightly darker girl.

"What else?" Kimber repeated in a louder voice.

"What else?" Exler reluctantly turned away from the wrestling match. "Well, all the court allowed Freisler to say was that the patrol returned to the RV at 1500 hours with the civilian work party and the Polish guide."

"What Polish guide?"

"Presumably the one who could take them through the Russian lines."

A Polish guide, a German patrol and a civilian working party; Zagorski's allegations could hardly be dismissed as the ravings of a mentally disturbed person if the civilian work party included the agent Major General Reinhard Gehlen had referred to as 'Phoenix'. There were a dozen questions he wanted to ask Exler but the blonde, who was flat on the canvas receiving a mud facial and shampoo from her opponent, was claiming all his attention.

His name was Charles Hazelton, but within 'Five' he was known as Keyhole Charlie because he had been trained as a locksmith, which was why MI5 had gone out of their way to recruit him. The tools of his trade were a massive collection of some fifteen thousand keys which he guaranteed would open any door, any filing cabinet and any safe other than one fitted with a Manufoil combination. When out on a job, he carried a wide selection of tools in a black bag which at one time had belonged to his brother-in-law who was a doctor. Any fool could break into a safe given the right equipment; it was Hazelton's proud boast that when he opened one up, no one could tell it had been tampered with.

Viner knew of his reputation but had never worked with him before and wished things could have remained that way for the foreseeable future. Personal animosity had nothing to do with his antipathy, for Keyhole Charlie was in fact a very likeable man. It was the nature of the assignment they had been given which bothered Viner. Mechanics like Hazelton only appeared on the scene when something illegal had to be done, like turning over the offices of *The Sentinel* in Varley Mall. For reasons which were not at all clear to him, their superiors didn't want to apply for a search warrant; instead, he and Keyhole Charlie were to break into the premises like a couple of thieves in the night.

A few minutes before nine, Viner picked up Keyhole Charlie from his flat in Highbury and drove north on Holloway Road. Things were never lively on a Monday evening and at that hour, there was very little traffic on the road, which in a curious way made him even more jumpy. Suddenly it became very important to know precisely how many other break-ins the locksmith had done in his time.

"It's not exactly a new experience for me," Hazelton told him cheerfully. "Truth is, I've lost count of the number of Fellow Travellers I've helped to bug since Burgess and Maclean did a bunk."

"Any bad moments?"

"Not so far."

Viner hoped he wasn't tempting providence. Approaching the intersection before Archway tube station, he moved into the inside lane and signalled he was going left in Junction Road. Turning right at the first T-junction, he drove past Number 6 Varley Mall and parked the unmarked Hillman Minx round the corner in Macdonald Drive.

"Well, here we are," he said unnecessarily.

Viner got out of the car, waited for Hazelton to join him, then crossed the road and entered the narrow earthen lane behind and parallel to Varley Mall. Wooden fences and overgrown privet hedges on either side, no street lights and a low overcast hiding the moon; they couldn't have asked for more favourable conditions, but he still didn't like it. The neighbourhood fell within 'E' Division and no one had warned the Detective Chief Superintendent, let alone the Borough Commander, that Special Branch and MI5 were operating in their manor.

The back gate to Number 6 Varley Mall was secured with a padlock and hasp on the inside. Hazelton vaulted over it without making a sound; Viner was less fortunate, caught his trailing foot on the gate, and landing awkwardly, blundered into the dustbin and knocked it over. Somewhere not too far away, a dog started barking.

"Christ."

"It's all right," Hazelton said quietly, "dogs are always barking. Besides, most of the houses around here are registered offices."

"The ones across the lane aren't."

"You worry too much."

Hazelton moved towards the house through knee-high grass and past a rose bed choked with weeds. Halting in front of the back door, he took out a pencil flashlight and trained the pinpoint beam on the lock, then stood there humming tunelessly under his breath.

"Trouble?" Viner asked softly.

"Not unless it's bolted on the inside. What we have here is an ordinary mortice a child of five could pick."

Hazelton opened his little black bag and selected a bunch of keys. The first three he tried didn't fit, the fourth one did but the door only moved fractionally after he had unlocked it.

"Draw bolts," he told Viner, "top and bottom. No way of shifting them."

"That's it then; let's get out of here."

"You give up too easily."

Hazelton sidestepped to the left-hand sash window, rummaged through his black bag again and came up with a tool which resembled a set of tappet gauges for measuring the valve clearance on an engine. Easing one of the blades between the upper and lower frames, he pushed the catch out of the housing and then lowered the top half of the window.

"See, nothing to it."

Viner glanced over his shoulder to make sure no one was watching him from the houses across the lane before he climbed into the room. Hazelton had already opened one filing cabinet and was about to start on the next when they heard a police car in the distance.

"It's not coming for us," Hazelton said confidently.

Viner cocked his head. Was that one car or two he could hear? Hazelton settled the doubt for him.

"Shit, that's it, I'm off."

Keyhole Charlie grabbed his bag, ran across the room and attempted to dive through the lower half of the window which was closed. He was still lying on the grass outside, bleeding like a stuck pig when the police arrived.

Kimber found the lock with his room key at the second attempt and opened the door, then groped for the light switch inside the hall. His hands encountered a bare wall and he moved sideways to the right, blundered into the bathroom and came out again, swearing under his breath. Thoroughly disorientated, he tripped over the luggage rack and measured his length on the floor. He raised himself up on hands and knees, reached out to get his bearings and touched the bed. He crawled round it towards the headboard, bumped into the bedside table and after a dint of groping, located the lamp and flooded the room with light.

The door was still wide open. A little unsteady on his feet, Kimber crossed the room, locked it and hooked the security chain into the slot above the mortice. His mouth was dry, there were a dozen little men inside his head working on a demolition job with sledgehammers and he felt utterly wretched and washed out. Champagne had always had this effect on him when he had drunk too much of it and Deutscher Sekt was no exception. He slipped out of his jacket, hung it up in the wardrobe, then removed the notebook from the inside pocket and tossed it on to the bed. Loosening his tie, he went into the bathroom and sluiced his face in cold water.

Exler had been too paralytic to drive his car when they had left the Club Erotisch and Kimber had flagged down a cab and delivered him safely to his flat in Altona near the S-bahn station before returning to the Fürst Bismarck. Gottfried had boasted that he was married to a very understanding woman, which was just as well considering the amount he had put away. Whether she would be quite so tolerant when she saw the lipstick on his face and shirt collar was another matter.

Kimber dried his face and hands on a towel and returned to the bedroom. "Phone me the moment you have anything. You have my home number so don't keep it to yourself just because it's outside normal working hours." Emmerson would regret having said that because it was two fifteen am in England, but Kimber didn't see why he should be the only one to suffer. Lifting the receiver, he called the hotel operator and asked her to connect him with Reigate 1927.

Emmerson answered the phone with something that sounded halfway between a croak and a strangled yawn. It was some moments before he was sufficiently alert to realise just who it was who had called him in the middle of the night.

"Do you know what time it is?" he said indignantly.

"Yes, it's twenty past three here in Hamburg."

"I hope this is important."

"It certainly is. Better get a pencil and paper ready because I need some information on the following people." Kimber opened his notebook at the right page, waited for Emmerson to tell him to go ahead, then said, "The first name is Wilhelm Freisler. He was a corporal serving in the 73rd Infantry Division who was court-martialled and shot for desertion in July 1944 together with three other soldiers. I want the name and last known address of his next of kin."

"That's a tall order."

"It gets taller. See if you can persuade the Bundeswehr to provide us with an extract from the war diary of the 73rd Infantry Division for the twenty-second to the thirty-first of July 1944 inclusive. I am particularly interested to know what was happening at a place called Wolomin, ten miles north-east of Warsaw."

"I'll see what I can do."

"I'd also like a trace on a Captain Rudolf Brack of the SS who was employed in the legal department of the Reich Security Main Office and prosecuted Freisler."

"Anything else?" Emmerson sounded like a man whose patience was rapidly being exhausted and was only controlling his temper with difficulty.

"Just Otto Dornberger. He was an Under Officer in the 73rd

157

Infantry Division and appeared as a friend of the accused at Freisler's court martial. My informant thinks Dornberger came from Rothenburg."

Emmerson muttered something under his breath and in the ensuing silence, Kimber heard Diana ask her husband just how much longer he proposed to keep her awake.

"I don't think we shall get quite the same quick response from Bonn this time as we did with Exler and Witzleben."

"No, I don't suppose we will," Kimber said.

"So what are your future plans?"

"I thought I would go down to Iserlohn and have a word with Erich Witzleben."

"Good. Let me know where you're staying in Iserlohn in case I need to get hold of you in a hurry."

"Right."

"And be careful, Michael. We don't want any histrionics from Bonn."

"Don't worry," Kimber said, "I've no intention of starting World War Three."

He replaced the receiver and lay back on the bed. The room started spinning and he felt as though he were floating weightless in space. It was not a pleasant sensation.

CHAPTER 16

The day started badly for Emmerson with a phone call from Ryeland at 54 Broadway and Queen Anne's Gate. Depending on what was currently in vogue, Martin Ryeland was 'Six' or the Secret Intelligence Service or MI6. In his sourer moments, Emmerson had been known to observe that the SIS had more fancy titles than a Ruritanian prince.

Ryeland in fact was not a spy; his job was to look after those who were. A wartime Intelligence Corps officer, he had made a name for himself in Field Security and had gradually moved sideways into the Service following a spell of duty with the Allied Control Commission in Germany. As the head of the department responsible for monitoring the vetting status and political reliability of SIS personnel, he had forged strong links with Special Branch and MI5, the security service.

The Zagorski affair had started life as a routine inquiry by uniformed officers of 'L' Division in Lambeth. Detectives of the local Criminal Investigation Department had been drawn into the case by the letter found on the body and, once that had been translated, the political implications had automatically involved Special Branch. They in turn had rapidly referred the matter to MI5 who had subsequently advised Ryeland after they had discovered that Kimber was in the Diplomatic. The final link in the circuitous chain had been Emmerson, and the day Martin Ryeland had walked into his office had been one of the worst he could remember.

The phone call he'd received soon after he'd arrived at the office that morning led him to think that perhaps the worst was yet to come. The moment his PA showed the man from 54 Broadway into the room, a premonition became an established fact. Ryeland was well equipped to be the bearer of bad tidings; he had a hooked nose, eyes that glittered like a bird of prey and a long thin face. Bad news could be gauged by the lack of warmth in his smile; this morning the grimace looked positively icy.

"We have a problem, Nigel."

Early on in their acquaintance, Emmerson had discovered that Martin Ryeland was a firm believer in the principle that a problem shared was a problem halved.

"You wouldn't be here if we hadn't," he said dryly.

"Then you won't be surprised to hear that things didn't go too well at *The Sentinel* last night. In fact, I'm sorry to say Viner and Hazelton, the technical expert we borrowed from 'Five', made a real pig's ear of it."

"Exactly what did they do wrong?"

"They got caught," Ryeland told him succinctly. "Viner knocked over a dustbin which roused one of the neighbours who then phoned the police. As luck would have it, there were two patrol cars in the area; worse still, the criminal fraternity appeared to be having a night off. So both mobiles responded and in no time at all, they had Varley Mall sealed up tighter than a drum. When he heard the sirens, the technical expert lost his head and went out through the bottom half of the window, completely forgetting it was only the top half he'd opened. He's in Whittington Hospital; one ear was practically sliced off and they had to put twenty-seven stitches into his right leg."

The gory details appeared to fascinate Ryeland and he left nothing out. Although Emmerson was not a squeamish man, the graphic description left him feeling distinctly queasy.

"Hazelton is comfortable enough now but he's going to have quite a few scars to show for his night's work. Ours, on the other hand, won't be visible, at least I hope they won't. The Borough Commander of 'E' Division is thirsting after blood and would like to have our heads, but I think we can smooth his ruffled feathers."

"When did he hear about the incident?" Emmerson asked.

"Well, put it this way, he was woken up in time to hear the dawn chorus, which didn't put him in the best of moods to begin with."

Since it was an illegal operation, Hazelton and Viner had not carried any means of identification on them. Furthermore, both men had given a false name and address to the arresting officers which Viner couldn't have got away with had his face been known in 'E' Division. Hazelton had been rushed straight to the casualty department at Whittington Hospital where, following emergency treatment, he had then been detained overnight with a police constable at his bedside. He had therefore had to rely on Viner to sort things out with the police at the Rosslyn Hill station. Unfortunately, the arresting officers knew they had an open and shut case and had been in no hurry to let him make a phone call.

"When they finally did, Viner called his immediate superior and of course there was a further delay while details of the incident were passed on up the line to the Deputy Assistant Commissioner in charge of Special Branch. Then it had to come all the way down again from the Criminal Investigation Department on the other side of the house, which meant that the arresting officers were practically on their way to the Magistrates' Court by the time they were told to drop the charges."

"Thank God for small mercies."

"It's going to be very difficult to contain the situation."

Emmerson thought he knew what Ryeland meant. It wasn't only the arresting officers who had to be muzzled. There was also the ambulance crew who had rushed Hazelton to hospital, the Intern and nursing staff of the casualty department who had treated him and the Sister in charge of the ward where he was now convalescing. To an already intimidating list he could add the kitchen maids, hospital porters and student nurses.

"When will Hazelton be discharged from hospital?"

"Some time next week, I imagine." Ryeland allowed a wintry smile to make a brief appearance. "You don't have to worry about the hospital staff shooting off their mouths," he added, as though reading Emmerson's thoughts. "They won't make a big production out of the incident."

"How can you be so sure?"

"Because it's not the first time they've seen a policeman sitting by a patient's bedside."

"But there's still the householder who reported the break-in."

"The police will thank him for his assistance and then he'll be told that, as the intruders were caught red-handed, he won't be required to give evidence in court."

"Good."

"That leaves us with Mrs Irena Puzak and I'm not sure what we can do about her."

The royal 'we' was in constant use but Emmerson had to concede it was justified in this instance. At the end of the day, he was the one who had told Kimber to see the owner of *The Sentinel* and was equally responsible with Ryeland for what had followed.

"We should have obtained a search warrant, Martin."

"I agree with you, but it's too late now for regrets. Anyway, who was it who said Zagorski's allegations had to be kept under wraps because they were so politically sensitive?"

"Don't remind me," Emmerson said wearily.

"How do you think Irena Puzak will react?"

"I honestly don't know." The only thing Emmerson did know was that Irena Puzak was shrewd enough to realise the attempted burglary of her premises was connected with Kimber's visit.

"What's the worst case, Nigel?"

"That's easy to answer. She could give her story to the national press and then we really would be in trouble."

"I wonder. Can Irena Puzak establish a Foreign Office connection? I mean, apart from Kimber's name, what else does she have?"

"Nothing."

"We're sure about that, are we? Kimber didn't give her any reason to think he was there in some official capacity?"

"No, he kept it entirely on a personal level; he talked to her about defamation of character and the possibility of a libel action by the survivors."

"Can you dump him?"

"Who – Kimber?"

"Yes. If we go on trying to preserve the favourable image Kimber has created with the Americans, we'll soon reach the point where we shall be in danger of giving credence to Zagorski's preposterous allegations. From here on we should be thinking of ways to limit the damage. It's not up to me to tell you how to run your department, Nigel, but in your shoes, I'd move Kimber to a less demanding position."

'A less demanding position' was a euphemism for a low grade appointment, the kind of slot reserved for a man who had reached his ceiling and was simply marking time until he was eligible for a pension. It was also an adroit way of informing an officer that he had no future in the Service.

"It's worth thinking about," Emmerson agreed.

"Does he have any influential friends or relations who could make life difficult for you?"

"I don't know of any."

Jean Kimber had inherited almost a quarter of a million from her father who had been a highly successful solicitor in a practice which had been in the family since the turn of the century. Her first husband hadn't left her short of a bob or two either, but none of her surviving relatives were in a position to bring pressure to bear on the Foreign Office. As for Kimber's people, his father had been a consultant engineer and a strong supporter of the Church. It had been his fund-raising activities for the preservation of Salisbury Cathedral which had enabled the family to live at 'Roselands' in the Close, a grace-and-favour house which his Austrian-born widow still occupied.

"So what's your decision, Nigel?"

"We'll dump Kimber and let Madame Puzak answer for Zagorski should his letter be produced in evidence at the inquest."

And if the attempted burglary of *The Sentinel* did make the headlines, it would be Kimber who would be left holding the baby. His was the only name Irena Puzak had.

"You're doing the right thing, Nigel."

Emmerson hid his thoughts behind a vague smile. He would be doing the right thing when he told the Senior Administrative Officer he needn't bother to draft a cable to the British Embassy in Bonn requesting the additional information Kimber had asked for.

"It would be helpful to know the date of the inquest, Martin."

"That's easy; it's been fixed for Thursday the fourteenth of August, ten o'clock of the forenoon at Lambeth Town Hall."

"You might have told me."

"I only heard myself just before I came to see you," Ryeland said irritably.

"I'm sorry." Emmerson's expression was suitably contrite. "I should have known you wouldn't keep it to yourself."

"That's okay."

"I do have one small request, though I hesitate to ask . . ."

"Name it."

"Could we have some forewarning of what the investigating officers are likely to say in court?"

"I can practically guarantee it," Ryeland said cheerfully.

The Chief Administrative Officer of the Arabian Department was one of those less demanding appointments which were reserved for those career diplomats who had reached their ceiling and were not yet of pensionable age. No one was more suited for the post than the present incumbent, Leslie Humberstone, a fifty-two-year-old First Secretary who had fallen off the promotion ladder at the critical age of forty. Every annual confidential assessment had referred to his calm, unruffled approach, which was another way of saying he lacked a sense of urgency. Even more devastating was the assessment written before the war by the Head of Chancery at the British Embassy in Brussels who had observed that, although he possessed many sterling qualities, Humberstone was completely lacking in initiative.

It was this lack of initiative that Emmerson was banking on when he sent for him minutes after Ryeland had left. The information on Exler and Witzleben had been obtained on his behalf by the European Department after Emmerson had been to see his opposite number. He had given the gist of the cable to Humberstone who had then fleshed it out and submitted the draft for his approval before it went across to the European Department to be topped and tailed.

"This cable I asked you to draft, Leslie," Emmerson began.

"It's gone," Humberstone told him with satisfaction.

"Gone?"

"Well, the notes you gave me were pretty comprehensive, Nigel."

Emmerson felt his jaw drop and hastily closed it. The notes were a series of jottings he'd made on the back of an envelope when Kimber had phoned him in the middle of the night. He had dropped the envelope on to Humberstone's desk and had told him to get a cable off to Bonn.

"Why didn't you show me a draft, Leslie?" Emmerson asked in what he hoped was a reasonable tone of voice.

"You didn't ask for one."

"But the European Department isn't at our beck and call. They did us a favour when we asked for information on Exler and Witzleben and we shouldn't have imposed on their goodwill without having first cleared it at the highest level."

Even to his own ears, Emmerson knew he sounded pompous.

"I'm sorry, Nigel," Humberstone said contritely, "it never occurred to me that the previous cable to the Embassy in Bonn was simply a one-off arrangement. As a matter of fact, my opposite number thought we had established a regular channel of communication on this particular subject. That's why he raised no objections when I gave him the text of our latest request."

"You said the cable had gone?"

"Yes. It was despatched at 0815 hours Greenwich Mean Time. I've got the receipted copy on file if you would like to see it?"

A faint hope that the cable might still be languishing in the European Department had been extinguished. To send another cable cancelling the request would only excite unwelcome speculation. The inquest was only nine days away and if past experience was anything to go by, it would take the Embassy in Bonn at least a week to obtain the information. If Kimber grew restless, he could always tell him the West Germans were proving unco-operative.

"Yes, I would like to see the file copy," Emmerson said presently, "but there's no hurry, Leslie. Any time will do."

He found it difficult to be pleasant to Humberstone. For the Chief Administrative Officer to have acted on his own initiative was so out of character that Emmerson couldn't help wondering if he had some ulterior motive.

*   *   *

The Rhineland Express arrived in Dortmund a little under four hours after departing from Hamburg. From the Hertz Agency on Koniswall opposite the Hauptbahnhof, Kimber rented a Volkswagen and drove the remaining sixteen odd miles to Iserlohn where, shortly after two thirty, he checked into the Engelbert Hotel. There were several Witzlebens in the telephone directory, but there was only one dentist amongst them. Erich Witzleben had two phone numbers, one for the surgery in Laarstrasse, the other for his private residence in Nordstrasse. According to the scale on the street map which the receptionist had given Kimber, the dental surgery was less than a quarter of a mile from the Engelbert.

Laarstrasse was in the old part of Iserlohn and like most of the small town, it had come through the war unscathed. The dental surgery at number 58 was near the Schillerplatz, a large open square at the top end of the street which was used as a market place every Thursday and where the British Army held a ceremonial parade once a year to mark the Queen's Birthday. The surgery itself was sandwiched between a leather goods shop and an optician and was a good deal smaller than either.

Kimber pushed the street door open and walked inside to find himself confronted by a young, attractive brunette in a white surgical coat. A small name tag above the breast pocket identified her as Katharina Voegel.

"Can I help you?" she asked politely.

"My name is Josef Krebbs," Kimber told her in fluent German. "I have just moved to Iserlohn from Hamburg and my new neighbours tell me that Herr Witzleben is a marvellous dentist."

Flattery had been known to open many a door and he had few equals when it came to laying it on with a trowel. He needed to make a dental appointment because Witzleben was unlikely to invite a complete stranger into his house, but it was no good pretending he had toothache because the German would know different the moment he looked into his mouth.

"Naturally, I didn't leave my dental records in Hamburg but I do seem to have mislaid them. Perhaps we could start again from scratch?"

"Certainly." Katharina Voegel started leafing through the appointment book, which was the last thing Kimber wanted.

"I would be very grateful if you could fit me in today," he said and smiled hopefully.

"I've got a cancellation at four thirty if you don't mind waiting, Herr Krebbs?"

"I don't mind at all," Kimber assured her.

The waiting room across the narrow hall was no different from any other he had seen. The assorted collection of upright chairs was arranged in regimental fashion along all four walls. In the centre of the room, a much-abused dining table groaned under the weight of last year's magazines. There were three other patients, a little girl with braces on her teeth who was accompanied by her mother, a plump middle-aged woman in a severe black suit, and a young man in corduroys and a check shirt whom Kimber took to be a student. By the time his turn came around, he had read two back numbers of the *Reader's Digest* and the latest issue of *Stern Magazine* which was a mere ten months out of date.

Erich Witzleben was forty-one years old, one of the few personal details the British Embassy in Bonn had managed to worm out of the Bundeswehr. He was slim, handsome, had dark brown curly hair and considerable charm. He also smiled a lot as if to assure his patients that, with proper care, they too could have bright and gleaming teeth like this.

"Katharina tells me you have just arrived from Hamburg, Herr Krebbs?"

"Yes, I'm setting up in business with my cousin – industrial cleaners – that sort of thing."

"Have you always lived in Hamburg?"

"I was born in Vienna."

"Ah." Witzleben nodded sagely. "I thought I recognised the accent. Now, if you would open your mouth a little wider, Herr Krebbs."

"I ran into Gottfried Exler the other day," Kimber said casually.

"Who?"

"He was a Feldwebel with the 385th Postal and Courier Unit. We both met your brother Karl Heinz when we were serving in Warsaw."

Out of the corner of his eye, Kimber could see Katharina Voegel seated at a small table, a dental chart in front of her, pen ready to record the details of Witzleben's examination.

"Please, Herr Krebbs," Witzleben said nervously, "I want you to open your mouth."

"Oh, I certainly will. I am going to shout it from the house-tops because I'm sick and tired of feeling guilty about crimes we never committed. I mean, take your brother; the Poles have indicted him for war crimes and there's a warrant out for his arrest. Right?"

"I think you had better leave, Herr Krebbs."

"Karl Heinz was captured by the Home Army the day the uprising began . . ."

"I'm going to ask Frau Voegel to send for the police . . ."

"They held him for almost a month," Kimber said, talking the older man down. "If he was a war criminal, why didn't they try him when they had the chance? Your brother wasn't an anonymous face, he was the head of the Civil Affairs Bureau and a big man in Warsaw. Don't you see, he was known to the Resistance."

Witzleben had his mouth open and was wheezing like an asthmatic struggling to draw breath.

"Will you please leave us, Frau Voegel," he said with difficulty.

"Certainly. Do you wish me to send for the police, Herr Witzleben?"

"No, that won't be necessary."

Kimber waited until they were alone, then said, "Maria Bolek was the only person whom Karl Heinz feared. He was present when she was interrogated by a Gestapo agent called Neurath and he was afraid she was going to denounce him to the AK."

"Who are you?" Witzleben demanded hoarsely. "You're not a German and you weren't born in Vienna and your name isn't Krebbs."

"Your brother was evacuated to a hospital in Berlin the day after the Home Army withdrew from the Old Town on the first of September 1944. He never served in Poland again . . ."

"What do you want . . . ?"

"In May 1945, he was taken prisoner by the British when patrols of the 7th Armoured Division entered Flensburg near the Danish border. Two months later, your brother escapes from a POW camp because the Poles have suddenly indicted him as a war criminal . . ."

"I want you to leave my surgery now."

"I think he was set up," Kimber went on, "and someone you know helped him to get away. I am also damn sure you know where he is today."

"Get out," Witzleben told him, but his voice was subdued and lacked authority.

"And you are going to tell me where I can find him." Kimber pushed himself out of the dental chair and towered over the older man. "Right now, you may think otherwise, but that won't last because I'm going to haunt you every waking minute."

"Get out, I shan't warn you again . . ."

"I'm going to ruin you, Herr Witzleben. Just think about that." He walked over to the door and opened it, then looked back and smiled. "By the way, my name is Kimber, I'm an Englishman and

I'm staying at the Hotel Engelbert. I only mention this because sooner or later you will want to talk to me."

Kimber closed the door behind him, went downstairs and walked out into the street, but not before the demure-looking Frau Voegel had called him a stinking dog's turd.

Because he was extremely conscientious, Exler was invariably the last to leave the post office in Altona at the end of the working day. However, this was one time when devotion to duty was not the sole reason why he had stayed behind. Despite his proud boast to Kimber, his wife, Christina, had not been at all understanding when he had arrived home blind drunk. The fact that he had subsequently thrown up before he could reach the bathroom had only increased her anger which had still not abated by the time he had left that morning. He had phoned Christina twice during the day to apologise for his behaviour and had been coldly rebuffed on each occasion.

Still wondering what sort of reception he would get from his wife when he arrived home, Exler walked out into the yard behind the post office, unlocked the offside door of his Opel Rekord and got in. Like a robot functioning in accordance with a pre-set programme, he switched on the ignition, cranked the engine and revved up. As he eased his foot on the accelerator, he suddenly discovered he had company.

"Don't look round, Herr Exler."

The stranger was directly behind him. Soon after the car park had emptied, he must have broken into the Opel and had been hiding there on the floor between the seats.

"Who are you?"

"Kriminalpolizei."

"Have you some means of identification?"

"How about this?"

Exler looked down at the SS dagger which had appeared at his throat, its needle-sharp point lightly pricking the thyroid cartilage. "What do you want?" he asked nervously. "My wallet?"

"I'm not interested in stealing your money; all I want from you is some information."

"About the post office?"

"I'm sure you are a very amusing man, Herr Exler, but I'm not in the mood for your jokes."

"No, of course not." Exler pressed his legs together in an effort to control his bladder but was unable to stop himself urinating into his trousers.

"Kill the engine."

"Yes, certainly." His hand trembling, Exler reached for the ignition key and switched it off. The urine had soaked his left leg and run down into his shoe and he felt shamed and humiliated.

"Good. Now tell me about your English friend."

"Herr Kimber, the writer?"

"If that is his name," the stranger said menacingly.

"Oh, it is; believe me, I wouldn't lie to you."

"Why did he come to see you?"

After Warsaw, Exler believed he knew what it was like to be afraid, but nothing he had experienced before compared with the abject terror that gripped him now. He didn't owe Kimber anything and what had passed between them was hardly a state secret he had to protect at the cost of his life. So he told the stranger all about the wartime court martial which had so interested the Englishman and repeated the questions he had asked.

"What was the name of this Under Officer in the 73rd Infantry Division?"

"Otto Dornberger."

"And you say Kimber seemed anxious to find him?"

"Yes, but I couldn't tell him where he was living."

"Quite so."

A hand suddenly closed over Exler's mouth, then the knife went into his chest, killing him instantly.

CHAPTER 17

Number 56 Nordstrasse, where the Witzlebens lived, was a solid-looking three-storey house enclosed by a tall privet hedge which effectively hid the rooms on the ground floor from passers-by. The master bedroom on the intermediate floor didn't enjoy the same kind of privacy. For reasons best known to the architect, it was situated at the front of the house so that the first thing Erich Witzleben saw when he drew the curtains back was a dark blue Volkswagen on the opposite side of the road. A hand waved to him from inside the car, then the door opened and the driver got out.

"Kimber." He made it sound like an expletive compounded of anger and fear.

"What was that, Erich?" Herta asked, half asleep.

"It's nothing."

But he was lying. The Englishman was carrying out his threat to haunt him every waking minute and there was nothing he could do about it because Herta would only start asking a lot of questions he couldn't answer without incriminating himself. He went into the bathroom and ran hot water into the basin, then stripped off his pyjama jacket and lathered his beard with shaving soap. He shaved quickly, his mind on Kimber and the stranger who had phoned him about the Englishman last night when he and Herta were about to have dinner. It had been the same man who had telephoned the surgery to warn him that some very nosy people in London had been asking after his brother, Karl Heinz. The menacing voice had chilled him the first time he had heard it and it had been no less intimidating yesterday.

Witzleben returned to the bedroom to find Herta seated at the dressing table, gazing blankly at her reflection in the mirror, hairbrush at the ready. Whether by design or pure absent-mindedness, she hadn't bothered to slip on a negligée over the all-too-revealing nightdress. She had gone out and bought it herself on the very day the stranger had rung the surgery while he was making love to Katharina Voegel. The skimpy black number with the lace panel all the way down the front was so unlike anything Herta had ever worn before that he wondered if she suspected he was having an affair.

"Who was that man, Erich?"

"What man?"

"The one who was standing by the dark blue Volkswagen across the road."

Witzleben moved to the window and looked out. Although Herta had implied as much, it was still a relief to see that Kimber was no longer there.

"There's no one there now," he said, managing to sound perplexed.

Witzleben knew he was in trouble when he heard the crackle of static electricity as Herta began to attack her hair with the stiff brush.

"Can't you do better than that? You must think I am a complete fool."

"Now, you know that isn't true."

"Whose husband is he?"

The question stopped him cold, like a punch under the heart. In the eighteen years they had been married, Herta had never once given him cause to suspect that she was aware of his extramarital activities. Recovering his composure, he turned away from the window and moved towards the dressing table to stand behind her.

"I really don't know what you are talking about, dearest," he said and placed both hands on her shoulders.

"You surprise me."

"No, it's the other way round. Don't you know I love you too much ever to be unfaithful?"

He moved his hands over her shoulders and down the front of the nightdress to cup Herta's breasts and tease the nipples which hitherto had never failed to arouse her. Making love to his wife was the last thing he wanted to do at that hour in the morning but it was the only way to allay her suspicions.

"Stop that." Herta struck his wrist with the hairbrush hard enough to bruise it.

"Zum Teufel!" Witzleben withdrew both hands and nursed the afflicted one against his chest. "What the hell did you want to do that for?" he demanded in an injured tone of voice.

"Because I'm not in the mood to be pawed by you."

He turned his back on Herta and stalked into the dressing room, furious that she had had the gall to rebuff him. He went through the tallboy, opening and closing the drawers with unnecessary force as he looked out the clothes he was going to wear. Still in a foul mood when he had finished dressing, Witzleben went downstairs and found fault with the breakfast their live-in housekeeper had prepared for him. The telephone in the hall started ringing before he had finished telling her what he thought of the so-called freshly ground coffee.

"Yes?" He snatched the receiver from the cradle and bellowed into the mouthpiece a second time. "Yes?"

"Good morning, Herr Witzleben. I was wondering if you'd given any more thought to your brother, Karl Heinz?"

"You . . . you . . ." Witzleben spluttered with rage and slammed the phone down. Before he could make it back to the breakfast room, it rang again. He wanted to ignore the strident jangle but this was something he had never been able to do.

"About Frau Voegel," Kimber said as soon as he picked up the phone.

"What?"

"Frau Katharina Voegel. I'm sure you heard me the first time."

"I've had enough of this . . ."

"Such a very attractive woman and so loyal to you . . ."

"I'm going to hang up . . ."

"But you should tell her to be a little more discreet," Kimber continued as though he'd not been interrupted. "Calling me a stinking dog's turd might have made her feel good, but she didn't do you any favours . . ."

A board creaked on the spiral staircase behind him. One of the children, or his wife? Glancing over his shoulder, Witzleben saw it was Herta and wondered how much she had heard.

"Your wife must be a very understanding woman . . ."

The insistent voice of the Englishman claimed his attention and he was glad of an excuse to turn his back on Herta.

"Of course, I'm assuming you have told her about Frau Voegel?"

And if he hadn't, Herr Kimber soon would, that was the implicit threat behind the question.

"You should phone me at the surgery," Witzleben said, and gripped the receiver even more tightly in an effort to stay calm. "I don't keep my appointments diary at home. I suggest you ring 3124 a half hour from now."

"I'll see you this lunchtime," Kimber told him. "One o'clock sharp, the entrance to the outdoor swimming pool near the Seilersee."

"That's correct, 3124," Witzleben said and hung up.

He turned about in time to see Herta before she disappeared

from view around the last spiral on the staircase and reached the landing above. Her face in profile looked set and determined which he took as a sign that she would not forgive him in a hurry. His first inclination was to tell her to go to hell, but it was her money that paid for the extra luxuries such as the live-in cook-housekeeper, the maid and the general handyman and gave him the freedom he enjoyed. He would need to make it up with Herta, but it would have to be done subtly, otherwise she would smell a rat and become even more suspicous.

Breakfast had lost all its appeal for him and the dishes of pickled herrings, sliced cheese, salami and ham made his stomach heave. He settled for a roll, two cups of coffee and a cigarette.

The houses in Nordstrasse had been built in the early nineteen-twenties when most people hadn't owned a car. Although Number 56 was at the top end of the street where the properties were more expensive, it too did not have a garage. Faced with the choice of leaving his car out on the street or finding a lock-up within reasonable walking distance, Witzleben had rented a garage from an elderly widow who lived round the corner in Viktoriastrasse and whose husband had left her in reduced circumstances.

Witzleben stubbed out his cigarette, called to Herta from the hall that he was leaving and, getting no reply, stalked out of the house. The fact that it was a bright sunny morning didn't improve his ill humour and the uphill drag to Viktoriastrasse made him even more irritable. He vented his anger on the wrought-iron gates of the drive and the garage doors, opening them with such force that the lady of the house was drawn to the window to see if there had been an accident. His temper unabated, he got into the Mercedes, raced the engine and backed out of the garage and on to the road like a racing driver breaking from the grid. A horn blared a warning and he stamped on the brakes in time for the Opel Kapitän to miss his rear end by a hair's breadth.

Thoroughly shaken, Witzleben left the Mercedes by the kerbside to close the garage doors and wrought-iron gates, then got back into the car and drove off in a more subdued frame of mind. He was halfway down Nordstrasse and approaching the Schillerplatz when he saw the dark blue Volkswagen in his rear view mirror.

Measured in a straight line, Harley Street was six and a half miles from South Lambeth; as far as most of the inhabitants of the borough were concerned, it was light years away. Detective Superintendent Gurnard had made the pilgrimage from 'L' Division to Harley Street because the name on the brass plate outside number 153A was Professor R. J. Allenby and it wasn't politic to send a Detective Constable to question a Fellow of the Royal College of Surgeons even if he had done all the spadework.

The Detective Constable was the one who had come up with an explanation for the bag of cement Zagorski had lashed to his body. His old three-wheeler van had not been moved from the outside of his digs in Ealing and no jury was going to believe he had travelled across London by tube train late at night carrying a half-hundredweight bag of cement with him. The last thing Gurnard, or any of the officers of 'L' Division, wanted was an open verdict, but that had been the odds-on favourite. At least, it had seemed the most likely result before the Detective Constable had begun to visit all the building sites in the neighbourhood.

He had assumed that Zagorski would have come up to town on either the District or Piccadilly Line and then changed on to the Northern to go south of the river. Suicides were always unpredictable and there was no telling where he had got off the train. But Stockwell happened to be the nearest Underground station to the housing estate where Zagorski had taken his high dive, and the DC had started from there and worked his way back towards the next stop up the line at the Oval.

Preece Brothers were a small firm of local builders who were currently developing a half acre plot in Thorney Drive off the South Lambeth Road. According to the clerk of works, the site was constantly being pilfered. Taps, pipes, guttering and tins of paint were the most attractive items but bags of cement had also frequently gone missing. Preece Brothers were reluctant to fence the site in, which meant that, apart from a nightwatchman, other security was virtually non-existent. Most of the pilfering occurred over a weekend and the nineteenth and twentieth of July had been no exception.

In fact, they had lost more than usual on the Saturday night because the nightwatchman had failed to turn up. Although one bag of Blue Circle cement looked pretty much like any other, the clerk of works had been in no doubt that several bags with the same batch number as the one found on the Pole had also been stolen that night.

The building site in Thorney Drive could be seen from the South Lambeth Road and was no more than six hundred yards from the housing estate. Although the DC had been unable to find any witnesses who had seen Zagorski carrying a bag of cement, there was enough circumstantial evidence to suggest he had helped himself to one from Preece Brothers. All Gurnard needed to clinch a verdict of suicide was a motive, something which he hoped Professor Allenby would be able to supply.

His appointment with the Harley Street specialist had been arranged for eleven forty-five. Gurnard's experience with the National Health Service led him to believe that he would be lucky to see Allenby much before half past twelve, but doctors with private patients did not allow their secretaries to overbook. Gurnard arrived at number 153A with two minutes in hand, which was just as well because time was money in Harley Street and the professor didn't believe in wasting it.

"What can I do for you, Superintendent?" he asked, simultaneously waving Gurnard to a chair.

"I believe a Mr Stefan Zagorski was one of your patients?"

"I'm afraid you've been misinformed."

"That's funny." Gurnard cleared his throat. "According to the monthly statement from the Ealing branch of Lloyds Bank, two cheques payable to R. J. Allenby were debited to his current account. The first, dated the twenty-seventh of May was for fifty guineas, the second, issued almost a month later, was for one hundred and eighty-nine pounds twelve shillings and sixpence."

"There's no mystery about it, Superintendent. Mr Zagorski paid the bills on behalf of his friend."

Zagorski the benefactor was an unexpected development which momentarily threw Gurnard. "May one ask his name, sir?"

"I don't see why not. His friend was a fellow Pole called Leopold Sosna. Apparently, they both came from Warsaw and had known one another from childhood."

"Do you have an address for Mr Sosna?"

"Not in England."

"He was domiciled abroad?" Gurnard was rapidly coming to the conclusion that prising information from the Harley Street specialist was like getting blood from a stone.

"Mr Sosna lives in Germany. He was over here on holiday, staying with his lifelong friend, Mr Zagorski, who persuaded him to come and see me. Mr Sosna had been ill for some months but was reluctant to see a specialist in Germany because his medical insurance didn't cover private consultations."

"So Mr Zagorski came with him and paid your fee on the spot?"

"I never met Mr Zagorski," Allenby told him calmly. "He telephoned to make an appointment for his friend and sent him along to my surgery with a certified cheque."

"What about the bill for the second visit?"

175

"I sent that to Mr Zagorski care of *The Sentinel* in Varley Mall. My secretary received his cheque two or three days later."

"Can you tell me what is wrong with Mr Sosna?"

"That's between doctor and patient, Superintendent. You should know better than to ask."

"You can tell me what he looks like, can't you, sir?"

"Tall, very thin, austere . . ."

"Would this be your Mr Sosna?" Gurnard reached inside his jacket, took out a photograph and placed it in front of Allenby.

"Yes, that's him."

"His name is Zagorski. A fortnight ago last Saturday, he jumped from the roof of an eight-storey block of flats in South Lambeth. We're pretty sure it was suicide but we'd be happier if we knew why he decided to take his life."

"He had lung cancer," Allenby said quietly. "It was terminal."

Kimber arrived at the rendezvous fifteen minutes ahead of time, parked the Volkswagen in the Seeuferstrasse and walked the rest of the way to the open-air pool. The noise level suggested that half the school population of Iserlohn had decided to go swimming and judging by the number of cars parked on both sides of the road outside the entrance, many of them were accompanied by a parent. None of the benches on the grass verge were, however, in demand and he chose the one farthest away from the litter bins and the marauding wasps.

He didn't know whether Witzleben would show up or not. Although the German had sounded thoroughly frightened on the telephone, he might have recovered his nerve sufficiently by now to call his bluff. Kimber supposed he might be able to step up the pressure through Katharina Voegel but she didn't strike him as the sort of young woman who would be easily intimidated. By the way the dentist had reacted, it was obvious that he was having an affair with her and didn't want his wife to know about it, but the unknown factor was Frau Witzleben. If she held the purse strings, then Witzleben would do anything to keep her sweet. On the other hand, if she was the kind of hausfrau for whom Kirche, Kinder and Küche were everything, she would probably tolerate a wayward husband and Erich would not have to try all that hard to placate her.

A Mercedes turned into the approach road and cruised slowly past Kimber, then veered across the road as the driver spotted a vacant slot at the kerbside. After shunting backwards and forwards to no avail, there followed a loud clunk as Witzleben deliberately bumped fenders with a Borgward Isabella to give himself enough room to squeeze the Mercedes into the space with a couple of feet to spare. He got out of the car and looked around as though anxious to make sure that there was no one in the vicinity who would recognise him, then crossed the road and approached Kimber.

"Here, take this," he said and pushed a thick brown envelope at Kimber. "It'll tell you everything you want to know about my brother."

It didn't look right, it didn't feel right, and Kimber knew it was all wrong the moment the German turned on his heel and started to walk away from him. Nevertheless, he opened the envelope, and that was his second big mistake because it contained thirty hundred-Deutschmark notes, and two plainclothes officers appeared from nowhere to grab Kimber before he had time to blink. While one policeman cuffed both wrists behind his back, the other frisked him, then went through his pockets. The British passport momentarily fazed him but he was quick to recover and his partner wasn't the least bit impressed by the lion and unicorn motif on the front cover. Grabbing hold of Kimber, they hustled him into a BMW saloon.

Police Headquarters was roughly a mile from the Seilersee. Situated between Sophienstrasse and Lange Strasse north of the Schillerplatz, it was about the size of a city block. Getting there took them just over five minutes; finding another eight men who were approximately the same age, height and weight as Kimber took much longer. The line-up was held in the inner courtyard and was a pure formality, which Frau Voegel enlivened by slapping his face when she picked him out. After that little touch of drama, Kimber was left to cool his heels in a cell while the police took statements from her and the dentist.

Two hours later, Kimber was wheeled into an interview room to be questioned by the arresting officers. Overhead lights, no windows, one table, two chairs; interview rooms were, he supposed, pretty much the same the world over, but it didn't make him feel any better.

"I'm Kommissar Prohl," the taller officer said, "and this is Detective Sergeant Veesenmeyer, Kriminalpolizei."

"I wondered when you were going to identify yourselves," Kimber said dryly. "I was beginning to think you'd forgotten your own names."

"This is not the time for jokes, Herr Kimber. You are in serious trouble."

There was no need for Prohl to tell him that. Witzleben had recovered his nerve and had set him up. Admittedly, he had been treading on thin ice, but the really galling thing was that he was the one who'd dictated the rendezvous.

"Frau Voegel has stated on oath that you went to Herr Witzleben's surgery yesterday afternoon and accused him of having an affair with her." Prohl picked up the folder that had been lying on the table in front of him and waved it under Kimber's nose. "She also claims that you threatened to inform their respective spouses unless they paid you the sum of three thousand Deutschmarks."

"How long am I supposed to have been watching them? I mean, you just don't walk into a man's surgery, accuse him of stuffing his receptionist and then demand a lump sum in the way of hush money."

"You rang Herr Witzleben's home number on several occasions and threatened him."

"Several occasions?" Kimber laughed. "Listen, I met him for the first time yesterday."

"So you say."

"I was in Hamburg yesterday. Talk to Gottfried Exler if you don't believe me."

"Who's he?"

"The postmaster of Altona," Kimber said tersely. "The number is 89 17 32."

Prohl stared at him for some moments, then turned to Veesenmeyer. "Keep an eye on him, Sergeant," he growled and walked out of the room.

Hamburg was not the other side of the world but Prohl was gone long enough to suggest that the Altona number was not the easiest one to raise. When he did finally return, his face was like stone.

"Your friend, Gottfried Exler, is dead," he said in a flat, hard voice.

"Wha . . . a . . . at?"

"He was found in the yard behind the post office early this morning. He had been stabbed through the heart."

"Jesus Christ." Kimber sat there numb with disbelief. Poor old Gottfried, poor Christina. What possible motive could anyone have for murdering him? "Had he been robbed?"

"No."

"Any homosexual implications?" Kimber wondered why he had asked when Gottfried had given him no reason to suppose he was that way inclined.

"Absolutely not. This was a professional job, clean and swift. No mess, no signs of a struggle. He was stabbed from behind while sitting in his car."

Something to do with Karl Heinz Witzleben then?

"I want to see the British Consul General in Düsseldorf."

"I bet you do," Prohl said. "The question is, will he want to see you, Herr Kimber?"

There had been a town on the heights above the River Tauber since about 500 BC when the Celtic tribes had established the first settlement on the hill. The foundations of a Franconian castle had been laid about 970 AD, King Conrad III had erected an Imperial castle on the site some seventy years later and Rothenburg had appeared in the Chronicles for the first time in 1144. Every year, thousands of visitors flocked to the medieval walled town, but the man who stood at the top of Galgengasse had not come to see the White Tower, the Franciscan church, the Castle Gate, the Meistertrunk clock or any other tourist attraction. His name was Rudolf Brack and he was in Rothenburg strictly on business.

Brack glanced at his wristwatch, saw that it was four minutes to six, and started walking towards the Galgen Gate. Halfway down the cobbled street, he stopped outside a bookshop-cum-stationer's and peered through the window to make sure the shop was empty before he went inside. The only assistant behind the counter was a young, dark-haired girl who looked no more than sixteen.

"Good evening, Fräulein," Brack said politely. "Am I right in thinking Herr Dornberger has a small printing business as well as this shop?"

"Yes, he has."

"Oh, good. Do you think I could see him?" Brack flashed her a warm smile. "Just say that his old friend, Willy, is here."

"My father's out," the girl told him. "He's gone to Nuremberg on business."

"Do you know when he will be back?"

"He left this afternoon shortly after two o'clock; we're not expecting him home much before seven thirty."

"That's a shame," Brack said and looked disappointed. "I was hoping to place a one-off order for some reunion cards."

"I could take it."

"No, these are rather special cards. I would prefer to discuss the lay-out with your father."

"Are you staying in Rothenberg, Herr . . . Willy?"

The momentary pause before 'Willy' was her cute little way of asking him for his surname. But she could wait until hell froze over and he still wouldn't tell her. There was, he thought, nothing to be gained by scaring the shit out of Otto Dornberger before they met face to face.

"No, I'm just passing through on my way to Ansbach," Brack said and smiled again. "I'm a sales representative for I. G. Farben."

"Oh." The girl nodded as though he had explained everything to her satisfaction. "Father will be sorry to have missed you."

"Well, I will be passing this way again tomorrow around the same time. Will Otto be in then?"

"Oh, yes."

"Good. Please give him my regards."

"Who shall I say was calling?"

"Tell him Willy. We served together in the 73rd Infantry Division during the war when you were a very little girl." Brack moved towards the door. "I'm helping to organise a reunion in Nuremberg for the local Old Comrades Association," he said, and walked out of the shop.

CHAPTER 18

Kommissar Prohl could not remember meeting anyone quite like the Englishman. At ten minutes past six last night, Kimber had been allowed to telephone the British Consul General in Düsseldorf; at five minutes to nine, the Police President of North Rhine Westphalia had called Prohl and ordered his immediate release. Not content with bringing political pressure to bear, he now had the gall to walk into Police Headquarters some twelve hours later and ask for his assistance.

"You want to trace a former Unter Offizier called Otto Dornberger?" he growled. "Get your friends in Bonn to do it; you seem to have all the necessary connections."

"Is that what Erich Witzleben has?"

"What do you mean by that, Herr Kimber?"

"I mean, Witzleben rings you up, says he is being blackmailed and will you please be there when he hands three thousand Deutschmarks to the extortionist outside the open-air swimming pool. If it had been anyone else, I think you would have wanted to know why this was the first time the police had heard about it."

"You are treading on very thin ice, Herr Kimber."

"So are you, Herr Kommissar. Normally, the victim would be told to play for time because the police would want to be very sure of the facts before they pounced, otherwise they might find themselves being sued for false arrest. But you jumped straight in with both feet . . ."

"I'm not going to warn you again . . ."

"Hell, you didn't even wire Witzleben for sound."

"That's where you're wrong," Prohl said, relishing the fact that this was one allegation he could deny with conviction.

"You certainly didn't hear me on the tape." Kimber smiled. "I bet you didn't hear Witzleben either."

"There were technical difficulties, the tape recorder malfunctioned."

"You mean he switched it off before he got out of his Mercedes."

"Save your breath, Herr Kimber. You may think that by making me feel guilty, I'll run a trace on Otto Dornberger, but it isn't going to work. I'm not interested in finding him."

"Your first concern is to protect the Witzlebens, is it?"

The jibe touched a raw nerve. Iserlohn was a small town and even though he was now eighty-six and going slightly ga-ga, old man Witzleben, the patriarch of the family, still had a lot of influence. The youngest son, Erich, was known to be a philanderer but the one who used the family name to good effect was Frau Charlotte, the widow of Major General Manfred Witzleben.

"I don't have to take any shit from you," Prohl said angrily.

"Erich Witzleben switched off the tape recorder because he knew I was going to ask him about his brother, Karl Heinz, and he didn't want you to hear that."

"Nonsense."

"What has Karl Heinz Witzleben done to command such loyalty from you?"

"Nothing, I've never even met the man. I came here from Dortmund on promotion in 1950. No one tells me how to do my job."

But that hadn't been the case yesterday when the Ober Kommissar had called him into his office. Witzleben had been there, so had the Assistant Burgomeister and a lawyer from the Prosecution Service. The whole thing had been handed to him on a plate; all he had to do was be there when Witzleben handed over the envelope. There had been a smell of bad fish about the set-up but even in post-war Germany, an order was still an order and he'd had to go along with it.

His worst fears had been confirmed when Sergeant Veesenmeyer had found a British passport on Kimber, and how he had managed to seem completely unruffled by the discovery was something he'd never know. Of course, he had had to take the Englishman in to Police Headquarters but he'd figured it had been a case of mistaken identity by Witzleben and had confidently expected the Chief of Police would apologise to Kimber and smooth things over. But no, the hot shot lawyer from the Prosecution Service had insisted they go through the whole rigmarole of holding an identity parade and obtaining affidavits from the two so-called victims. And who had been left holding the baby when it had gone political? Why, that dummkopf Fritz Prohl. The Englishman was going to bring him down, but it was irrational to blame him for what was going to happen when it was his own Ober Kommissar who had dropped him in it. It was, however, a little difficult to remain quite so objective when the Englishman was trying to manipulate him exactly as Witzleben had done and with a story that was even more far-fetched.

"Don't let him do it to you a second time," Kimber said.

"Do what to me?"

"Put you in a position where it's your neck on the chopping block. The dentist was a lot cleverer than I gave him credit for; he wasn't trying to put me inside on a trumped-up charge of blackmail, he wanted me out of the country and creating a low-key diplomatic incident was the best way of achieving it. Witzleben was going to say he'd mistaken me for someone else, and you would have taken the blame. Only Frau Voegel got carried away and hammed it up."

Prohl thought the Englishman was wrong in one respect; Erich Witzleben didn't have the imagination or the Machiavellian turn of mind needed to conceive such a plan. But Frau Charlotte, the General's widow, did, and he was prepared to bet that it was she whom Erich Witzleben had consulted when he hadn't known what to do about Kimber.

"You really think this Otto Dornberger is in danger?"

"I don't think you should reject the possibility out of hand," Kimber said.

He wished the Englishman had some tangible evidence to support his contention but if he seized on this as an excuse for doing nothing, his head would still roll if the former Unter Offizier ended up in a morgue.

"Look, time is running on and a man's life could be at stake. If you won't put a trace on Otto Dornberger, say so, and I'll try the Police President of Hamburg. Maybe I can persuade him to do something."

Prohl sighed. What the hell, he was probably going to end up in the mire no matter what he did and, in a way, he owed this man a favour.

"Are you still staying at the Hotel Engelbert, Herr Kimber?"

"Yes. Does this mean you will try to locate Otto Dornberger?"

"Is there any other way I can persuade you to leave me in peace?"

Kimber smiled. "Absolutely not," he said.

"All right, I'll let you know the minute I have anything."

"I'd sooner you told the local police first."

Prohl sighed for the second time in as many minutes. "Let's do one thing at a time," he said. "We don't know if he's still alive yet. It's possible he never came home from the war."

The bulk of Dornberger's income came from the printing business down the road from the bookshop and stationer's. With few overheads and virtually no labour costs, he had been able to undercut a much larger firm in nearby Ansbach and, as a result, had secured contracts to print and supply stationery for the Burgomeister's office, local branches of the Kreissparkasse, Dresdener and Commerz Banks and the Rathaus. He also produced leaflets for the Tourist Information Office, local guidebooks, hotel brochures and invoices for the majority of private businesses in town. Consequently, Dornberger spent most of his time at the printing works, leaving his wife, Gisela, to look after the bookshop and stationer's. In this, she was assisted by Ella, their sixteen-year-old daughter who helped out on Saturdays and school holidays.

Books, writing pads and envelopes, sealing wax, fountain pens and pencils, rulers and erasers had absolutely no appeal for Ella. Had the Dornbergers owned a record shop, she would have been in her element and would have taken an interest in the family business which would be hers one day. As it was, she walked around in a dream half the time, her mind on Elvis Presley. If left in charge of the shop towards the end of the day when her mother was preparing the evening meal, there was a strong possibility that customers would either be undercharged or overcharged on the goods they purchased. She could, however, be relied upon to deliver orders which her mother received at the shop. Dornberger was, in fact, just finishing a print run of five thousand copies of a leaflet for the Tourist Information Office when Ella walked in with an order.

"From the Reichsstadt Museum," she said, handing him a memo.

"Thank you." Dornberger glanced at the order and gave a low whistle. "This will help to keep the wolf from the door, Ella."

"You're pleased with it?"

"Very." Dornberger was tempted to ruffle her hair in affection, then remembered in time that she no longer considered herself a little girl.

"Did I tell you about Herr Willy, Papa?" she asked, suddenly recalling the mysterious stranger.

"Willy who?"

"He wouldn't give his surname."

"Do you mean he refused?"

"Not exactly, he just seemed to think it was unnecessary. He said you and he had served in the same Division during the war." Ella frowned. "I think Herr Willy said it was the 73rd Infantry Division; anyway, he's organising a reunion and wants you to print the invitations."

"When did this happen?"

"Yesterday evening while you were in Nuremberg. It must have been about six o'clock because I was thinking of closing the shop." Her frown became a little deeper. "Are you sure I didn't tell you about him, Papa?"

"Quite sure."

Ella had chattered like a magpie all through supper and had been equally voluble at breakfast but she had never once mentioned anyone called Willy.

"He's a salesman for some big company."

"That's a big help."

"I told Herr Willy you would be sorry to have missed him, Papa, but he said he would be in Rothenburg again this evening."

"I must remember to avoid him," Dornberger muttered.

"What did you say, Papa?"

"Nothing, Liebchen. You'd better get back to the shop, I expect your mother could do with a helping hand."

Dornberger lit a cigarette and sat down on an upturned packing crate. The 73rd Infantry Division had not been the happiest outfit he had ever served with and he had made very few friends, none of whom had been called Willy. He had joined the Division a bare three weeks before the battle of Warsaw had begun, one of many replacements plucked from holding units, training establishments and convalescent depots. He had fought alongside strangers and his battalion had been shunted from sector to sector as the Divisional Commander strove to plug the gaps in the line. The 73rd hadn't performed at all well and had incurred the displeasure of the Führer himself. Officers and men alike had been denied leave and promotion. Neither punitive measure had affected him; on the twenty-seventh of September 1944, he had been captured by the Red Army and had spent the next eight years in captivity.

Eight years. Ella had been nearly ten when he had returned to Rothenburg in January 1952, a gaunt stranger, old before his time. She had referred to him as 'that man' and had asked her mother when he would be leaving, as though he was some sort of transient lover who had outstayed his welcome. It had taken her until the following December to accept him as her Papa, but that was hardly surprising. Ella had been sixteen months old on his last furlough in June 1943 and couldn't remember him.

Some people had happy memories of the past but he had no wish to remember the locust years from '44 to '52 and would make sure he was out when this man who called himself Willy passed through Rothenburg.

*   *   *

185

Kimber waited until ten forty-five before he asked the hotel switch-board operator to place a call to London. Emmerson was usually in his office by nine thirty and Iserlohn was an hour ahead of British Summer Time. The extra fifteen minutes was intended to give him time to read any overnight cablegrams from various embassies and diplomatic missions in the Middle East and Persian Gulf. As usual, his PA intercepted the call and, as she put him through, Kimber heard her warn Emmerson that he was coming through on an unguarded line. His first question was entirely predictable.

"Where are you phoning from, Michael?" he asked.

"The Hotel Engelbert in Iserlohn."

"What are you doing there? You should have left for the airport hours ago."

"I had some unfinished business to attend to," Kimber said and could tell by the tongue-clucking that Emmerson didn't like it.

"Surely you are aware of the situation?"

Although Bonn hadn't actually said they were going to deport him, they had made it abundantly clear to the Consul General in Düsseldorf that they wanted Kimber out of the Federal Republic on the first available flight. In fact, a Consular official had made the hundred-mile round trip to Iserlohn to deliver this message in person shortly after Kimber had been released. He had also relayed a message from Emmerson ordering him back to London.

"I know that a man was murdered less than twenty-four hours after I had been to see him. I also know it's not up to the Police President of North Rhine Westphalia to say that I'm free to go; Hamburg is outside his bailiwick and he has no jurisdiction over the investigation."

"Be careful what you say," Emmerson warned, "this is not a secure link."

"So I heard."

"There's a Lufthansa flight to London departing from Düsseldorf at 1405 hours." Emmerson paused, muttered something off-stage, then said, "Failing that, you can catch the British European Airways flight from Cologne an hour later."

"You have a very efficient PA, Nigel, but you can tell her to put the timetables away. I just can't leave here today; before I come home, I want to make sure that Otto Dornberger isn't being left out on a limb."

"What exactly have you done now?" Emmerson asked in a re-signed voice.

"I've simply persuaded the Kriminalpolizei to find out where Dornberger is living, assuming he came home from the war."

"And all this stems from the court martial Exler told you about?"

"Let's not forget Stefan Zagorski's interest in the trial."

"You can forget what he put in his letter, that was pure malice."

"What do you mean?"

Emmerson was reluctant to go into too many details over the phone but Kimber dragged it out of him a bit at a time. The police had been looking for a motive which would lead a coroner's jury to bring in a verdict of suicide, and they had found one. Zagorski had been to a specialist who, after examining his X-rays and the results of various sputum tests, had subsequently informed him that he had terminal lung cancer. Knowing this, it was easy to dismiss the letter he had written as Stefan's way of taking it out on everyone he knew.

"It'll all come out at the inquest a week from today," Emmerson said, winding up.

"So why did it take the police so long to find this out?"

"Because he had covered his tracks and led the specialist to believe that Zagorski had retained him to examine his friend, Leopold Sosna. We haven't found the policy yet, but I imagine he was insured and was anxious to ensure the claim wasn't invalidated."

Leopold Sosna – Halina's father. Kimber wondered what Stefan had had against him.

"Anyway, I want you to pack your bags and come straight home. This farce has gone on long enough."

Leopold Sosna had been one of the two thousand hostages who had been shot in July 1944 in reprisal for acts of sabotage committed before the uprising had begun. His execution was the reason why Halina had gone on hating the Germans after the war had ended.

"Did you hear me, Michael?"

"I'm afraid not."

"I want you back in London, not tomorrow but today."

"Then you had better square it with the Chief of Police in Hamburg," Kimber said and hung up before he had a chance to come back to him.

Rudolf Brack walked through the Volkspark and entered the Nuremberg stadium, once the heartland of the National Socialist Party but now reduced to a vast, dead amphitheatre. The eagles were still there on the concrete columns of the review dais but the swastika emblem within each laurel wreath had been defaced. He remembered how it had been at the Party rallies of '36, '37 and '38, the torchlight parades through the streets of old Nuremberg, the massed ranks of the SS Leibstandarte in full field marching order, the political speeches to the faithful, the sense of history being made and the revitalisation of Germany. Hawkers had done a roaring trade selling postcards showing Frederick the Great, Bismarck, Hindenburg and Hitler. Beneath the pictures, the legend had said, 'What the King conquered, the Prince formed, the Field Marshal defended, the soldier saved and unified'. Nowadays, you could travel the length and breadth of the country without finding a soul who would admit to having voted for the Führer.

And chicken shit like Doctor Konrad Adenauer, ex-Lord Mayor of Cologne, leader of the Christian Democrats and Chancellor of West Germany since 1949 had seen to it that he had been dragged through the denazification courts. Anyone who aspired to public office had to be as pure as the driven snow, and he had made the big mistake of allowing his name to go forward as a Christian Social Union candidate in the elections for the Bavarian Länder in 1950. Quakenbrück was the man who had pointed a finger at him; Emil Quakenbrück, the dedicated civil servant in Bonn who had found his SS personal file in the archives of the Ministry of the Interior and had presented the facts to the Minister himself. Naturally, Franz Josef, leader of the CSU, had immediately withdrawn his endorsement of his candidature and, after being dragged through the courts, he had been sentenced to two years' imprisonment. This had subsequently been reduced to six months and, with time off for good behaviour, he had been released after four.

Apart from finishing him as a budding politician, the prison sentence had also had an adverse effect on his career as a lawyer. His partners had seen him as a liability and had lost no time in asking him to leave the practice. Fortunately, a sympathiser had found him a job as a corporate lawyer and he had left Munich for Stuttgart to begin a new life. Within two years he was on the board of directors and people who had known him in Munich were saying that he had fallen on his feet. Brack would have agreed with them but for the delayed-action bomb that was buried deep in the historical archives of the Bundeswehr.

The delayed-action bomb was the unexpurgated transcript of the trial in which he had prosecuted four soldiers of the 73rd Infantry Division for desertion in the face of the enemy. The court martial had been held on Wednesday the twenty-sixth of July, six days after the arch-traitor Stauffenburg had planted a bomb in the conference room at Rastenburg in a vain attempt to kill the Führer. The conspiracy to overthrow the Government and sue for peace had been hatched by senior army officers at the Bendlerstrasse Headquarters of the Reserve Army in Berlin. But the cancer hadn't ended there. Had the Führer been killed, swine like Field Marshal Günther von Kluge, Commander in Chief of Army Group B in Normandy, would have participated in the coup d'état. With most of the Prussian-dominated General Staff implicated to varying degrees, the National Socialist Party had been forced to assert its complete authority over the Army. The court martial had been part of that process; with the President, Judge Advocate and Prosecutor all members of the SS, the Army had been shown who was the boss.

He had accepted the case for the prosecution at face value; it hadn't bothered him that of the four accused, Wilhelm Freisler had twice been decorated with the Iron Cross Second Class. The principal witness had been a respected Gestapo officer and his testimony had been good enough for him. Besides, he had considered it an honour to be the Prosecutor, especially as he had been told on good authority that Heinrich Himmler was taking a personal interest in the case. Nothing could have been farther from the truth, but that had only become evident in the last few weeks of the war. Even so, the knowledge that he had probably sent four innocent men to their deaths hadn't troubled his conscience. The 73rd Infantry Division had had a poor combat record and it had been necessary to make an example so that the rank and file would know what would happen to them should they fail to show the proper fighting spirit.

It was fortunate that Emil Quakenbrück had not been aware of the court martial proceedings when he had dragged him through the denazification court, otherwise his sentence would not have been nearly so lenient. The falsification of official records to give them some semblance of legality and the destruction of those which had been particularly incriminating was one thing, participating in what amounted to the murder of four innocent men was quite another.

Brack sat down on the steps leading to the dais and lit a cigarette. How the unexpurgated copy of the trial proceedings had ended up in the Army's historical archives, when every copy of the edited version had been accounted for, was beyond him. But its existence had been made known to him back in May when some Pole he had never heard of had walked into the West German Embassy in London and asked the First Secretary to obtain a copy for his benefit. He had owed that timely warning to an unknown informant in the historical section whose first loyalty undoubtedly lay elsewhere. The same source had alerted him again when the British

Foreign Office had inquired after the whereabouts of Karl Heinz Witzleben and Gottfried Exler.

Chances were that his anonymous benefactor had expected him to quietly disappear, but he was forty-five and far too old to start again; he also had too much to lose. He wasn't only faced with the prospect of a long prison sentence; the way things were going in Adenauer's Germany, the surviving next-of-kin of Freisler and the other soldiers could sue him for every pfennig he had. So, once Exler had confirmed his worst fears, he had to go; the same applied to ex-Unter Offizier Otto Dornberger. It had been a question of weighing the risks, and denying the information at source was a lot safer than eliminating an English diplomat.

Brack dropped his cigarette and trod it underfoot. All the same, he wished he could have got to Dornberger yesterday. Rothenburg was just too damned small for comfort. He also had a nasty premonition that time was running out for him.

CHAPTER 19

Kimber walked into Police Headquarters on Sophienstrasse, told the officer on the desk that Kommissar Prohl was expecting him and waited while he checked with the Kripo chief. Kimber had read every news item in the *Westfälische Rundschau* and the *Rheinische Post,* had drunk enough coffee to float a battleship and had just told the hotel manager that it looked as though he would be staying one more night at the Engelbert when he had been paged by the bellboy.

Other than telling him that Bonn had come up with an address, Prohl had been fairly uncommunicative on the phone. He hadn't mentioned Dornberger by name and the whole tenor of what he had said suggested he was being ultra-cautious in case there was an eavesdropper on the line. Even now Kimber wasn't sure if he had been asked to call round merely to sign a disclaimer or whether Prohl was simply using this as a smokescreen to blind his superiors. It still remained in doubt after Kimber was shown into his office.

"Thank you for coming, Herr Kimber." It was all very formal. Prohl came round the desk to shake hands, gave a slight bow as he did so, then waved him to a chair before producing a two-page document. "I've been asked to give you this," he said.

The disclaimer had been cobbled together by lawyers representing the police authority who were anxious to head off a possible writ for wrongful arrest. In addition to a fulsome apology, the Chief Commissioner was of the opinion that the arresting officers had acted precipitately and an observation to this effect was to be lodged in their personal files.

"They've really dropped you in it, haven't they?" Kimber said.

Prohl shrugged his shoulders. "These things happen."

"They certainly do."

"Perhaps you would like to read the translation before you sign both copies?"

Dornberger's address had been handwritten on a page torn from a small notebook and then attached to the translation with a paper clip. But to Kimber, the way Prohl had chosen to pass this information to him was even more revealing.

"Why haven't you phoned Rothenburg?" he asked.

"We have no reason to do so."

The 'we' was also significant; it told him that the German had been over-ruled by his superiors.

"I'm sorry, Herr Kimber, but there is nothing to connect this man with your friend the postmaster."

Kimber leaned towards the other man and kept his voice down. "Exler was stationed in Warsaw and knew of him, that's the connection. Gottfried was killed because he was insatiably curious and was cursed with a photographic memory. I'll tell you something else; he looked after Karl Heinz Witzleben when he was wounded, and we all know what happened when I tried to question Erich about his brother who is, after all, an escaped war criminal."

"We deal in facts," Prohl told him, "not suppositions and inferences. If we did contact our colleagues in Rothenburg, what could we possibly tell them? Nothing that would make any sense to them."

"Is that your considered opinion?"

"I've no authority to call Rothenburg; it's in a different Land and it would be up to the Police President of North Rhine Westphalia to advise his opposite number if he saw fit."

"And the same goes for Hamburg?"

"But of course."

"Surprise, surprise."

"Are you going to sign the disclaimer?" Prohl inquired politely.

"Sure." Kimber uncapped his fountain pen and scrawled his signature at the foot of page two on both copies. "How far is Rothenburg from here?"

"Four hundred and thirty-six kilometres."

Prohl had obviously anticipated that he would go there. Confirmation of this followed in the next breath.

"Your best route is through Hegen, Siegen, bypass Frankfurt and follow Route 6 into Würzburg, then head south-west to Uffenheim."

"Right."

"Have you got a map?"

"Not of that area."

Prohl opened a drawer in his desk and took out an ADAC, the German equivalent of the AA members' handbook. "You'd better borrow this," he said. "You can post it back to me when you've finished with it."

"Thanks."

Four hundred and thirty-six kilometres, say two hundred and

seventy miles. Kimber glanced at his wristwatch; allowing for an occasional hold-up on the way, he ought to be in Rothenburg by six thirty.

"Don't forget your copy of the disclaimer, Herr Kimber."

Prohl shook hands again, wished Kimber good luck and urged him to drive safely. When he got back to the hotel, he found that as well as Dornberger's address, he had also been given his telephone number.

A heavy-set man just beat him to the only pay phone in the lobby. Collecting his key from the desk clerk, Kimber went up to his room on the second floor and got the hotel switchboard operator to put him through to Rothenburg 0521. The number rang out for quite some time before a girl whose voice suggested she was in her early teens lifted the receiver and repeated the number. Kimber said good afternoon and asked if he could speak to Herr Dornberger.

"My father's not here at the moment," the girl told him, "but if you want to place an order, I can take it down."

"Well, this is more of a personal thing, Fräulein . . . ?"

"Ella Dornberger," she said under his prompting.

"And my name is Kimber, Michael Kimber. As you might expect with a name like that, I am English."

"Natürlich."

"I've never met your father, Fräulein Ella, but I know a great deal about him. For instance, he was an Under Officer in the 73rd Infantry Division and served on the Eastern Front. In 1944, while in Warsaw, he defended four soldiers who were being courtmartialled for desertion. One of them was a Gefreiter called Wilhelm Freisler."

"Willy?" Ella sounded pleased and excited. "Herr Willy is a friend of yours?"

Her question brought him up sharp. Ella couldn't possibly be talking about the same man; Freisler had been shot by a firing squad fourteen years ago.

"Wilhelm is a common name," he said, temporising. "Can you describe the one you know?"

"Well, he's quite old . . ." Ella began, then broke off. Before she cupped a hand over the mouthpiece, Kimber was pretty sure he heard someone ask her who was calling. A fairly lengthy silence ensued and he wondered if she was going to hang up on him.

"Are you still there?" a loud voice demanded.

A much older woman by the sound of her voice; probably Ella's mother, he decided.

"Frau Dornberger?" Kimber said tentatively.

"My husband doesn't want anything to do with you or the other old comrade who was asking for him yesterday. The war is over and he does not wish to remember it." She slammed the phone down, cutting him off before he had a chance to get a word in.

'Willy' was quite old according to Ella but when you are in your early teens, anyone over thirty seems positively ancient. This 'Willy' was perhaps his age or her father's age. And some time in the last twenty-four hours, he had gone to see Dornberger and had missed him. He must have said something to the girl that had put the fear of God into her father when she told him about it, which would explain Frau Dornberger's hostility a few moments ago. Kimber toyed with the idea of calling Prohl but the Kommissar was only interested in facts and he was conspicuously short of those. He buzzed the operator, said he had been cut off from Rothenburg and asked her to reconnect him. This time the phone was promptly answered by Frau Dornberger.

"Don't hang up," Kimber told her, "just listen to me for one moment because this could be a matter of life or death."

"I have nothing to say to . . ."

"Ask your husband about Wilhelm Freisler . . ."

"I'm going to call the police . . ."

"Yes, you do that. Ask your husband about Gefreiter Freisler and then call the police."

"I've had enough of this nonsense," Frau Dornberger told him and broke the connection.

Two hundred and seventy miles to Rothenburg and precious little of it on the autobahn. It could be said that he had done everything in his power to warn Otto Dornberger, but that sounded like the kind of excuse offered in self-justification when you backed away from a situation. He picked up the ADAC handbook which Prohl had given him, went down to the lobby and left his room key with reception. Two minutes later, he backed the Volkswagen out of the parking slot and drove off towards Hegen.

Gisela Dornberger poured herself another Schnapps from the bottle on the sideboard and downed it in one go. Apart from the very occasional glass of hock, she rarely touched alcohol from one year's end to another, but the two phone calls had unnerved her and a stiff drink had seemed the very thing to calm her down. She had never heard Otto mention a soldier called Feisler or Freisler but there were things she had kept from him too.

There had been a limit to the length of time she could cherish the memory of his last furlough back in the June of 1943 and it had

194

been hard for a young, healthy woman to keep the faith. This had been especially true in 1948 when the men were coming home from Russian POW camps and there had still been no word of her husband other than the original telegram informing her that he was missing in action. No one had ever known of her affair with Joachim, whose wife was paralysed from the waist down as a result of spinal meningitis. Two lonely people with two good reasons for being very discreet because Ella had reached the age when she noticed things.

Gisela raised her eyes, looked at the clock on the wall above the sideboard and came to with a jolt. What the hell was the matter with her, daydreaming at a time like this? She put the bottle of Schnapps away, instinctively patted her hair to make sure it was tidy, then went downstairs and told Ella to look after the shop.

"Is everything all right, Mutti?"

"Of course it is," she assured Ella. "I just want to have a word with your father."

Gisela walked out of the shop and made her way along the Galgengasse to the small lock-up where, with the aid of a loan from the Dresdener Bank, they had installed a fully-automated press. When she let herself in, Otto was seated at the workbench setting the Burgomeister's name and private address in upper case figures prior to running off the latest order for headed notepaper.

"I've had another phone call, Otto."

"Who from?"

"The same man who rang just as you were leaving after lunch. He told me to ask you about a soldier called Feisler."

"Never heard of him."

"It could have been Freisler; his first name was Wilhelm and he was a Gefreiter."

There was no reaction. Otto had his back to her and it was impossible to guess what he was thinking. The silence grew and became an invisible wall between them.

"He advised me to go to the police," Gisela said quietly. "Why would I do that, Otto?"

"I can't imagine," he told her in an equally low voice.

"What did you do to this man Freisler?"

"Nothing." He turned slowly about to face her. "I was detailed to represent him and three other soldiers who were being courtmartialled for desertion. I met the four accused for the first time the night before the trial and I had no idea what evidence was going to be offered by the Prosecutor, who was an SS Hauptsturmführer, until I walked into court. The Judge Advocate and the President of the court martial were also SS, which should tell you what sort of trial it was."

"What happened, Otto?"

"Well, the result was a foregone conclusion; I lost the case and the four accused were sentenced to death. They were shot that same afternoon."

"Were they guilty of desertion?"

"What does it matter now?"

"I think it matters to us," Gisela said fiercely. "Freisler was a very brave soldier and he had a chestful of medals to prove it. Men like him don't suddenly run away from the enemy."

But Freisler had obviously been a difficult NCO which had explained why he was still only a Gefreiter. Officers had to earn his respect; until they did, the fancy epaulettes on their shoulders were just a tailor's handiwork.

"Freisler certainly wasn't cowed when he went into the witness box to give evidence on oath. The Judge Advocate didn't like what he was saying and kept hammering the table with his gavel, but it didn't bother him any."

According to Freisler, he and the other three soldiers from the Divisional Reinforcement Unit had been detailed to carry out a special mission in the Wolomin area. Apart from providing them with a Kübelwagen, the officer commanding the Reinforcement Unit had left the briefing to an unidentified official from the Civil Affairs Bureau who had simply given him a map reference of the rendezvous on the outskirts of Praga. There the patrol had linked up with a working party composed of four inmates from the Pawiak Prison under a Scharführer who had a couple of Azerbaijani storm-troopers in tow. There had also been a Polish guide. The Scharführer had loaded the prisoners on to an Opel Blitz truck and the combined party had then set off for Wolomin.

"Soviet tanks had been seen in the area but the situation was very fluid and the Red Army had outstripped its supplies and was running out of steam. The Polish guide led them to an estate in a wooded area some distance from Wolomin. The house was damn nearly as big as a Schloss but it had been knocked about and most of the slate roof was missing. Anyway, Freisler was told to establish an observation post on the north-east fringe of the wood in order to raise the alarm should the Russians start probing in their direction. The prisoners had been issued with picks and shovels so it wasn't too difficult to guess that something pretty valuable was buried somewhere in the grounds."

A little over five and a half hours after they had established their

OP, Freisler and the other soldiers heard a fusillade of shots in the vicinity of the house to their rear. Shortly thereafter, the Scharführer had sent one of the Azerbaijanis over to their position to let them know that the mission had been completed.

"When they returned to the vehicles, there was no sign of the prisoners and the Polish guide had also disappeared. The Scharführer didn't offer any explanation, but then he didn't have to. So they drove back to Praga, crossed the Vistula and went on to the freight yards near the Central Station where they transferred a number of packing crates from the Opel truck to a boxcar. By this time it was getting dark, so Freisler wasn't too surprised when he was told that his patrol would be staying the night at Garrison Headquarters. He was, however, surprised when the civilian who had briefed him showed up to express his appreciation for a job well done. And he was absolutely astounded when he was told that they were to be granted ten days' furlough and would be departing for Berlin on the twenty-fifth of July. All four were arrested by the Military Police at the Central Station as they were about to board the train; according to the prosecution, the leave passes in their possession were forgeries."

"Did you believe his story, Otto?"

"Oh yes, it rang true." Dornberger scowled. "But what really convinced me was the way the Judge Advocate tried to shout him down."

After the trial was over, he had reported his misgivings to the battalion commander but he hadn't wanted to know. "We are fighting a war, Dornberger," the Major had told him, "and sometimes mistakes are made. The thing you must remember is that you did the best you could for those men, and now you owe it to your company to do the best you can for them."

"Do you remember their names?" Gisela asked.

"Who? The Prosecutor, President and Judge Advocate?"

"And the others."

"The Scharführer never gave me his but he called the Polish guide Herr Sosna every time he addressed him."

"Write them down, Otto."

"Why?"

"Because we are going to see the police," Gisela told him, "and we'll have to show them something when we ask for protection."

The cable from the British Embassy in Bonn reached Leslie Humberstone at five pm via the European Department and one of the internal messengers who collected and delivered mail from other sections and the post room. The date time group was 071415Z hours August '58, which meant it had taken the Embassy a little over fifty-five hours to obtain the information Emmerson had asked for. Pinned to the cable was a brief memo which said: "Leslie, this is the quickest response I've ever known from Bonn but of course the content is pretty low grade in more senses than one." By the time he had read the cable, Humberstone was inclined to agree with his opposite number in the German Section.

Of all the information in the cable, Humberstone found the thumbnail sketch of Wilhelm Freisler the most interesting. The Gefreiter had been born on the second of April 1916 at Floha in what was now East Germany. He had been called up for military training shortly after his nineteenth birthday and had been released two years later. Mobilised with the rest of his class of '16, he had seen action in Poland, the Low Countries and on the Eastern Front. He had been decorated with the Iron Cross Second Class for conspicuous bravery in September '41 and had been awarded a bar to the medal nine months later. His other decorations had included the 1941–1942 Winter Campaign Medal for service on the Russian Front, the Crimea Shield and the Close Combat Badge for having destroyed five Soviet T34 tanks single-handed. His family had been informed that he was killed in action on the twenty-fifth of July 1944. Next of kin had been his mother whose last known address was in Karl Marx Stadt, formerly Chemitz.

Whoever had been responsible for keeping the war diary of the 73rd Infantry Division up to date had evidently been doing something else from the twenty-second of July to the thirty-first. The bare words "Patrol Activity" appeared on five consecutive days until the twenty-seventh of July when he briefly reported that two battalions were engaging units of the Soviet 2nd Tank Army on the Swidra River forty miles south-east of Warsaw. Three days later, General Fritz Franck, commander of the 73rd Infantry Division had been captured at Zielonka, twenty miles east of the capital, when elements of the Soviet 3rd Tank Corps had broken through the weakly-held forward defended localities. The writer had omitted to say who had subsequently taken over command.

What Bonn had been able to tell them about Rudolf Brack and Otto Dornberger amounted to a couple of sentences in each case. The former Hauptsturmführer had moved to Stuttgart after serving four months of a two-year prison sentence handed down by a denazification court. No longer active in politics, he was said to be a corporate lawyer with Rheinmetallgesellschaft. A printer by trade, Otto Dornberger had returned to Rothenburg following his release from a Russian POW camp in 1952. According to the West German Social Security Office, his present address was 16 Galgengasse.

Humberstone put the cable in the special branch memorandum that had been opened for the subject, numbered the folio and walked the file down the corridor to Emmerson. He had to go through the PA's office first, but, since she was on the phone, he merely gave her a sweet smile, pointed to the communicating door, gave it a perfunctory rap and went straight in.

"A cable from Bonn, Nigel," he said brightly.

Emmerson looked up from a draft report he was correcting with a red biro, clearly annoyed at being interrupted. "Put it in the in-tray," he said curtly and went back to the report.

"Yes, of course." Humberstone moved a little closer to the desk, placed the BM in the tray. "Sorry if I disturbed you," he mumbled. "I didn't know you were busy."

"That's all right, Leslie." Emmerson waited until he was on the way out of the office, then said, "Oh, by the way, you can shred that BM file on the fifteenth of August."

"A week tomorrow." Humberstone turned about. "Anything significant about the date, Nigel?"

"Not particularly," Emmerson told him. "I just don't see that we shall need it after the inquest on Zagorski has been concluded."

Gisela curbed her impatience and waited for Joachim to finish reading the account of the court martial which Otto had prepared at her instigation. By the time he had written it up, the idea of going to the police to ask for protection had struck them both as absurd. "You know what their reaction will be when they see this?" Otto had asked and had immediately answered his own question. "They will say: 'This is all very interesting, Herr Dornberger, but has anyone actually threatened you?'" And of course no one had; and that was the reason why she had gone to Joachim to seek his advice. Nowadays, he was in the picture-framing business, but until his retirement a few years ago, Joachim had been a highly respected member of the local constabulary.

"Otto is right," he said presently. "The police won't take any notice of this. The most they will do is pass this letter on to the Ministry of the Interior for possible investigation, though I'm not at all sure this wartime incident isn't covered by the statue of limitations."

"That's all very well, Joachim, but what are we supposed to do?"

"You really think this man who spoke to Ella when she was alone in the bookshop means to harm you?"

"How long is it since Otto returned from the east?"

"Six years," Joachim said wistfully and gently placed a hand on her knee.

"Six years, and no one who knew Otto while he was in the army has ever tried to get in touch with him since he came home. Now, suddenly, this man who calls himself Willy is anxious to renew a friendship which my husband claims has never existed. Wouldn't you be worried?"

"I can't say, because it's outside my experience. I spent the entire war here in Rothenburg."

Although his hand was still resting on her knee, Gisela made no effort to remove it. There was something very comforting about his discreet yet intimate touch as though he were protecting her. How many times in the past had they sat here in Joachim's office behind the showroom, his wife upstairs confined to bed?

"Can't Otto take you away for a week or two until this thing blows over?"

"Can you see my husband closing up the shop for a fortnight and losing all that business? Besides, this Willy told Ella he would probably be passing through Rothenburg again this evening."

"That puts a different complexion on it." Joachim removed his hand and walked over to the small roll-top bureau. He took out a key, unlocked the top right-hand drawer and reaching inside, brought out a pistol wrapped in a piece of calico. Extracting the magazine from the butt, he loaded it with four loose rounds. "This is a 7.65mm Sauer Bohorden Modell," he said. "All automatics have the same basic mechanism so Otto will know how to handle it in an emergency."

"Where did you get this?" she asked in a hollow voice.

"Call it a souvenir from my days with the police." He opened the handbag on her lap, tucked the pistol inside and snapped the catch shut, then helped Gisela to her feet. "Tell you what, if you leave this statement of your husband's with me, I'll see what I can do. I still have some influence with the police; maybe I can persuade them to take it seriously."

"I don't know how to thank you, Joachim."

"Oh, I think you'll find a way," he said and patted her behind as she moved towards the door.

Gisela quickened her steps, anxious to reach the street before he could fondle her again. Her face pinking with embarrassment, she left the gallery in the Kopellenplatz and hurried back to Otto. At that precise moment, Rudolph Brack was just turning into the car park below the tower at the foot of the Galgengasse.

CHAPTER 20

Brack locked the Mercedes and started up the hill towards the tower at the bottom of the Galgengasse. It was only a minute or so before six, but the number of visitors hadn't thinned out all that much and he was just one more stranger among hundreds. He was dressed like any other tourist, slacks, open-neck sports shirt, the sleeves folded back above the elbows, a lightweight anorak draped over one arm in case it came on to rain. He even carried a camera slung from his right shoulder by a thin leather strap. He was, however, pretty sure that no other tourist was walking around the town with an SS dagger taped to an inside calf.

Dornberger had to be eliminated because he possessed certain knowledge which would undoubtedly destroy some very important people. The former Unter Offizier wasn't aware of this power otherwise he would have surely used it long ago, but the Englishman only had to ask the right questions of him to set off a chain reaction.

Brack walked through the passageway under the tower and emerged into the Galgengasse in time to see a woman enter the lock-up where the printing was done. Late thirties, pushing forty, dark curly hair, rounded face, good legs, figure beginning to thicken around the waist. Ella's mother; he saw the likeness in a flash and swore under his breath. He had planned to hit Dornberger when he was alone in the print shop and her presence was a hazard he could do without. Even with a knife to balance things up a bit, the odds of one against two were not to his liking. If Frau Dornberger did nothing else, she could probably scream loud enough to raise the roof.

He walked on at a brisk pace, threading his way through the slower moving pedestrians in the cobbled alley. One minute to six; he had dallied too long in Nuremberg killing time and Ella would be closing up any second now, if she hadn't already done so. He reached the bookshop just as she was closing the door and managed to get a foot in the jamb before she could shut it properly. He placed a hand on the glass pane and exerted enough force to push the door open and send Ella staggering backwards into the shop. Moving swiftly, Brack stepped inside, tossed his anorak and camera on to the floor, then closed the door and tripped the catch.

"Herr Willy . . ." Her eyes looked as though they were about to pop out of their sockets and her mouth kept opening and closing like a fish starved of oxygen.

He should never have told Ella that he had served with her father in the same infantry division during the war. Worse still, he should never have said that his name was Willy. That had been plain stupid because Dornberger might just have made the connection and wondered how it was that Wilhelm Freisler had risen from the dead.

"What do you think you are doing, Herr Willy?"

"I've come to place my order," he said easily. "The invitations to the reunion of the 73rd Division – remember?"

"The shop is closed."

"Yes, I closed it." Brack tried to move nearer but she backed away from him. "It's all right, Ella," he said smiling. "I'm not going to hurt you."

But that was precisely what he intended to do. He reached out, grabbed a wrist and pulled Ella forward on to a short arm jab that went deep into the solar plexus and knocked every ounce of breath out of her body. She folded at the waist, sank down on to her knees and moaned in pain. Still holding on to a wrist, Brack twisted the arm behind Ella's back and hauling the girl upright, frogmarched her behind one of the free-standing bookshelves towards the rear of the shop, then forced her to sit down on the floor where she couldn't be seen from the street.

"Don't scream for help, don't open your mouth and don't say anything until you're spoken to. Obey those rules and you won't get hurt. Okay?"

"Yes." The word came out in an agonised gasp.

"Good. I knew we'd get along." He smiled again, revealing a set of gleaming teeth that looked as though they had been capped and polished, then crouched beside her. "First question – what's behind the door at the back of the shop?"

"The stockroom."

"And you live in the flat above?"

"Yes." Talking wasn't quite such an effort now and some of the colour was creeping back into her cheeks.

"Okay, question number three. Do you have to come through the shop to get to the flat?"

Ella shook her head. "There's another door between us and the adjoining shop. It opens into a covered passageway. From there you enter the stockroom where there's a staircase to the flat above."

"Good girl." Brack patted her face. "Now, you are going to behave yourself, right? If the telephone rings, you will answer it and ask if you can take a message. I'll be standing by your side and I want you to hold the phone out so that I can hear what the caller is saying. You understand?"

"Yes."

"And when your parents come through the back door, I don't want you calling out to them." He patted Ella's face again, then pinched her cheeks between thumb and index finger, forcing her mouth open. "Do I make myself clear?"

An animal-like grunt escaped her; unable to communicate properly because he was squeezing her mouth, she nodded emphatically to avoid any possible misunderstanding.

"Okay. Now I want you to sit cross-legged on the floor with both hands clasped together on top of your head."

Brack released her mouth and waited until she had adopted the position before he hoiked his right trouser leg and ripped off the adhesive plaster he had taped across the SS dagger.

Otto had listened to her in total silence, his face set like stone, his eyes staring blankly at the calendar above the workbench. The 7.65mm automatic lay within reach but he hadn't looked at the pistol since she had taken it out of her handbag. For all Gisela knew, he hadn't heard a word she had said.

"Have you been listening to me, Otto?"

"Of course I have."

"Well then, say something."

"Why did you have to go to Joachim?"

Gisela flinched as though she had been struck. The question had caught her off guard and she couldn't think what had prompted it, but the venom in his voice was ominous and there were butterflies in her stomach. "Because he used to be a policeman," she said nervously, "and I thought he could help us."

"Oh, he's a very helpful fellow is Joachim." Otto turned sideways and pointed an accusing finger at her. "At least where you're concerned, he is."

"What do you mean?" Gisela asked, even though she already knew the answer.

"I'm talking about how Joachim looked after you while I was away, I'm talking about the number of times you dropped your pants for him while I was stuck inside a POW camp."

"Someone has been spreading malicious lies . . ."

"Don't add insult to injury, Gisela. You think I wasn't aware of all those knowing looks from the neighbours when I came home, the innuendoes, the sly digs? Give me credit for some intelligence."

"You never said a word about it to me."

"I had been away eight years and you had every reason to suppose I was dead. I could understand how lonely you must have been and I just wanted to pick up the pieces and start again."

"So did I," Gisela whispered.

"But I could never forgive Joachim. What the hell could you see in him?"

"He was kind."

"He's a bastard by any definition. Look how he avoided the war. First he persuades the medical board that he is unfit for military service because he has fallen arches, except that the doctors dressed it up in fancy language. What did they call it – displaced metatarsal bones?"

"Something like that."

"Then when things got really tough and they were drafting the halt, the lame, the sick and the near blind, he used his wife's illness as an excuse to obtain a further exemption even though the Reich Labour Office could have found a live-in nurse to look after her. Still, let's not forget he had always been a staunch member of the National Socialist Party, so perhaps the decision wasn't altogether surprising."

"Otto, you've got to stop torturing yourself like this." Gisela crouched beside him and put an arm around his shoulders. "It's all in the past. Whatever there was between Joachim and me died a long time ago."

"Is that why you went running to him?"

"I did nothing of the kind . . ."

"No? You could fool me." He removed her arm and distanced himself from her. "You seem to forget we both know there was no point going to the police with what we had. So why the hell bother with Joachim unless there is still something between you two?"

"You'll have to believe what you want to believe," Gisela said wearily.

"What kind of answer is that?"

"What are we going to do, Otto?"

"I don't know about you, but I propose to sit here and get very drunk. Now get the hell out of my workshop and leave me alone."

"If that's what you want."

Gisela stood up, turned away from him and walked towards the judas gate, her footsteps becoming quicker and quicker until she was practically running. The door slammed behind her, making a noise like a pistol shot. In the long silence that followed her departure, Dornberger opened the drawer of his workbench and took out a three-quarter-full bottle of Schnapps which had been there since the Christmas before last. Unscrewing the cap, he poured a large measure into a cup and downed it in one go.

He had wanted to lash out and hurt Gisela without really knowing why and he had succeeded only too well. His eyes fell on the Sauer Bohorden Modell pistol and in a sudden fit of rage, he picked up the automatic and hurled it against the wall.

The back door opened and closed, the light in the stockroom came on and Brack heard the sound of a woman's footsteps moving towards the staircase.

"It's only me, Ella," she called out.

No Herr Dornberger. Brack looked at the girl and placed a finger across his lips, warning her to be silent, then he inched closer to whisper in her ear while threatening her with the dagger.

"You do what I tell you and no one will get hurt. Understand?" Ella licked her lips and opened her mouth. "Just nod your head," Brack told her.

"Ella?" Frau Dornberger went on up the staircase. "Where are you, Ella?" Her anxious voice floated down from the landing above.

"Okay, call out, tell her where you are and be natural."

"I'm down here, Mutti, in the shop."

"What on earth are you doing, Ella? You should have closed up long ago. Do it now and come upstairs."

"Tell her you can't," Brack whispered. "Say you fell over and twisted your ankle."

"I can't, I've hurt my ankle. I twisted it when I fell over."

Although it wasn't exactly what he had told her to say, at least she hadn't sounded hysterical. A little nervous perhaps, but anyone who didn't know there was a knife at her throat would think she was still shaken up after her fall and in some pain. From the urgent footsteps and the reassuring noises she was making, it was evident Frau Dornberger thought so; yanking Ella to her feet, Brack moved to one side of the door so that her mother would have to enter the shop before she saw them.

The door swung open on creaking hinges and Frau Dornberger stood there in the entrance silhouetted by the light behind her in the stockroom. She peered into the shop but her eyes were not focussing properly in the gloom, and her hand automatically found the switch on the inside wall as she stepped across the threshold.

"Ella?"

"She's right here," Brack said coolly. "What happens to her in the next few seconds is entirely up to you. If you try to raise the alarm, she'll be dead before you have time to blink."

"Who are you – the Herr Willy Ella told us about?" Her voice was hoarse and sounded as though she had a sore throat. "What do you want?"

"My name doesn't matter, Frau Dornberger. What I want is for you to back off into the stockroom and do exactly what I tell you."

There was never any question that she wouldn't obey him. He had the advantage of surprise and was armed with a knife, and no mother worthy of the name would do anything which might jeopardise her child's life. The same applied in reverse; as soon as they were in the stockroom, he closed the door behind him and told Ella that she had precisely one minute to find some twine before he slit her mother's throat. She was back in less because Frau Dornberger told her where there was a ball of string.

"Very good, Ella." Brack steered Frau Dornberger to an old chair which they used to reach the top shelves in the stockroom and forced her to sit down. "Now tie your mother's hands behind her back and be sure you make a good job of it. I want to see that string bite into her wrists."

The girl started crying and her hands were shaking so much that by the time she had finished, a nine-month-old baby would have had no difficulty in freeing itself. He made her do it again and again until at last he was finally satisfied.

"The elbows next, then the ankles and knees."

"You are filth," Frau Dornberger told him.

"Let's talk about your husband," Brack said, unmoved. "When is he coming home?"

"Tomorrow. Otto is away on business in Stuttgart; he has a contract to supply . . ."

"That isn't what Ella told me while you were out."

"Ella doesn't know everything."

"She knows when not to lie, and that's more than you do." He stooped, grabbed hold of a rung and upended the chair, tipping Frau Dornberger on to the floor. Her head struck the bare boards with a resounding crack that left her feeling dazed and frightened. "So stop trying to be clever and tell me when we can expect to see him."

"My husband is busy getting drunk with a bottle of Schnapps in the lock-up," she whispered. "I don't know when he's coming home or even if he is."

The breaks were going his way. They had had a quarrel and now Otto was drowning his sorrows. The only thing he didn't like was the possibility that Dornberger might not come home. Still, he could afford to wait an hour which would give Otto time to sink the bottle and get half paralytic. The time was now ten minutes after seven; if Dornberger hadn't shown up by eight, he would have to call on him at the print shop. Meantime, he would have to ensure that Frau Dornberger kept her mouth shut. He glanced at Ella, saw that she was wearing ankle socks and ordered her to remove one.

"Sorry about this," he said indifferently, then stuffed the sock into Frau Dornberger's mouth and used the ribbon from Ella's hair to tie it in place.

Kimber came in on Route 25 from Würzburg, shot past the parking area outside the walls and driving through the passageway under the tower, entered Galgengasse. After allowing for the odd delay, he had reckoned to be in Rothenburg by six thirty, but extensive roadworks on the autobahn and a pile-up between a luxury coach and a juggernaut had added a good forty minutes to the overall time for the journey.

He eased his foot on the accelerator and glanced left and right, hoping to see a sign or a number above a doorway which would tell him he had found Dornberger. Spotting the bookshop on the right-hand side of the roadway halfway along the lane, he looked for somewhere to leave the Volkswagen and was obliged to follow the directional arrows for the parking lot in the Schrannenplatz. He went into the first available space, locked the car and doubled back to Number 16 Galgengasse.

There were no lights in the shop or the flat above and the curtains upstairs hadn't been drawn either. Evening was rapidly closing in and he couldn't believe the Dornbergers, mother, father and daughter were sitting there in the near-dark. Kimber moved into the entrance; there was a hanging card in the window which said 'Offen' but the door itself was locked. He peered through the glass panel, saw a crack of light at floor level towards the back of the shop and rapped on the door. There was no reaction and he tried again, this time pounding the woodwork until the glass rattled in the frame. Still no one came to the door but some of the passers-by looked at him suspiciously.

The Dornbergers had gone out, or so it seemed, but they had evidently left a light on somewhere and hadn't bothered to draw the curtains. When they'd closed the shop, they had forgotten to reverse the hanging card in the window, which meant they were either very careless and disorganised people or else something wasn't quite right. Kimber stood back and looked at the window displays on either side of the entrance. Neat, well presented, eye-catching even; in the failing light it was impossible to get more than a general impression of the shop itself, but from what little he could see of the interior from the street, it compared very favourably with any small bookseller's in London.

All the evidence suggested that the Dornbergers were neither careless nor disorganised. He turned about and walked towards the town centre looking for the nearest pay phone.

Brack slowly exhaled, which was as close as he was ever likely to come to heaving a sigh of relief. Who had come knocking at the door – a friend of the Dornbergers? Surely a friend would have used the passageway.

"Were your parents expecting anyone to call on them tonight?" he asked Ella.

"No."

He believed her for the simple reason that she was far too terrified of him to think of lying. Could it have been a drunk then? No, the man had been too well-behaved; if he'd had too much to drink, he would have been raucous, shouting at the top of his voice for someone to let him in. Suddenly, another possibility occurred to him and he wondered if it had been the Englishman Exler had told him about shortly before he had driven the knife into the postmaster's chest.

"I want you to think very carefully about this question before you answer it, Ella." Brack raised her chin with the dagger and forced her to look him straight in the eye. "Have you ever heard of an Englishman called Kimber?"

The astonished expression in her eyes gave him the answer before she spoke.

"When did you first hear his name?" he asked.

"Today." Ella swallowed, then went on staccato-fashion as though out of breath. "He telephoned at lunchtime and asked to speak to father . . . Mutti told the Englishman that he didn't want anything to do with him because . . . the war was over and he had no wish to remember it . . . when Herr Kimber rang again a few minutes later . . . Mutti told him she would call the police if he didn't stop pestering us."

"And did she?"

"No, he didn't phone again."

Kimber hadn't bothered to ring a third time; instead, he had got into his car and driven to Rothenburg. It might seem a little far-fetched but only a fool would ignore the possibility.

The telephone shattered the silence, cut into his train of thought and made him flinch; the one in the shop and the extension upstairs in the flat stridently demanding an answer. Should he ignore it, or what? Maybe if he waited long enough, the caller would eventually hang up. But if it was the Englishman, he would go on and on and on. Brack looked at Ella, decided that with proper coaching she could answer the phone, and pushed her towards the staircase. The phone in the shop was nearer but no one could see them if he used the extension in the flat.

Kimber watched the second hand on the Omega notch up another minute. Two minutes had now elapsed since the number had begun to ring out and it was beginning to look as though the Dornbergers were not at home after all. But, even as he came to this conclusion, someone lifted the receiver and a small voice said, "Rothenburg 0521."

"Is that you, Fräulein Ella?" he asked.

"Yes, who's that?"

"It's me, Herr Kimber. We spoke on the phone this morning, remember?"

"Yes."

"You sound breathless – is everything all right?"

"I've just come in . . ." Ella paused for what seemed an inordinately long time, then said, "I heard the phone ringing so I ran upstairs to answer it."

Ella was being coached, someone was telling her how to respond after listening to what he had said. He couldn't hear the interloper but he was there at her side, probably writing her lines, then holding them up like a cue card for her to read aloud. It accounted for the long pause and then the lucid explanation.

"Is your father there?" he asked.

"No . . . both my parents are out . . . they will be home at eight thirty."

Kimber frowned. Was that the kind of reply he would expect from a young teenager? In the same circumstances, would his own stepdaughter, Alison, have volunteered more information than she needed to? He looked at his wristwatch again. Why give him the precise time she expected her parents to return? And why should it be a good hour from now?

"Would you do something for me, Ella? Would you tell your father that I'd like to see him?"

Another pause. "I'll give him your message, Herr Kimber . . . but I don't think he will change his mind about seeing you."

That certainly rang true but it was too sophisticated for a young girl like Ella. But if he told the local police that and then asked them to break into the shop, they would either fall about laughing or threaten to lock him up for wasting their time. That left him with two choices; either he walked away and forgot the whole business or else he backed his hunch.

"I'll be seeing you, Ella," Kimber said and hung up.

Brack took the receiver from Ella and placed it on the cradle, terminating the continuous burr. "You did well," he told her.

But could he say the same for himself? If Kimber was as suspicious as he had sounded on the telephone, would he wait until eight thirty or would he be knocking on the door long before then? Brack fingered the stubble on his jaw. He could walk Ella down the street and use her to get to Dornberger, but there were still too many people about and she might just open her mouth and scream for help.

Provided he waited long enough, Otto was bound to come home some time; it was the damned Englishman who was the joker in the pack. It was the possibility that Kimber could blunder on to the scene that was forcing him to act prematurely. Then his legal training came to his rescue and Brack realised that he was panicking unnecessarily. Kimber had never seen the man he was looking for and with Ella's help, he could pass himself off as her father. In simple terms, he told Ella exactly what he wanted from her and made it abundantly clear what would happen if she disobeyed his instructions or failed to co-operate. Leaving the lights on in the flat, he then took her down into the stockroom.

Dornberger held the bottle of Schnapps up to the light to see if it really was empty, then turned it upside down over the cup to make absolutely sure. A dewdrop collected in the neck of the bottle, detached itself from the lip and missing the cup in his unsteady hand, landed on the workbench to form a tiny damp star on the wood.

"Party shover," Dornberger announced in a slurred voice.

He could not remember a time when he had felt so on top of the world. Right now, he could win the giant slalom at the next Winter Olympics, break ten seconds for the hundred-metre dash, or take

Joachim apart with his bare hands. There was nothing he couldn't do, he could even forgive Gisela for screwing around which just showed what a magnanimous fellow he was.

"You're okay, Dornberger," he told himself. "You're jus' too easy-going, tha's all."

Well, he would soon show Gisela he wasn't a man to be trifled with; he'd teach her who wore the trousers in their household, something he should have done years ago. And after Gisela had been brought to heel, he would call on that reptile, Joachim, and sort him out.

Dornberger got to his feet, lurched along the workbench, then stooped down to pick up the Sauer automatic. He would also let the bastard have his pistol back but not until he had made him crap in his pants. The mental picture of Joachim dancing around in soiled pants appealed to him so much that he couldn't stop laughing. With some difficulty, he pulled the slide back to chamber a round and applied the safety catch. Tucking the automatic, barrel first, into the waistband of his slacks, he started towards the judas gate on legs that felt distinctly rubbery. A few minutes' rest and a quick drag and he would be as right as rain. Dornberger sank down on to the chair, found a packet of cigarettes and managed to light one at the second attempt.

Kimber looked up at the flat above the bookshop. The curtains had been drawn in one of the rooms facing the street and he could see a chink of light in the narrow gap between them. The hanging card in the shop window was still showing 'Offen' but perhaps Ella hadn't noticed it when she had returned home. He rapped on the glass and was pleasantly surprised when the lights came on in the shop. He had been told that Otto Dornberger refused to see him, but there he was, large as life, with his daughter, Ella. He was about five feet nine and a once-athletic body had begun to thicken at the waist. Kimber reckoned he was in his mid-forties and the absence of any grey in his short, dark hair suggested he was vain about his appearance.

"Herr Kimber, I presume?" he said after Ella had let him into the shop.

It wasn't the warmest greeting Kimber had known. He tried a disarming smile and wasn't too surprised when the German ignored his outstretched hand.

"I'm afraid so," Kimber admitted.

"Did no one tell you the war has been over for thirteen years, Herr Kimber?"

"It ended for Wilhelm Freisler and the other soldiers you defended in 1944."

"I did the best I could for them."

"Tell me about Brack."

"Who?"

"Hauptsturmführer Rudolf Brack, the Prosecuting Officer. What sort of man was he?"

"A typical SS lawyer. He believed the men were guilty as charged and the sooner the court agreed with his opinion, the better it would be for all concerned."

Dornberger was making all the right noises but his words seemed to lack conviction. Kimber also thought it was odd that Ella should be present. He could have understood it if Frau Dornberger had been there to lend moral support, but a sixteen-year-old girl? And why was Dornberger sticking so close to his daughter? He was standing half a pace behind Ella's right shoulder, shielding her from the door at the back of the shop. Unable to move to her left because of the long counter where the stationery was displayed, she was effectively boxed in.

"I knew the accused were being railroaded," Dornberger continued in a curiously flat voice. "Freisler's story was so fantastic, it had to be true, but it was the fact that the Judge Advocate kept shouting him down that really convinced me he was innocent."

"The Judge Advocate was SS?"

"Yes, so was the President of the Court."

"Do you remember their names?"

"It's a long time ago and I had other things to think about when I was a POW in the USSR."

"Some names you don't forget," Kimber said, his eyes on Ella. Her face was very pale and she was gnawing the inside of her bottom lip.

"The Judge Advocate was a Standartenführer called Lohse, or was it Lutze?" A puzzled frown creased his brow and was followed by a half-apologetic shrug. "Anyway, he was about forty or so in those days and I remember that he outranked the President . . ." Dornberger suddenly dried up.

A door had opened somewhere and Kimber heard the clump of footsteps in the back room. Then a loud, drunken voice said, "I want a word with you, Gisela."

"Papa," Ella screamed. "Papa."

The impostor lashed out and sent her reeling with a vicious forearm smash which caught Ella high up on the right side of her head. She cannoned into the display counter, shattered the glass and collapsed on to the floor bleeding profusely from the left shoulder. Almost in the same instant, the door to the stockroom flew open and Dornberger charged into the shop brandishing an automatic pistol. He looked neither left nor right and saw only Kimber standing directly in his path.

Kimber read his intentions and threw himself sideways and rolled out of the line of fire a split second before he snatched the trigger. The bullet whunked into the door frame, a second round ploughed into the ceiling and brought down a slab of plaster. When he looked up, Dornberger was performing a ballet dancer's spin of his own creation, pirouetting on his right heel, both hands tugging at the dagger buried deep in the side of his neck. The only sound to come from his open mouth was the gurgle of a man who was drowning in his own blood; then his legs became inextricably entwined and he went down like a spindly tree in a hurricane.

The pistol was lying some twelve feet beyond Dornberger under a pyramid display stand of paperbacks. Kimber went after it, scrabbling across the carpeted floor on hands and knees in a desperate attempt to grab the automatic before the impostor did. The odds were stacked against him; it was Ella who evened them up. Showing remarkable presence of mind, she flung herself at the impostor and wrapped both arms around his right leg. Somehow Brack managed to retain his balance while he turned about and kicked out with his left foot. The toecap of his shoe went into Ella's ribs and made her grunt with pain. A second kick delivered with even greater ferocity connected with her right elbow and paralysed the arm. Breaking free, he launched himself at Kimber in a low, flat dive.

Kimber almost had the barrel within his grasp when the German landed on his back and pinned him to the floor. He had seen him whip out a dagger and hurl it at Dornberger and knew that, given half a chance, he would kill him too. A pair of strong hands encircled his throat and he instinctively hunched both shoulders and pressed his chin into his chest in an attempt to break the grip on his windpipe. Fear set the adrenalin flowing and gave him added strength; reaching up, he pried a finger loose and bent it back until it snapped out of joint.

Brack screamed, lost his stranglehold and was thrown forward as Kimber arched his back and heaved him head first into the display stand. Blood dripping from a gash above his right eye, he rolled clear, slammed a foot into Kimber's side and snaked towards Dornberger on his stomach. He reached out, plucked the dagger from the dead man's neck, came up into a crouch and swivelled about to lunge at the Englishman with the knife.

The automatic was still lying under the display stand; one arm nursing his injured ribcage, Kimber groped for the pistol with the other and pulled it out barrel first. He slipped the index finger inside the trigger guard, folded the butt into his palm and sat up facing his adversary. The German was just six feet away when he squeezed the trigger and shot him in the head.

He was still squatting there holding the automatic when the police broke into the shop. The senior patrolman was not the sort to take unnecessary risks. There were two bodies on the floor, an hysterical young girl and a man with a smoking gun in his hand. Raising his nightstick, he clubbed Kimber across the skull and laid him out cold.

Chapter 21

Kimber turned into King Charles Street, placed the bowler on his head and, without breaking his stride, adjusted it to a slightly more comfortable position so that it was not pressing on the still tender bruise on his skull. Assistant Under Secretaries and above were required to wear black jackets and striped pants; lesser mortals were allowed to wear dark three-piece suits. The bowler hat was, however, de rigueur for all grades and was practically a badge of office. Without one, you were likely to be asked for proof of identity by the commissionaires, especially if there was a new one on duty.

Kimber walked on towards the entrance near the Clive Steps and went inside the building. The commissionaire was ex-Navy; among the medal ribbons he wore on his uniform were the 1939–1945, Atlantic, Middle East and Pacific Stars. He had been with the Foreign Office long enough to know most people by name.

"Nice to have you back, Mr Kimber, sir," he said cheerfully. "I trust you had a good holiday?"

"Marvellous, Fred. Only thing that spoils it is coming back to this place." Removing his hat, he went on up to the Arabian Department and looked in on the Administrative Officer.

"Well, hello stranger," Humberstone said. "I'm glad to see you're still in one piece." He looked him over, an amused smile on his face. "You are in one piece, aren't you, Michael?"

"More or less. They kept me in hospital for a few days under observation. I think the Police Authority was worried I might sue them."

"Really? We heard the police were going to charge you with manslaughter or whatever the West Germans call it. Nigel was very concerned."

"I bet he was."

"Some of your colleagues were suggesting you had joined the wrong profession." Humberstone grinned. "Diplomats are supposed to establish cordial relations, not kill people."

"Yes, well, unfortunately the late Hauptsturmführer Brack wasn't exactly friendly."

"Quite. But did you have to shoot him between the eyes?"

There had been no time for any niceties. Brack had been in a crouching position, poised to stick the knife into his chest and he had picked up the automatic and fired.

"I don't see that it's any business of yours, Leslie," he said mildly.

"No, of course it isn't. And believe me, I certainly wasn't meaning to sound critical." Humberstone got up and moved round his desk to open the extreme top left-hand drawer among the bank of filing cabinets lining one wall of the office. "You might be interested to see this," he said and plucked out a branch memorandum.

Kimber recognised the gesture for what it was, a peace offering. Opening the slim file, he found the top folio was a cable from Bonn which answered most of the questions he had raised with Emmerson.

"I'm supposed to destroy the file tomorrow."

"Why?"

"Nigel's orders; he said it wouldn't be needed after the fourteenth of August."

Kimber wondered what was so special about the date, then recalled Emmerson telling him that the inquest on Zagorski had been set for the fourteenth. Since there was every prospect that the coroner's jury would bring in a verdict of suicide, he could understand why Nigel would consign the file to the shredder. He thought of asking Humberstone to make a copy of the signal from Bonn, but apart from the information about Freisler's next of kin, it didn't tell him anything he hadn't already learned from Frau Dornberger.

"Seems a pity to destroy the file so soon after opening it," Humberstone observed.

"If you didn't do a little weeding now and then, Leslie, you wouldn't be able to get into your office."

"Quite." Humberstone broke off, listened to the footsteps in the corridor, then glanced at his wristwatch. Snatching the file from Kimber, he hastily put it back in the filing cabinet. "I think that must be Nigel," he said, as if an explanation was necessary.

"What are you so worried about?" Kimber asked him. "I'm the one who's on the mat."

But it didn't turn out like that and, in fact, Emmerson couldn't have been nicer. The bottle of Tio Pepe, the silver salver and Waterford sherry glasses which his PA kept in her office, were normally reserved for VIPs along with the freshly-ground coffee. For reasons which did not become clear until he was about to leave, Kimber was treated like an honoured guest.

"You are to be congratulated, Michael."

"I am?"

"Yes, it's not every day that a First Secretary receives a letter of commendation from the West German Minister of the Interior." Emmerson raised his glass and took an appreciative sip. "Whether they will still be grateful a month from now depends on what comes out of the woodwork. I think they would have been happier if the affair could have begun and ended with Rudolf Brack."

"He did his best to contain it. The only name Brack gave me was Standartenführer Lutze, the Judge Advocate who, it transpires, went out and hung himself the day Himmler committed suicide. He had a convenient lapse of memory concerning the identity of the President of the court martial."

"Because Oberführer Helmuth Morgen is still alive." Emmerson shook his head. "Odd that Brack should go out of his way to protect Morgen."

"I believe he was hoping to protect himself, Nigel. He wanted me to think he was Dornberger so he named Lutze to give himself credibility. If Ella's father hadn't turned up, he might have carried it off and I would have gone on my way, looking for a man who was already dead."

"The word 'if' is the biggest and most useless conjunction in history, Michael."

Emmerson was right. If Dornberger had been home the first time Brack had called at the shop, he would have killed the last witness who could point a finger at him. Then, he and ex-Oberführer Helmuth Morgen would have been safe for all time.

"I wonder who warned Morgen and Brack that we were looking for them?"

"Who knows?" Kimber shrugged. "It depends on whether Morgen is prepared to betray his source. Anyway, we weren't the first to go after them. According to Bonn, Zagorski set that particular hare running when he walked into the West German Embassy in London back in May."

And there was another big 'if', because the story would have had a very different ending had Brack taken action to eliminate Exler and Dornberger there and then.

"Well, it's not our problem any longer, thank God."

"What do you think they will do about Karl Heinz Witzleben?"

"That's up to the Poles, Michael. If they feel strongly enough about his alleged war crimes, I dare say the West Germans will do all they can to trace him." Emmerson finished the rest of his sherry and put the glass down on the salver. "I'm afraid this business has

217

messed up your holiday a bit, but you'll be able to get away after you have seen the Deputy Under Secretary on Friday morning."

"What does he want to see me about?"

"It's supposed to be confidential but you are leaving us to join the UK delegation to the UN in New York. It means promotion to Counsellor." Emmerson smiled. "Try to act surprised when the DUS informs you officially."

"Yes, I will." Kimber shook his head. "I don't know what to say . . ."

"You deserve it, Michael, you were always a potential flier. And now that has been recognised by the people upstairs."

Or was it because Emmerson had taken his coat off and gone to work on his behalf in order to be rid of him? You're getting paranoid, Kimber told himself; back door influence alone would never have got him the job had not the DUS thought he was up to it. Still in a daze, he walked back to his office and was about to clear out his desk when Humberstone poked his head round the door.

"You left your bowler in my office," he said.

"Thanks."

"Still in one piece then?"

"No blood was shed on the carpet, Leslie."

"Good." Humberstone continued to linger in the rapidly diminishing hope that Kimber would tell him what had happened. "Did I mention I had a phone call from a Mrs Irena Puzak while you were away?"

"No. What did she want?"

"I rather gathered it was you who wanted something from her. Anyway, she asked if you would phone her some time."

"Thank you, Leslie."

"My pleasure," Humberstone said, finally conceding defeat.

Irena Puzak had come up with something and wanted him to call her. Kimber thought he could do better than that; lifting the phone, he rang Emmerson's PA and told her that there were certain matters he had to attend to following his conversation with Nigel. The message was sufficiently vague to account for his absence while in no way alarming Emmerson.

Nothing had changed since the last time Kimber had visited the offices of *The Sentinel* in Varley Mall. No one had been appointed to replace Zagorski and the desk he had once occupied remained empty as if in memory of a man few would remember. Since there were no reporters on the staff, he wondered if Mrs Puzak was now compiling the news from Reuters, Associated Press and the BBC Overseas Service as well as writing the leader column.

"I thought I'd drop by in person instead of phoning you," Kimber told her. "I hope that's all right?"

"I'm always delighted to receive visitors during working hours." Her eyes twinkled. "It's the ones who call after the office is closed who can be troublesome."

"I'm not sure I know what you mean," Kimber said, though he had a pretty good idea.

"We were burgled a week ago yesterday." She waved a hand indicating the sashcord window. "They forced the catch and climbed in. Fortunately, one of the neighbours spotted them and rang the police. They caught one of the burglars, the other ran off." Her eyes positively sparkled with amusement. "I think they must have been amateurs," she said dryly. "After all, what could a proper thief hope to find in this office?"

Mrs Puzak had got it wrong. They had been hoping they wouldn't find anything which would substantiate Zagorski's allegations.

"When does the case come up?" he asked.

"I don't know. The police told me I wouldn't be required to give evidence because they had caught the thief red-handed. They said he had also made a full confession and asked for nine similar offences to be taken into consideration."

A suspicion that MI5 had been responsible for the break-in became a certainty. The only thing that surprised Kimber was that, so far, Irena Puzak hadn't accused him of instigating it.

"I have consulted my solicitors, Mr Kimber, and they assure me that no one can bring an action for libel against a dead man."

He couldn't believe this was the reason why she had left a message with Humberstone asking him to ring her. The fact that Zagorski was dead was irrelevant; as the owner of *The Sentinel*, Irena Puzak could still be sued for libel if she published his allegations, and she had been around long enough to know it.

"And I've no intention of publishing Stefan Zagorski's allegations." She was still fencing with him but he went along with it, knowing that sooner or later she was bound to show her hand.

"I'm glad, it would only have hurt a lot of innocent people. I also think that those who knew Stefan in Warsaw would like to remember him the way he was then instead of the warped and bitter man he became when he learned he was dying."

"Dying?"

"He had cancer, Mrs Puzak; a Harley Street specialist called

Allenby told him it was terminal. It will all come out at the inquest tomorrow."

"So you are no longer interested in tracing the other people Stefan named in his letter?"

The issues Zagorski had raised would be buried with him when the coroner's jury in South Lambeth returned their verdict. Emmerson no longer cared whether 'Phoenix', the Soviet agent in the AK High Command, had really existed, or whether he had simply been a character invented by General Reinhard Gehlen for the purposes of black propaganda. What had happened in Warsaw in 1944 was ancient history which was only of academic interest in 1958. And yet something in Irena Puzak's voice rekindled a feeling that he ought to keep plugging away until there were no more loose ends that begged an explanation.

"I didn't say that," Kimber told her. "I'd still like to know what happened to Adam Nowotko and the Resistance leader who was known as 'Wolf'."

"And Karol Bolek?"

"Is he related to Maria Bolek?"

"Karol is the younger of her two older brothers. He escaped from Poland in October 1939 and made his way to England via Romania, Yugoslavia, northern Italy and France. He joined the RAF, became a pilot and served in Bomber Command. He stayed on in the Air Force after the war."

Kimber was sitting on the rickety ladderback chair half facing the garden, but he was unaware of the knee-high grass and the weed-infested rose bed. Instead, he saw the police station near the junction of Dluga and Miodowa Streets in the Old Town and remembered Maria rousing him from a dead sleep that hot Sunday morning in August. Some time during their conversation she had asked him how long he had known Halina and if she had ever mentioned a Count Ladislaw Nowotko.

"Do you know where I can find Karol Bolek?"

"He's at the Air Ministry here in London."

"I'd like to see him."

"He would also like to meet you." Irena Puzak glanced at the phone on her desk. "Would you like me to arrange it?" she asked.

"Yes, please.' "

Kimber began to regret his decision moments after he'd made it. What was he going to say to Maria's brother? I was there when they fished your sister out of the sewers on the outskirts of Zoliborz? She had been in the water over a fortnight and the only way her husband could identify her was by the curtain ring he'd given her when they were married during the siege? He remembered how Maria had looked the first time he'd seen her at Zagorski's headquarters in the post office, her nose still swollen from the beating she had received, the bruises on both cheekbones the colour of over-ripe bananas. Then he heard Mrs Puzak hang up and it was too late for second thoughts.

"Karol Bolek will meet you at twelve thirty outside the side entrance to the Air Ministry on Horse Guards Avenue." She paused, then added, "I hope that's convenient?"

Kimber nodded. "It's good of you to go to so much trouble," he said. "In fact, one hesitates to ask if you know the present whereabouts of Adam Nowotko?"

"He's living in Warsaw and has a teaching post at the University."

According to Irena Puzak's source of information, Adam Nowotko had not marched into captivity when the garrison defending Zoliborz had surrendered on the thirtieth of September. Along with roughly a hundred members of the People's Army, he had broken through the German lines to reach the Vistula where they had been picked up by assault boats crewed by men of General Berling's 1st Polish Army in Praga.

"If he hadn't been a member of the Communist Party before 1944 he certainly became one immediately after the war. Stefan could not believe that a member of the aristocracy would do such a thing. I think he really hated him for it."

And had therefore made Nowotko a leading light in the conspiracy to betray the Home Army. It was just one more insight into the twisted way Zagorski's mind had been working before he took the high dive.

"And the man who was known as 'Wolf'? Do you have any idea who he is, or was?"

"Why do you want to know, Mr Kimber?"

It wasn't the easiest question to answer and he was aware that what he was saying didn't sound particularly cogent.

"There was no conspiracy. Stalin allowed the Germans to destroy the Home Army because they were loyal to the Polish Government in Exile and he was determined that the Moscow-backed Committee of National Liberation in Lublin were going to be the future rulers. But Stefan wasn't a complete looney; a crime was committed in Warsaw and even now, fourteen years later, the killing hasn't stopped. If you want to know what my motives are, I guess I would have to say that I don't see why men like Witzleben should be allowed to get away with it." Kimber looked her straight in the eye. "Does that make any sense to you?" he asked.

"'Wolf' was the codename used by my husband, Michal Puzak."

"What?" Kimber felt his jaw drop.

"You may have seen him the first time you called. Michal handles the advertising side of the business and works in the front office."

"Will he talk to me?"

"I don't see why not, Mr Kimber. Let's go next door and I'll introduce you."

Advertising manager was a somewhat glorified title for a clerk who sat by a telephone compiling the list of engagements, marriages, births and deaths for a readership of just over two thousand. Puzak had met Irena in London a few months after her first husband had died of pneumonia in September 1948. Four years before that, he had commanded the company which had stormed the Civil Affairs Bureau in Krasinski Square.

"I remember Maria Bolek," he told Kimber. "Two of my men found her wandering about the garden. We thought she was a collaborator like the other Poles who worked for the German-run Civil Affairs Bureau, but she claimed she was in the AK and was being interrogated by a Gestapo agent called Neurath shortly before we captured the building."

"Neurath wanted her to identify some of the people the Gestapo had secretly photographed."

"She told you?"

"Yes. Maria said she recognised Halina Sosna in one of the snapshots. You ever heard of her?"

"No, I can't say I have."

Kimber tried a different approach. "There's something I don't understand," he said. "Why didn't the Home Army try Witzleben after they had captured him?"

"What for?"

"He's a war criminal."

"He was a thief, not a mass murderer."

He had not been in the same league as Goering who had looted practically every art gallery and museum in Occupied Europe, but he had evidently skimmed some of the cream off the milk. It was, Puzak said, a matter of public record.

"God, I can't believe how stupid I've been." Kimber shook his head in disbelief. "All this time and it never occurred to me that it was all about a small fortune. Do you know the names of the principal witnesses?"

"I could get them for you if you are really serious about finding Witzleben?"

Kimber went through his wallet until he found a card, then wrote his home number on it. "Perhaps you would call me on Camberley 233 any time after seven o'clock?"

"You haven't answered my question."

"One of Witzleben's friends tried to kill me," Kimber said tersely. "Is that serious enough for you?"

Karol Bolek had been born in October 1915, some thirteen months before Maria. He was about five feet eight, had dark curly hair like his sister's and, as with most ex-Lancaster bomber pilots, suffered from back trouble. Bolek had had four good reasons for not returning to Poland after the war; through the International Red Cross he had learned that, as well as Maria, both his parents had been killed during the uprising and his elder brother, Konstantin, had been among the four thousand Polish officers murdered by the NKVD in the Katyn Forest. He had one very good reason for staying in England. In 1943, while based at RAF Hucknall, he had met and subsequently married a WAAF radar technician.

Most of this Kimber had learned from Irena Puzak before leaving *The Sentinel*, the rest he had got from Bolek himself as they walked down Horse Guards Avenue to the gardens on Victoria Embankment. Recognising the Polish exile had been easy enough; he was a mirror image of his sister and had been the only man in a dark suit outside the Air Ministry who had appeared to be waiting for someone.

"Tell me everything you can remember about Maria," he said, and Kimber did just that. He spoke of her courage and unflagging morale and told him about Leon Jarrell, the twenty-two-year-old American she had married during the siege and how happy they had been together. He lied about her death and deliberately led him to believe that Maria had been killed in a fire damp explosion, because it altered nothing and it was kinder to gloss over the more harrowing details.

"The only person Maria had no time for was a Count Ladislaw Nowotko. She called him an evil old man. I gathered there was some suspicion that he was a collaborator."

"It wouldn't have surprised me," Bolek said.

"You knew him?"

"Not personally. The Nowotkos were landowners and moved in different circles. Their wives down through the generations were more noted for their wealth than their beauty which would explain how the family acquired estates at Kepno near the old German border and at Wolomin. Ladislaw Nowotko was reputed to have had one of the most valuable collections of paintings outside the National Museum."

And somehow Witzleben had got to hear that the collection was buried in the grounds of the house at Wolomin and had decided to help himself to it with a little help from Neurath and certain ranking officers in the SS. But who had told him, and why? The questions kept bugging him long after he parted company from Karol Bolek and walked back to his office.

In May 1945, Witzleben had been put into the bag. Two months later he had escaped from the internment camp by hiding in one of the swill bins which were collected from the cookhouse every evening. Since then, he had not been seen or heard of. To trace him now would be akin to looking for the proverbial needle in a haystack, but it wasn't an entirely hopeless task.

Kimber opened the centre drawer of his desk, took out a sheet of official notepaper and, deleting the King Charles Street address, inserted his own. Then he wrote a brief letter to Kommissar Fritz Prohl asking him to find out what had happened to Frau Witzleben after her husband had disappeared. After what had happened at Rothenburg, he knew he could rely on him to do his best.

Hillcrest without Jean and the children was as dead and as quiet as the grave. When the house was full, two of the five bedrooms upstairs and the playroom looked as though a hurricane had passed through and their daily help had her work cut out to establish some semblance of order. Now, the whole place smelled of furniture polish and every room was neat and tidy.

He opened the windows in the study to let in some fresh air, then fixed himself a whisky soda before booking a call to St Malo, the third in almost as many days.

"I've got some good news for you, darling," he said when Jean answered the phone.

"That makes a nice change."

"I'm catching the night boat from Southampton on Friday."

"Well, that is good news."

"Something else. I'm being posted to the UN in New York." He paused, then added somewhat diffidently, "It means promotion."

"Now that really is marvellous . . ."

Kimber listened to Jean enthusing but couldn't really believe what he was hearing. There was no mention of how his stepdaughter, Alison, would react to the posting but he didn't need Jean to tell him that it would be greeted with something less than enthusiasm. It meant leaving all her friends, changing schools, and doubtless there would be a hundred and one other objections she would raise.

"What about Alison?" he asked.

"Our daughter," Jean said firmly, "will do as she's bloody well told and come with us."

Michal Puzak telephoned him at home the night before he left for St Malo. Of the witnesses who had submitted affidavits concerning the activities of Karl Heinz Witzleben while head of the Civil Affairs Bureau in Warsaw, only Halina Sosna had accused him of premeditated murder. The information didn't come as a complete surprise to Kimber. According to what Dornberger had told his wife, it had been her father who had shown the Scharführer where the paintings were buried and had ended up in a shallow grave for his trouble. What did surprise Kimber was that, according to the Polish Embassy in London, she had subsequently withdrawn the allegation in 1950 after being interviewed in New York by an official from the State Department.

Kommissar Fritz Prohl was not quite so quick off the mark. His letter was lying on the hall table among several circulars and the telephone bill when Kimber returned from St Malo on the thirtieth of August. Brief and to the point, it informed him that Margarete Witzleben had divorced her husband in October 1946 on grounds of desertion. She had then remarried a widower called Franz Burgdorf and had emigrated to South Africa in 1948 where the couple were now believed to be living in Johannesburg.

1958

NEW YORK
LOS ANGELES
SAN FRANCISCO

Tuesday 7 October
to
Friday 10 October

CHAPTER 22

Some people liked to eat before going to the theatre, others preferred to dine after the show; Kimber had booked a table at Sardi's for eight fifteen to avoid both factions. A generous tip had secured him a corner table upstairs and had guaranteed his guest would receive VIP treatment when he arrived.

The last time he had seen Leon Jarrell, the American had been wearing a pair of scuffed shoes, baggy grey slacks with frayed turn-ups, a shirt which had beggared description and a moth-eaten sleeveless sweater with more holes in it than a piece of Gruyère cheese. The clothes had looked several sizes too large for him because, like the rest of the Zoliborz garrison, he had been close to starving, his skin had been the colour of paste ingrained with dirt and he had also been suffering from a bad case of ringworm.

Fourteen years later, the man the head waiter steered towards Kimber's table was wearing hand-made Italian shoes, a Brooks Brothers suit and a button-down shirt that hadn't come from a chain store. At a rough guess, he reckoned Jarrell now weighed a hundred and fifty pounds, but it didn't show too much even though he was under five feet seven. In 1944, his youthful appearance had suggested that he should still be in High School; at thirty-six, he looked his age but hadn't lost the infectious smile.

"Hi, Michael, isn't this something?" He pumped Kimber's hand and clapped him on the shoulder. "I just can't get over it – you haven't changed a bit – well, maybe your hair isn't quite so coppery as it used to be."

"I'm not quite as young as I used to be."

"Yeah – how long is it since we last saw one another?"

"Over fourteen years."

"Over fourteen years – a lifetime. And now you're here in New York with the UN."

Jarrell had said much the same thing when he had phoned him on Monday at his apartment on East 66th between Fifth Avenue and Madison.

"We've got a lot of catching up to do, Michael."

"That we have. Meantime, what would you like to drink?"

"What's that you're drinking?"

"Scotch on the rocks."

"The same for me then." Jarrell pulled out a chair and sat down. "What exactly is your job at the UN, Michael, or is it a secret?"

"How could you keep anything secret at the UN? It's the biggest coffee house in the world. But to put it in a nutshell, I'm a dogsbody with the Special Political Committee. We do the donkey work for the General Assembly."

Of the standing committees dealing with such diverse subjects as Economics, Social, Humanitarian and Cultural Affairs, Decolonisation, Administrative, and Legal, the busiest one was that concerned with Political and Security matters. The Special Political Committee had, in fact, been formed in order to relieve this group of some of the burden.

"I guess they keep you pretty busy, huh?"

"We come up for air every now and then."

"Well, I'm glad you made the time to find me, Michael. How did you do it?"

"It wasn't all that difficult. I have a good friend in the State Department who paved the way, and the Pentagon were very helpful."

"But they wouldn't know that I left Chicago in '53."

"You're right, they didn't. I had to hire a private detective from the Burns Agency to run you to ground."

Jarrell raised an eyebrow. "That must have cost you," he said in a neutral voice.

The agency had charged him six hundred and thirty-eight dollars seventy-four on the basis of fifty a day plus expenses. "It was worth it," Kimber told him.

"I bet they gave you more than the address and phone number of my apartment."

"They told me the name of the advertising agency you work for."

Leon had been repatriated in June 1945; nine months later, he had been discharged from the Army Air Corps and had gone to the University of Chicago under the GI Bill of Rights. He had majored in Art and taken a course in Graphics which had helped him to land a job with a minor agency after he had graduated.

"Did the Burns people tell you that I started out as an illustrator?"

"No."

"Only opening I could get. I'd learned the rudiments in Warsaw producing instructional manuals for the Home Army, so at least I could tell them I'd had some practical experience. It was another eighteen months before they gave me a shot at writing the copy."

Jarrell broke off while the waiter took their orders after bringing him a Scotch on the rocks. He heard Kimber order a filet mignon, French fries and a side salad and decided to have the same but wanted his steak medium rare.

"Where was I?" he asked Kimber.

"You had just become a copy writer."

"Yeah, that was back in 1950. I married a girl called Krysia later the same year but it didn't work out and we split up in 1953."

"And you then came to New York and made a name for yourself on Madison Avenue."

"I'm doing all right. How about you, Michael?"

"I'm happily married with a fourteen-year-old stepdaughter and a six-year-old son. I was posted to the UN five weeks ago and we're living in a very attractive house on Whitney Avenue in New Haven. I get home most nights but if we do have to work late, there's always a bed for me at our offices on Third Avenue."

"So where does your wife think you are tonight?"

"Oh, Jean knows I'm having dinner with you." Kimber paused, then said, "One of the reasons I wanted to find you is that I ran into Karol Bolek shortly before I left London."

"Maria's brother?" Jarrell gave a low whistle. "That's one hell of a coincidence, isn't it?"

"It didn't happen by chance, Leon. The wife of a man called Puzak told me where to find him; when her husband was with the AK, his codename was 'Wolf'."

Jarrell stared at him as though he'd seen a ghost. "That's the son of a bitch who damn nearly had Maria shot as a collaborator."

"Yes."

"Did you know him in Warsaw?"

Kimber shook his head. "I met him in London for the first time seven weeks ago."

"And I bet that didn't happen by chance either?"

"Right again."

Kimber told him how Zagorski had committed suicide and the allegations he had made about Tatar, Orska, Nowotko, Maria, Halina and himself. "He even threw you in for good measure."

"What was he – a candidate for the funny farm?"

"Oh, he was unbalanced by his obsession with what happened in Warsaw, but not everything he put in that final letter to me was a hundred per cent gibberish. I think certain members of the Home Army did make a deal with Karl Heinz Witzleben and he walked away with a small fortune in paintings belonging to the Nowotkos. I don't know what the Resistance was supposed to get in return, but there's no doubt that they were double-crossed, and Halina's father was one of the victims."

"Maria never trusted her," Jarrell said thoughtfully. "When she was being interrogated by Neurath, he showed her a number of photographs of Halina taken by the Gestapo that were pretty compromising."

"I know about the one taken of her arm-in-arm with Ladislaw Nowotko in Lazienki Park."

"They also snapped her outside Kuba's Café. It had to be in the height of summer because she was wearing a dress with short sleeves and you could see her shadow on the sidewalk. Probably June or July '44 because once the Krauts began to use the information Halina was giving them, it wouldn't have taken the AK very long to figure out that she was working for the Gestapo. At least, that's what Maria reckoned."

There was more, a whole lot more, but much of it was repetitive and Kimber was only vaguely aware of what the American was saying. Kuba's Café on Jasna Street had belonged to Stefan Zagorski and the headquarters of the 5th battalion had been established in the flat above. But that was beside the point. What was it Daniel Tatar had said to him a few weeks ago in Blackpool? The café was the perfect cover for a Resistance leader. Damn right it was; people could come and go during the hours of daylight without arousing suspicion. Hell, the café could have been used as a postbox by more than one Resistance cell.

"Then there was this guy in shirtsleeves they photographed getting off a tram. The definition was so lousy that Maria couldn't place him for a long time, but the more she thought about it, the more she was convinced it wasn't the only shot they'd taken. She described the other picture so clearly that I had no difficulty in recognising the guy when I eventually came face to face with him in Zoliborz the day you accompanied his recce patrol across the Vistula."

"Adam Nowotko?"

"Got him in one, Michael."

Maybe the deal with Witzleben had been initiated by the Communist People's Army? But where had Maria Bolek fitted into the picture? Usually, anyone suspected of being in the Resistance was taken to the Gestapo headquarters on Szucha Avenue or to the Pawiak Prison in the old Jewish ghetto, but she had been interrogated at the Civil Affairs Bureau in the presence of Witzleben. Why was that? Had Witzleben believed she possessed the means to threaten him in some way?

"What exactly did Maria do at the Civil Affairs Bureau?" Kimber asked.

"Clerical work – typing, filing, that sort of thing." Jarrell broke off while the waiter served them, then said, "Of course, whenever the Germans introduced a new regulation affecting the civilian population, Witzleben would get her to check that it had been translated correctly into Polish. That's how Maria was able to give the AK advanced warning."

"What about the mail?"

"It went through the Army's field post office in Napoleon Square. Letters and parcels addressed to the Civil Affairs Bureau were supposed to be delivered to the chief clerk who was a German, but he was a drinker and wasn't always there to receive the post first thing in the morning." Jarrell cut his steak into manageable portions, then speared a piece with a fork. "Exler used to hand the mail over to Maria whenever the chief clerk was absent."

"What about Witzleben's personal mail?"

"It came through the same channels as the official stuff, but there was no way Maria could open the envelopes without him knowing she had been reading his letters. There were too many Polish collaborators in the same office who would have been only too ready to inform on her the moment she was seen tampering with the mail."

Every promising lead finished up as a blind alley. But no matter what Leon told him, Kimber couldn't forget that Maria Bolek had not been treated like any other suspect, and there had to be a reason.

"What did Maria think of Witzleben?"

"A real creep. Maybe those weren't her exact words but they certainly represent her opinion. He kept a photograph of his wife on his desk and a succession of mistresses in his bed. He talked brave but he was just as chicken-hearted as all the other thousands of German civilian officials who fled the city when the Russians were approaching Wolomin. Except that he was a bit slower off the mark; by the time he got around to ordering a boxcar from the Railway Transportation Organisation, the Governor and the Mayor had returned to the city."

"A boxcar?"

"Yeah. Witzleben lived in a commandeered house near the Brühl Palace; Maria reckoned he was planning to strip the place bare."

"When was this?"

233

"You're not asking me to put a date on it, are you, Michael?" Jarrell shook his head. "Hell, it was fourteen years ago, how's a man supposed to remember details like that?"

"Make a stab at it. Was it ten days before the uprising began?"

"No, I'd say it was more like a week."

"How did Maria know about the boxcar?"

"She took a phone message from the RTO correcting the information given to Witzleben. Apparently, the Movement Control Officer had told him that the boxcar would be positioned in the sidings at the Danzig Station, instead of which, it was in the marshalling yards near the Central Station. The caller thought he was talking to one of the German civilians."

"One last question," said Kimber. "Who did Maria tell?"

"The chief clerk, I guess."

"Not Witzleben?"

"Naw, she never went near him if she could help it – said his eyes were always mentally undressing her. Like I said, he was a real creep."

The telephone call was the reason why Maria had been taken in for interrogation by Neurath. Somehow Witzleben had learned that she was the one who had taken the message from the RTO and he had wanted to find out if she had appreciated its significance.

"Don't you see, Leon, the photographs were a ruse. Ladislaw Nowotko wasn't a member of the AK or the People's Army; his picture was included in the pack because they wanted to see if she knew the Count. Neurath was going to kill her because Maria had recognised him, and they feared she would make the connection and realise they intended to ship his art collection back to Germany in the boxcar."

"So?"

"So they weren't planning to send the paintings home for Reichsmarschall Goering's benefit, nor were they destined for the Führer's museum at Linz. So Maria had to die because they believed she knew too much."

Jarrell removed a tiny piece of lettuce which was clinging obstinately to his lower lip and inspected it closely. "That's a very neat theory, Michael," he said eventually. "Have you got one to fit Halina?"

"I'm still working on it," Kimber told him. "Only she can tell me what the Resistance was hoping to get from Witzleben in exchange for the paintings."

"Don't tell me you've got the Burns Agency looking for her too?"

"Yes. She was here in New York in 1950. She was in the fashion business, had a place in the Village which she called The Thrift Shop, sold last year's haute couture models from Paris at knock-down prices. Don't ask me how Halina got hold of them, but she obviously made a success of the enterprise judging by the amount the new owners paid her when she sold up and moved to California."

"Do you have an address for her out there?"

"Not yet."

"Uh huh." Jarrell signalled the waiter to remove his plate, then lit a cigarette. "I always smoke between courses," he said. "You don't mind, do you?"

"Not a bit."

"You want to tell me how you discovered Halina was here in '50?"

Kimber told him about the list of war crimes attributed to Witzleben which were still outstanding and how she had retracted her allegations after being interviewed by an official from the State Department.

"Interesting," Jarrell said. "What was she trying to hide?"

"Nothing. I talked to the official who'd interviewed her. Halina withdrew her allegations because she was the only one to have accused Witzleben of murder and she was told there was no way the charge could be made to stick should he ever be apprehended."

The hooker liked to call herself Gene because she hated her given name of Ruth and also because she was a fan of Gene Tierney and believed that, like the movie star, she too had style and class. One day she too would be a star of the silver screen; meanwhile, in her other line of work, she cruised the bars on Hollywood Boulevard between Hudson and Sycamore Avenues. In keeping with her self-esteem, Gene charged seventy-five dollars a trick which, on the basis of four lays a night from Monday to Saturday, meant that she could earn as much as eighteen hundred a week. And at 1958 prices, that wasn't exactly chicken feed.

There was never a shortage of 'Johns'. She had the longest and best-looking legs in the business and the kind of tight little ass which unfailingly drew admiring glances whenever she chose to wiggle it. The cops never gave her any trouble because she took care of the patrolmen and could spot a plainclothes Dick a mile off. A five spot from the John kept most desk clerks happy and pre-empted questions concerning the absence of any luggage. She also made it a rule never to use the same room twice in an evening which was another reason why hotel staff and the like were prepared to turn a blind eye in her direction.

If anyone gave Gene a hard time, it was usually a John who either wanted a refund or got overheated when she refused to accommodate a particularly nasty kink. She liked to think she could size up a weirdo long before he thought of approaching her, but no one is infallible and once in a while she made a mistake. Tonight, she had made one with her first trick of the evening. "Call me Ray," he'd said when she had picked him up in Leroy's Bar near the Roosevelt Hotel, and she had liked him on sight.

Ray was in his early forties, had jet black hair, was over six feet and weighed about a hundred and ninety pounds, all of it muscle. With his neat moustache, he reminded her of Clark Gable, except that now she came to think about it, his face was a lot harder. But there had never been the slightest suspicion in her mind that he was anything other than a gentleman when they'd driven out to the motel on Laurel Canyon in his Oldsmobile.

Most Johns liked her to put on a show for them and she had lost count of the number of times she had paraded around a room in stockings, garter belt and high-heeled pumps. Gene didn't mind going through the motions of playing with herself if that was what turned Ray on, but she figured it was time to draw the line when he unplugged the phone and looked as though he was about to use the cord on her.

"What the hell do you think you're going to do with that?" she snarled.

"Nothing," he said, still smiling amiably.

"Drop it then."

"Sure." He tossed the flex on to the floor near the divan, then stood there in the centre of the bedroom, waiting passively in his shirt-tails for her to make the next move. "All I want is for you to screw me," he said hoarsely.

"Right now?"

"Right now."

Gene walked over to the dresser, opened her handbag and taking out a condom, rolled it delicately over his erect penis. Then she tickled his scrotum with a feather-like touch which excited him and made his thighs tremble.

"How does this grab you?" she asked and tweaked him gently.

"Not as much as this," Ray whispered and walked her backwards towards the divan.

It was going to be all right after all. She was in control and could put the son of a bitch on the floor writhing in agony if he tried any funny business. One hard squeeze, that's all it would take to cool his ardour.

Gene was still savouring her sense of power over him when he suddenly spun her around and she ended up face down on the bed. A knee pinned her there while he twisted both arms behind her back, reached for the flex on the carpet and lashed her wrists together. She tried to scream, but her mouth was pressed into the bedcover and she could hardly breathe let alone cry out. He grabbed a handful of her blonde hair, twisted it in a knot and hauled her upright.

"You mother . . ."

There was a whole lot more she wanted to say but the bastard cuffed her about and used the heel of his right hand on the five-hundred-dollar nose job she'd had from one of the best plastic surgeons in Hollywood. The blood ran down her chin and dripped on to her chest, mesmerising her long enough for him to stuff her lace-trimmed panties into her mouth. Before Gene realised what was happening, she was in the bathroom and he had ripped her nylons to shreds and was using a strip to tie the gag in place. She tried to backheel him in the groin but this Ray guy knew how to hurt people and she almost passed out when he dug a fist into each kidney. He raised the toilet seat, shoved her head into the pan and held it there.

"Okay, kike," he grunted. "Let's see if we can't do something about the way you stink."

Kike? How did this disgusting piece of filth know that she was Jewish?

"I can make a Yid like you a mile off," he said, as if reading her mind. "Believe me, I've had plenty of practice."

She could feel his hatred like a physical presence and was afraid. Then he reached for the lever, flushed the toilet and pushed her head right down into the bowl. The water rose above her ears and she was convinced she was going to drown. "Don't panic, hold your breath," she told herself; sound advice but difficult to follow when you were terrified out of your wits and your lungs felt as though they were going to explode. The pressure on her neck eased as he transferred his grip to both ankles and lifted her legs until she was practically standing on her head; then he pumped her up and down as though she was a plunger and he was trying to clear a blockage in the outlet. Tiring of that game, he punched her twice in the stomach and her world was suddenly a very dark place.

When she came to, the water had subsided and she found she was on her knees again. She tried to stand up but slipped on the wet tiles and sat down on her rump hard enough to bruise it. Tears

237

ran down her cheeks and mingled with the blood still trickling from her nose. Self-pity wasn't going to help her, she decided, and began to work on her wrists, rotating them in opposite directions gradually to loosen the flex. Finally, she managed to free the little and third fingers of her left hand and the rest was easy. She found the knotted end of the nylon stocking and after a lot of fumbling, finally succeeded in undoing it. She pulled the makeshift gag from her mouth, filled her tortured lungs with air and sat there on the floor, shivering as though in the grip of malaria.

A door closed. Moments later, she heard the whirr of a starter motor followed by the deep throbbing noise of an eight-cylinder engine. Tyres crunched on the gravel and then the bastard was gone and she was still alive and that was all that mattered.

Ray Inglis went on down Laurel Canyon and turned right on Sunset Boulevard. He hadn't figured Gene for a Jewess when he'd picked her up in Leroy's Bar but that just showed how even an expert like himself could be fooled. It was only when they were on their way to the motel and she had been making small talk about the things she liked to eat that he had begun to suspect she was a kike. Gene was short for Eugene and came from the Greek meaning 'well born'. He threw back his head and laughed; well, there was one Yid who certainly wasn't well born and knew what happened to those who gave themselves airs and graces. All the same, it was a real crock of shit to end up with one of the surviving Untermenschen when you'd gone out on the town looking for a good, clean lay.

He switched on the car radio and searched the dial until he found a station playing Country and Western. Tapping the steering wheel in time with the rhythm, he drove on through Beverly Hills, skirted the UCLA campus, and still on Sunset, rolled into Brentwood Park. The sole proprietor of a used-car business in Santa Monica, the Spanish-style villa on Posetano Road off the Pacific Coast Highway was just one visible sign of his success. Membership of the Brentwood Country Club was an indication of his social status.

Inglis ran the Oldsmobile up on to the driveway, cut the engine and got out. A quarter to eight; the tired businessman home at last after a busy day at the office. He let himself into the empty house and switched on the hall light; glancing automatically at the phone, he saw that someone had left a message on the answering machine. Rewinding the tape, he punched the play button and a voice he hadn't heard in months said, "I hate these machines, call me on 331–0922 the minute you get in, Ray. It's urgent."

He rewound the tape again, switched off the answering machine

238

and dialled the number in Sausalito. He didn't have to wait long for an answer.

"Hi," he said, "I got your message. What's the problem?"

"The problem is an Englishman called Kimber."

"I've never heard of him."

"You have now. He hired a private detective who has managed to find our Polish friend."

"So what do you want me to do about it?"

"I want you to take care of that particular problem, something you should have done long ago when you were presented with a golden opportunity."

"Let me think about it," Inglis said.

"There's no time for that, I want you on the first flight to San Francisco tomorrow morning. I'll meet you at the airport."

Inglis frowned. If the high-pitched tone of voice was any guide, the man in Sausalito was practically shitting himself and there was no telling what the clown might do in a panic. "All right," he said, "but we'll do it my way. You sit tight until I tell you where and when we're going to meet."

"But . . ."

"No arguments," Inglis said and hung up.

Ray Inglis had been born Rolf Ingelmann on the sixteenth of October 1914 at Stettin on the Baltic. He had arrived in California eight years ago by way of Italy, South Africa and Mexico. In 1944, he had been a Scharführer commanding a platoon of Azerbaijanis. Amongst a long list of war crimes he had committed which carried the death penalty was the cold-blooded murder of Halina's father, Leopold Sosna.

CHAPTER 23

Ever since he had broken the news of his forthcoming trip to California, Kimber had been wondering if he should tell Jean just how it had come about. It would be easier to leave her with the impression that he was going to San Francisco at the behest of the Special Political Committee, but it would be less than honest, and she had a right to know the truth. It was, however, a little late in the day to exorcise a guilty conscience and he wished he had told her last night instead of driving it up to the last minute.

"More coffee, Michael?"

"Please." There was time for another cup but not much else. In another fifteen minutes, Jean would drive him to the station and he would board a train for New York and a cab ride to La Guardia. "This trip to the West Coast," he began.

"It's all right, Michael. I know you don't like the idea of going off for three or four days when we've had so little time together since we arrived in America, but it's your job and I understand. After all, it isn't as if you had volunteered, is it?"

He had a choice: he could sit there and say nothing, or he could do what was right. "I brought it on myself by deliberately re-opening a lot of old wounds. I played the Polish Delegation off against the West German and drew in the South African."

Jean left the coffee pot on the ring and sat down at the kitchen table. "What's this all about, Michael?" she asked quietly.

"It's about a woman who divorced her husband, married a widower called Franz Burgdorf and emigrated to South Africa in 1948. I wanted to know if they were still living in Johannesburg."

"And?"

"They aren't. The Burgdorfs moved on to California in August 1950. Only, by then, Burgdorf's first name had become Erwin because Franz had succumbed to a heart attack five months after arriving in South Africa. And, surprise, surprise, his widow married his younger brother in March the following year. Seems miracles do happen because according to the Public Records Office in Bonn,

Erwin Burgdorf was killed in an air raid on Hannover in December 1943."

"Could the name of her first husband have been Witzleben?" Jean asked.

"Yes. I believe she remarried him in South Africa."

"And he's still wanted for war crimes?"

"Technically speaking." He caught her raised eyebrow and knew Jean wouldn't let it go at that. "Witzleben was the head of the Civil Affairs Bureau when the SS wiped out the Jewish ghetto in Warsaw, but he wasn't responsible for implementing the Final Solution, so his hands are relatively clean. That's not to say he didn't know what was going on, but the fact that he did nothing about it is not an indictable offence. When the International Military Tribunal was established in August 1945, the only thing they had against him was the plunder of private and public property plus one allegation of murder which Halina Sosna subsequently withdrew in 1950."

The name which had become a bone of contention between them was out in the open. He looked into Jean's eyes for the warning signs of the slow-burning fuse that would initiate the explosion, but she merely appeared thoughtful.

"I assume Halina is in San Francisco?" she said presently.

"Yes. But you don't have to worry about that; she's married to her business partner, and anyway, I'll be accompanied by Leon Jarrell."

Kimber groaned inwardly; he had wanted Jean to know that there was nothing between them, instead of which he'd managed to make it sound as though he had something to hide. Had he deliberately set out to plant a seed of suspicion in her mind, he couldn't have done a better job.

"Who told you?"

"The private detective I hired to find her . . . and Leon Jarrell of course." He shouldn't have paused before mentioning Leon, it made it sound even worse.

"How much did it cost us, Michael?"

"Quite a bit." Although the Burns Agency hadn't presented their final account yet, the fee for locating Leon had amounted to almost six hundred and forty dollars. He could therefore reckon on as much again for the work they'd done in California. "There won't be much change left from the Disturbance Allowance we received from the Foreign Office."

"Fifteen hundred dollars . . ." Jean said in a hollow voice.

"I'll be reimbursed . . ."

241

"I don't understand you, Michael. Why can't you leave this sort of thing to the professionals?"

She had said the same thing after Detective Inspector Viner had been to see him and hadn't been impressed by his answer then.

"If the Poles are showing little inclination to bring Witzleben to justice, why should you be so concerned?"

"Because a lot of men have died to satisfy his greed – four inmates from the Pawiak Prison, four enlisted men of the 73rd Infantry Division, Leopold Sosna, Gottfried Exler and Otto Dornberger -- and I don't see why he should get away with it."

"Perhaps not, but you are a guest in this country, Michael, and finding him is a job for the FBI."

"I don't think they would be interested."

"What do you mean, they wouldn't be interested?"

"The Witzlebens came to California in 1950 when there was a full-scale war going on in Korea, we were fighting the Communist terrorists in the jungles of Malaya, the French had their hands full in Indo-China and the Russians had got the atomic bomb. World War Three was on the horizon and every Western Intelligence Agency was hungry for information about the potential enemy. From his wartime experience as head of the Civil Affairs Bureau, Witzleben was uniquely qualified to brief the Americans about the men who are now running things in Poland. I'm pretty sure he convinced the CIA of this and, as a reward, they undoubtedly gave him and his wife a new identity."

"And you think Halina Sosna was pressured into withdrawing her allegations?"

"I'm certain of it."

Kimber was equally certain that the State Department official had felt so badly about it that, if he hadn't actually told Halina where the Witzlebens were living, he'd hinted where she ought to start looking for them. In fact, he was going to San Francisco on the premise that she had traced them.

"You've got a train to catch, Michael. It's time we were going."

It was difficult to know what Jean was thinking. Her voice was flat, impersonal, wooden, like a person in shock. He collected his bag from upstairs, checked to make sure he hadn't forgotten his wallet and traveller's cheques, then closed the front door behind him and joined Jean in the Chevrolet station wagon. It was a typical Fall day, deceptively bright sunlight, a clear blue sky and a sharp nip in the air that let you know winter could not be far away.

A cold front appeared to have already settled inside the car and they hardly exchanged a word all the way from Whitney Avenue to the railroad station. It seemed to him that the most he could hope for was a frigid peck on the cheek; consequently, he was unprepared for the warm embrace and the terms of endearment.

"I think you're crazy," Jean told him, "but I don't know what we would do without you. So take care of yourself because we want you to come home in one piece. No lumps on the head or anything like that. You hear?"

"I hear you," he said and kissed her again before he got out of the car and ran for the train.

Inglis arrived in San Francisco much later than he had anticipated. Fog over the bay held his flight for an hour and ten minutes until it was dispersed by a light westerly breeze and they were cleared to land. Travelling light, with only one piece of hand baggage, he walked on past the carousel and followed the signs for the exit. From a pay phone in the arrivals hall, he rang the number in Sausalito where Peter Hase, previously known as Erwin Burgdorf and Karl Heinz Witzleben from Iserlohn now lived.

When he answered, Inglis said, "It's me – Ray. I've just got in."

"You're lucky, we're still fogged in here."

"No problem, we'll meet halfway. The cocktail bar of the Huntington Hotel on California Street as soon as you can make it. Okay?"

"Yes."

"Don't keep me waiting too long then," Inglis said and hung up.

He went over to the Avis desk, rented a '58 model Ford Thunderbird and, taking delivery of the car outside the terminal building, headed into town on US Highway 101. It seemed to Inglis that he had been wet-nursing Witzleben ever since they had met back in July 1944. He'd certainly more than earned the hundred thousand dollars he had received for his part in the Wolomin affair, but at least he'd been luckier than poor old Walther Neurath, the Gestapo agent who had recruited him.

"The war is lost," Neurath had said. "You know it, I know it, the Generals know it. Naturally, we shall go on fighting to the very end, but we have got to look out for ourselves and put a little by for the future." Then he had mentioned the art collection that was theirs for the taking and had assured him that Oberführer Helmuth Morgen, commanding the SS Field Police in Warsaw, was behind the operation, which had set his mind at rest.

But Witzleben had been the principal architect and he had made it a condition that there should be no witnesses who could finger him. Between them, Neurath and Morgen had taken care of the four riflemen from the 73rd Infantry Division and he'd eliminated the Polish guide and the four inmates from the Pawiak Prison. Even though the two Azerbaijanis hadn't understood what the hell was going on, they too had been silenced. However, in their case, he'd simply kept them out on point duty twenty yards ahead of his platoon of stormtroopers until they'd fallen victim to an AK sniper.

Eleven months later, he'd had to bail Witzleben out again after the British had stuck him in an internment camp near Bremen. Morgen had planned the escape; he had executed it, driving into the compound to smuggle Karl Heinz past the guards in a pig-swill bin. Had it not been for the fact that both he and the ex-Oberführer had still been waiting to receive their share of the Wolomin paintings, they would have left him to rot behind the barbed wire. But money is a powerful inducement and Witzleben had used it to good effect. He had bought his services to get him to South Africa via Italy, and he had used him again when he had decided to settle in California.

Inglis turned off US Highway 101 into 7th Street and drove past the Main Post Office and the Greyhound Bus Terminal to make a right turn on Market Street. At the junction of Powell Street, he headed north towards the Nob Hill District, then turned left by the Stafford Court Hotel into California Street. Approaching Grace Cathedral, he overtook a cable car on the inside, turned right into Taylor Street and eased the car into the first vacant space on the steep hillside. As a safeguard in case the parking brake failed, he angled the front wheels into the kerbside, then got out of the car and walked back to Huntington Park from where he could watch the hotel across the street.

Ten minutes went by, then another ten. The fog had completely dispersed by now and he was beginning to wonder what had happened to the Herr Doktor when he spotted the six-year-old powder blue Cadillac that was seemingly his pride and joy. Anyone else would have traded it in for a new model a couple of years back, but Witzleben wouldn't consider parting with good money until the car was on its last legs. He waited until the plump, grey-haired figure had disappeared into the lobby before he rang the hotel from a pay phone down the street and asked the desk clerk to page Mr Peter Hase. It was the oldest trick in the book but Witzleben sounded bewildered as though he'd never played it before.

"Who is this?" he asked.

"It's me – Ray," Inglis told him. "Listen, I'm sorry about this but my secretary made an error and booked a table for two at the 'Sir Francis Drake'."

"Is that where you are now?"

"Hell, no, I'm still at the office but I'll join you in fifteen minutes. Wait for me in the lobby."

Inglis put the phone down, ran back to the car and made two right turns to approach California Street from Mason Street. The hotel on Powell and Sutters was only a quarter of a mile from the Huntington; if Witzleben was being followed, Inglis figured the short journey might well catch the shadow off guard.

The powder blue Cadillac came on down the street with a Pontiac in tow; while Inglis waited for the lights on Mason, a Chrysler joined the caravan. Both vehicles followed the Cadillac into Powell but carried straight on when Witzleben stopped outside the 'Sir Francis Drake'. Inglis tagged them as far as Union Square where he parked the Ford and went in search of another pay phone. This time, he sent the Herr Doktor to Pier 45 on Fisherman's Wharf.

It was a straight mile and a half run all the way down Powell to Jefferson Street and across to the Pier. Nothing untoward happened on the way there, no one paid any attention to Witzleben after he left the Cadillac in the parking area and walked over to Pier 45. Even so, Inglis allowed him to cool his heels for a further ten minutes before he made contact.

"Admiring the view?" he asked laconically and pointed to Alcatraz Island.

"I don't find that particularly amusing. What the hell kept you?"

"I wanted to make sure you were clean; a man in my position can't be too careful." Inglis turned his back on the view, nudged the older man in the ribs and steered him towards the rented Ford. "We'll use my car, yours is too conspicuous."

Leaving the parking area, he drove past Ripley's 'Believe it or not Museum', headed south on Taylor as far as Bay Street, then cut across to Van Ness Avenue.

"All right, Karl Heinz," he said presently, "suppose you tell me what all this shit is about. Who the hell is Kimber?"

"An Englishman the Polish bitch knew in Warsaw. A couple of months ago, he was in Germany asking questions about the Wolomin episode, then he comes to America and hires a private detective to find her."

"Who told you all this?"

"The Sosna woman."

"She made it up, hoping to frighten you."

"No, it's all true. I checked."

Inglis gripped the steering wheel, his knuckles turning white. The stupid bastard had telephoned his relatives in Germany, probably called his younger brother, Erich. That had to be it; no one else was in a position to verify the story. "So what does Sosna want from you?" he asked.

"She owns a string of fashion salons in San Francisco, Monterey, Carmel by the Sea and Santa Barbara. Now she's thinking about opening one in Ventura. No sum has been mentioned yet but she will expect me to put up some of the capital as usual."

Witzleben was never going to admit it but he had obviously been a silent partner in Sosna Fashions from the moment the Polish woman had arrived in San Francisco. The way he told it, she had simply turned up on the doorstep of his house in Sausalito one day and had had a long talk with Margarete while he was down the road looking after their art gallery opposite the landing stage.

"I kept asking myself how she had found us, and the only explanation I could come up with was that we had been betrayed by the official from the State Department who had persuaded Sosna to withdraw her ridiculous accusations."

"You should have contacted your guardian in the CIA and told him what had happened."

"It was too late for that," Witzleben said irritably. "I was already compromised."

"How?"

"Does it matter?"

"I wouldn't know."

Inglis turned off Van Ness Avenue into Turtle Street and headed towards the University. He could pump the old fart from now until New Year's and would still end up being none the wiser.

Witzleben said, "Kimber has never met me, doesn't know my assumed name, what I look like or where I live. Kill Sosna and her husband and we are both safe."

Inglis noted the 'we'; it implied they were both in the same boat whereas Karl Heinz had always looked after number one. After sending him ahead to try out one of the forged passports on Immigration, the first thing Witzleben had done after arriving in California was to make a deal with the CIA.

"This Kimber knows even less about me, Karl Heinz."

"I wouldn't bank on that."

The threat was implicit; if the Sosna woman delivered him to Kimber, he wouldn't be the only one to go down. The Polish woman and her spouse or the Herr Doktor and his? Inglis thought it would be safer and far easier to take out the Witzlebens.

"I've sent Margarete away for a day or two until this affair is settled," Witzleben announced casually.

246

Inglis wondered if the remark was as innocent as it sounded or whether it was meant to be a veiled warning that he would have to reckon with Frau Witzleben should the Herr Doktor meet with a fatal accident.

"All right, Karl Heinz," he said grimly, "where do the Sosnas live?"

"Pacific Heights. They have a place on Buchanan Street."

"You want to show me?"

"I certainly do. When we get to the University, make a right turn into Masonic Avenue and I'll give you directions from there."

Witzleben's sense of direction wasn't all that hot and a couple of wrong turnings resulted in a five-mile journey becoming eight. The Sosna residence on the corner of Buchanan and Pacific Avenue was called 'Praga' and resembled a Spanish hacienda. A tall privet hedge effectively concealed most of the grounds which included a tennis court as well as the inevitable swimming pool. There was a television camera mounted on one of the gateposts and a burglar alarm was prominently displayed above the front porch. If that wasn't bad enough, the house was situated in the kind of exclusive neighbourhood where the residents employed their own security guards to protect their properties rather than relying entirely on the San Francisco Police Department.

"This is no good," Inglis snarled. "The house is a goddamn fortress. I'd either be dead or on my way to jail as soon as I crossed the threshold."

"They've got a weekend cottage at Carmel by the Sea which is pretty isolated," Witzleben said in an effort to be helpful.

"A weekend cottage and today's Thursday. You're the one who's been crying wolf – you think we can afford to waste twenty-four hours on the off chance they might go down there tomorrow night?"

"No."

"Damn right; any other answer and I'd have shoved you out of the car while it was still rolling." Inglis turned into Pacific Avenue and headed east towards Van Ness. "They have to come to us," he said, thinking aloud. "Somewhere quiet, somewhere off the beaten track."

"That's easier said than done."

It was the kind of barren comment Inglis could do without. On a more positive note, he needed to acquire a shotgun and a .32 piece with a short barrel, say two and a half inches. Both weapons could be bought over the counter at a gunshop but would be traceable. That wouldn't matter provided they were never found. The Ford Thunderbird was something else; someone might recall the licence number. The only answer was to rent another car and switch the plates for false ones. The ideas started to come thick and fast until he knew what he was going to do.

"We use one as bait to draw the other to us," Inglis said.

"What?"

"I was referring to the Sosna woman and her husband, which means I want you to tell me everything you know about them."

Jarrell slept fitfully, his chin making contact with his chest whenever his head lolled forward. Beside him, Kimber tried to pass the time reading an in-house aviation magazine as their plane flew steadily westwards into the sun. He had started reading an article praising the Boeing 707 shortly after their flight had taken off from La Guardia and now, an hour and fifty minutes away from San Francisco, he was still only three quarters of the way through it.

Halina Sosna was to blame, she kept intruding on his thoughts, making it impossible for him to concentrate on the mundane. He had lost her when the Home Army had marched into captivity, found her in charge of a refugee camp for displaced persons after he'd been released from Colditz, and lost her again in Paris one wet afternoon in July '46. In between, he had been very much in love with Halina; now he had found her for the second time and his feelings were very different. At least, that was what he wanted to believe.

Kimber found himself thinking about Harvey Yeo, the man she had married five years ago. According to the Burns Agency, he was thirty-two, which made him eight years younger than Halina. He was described by business associates as plain, quiet, colourless and ineffectual, characteristics that made Kimber wonder what she had seen in him. Maybe it had been the attraction of opposites, because Halina was everything that Harvey Yeo seemingly was not. Ineffectual? Not Halina. She had joined the hundred members of the People's Army who had broken through the German lines and crossed the Vistula when the rest of the garrison defending Zoliborz had surrendered. She had then become an auxiliary in General Berling's 1st Polish Army and had accompanied them all the way to the old pre-war frontier with Germany. In February 1945, she had absented herself from the Women's Auxiliary Transport unit and headed west in the wake of the Red Army.

"I could see the writing on the wall," she had told him later. "I knew Churchill and Roosevelt would abandon Poland and tell us to reach an accommodation with the Soviets and I didn't want to live under a Moscow-appointed government."

Halina had also told him how she had had to live off the land, sometimes taking at gunpoint what she needed from those few German civilians who remained in the rear area. On one occasion, two Russian deserters from Marshal Chuikov's Eighth Guards Army had tried to rape her and she had shot them both, one in the head, the other in the back as he tried to run away. Finally, on May the seventh, twenty-four hours before VE Day, she had slipped through the Russian lines near Stettin and made contact with a troop of Royal Engineers belonging to 7th Armoured Division. Taken to Divisional Headquarters, she had immediately made a sworn statement accusing Witzleben of murder.

"A penny for them," Jarrell said, making Kimber jump.

"I was thinking about an enigma whose name is Halina . . ."

"Yeah, that's one lady who is a real puzzle. But that's why we're going to San Francisco, isn't it, to find out what makes her tick?"

CHAPTER 24

Harvey Yeo in no way resembled the stereotyped image of the typical fashion buyer. He did not wear outrageous clothes, nor did he affect any flamboyant mannerisms. A slim five feet seven, he had straight brown hair and wore horn-rimmed glasses which made him appear studious. Strangers who were unaware of his occupation before they were introduced, took him for either an accountant or a High School teacher. In 1950, when Halina Sosna had opened her first boutique in San Francisco, he had been a fashion buyer for a large retail chain and they had met when she had gone to him seeking advice. Her flair and his know-how had made a formidable combination and she had opened a second branch on Sutter Street less than a year later.

The original establishment at 1098 Market Street was now a men's outfitters, a new venture they had started at the beginning of the year. This side of the business was entirely Yeo's province; Market Street was where he spent his working day from eight in the morning to six in the evening with three quarters of an hour off for lunch. He worked longer and harder than any of their employees; his only indulgence was a Jaguar XK120 sports car which he garaged in the underground lot in Marshall Square less than five minutes' walk from Sosna's Men's Outfitters. Because his routine never varied, Witzleben was able to point him out to Inglis when he left the store promptly at twelve fifteen to walk to Merlin's Express Diner on 7th Street and Golden Gate Avenue where he lunched every day.

With his previous experience in the SS, Inglis needed only a brief glimpse to be sure of recognising him again. He started the Ford Thunderbird, pulled out from the kerb and continued on down Market Street as far as Mason where he dropped Witzleben off with orders to rent a car from Budget and meet him again at the World Trade Centre on the waterfront. No stranger to San Francisco, he knew his way around town well enough not to get lost, but without

Witzleben's local knowledge, he could have wasted hours looking for a gunsmith.

The gunsmith on 6th Street near the China Basin sold everything from a dinky little .22 revolver with an inlaid mother-of-pearl pistol grip to a high-powered rifle that could stop an elephant in its tracks. Inglis showed his permit from the LAPD to one of the assistants, told him he was a member of a gun club in Santa Monica and was looking for a .32 calibre revolver which he could use in competition shooting as well as for self-protection. After examining several models, he settled for a Colt Diamondback with a two-inch barrel. When it came to choosing a shotgun, he opted for a 12-bore Ithaca M37 pump-action. To maintain the pretence that he wanted both weapons for sporting purposes, he purchased far more ammunition than he needed and paid the bill with his credit card.

Inglis made two stops on the way to the World Trade Centre. At a hardware store, he bought a clothes line, a pair of scissors and a small fire-extinguisher, then from a druggist's farther along the same street, he purchased a bottle of Ronson lighter fuel. When he arrived at the rendezvous five minutes later, an anxious-looking Witzleben was waiting for him with a Dodge sedan.

"I was beginning to think you'd run out on me and gone back to LA," he said and laughed nervously.

"Don't make me wish I had," Inglis told him.

"I was only joking."

"Yeah? Well, suppose you do something useful, Karl Heinz, and open the trunk of your car. You think you can do that without me holding your hand?"

"There's no need to be sarcastic," Witzleben said in an injured tone of voice.

Inglis walked round the Ford Thunderbird, opened the trunk and transferred the cardboard boxes containing the shotgun and Colt revolver to the Dodge sedan, and returned for the small items he'd purchased at the hardware and drug stores. Then he swapped keys with Witzleben.

"Do you remember what you've got to do?" he asked.

Witzleben nodded. "I follow you up Market Street and wait outside the garage. When you reappear, I'll know everything's okay if the front offside window is down and you are driving one-handed, left elbow resting on the door. In that event, I follow you out of town; otherwise, I return to Fisherman's Wharf and wait for you there."

"Good."

"Do you think this plan of yours is going to work?" Witzleben asked.

"It's the only one we've got, unless you can think of something better."

Inglis didn't wait for an answer; he got into the Dodge, backed out of the parking slot near the ferry building and negotiating the one-way circuit around the Justin Herman Plaza, drove up Market Street. At Marshall Square, he turned into the underground parking lot, collected a ticket from the vending machine and made the rounds until he found a vacant space on the second level. Five after three: the slack hour of mid-afternoon and no one about, but that didn't mean he would have the place to himself for ever.

He opened the trunk, found a box spanner in the toolbag and removed both licence plates, then went looking for a replacement set on the bottom level. It was more time-consuming but a whole lot safer than stealing them from a car in the vicinity of the Dodge. A Lincoln Premiere with a Nevada licence number caught his eye and walking behind the limousine, he tackled the rear plate first. Halfway through the task, the sudden squeal of tyres negotiating a tight bend alerted him and he had time to duck out of sight behind a pillar before the vehicle came on down the ramp and cruised slowly past. The driver parked around the corner from his position and cut the engine. A car door slammed, footsteps gradually receded into the distance; then he heard the man close the stairwell door behind him and breathed a little easier. He unscrewed the second bolt, moved round to the grill and removed the other plate.

Back on the second level, Inglis wasted no time in transferring the stolen plates to the Dodge. Then he opened the cardboard box containing the .32 Colt Diamondback, loaded the cylinder with six rounds and stuffed the revolver into the waistband of his slacks. Three forty-one: the minutes were running away from him and he still had to locate the two-door Jaguar XK120. No sweat there, he told himself. How many jerks were riding around town in a British sports job? Armed with the bottle of Ronson lighter fuel and the fire extinguisher, he started looking for Yeo's pride and joy and was lucky enough to find the car on the same level near the up ramp some twenty odd feet from the pedestrian stairwell.

"Now for the tricky bit," Inglis muttered, as though everything up until then had been child's play.

An export left-hand drive. Yeo hadn't bothered to reverse into the bay which meant that the offside door was farthest away from the stairwell. Inglis moved round to the nearside window, used the fire extinguisher to smash the glass and emptied the bottle of lighter fuel over both seats and the walnut dashboard. Then he struck a match and set fire to the interior. Although he waited until the flames had burned through the leather seats to the horsehair stuffing, he was careful to smother the blaze with the extinguisher before the acrid smoke could reach the attendant on the first level. Satisfied with his handiwork, he then rang Sosna's Men's Outfitters from a pay phone at the top of the stairwell.

"My name's Glossop," he told Yeo when they were connected. "We've never met, but you own a XK120. Right?"

"I have a Jaguar –"

"I'm calling from Marshall Square," Inglis said, cutting him short. "I think you'd better get down here, Mr Yeo. There was a lot of smoke coming from inside your jalopy so I broke the nearside window and put out the fire."

"Fire?"

"Yeah. Looks as though it started behind the dash and spread to the carpet and seats."

"How did you know –?" Yeo began.

"Your name was on the registration slip attached to the steering column, the attendant on the check-out booth told me where you work." Inglis paused, then said, "Look, I don't want to seem pushy, Mr Yeo, but I've got things to do and I don't want to cool my heels here all afternoon."

"I'm coming right now."

"Good, I'll wait by your car," Inglis said and hung up.

He ran down the stairwell to the second level and reached the Jaguar just in time to stand in front of the damaged window as a vehicle headed towards the exit ramp from the floor below. What he didn't need right now was two or more onlookers discussing what had caused the fire; what he did need was some privacy so that he and Yeo could have a secluded chat. Maybe he had overdone the visual effects, but he had to grab Harvey Yeo's attention and distract him just long enough to make the snatch.

Three fifty-eight: what the hell was keeping the jerk? Had he rung his insurance agent, stopped to ask the attendant on the check-out if he'd heard anything about a fire, or what? The heavy clang of the stairwell door, urgent footsteps coming towards him; Inglis looked up and instantly recognised Harvey Yeo, as neat and dapper in a gaberdine suit, button-down shirt and necktie as one of the dummies in his shop window.

"Mr Glossop?" he asked while still a good ten feet away.

"That's me," Inglis said and stepped aside to let him see the damage.

"Oh, my God." Yeo ran forward. "Oh, my God," he repeated and started to open the door.

Inglis drew the .32 Colt Diamondback, rammed the barrel into Yeo's ribs and watched the expression freeze on his face as comprehension slowly dawned. "It's loaded," he whispered, "just in case you had any doubts, Harvey. Only a .32 calibre but it'll still make one hell of a mess of your insides."

"My billfold's in the breast pocket."

"I'm not interested in your money," Inglis told him. "It's you I want."

"Me?" Yeo said and swallowed audibly.

"We're going to stroll over to my car and you're going to act like we're old friends. The gun'll be in my jacket pocket but don't get any wrong ideas. Try to run away or call for help and you're dead meat. You understand what I'm saying?"

"Yes."

"Okay, let's get with it."

He walked Yeo round the level to where the Dodge was parked, then made him crouch down below the rear fender, his hands crossed behind his back. Opening the trunk, Inglis cut a length of rope from the clothes line and used it to tie his wrists. Then he removed the neatly folded handkerchief which was peeping from the top pocket of the gaberdine jacket and gagged him with it.

"Time for you to have a nap," Inglis murmured and clubbed him behind the right ear with the pistol grip.

He bundled Yeo into the trunk, cut another hank from the clothes line and hog-tied both ankles to his wrists so that he couldn't move a muscle. The clack of high heels on concrete and the indistinct voices of two women in conversation provided all the incentive he needed to slam the lid down and tumble into the car. Ignition on, starter button, gun the engine, handbrake off, shift into first, clutch out. The two women reared back and shouted after him as he shot out of the parking bay, turned right and roared off down the straight. Tyres screaming, he took the first bend at over thirty.

The voice of reason counselled him to calm down and he eased his foot on the gas pedal and obediently followed the exit signs. Coming out of the last upward spiral, he lowered the window on his side and kept it down after paying the man in the check-out booth. One hand on the wheel, left elbow on the doorsill; the signal Witzleben was expecting to see when he reappeared on Market Street. A right turn, then three blocks south-west to Van Ness Avenue. Where the hell was Karl Heinz? He searched the wing and rear view mirrors, gave a sigh of relief when he spotted the Ford Thunderbird four vehicles back.

Inglis filtered right into Van Ness and headed north past Symphony Hall, the Opera House, City Hall and the State Building. Beyond the intersection with Golden Gate Avenue, Van Ness became US Highway 101 and from there on, it was pretty well a straight run all the way out to the Presidion and the Golden Gate Bridge.

Inglis had just passed the turn-off for Sausalito, north of the bridge, when he remembered he'd left the shotgun and box of shells in the trunk. One blast from the 12-bore at point blank range – that's all it would take to blow his head off when he raised the lid. And that was what he could expect if Yeo managed to break free on the journey.

The telephone call, which Halina had been expecting ever since she'd been interviewed by the man from the Burns Agency, was put through to her office at the branch of Sosna Fashions on Sutter Street a few minutes before five o'clock. The last time she had spoken to Kimber was when they had said goodbye in a small apartment in the Rue de Londres behind the Gare St Lazare; now, over twelve years later, he sounded just the same.

"Michael, Michael," she said with genuine tenderness. "How wonderful to hear your voice again after all these years. Where are you calling from?"

"The King George Hotel."

"You're here in San Francisco?" Some of the warmth left her voice when she said, "God, that's marvellous."

"I need to see you, Halina."

How like Michael, she thought, to get straight to the point without any false expression of sentiment. In pursuit of the truth, he was the most dangerous man she had ever met. Not for the first time, she wondered why on earth he had joined the Diplomatic Service when, apart from his language qualifications, he was so obviously unsuited for it.

"I need to see you," he repeated, this time with what she thought was something akin to longing in his voice.

"When?"

"Tonight."

"We're meeting some people for dinner at seven thirty."

"Please, Halina, it's very important. Couldn't we take up half an hour of your time beforehand?"

"We?"

"Leon Jarrell is with me."

"You mean to say you've kept in touch all these years?"

"Hardly."

Halina smiled to herself. Michael never did things by half; he had hired the Burns Agency to find Leon just as he had with her.

"Do you know where we live, Michael?" she asked.

"You have a house on Buchanan Street and Pacific Avenue."

"The Burns Agency has certainly done you proud," she said dryly.

"I believe they have a reputation for giving value for money."

"The house number is 2294, I'll expect you both at six thirty."

"I'll look forward to seeing you again." A slight pause, then, "It's been a long time."

"Too long," Halina murmured and slowly put the phone down.

Twelve years: Michael had taken up his place at Oxford again but had switched from English to Modern Languages. He had come out of the Army not really knowing what he wanted to do and someone he'd met at Colditz had steered him towards the British Foreign Office. But he had spent all his gratuity and run up an overdraft commuting to Paris by boat and train to see her every weekend he could. And every weekend had been forty-eight hours of tempestuous love-making, laughter, tears, arguments and fights because Michael couldn't understand why her one purpose in life, more important than anything or anyone else, was to seek out and destroy the men who had destroyed her family.

"This hatred you feel is a cancer that will eat you up. For God's sake, let go." Michael's words, but it had been him she had let go one wet afternoon in July '46 after she had received a letter from Adam Nowotko in Warsaw confirming that her mother had been gassed at Auschwitz in November '44.

Halina shook her head as if it would rid her mind of the past, reached for the phone and rang the house on Buchanan Street to warn Luis, their Filipino houseboy, that two guests would be arriving for drinks at six thirty. Then she called the branch on Market Street and got David Carman, the assistant manager.

"I really wanted to speak to Harvey," she told him.

"He went out about an hour ago, Miss Sosna, some problem with his Jaguar." Carman paused, then said, "Can I give him a message?"

"Yes. Would you tell him that two old friends are having drinks with us tonight and would he please try to be home by six thirty. Also, I'm going to book a table at the Top of the Mark for seven thirty."

"All four of you are going on to dinner?"

"No, David, just Harvey and me. It's a way of making sure our guests don't outstay their welcome."

Halina put the phone down and left her desk to open the small combination safe behind the painting by Jan Styka, the Polish artist, in her office. Sifting through the contents, she took out a manilla envelope and opened it. The glossy photograph inside had been taken on the United Nations Plaza in New York and showed a portly-looking man handing a package to a young, fair-haired male. The package contained twenty-five thousand dollars, the recipient was a Polish Intelligence officer attached to the Delegation, and the donor was Karl Heinz Witzleben.

Thirty-seven miles north of San Francisco, Inglis turned off US 101 on to State Highway 37 and headed north-east to cross the Petaluma River into Sonoma County, the wine-growing country. Everything was looking good; the Ford Thunderbird was roughly thirty yards in rear, the road ahead was deserted and Yeo was being as quiet as a dormouse in the trunk. At Sears Point, he headed north on Highway 121 and continued on past the racetrack towards the Sonoma Valley Airport.

The sun was just above the ridge line now, throwing the brown mountain tops into sharp relief. Below the crest, it cast fingers of light through the wide belt of fir trees; in the valley floor, the grape vines were already in shadow.

In 1940, when an Unterscharführer with the Leibstandarte Regiment, he had drunk the Loire Valley dry, but no matter what the French liked to think, they didn't have a monopoly on good wine. The Chardonnay, Sauvignon and Fume Blanc white grapes didn't come any better than they did in the Napa and Sonoma Valleys; and if you were into red, the Cabernet Sauvignon and Pinot Noir took some beating. He should know, he had been up and down these valleys on vacation a good few times in the last eight years, and no one had sampled more wines than he.

Big Bend, across the head of Sonoma Creek and on towards Schellville; the narrow highway was running in an easterly direction now, the signs of habitation few and far between. Angelo's Wine Country Deli with a large red cow on the roof, a winery and a store with a faded sign he couldn't read in the half light. Three miles beyond Schell Creek, Inglis spotted a narrow track leading into the pines and quickly braked to a halt. He shifted into reverse, forced Witzleben to back up, then signalling a left turn, he pulled off the highway. The track dipped below the road, carved a zig-zag path through the trees and led to a fire-break that was wide enough for him to swing the Dodge completely round. He switched off the engine, then waited for Witzleben to draw up alongside before he got out of the car.

"You want to open the trunk, Karl Heinz?" he asked and tossed the keys to the older man.

Inglis positioned himself off to one flank and trained the Colt revolver on the target area. If Yeo had managed to free himself, the Herr Doktor would be the one who got blasted with the 12-bore. The American, however, would be dead a split second after Witzleben bought it. In the event, the projected scenario didn't materialise; when the trunk was opened, Yeo was still hog-tied, unable to move his limbs.

Inglis pocketed the Colt revolver, took out the pump-action shotgun and breaking the seal on the box of cartridges, loaded the magazine with five shells.

"Hold this," he told Witzleben, "and try not to blow your head off."

"What are you planning to do?"

"We're going to need all the co-operation we can get from that tailor's dummy so I'm going to convince him why he should give it freely."

"You mean to hurt him?"

"That's the general idea, Karl Heinz. If you feel squeamish about it, take a walk in the woods while I'm attending to Harvey."

Inglis cut the rope which hog-tied Yeo's wrists and ankles with the pair of scissors, then he grabbed a fistful of hair and hauled him out of the trunk. The gag reduced an agonised cry to a muffled grunt but even had he been allowed full voice, it would have had no effect on Inglis. Two years on anti-partisan duty in Poland and the Ukraine had anaesthetised any feeling of compassion he might once have had. When it came to inflicting pain, he was the kind of expert who enjoyed his work. Propping Yeo against the car, he used him as a punchbag, hooking with both fists into his stomach and ribs until he went down.

"That's just for openers," Inglis said, dragging him to his feet. "Now the questions begin. First thing I want to know is how much cash you keep in the house, then I want a comprehensive list of your wife's jewellery – diamonds, sapphires, emeralds, rubies and pearls. You get the drift?"

Yeo was way ahead of him and was anxiously nodding his head long before he posed the question.

"Good." Inglis smiled grimly. "One other thing – don't start screaming the moment the gag is removed or I'll give you something to really yell about."

The threat was unnecessary. Yeo could see they were off the beaten track and would guess they were miles from anywhere. Even if he were stupid enough to shout for help, the chances of anyone hearing him were next to zero.

"Whenever you're ready, Harvey," he said casually.

Yeo licked his lips. "There's probably about nine hundred dollars in the bedroom safe. I don't know how much Halina keeps in her purse."

"Nine hundred?" Inglis shook his head. "That's pretty disappointing. What about your wife's jewellery?"

"She has a two-carat solitaire, a half hoop of diamonds, a sapphire and diamond ring, an emerald brooch and ear rings, a string of pearls, some opals – I can't remember everything, but all her jewellery is insured for twenty thousand dollars."

"It'll do as long as the lady delivers the stuff in person."

"I doubt if Halina will agree to do that."

"I think she will if you ask her nicely." Inglis gagged him again, reached inside the trunk for the pair of scissors and opened the blades. "Hold still, Harvey," he said in a soothing bedside manner worthy of the archetypal country doctor. "I don't want to hurt you more than is strictly necessary."

He eased one of the blades into the right eardrum, then jabbed the point into the tympanic membrane. It was one of the persuasive techniques he had used on the Untermenschen during the war and he knew the pain was agonising. Yeo stood on tiptoe, his eyes bulging out of their sockets, blood trickling from the ruptured eardrum.

"I want you to remember how much that hurt when you talk to Halina," Inglis said, then bundled him into the trunk and closed the lid.

"Did you have to do that?" Witzleben asked.

"You were watching then?"

"From a distance; I didn't like what I saw."

Inglis lit a cigarette, drew the smoke down on to his lungs and slowly exhaled. "You don't like the heat, you shouldn't have lit the fire."

"That's no answer."

"Aw, for Christ sake, Karl Heinz, what are you making a fuss about? We're going to kill him and the Sosna woman before the night's out."

"What you did was unnecessary."

"No." Inglis wagged a finger under his nose. "No, you're wrong. As a result of the pain I inflicted on him, Yeo is going to be very convincing when he telephones his wife."

"From where?" Witzleben demanded agitatedly. "How many pay phones have you seen on Highway 121?"

"There's a General Store a mile back down the road, we'll borrow theirs."

"You don't think the owners will object? Perhaps you are also hoping they won't remember our faces?"

"Who said I was planning to leave any witnesses behind?" Inglis said icily.

CHAPTER 25

The Pontiac had been delivered to their hotel by the Rent-a-Car agency on Mason at O'Farrell. The 'San Francisco Street, Recreation and Info Map in Superscale' had been purchased by Kimber from a small bookstore near the King George largely because Jarrell preferred driving to navigating.

"You get me to Buchanan Street and I'll help you look for the house number, whatever that might be."

"2294." Kimber pinpointed their position on the map, then said, "According to the Burns Agency, it's called 'Praga'."

"'Praga'? Wasn't she born there?"

"Yes, near the Wilno Station."

"Well, I'll be damned, who'd have thought Halina would be that sentimental?"

Kimber doubted if sentiment had anything to do with it. Halina's father had wanted to be a concert pianist but lacking that indefinable touch that would have singled him out from the rest of the field, had ended up scratching a living as a music teacher. Her mother had been trained as a seamstress and had supplemented the family income dressmaking for some of their wealthier neighbours. Halina had been an only child and they had wanted to do the best they could for her; in calling the house 'Praga', she was almost certainly reminding herself of how far she had come.

"I think we should turn left on Jackson Street up ahead," he said.

"You're the one with the map," Jarrell told him and tripped the traffic indicator.

Every road was a scenic roller-coaster climbing from narrow plateau to narrow plateau, only to drop away sharply from the hillcrest to afford peep views of the ocean. After leaving the hotel, they had made a series of right turns to head north on Taylor Street and on through Nob Hill. Once on Jackson, they would head due east to Pacific Heights.

"How are we doing for time, Michael?"

"No need to put your foot down. The house is less than a mile away and we've got over ten minutes in hand."

"Funny. I thought you'd be in a hurry to see the lady again."

"There's nothing between us any more . . ."

"Oh, sure."

"Listen, I know you didn't come along just for the ride, Leon, but let me do the talking. Okay?"

"So long as you don't let her twist you round her little finger," Jarrell said.

The house on Buchanan Street was exactly what the Burns Agency had said it was, half a million dollars' worth of prime real estate and the nearest thing to a Hollywood set Kimber had seen. Palm trees, lush green lawn, geraniums, exotic azaleas, red and purple bougainvillaea; the garden surrounding the pool was a riot of colour even in the half light of dusk. Against such an opulent backdrop, the Chevrolet station wagon parked outside the integral double garage looked unduly modest.

"I think I could get used to living in a place like this," Jarrell observed dryly.

A Filipino houseboy responded promptly to the door chimes and led them through a hall that was bigger than most New York apartments to an equally impressive drawing room complete with grand piano. There was no doubting that Halina belonged in such a room in such a house. She was wearing open sandals with two-inch heels, a flared black skirt and an oyster-coloured satin blouse. A black patent-leather belt with a gold buckle cinched a narrow waist.

"Michael . . . Leon." She hugged them both in turn, then stepped back a pace and ran a hand through her ash blonde hair. "I can't get over it, neither of you has changed a bit."

Kimber thought it was certainly true of Halina. Forty years of age and there wasn't a line on her face, not a pouch under her green eyes, not a crease mark on her neck. And she was as slim now as she had been in Paris back in '46.

"What will you have to drink, Michael?"

Kimber jerked his head, roused from his reverie. "Oh, a whisky, I think."

"Scotch or Irish?"

"Scotch, please – on the rocks."

"Leon?"

"The same."

"Me too, please, Luis," she said to the Filipino houseboy. "Then you may leave us."

There's nothing between us any more . . . So long as you don't let her twist you round her little finger. Echoes of a conversation not ten minutes old which Kimber preferred to forget because Halina could still mould him like putty, and suddenly it was as if he had never met Jean, never become a stepfather to Alison and never sired a child called Richard.

"I can't think what's keeping Harvey, but he should be –"

"I know what happened at Wolomin," Kimber said abruptly, cutting Halina off in mid-sentence. "Now I'd like to know exactly what sort of deal was made with Witzleben."

Halina turned away from Jarrell, her eyes glinting dangerously. "Just what the hell are you accusing me of, Michael?" she demanded angrily. "Are you implying that I was a traitor?"

"Of course I'm not. But there is evidence that points in that direction. The Gestapo photographed you in Lazienki Park and again outside Kuba's Café some time before the uprising began, yet they never arrested you. Why was that?"

"Because I was negotiating with them on behalf of the Home Army."

"Now I've heard everything," Jarrell said acidly.

"No, you haven't. On or about the eighth of July 1944, three senior officers of the Home Army who had been arrested in the November of the previous year, were suddenly released from the Pawiak Prison. They couldn't think why the Gestapo had let them go, neither could the AK High Command. One theory being mooted was that the Germans had freed the officers in the hope of improving the climate with the Polish Nationalists and were banking on the Katyn massacre to help them form an anti-Bolshevik coalition. Anyway, some ten days later, an intermediary acting with the authority of Oberführer Morgen, commanding the SS police in Warsaw, let it be known they were willing to release a number of high-ranking political prisoners for a consideration."

One of the names on the list had been the Military Liaison Officer from the London-based Polish Government in Exile. The Resistance had therefore been prepared to pay a small fortune to learn what, if anything, he had been forced to tell the Gestapo about the contingency plan for an uprising.

"The small fortune was to be provided by the Nowotko family, without their knowledge of course. Ladislaw Nowotko was known to the Nazis; he was a fanatical anti-Communist, so much so that he became pro-German when they invaded the Soviet Union."

Halina was aware that the Gestapo had photographed her walking arm-in-arm with him in Lazienki Park. Consequently, she had

263

not delivered or accepted any messages for over two months while they checked her out.

"Since I lived with Ladislaw, the Gestapo eventually came to the conclusion that I was of a like mind. As a courier for the AK, I could not have had a better cover. That's why the Home Army refused to authorise his assassination."

"They just traded his art collection to buy their man out of the Pawiak Prison instead." Kimber smiled. "A classic example of poetic justice."

"So a lot of people thought."

"Why did the Home Army choose you as a go-between?" Jarrell asked.

"Because I was already known to the Gestapo and was considered expendable. I was briefed by an Intelligence officer from AK Headquarters who told me I was to spend an hour every morning at Kuba's Café between ten and eleven until the Germans contacted me."

After two uneventful days in succession, it had begun to look as though the deal was off. Then, on the third morning, a twelve-year-old boy had walked up to Halina's table with a note instructing her to go immediately to Chopin's statue in the Saxon Gardens where she would be met by a guide.

"The man who was waiting for me had a cast in his left eye and had Gestapo written all over him. He led me over to an enclosed, steel-bodied army radio truck that was parked a hundred yards or so down the road from the Brühl Palace and told me to get in the back. That's where I met Witzleben and I told him about 'The Garden Bench' by Tissot and the other paintings by Renoir, Monet, Rembrandt and Holbein my father and I had buried on the Nowotko estate at Wolomin. He then informed me when and where the prisoners would be released and I was allowed to go in order to inform the Home Army."

The whole thing had been an elaborate double-cross; the Military Liaison Officer from the Polish Government in Exile had not been released, Halina's father had been forced to show the SS exactly where the paintings had been buried and had then been shot. It had also become rapidly evident to Halina that the Intelligence officer who had briefed her, had done so without first clearing the operation with the AK High Command.

"The man who met me in the Saxon Gardens was Walther Neurath, though I only learned his name on the day when the uprising began and we happened to walk into that checkpoint near Jasna Street."

"They could have been waiting for you," Kimber said slowly.

"No." Halina shook her head. "No, we walked into that road block by pure chance. Of course, I knew Neurath and Witzleben would be looking for me after I discovered they had arrested my parents; that's why I didn't go near the villa in Zoliborz until several days after the uprising had begun."

"And now Witzleben is here in San Francisco."

"Yes, he lives in Sausalito."

The telephone on the occasional table started to ring with a low-pitched insistent burr that was difficult to ignore. Kimber waited to see if Halina was going to answer it but apparently that was something she expected the servants to do.

"And what have you done about him?" he asked when the burring tone ceased.

"I've made him suffer."

"Damn right," Jarrell said angrily. "She's been shaking him down; he's the money tree behind her business."

"Oh, yes, I've bled him white over the years, and you know the best thing about it, Leon? All his money has eventually been channelled back to Poland to help rebuild Warsaw, and he knows it." Halina broke off as Luis entered the room. "Yes, what is it?" she demanded.

"You're wanted on the telephone," Luis told her.

"By whom?"

"A friend of Mr Harvey's. He said it was urgent."

"All right, Luis, I'll take it in here."

With a murmured excuse, Halina lifted the extension on the occasional table by her armchair. The subsequent conversation was entirely one-sided except when punctuated by the occasional terse yes or no from Halina. She didn't have to tell Kimber it was bad news; the way the colour had drained from her face, the strained expression which had replaced it and the way she had suddenly gripped the receiver and pressed it close to her ear said it all for her.

"What's happened?" he asked her quietly.

"It's Harvey . . ." She stood up, causing them both to get to their feet automatically. "He's had a bad accident."

"Which hospital has he been taken to?"

"Hospital?" Halina stared at him blankly, then recovered. "Oh – the San Francisco General."

"We'll drive you there."

"No, Michael." She flapped her hands. "No, I need some time to myself."

"Hey, come on, Halina," Jarrell said. "We're your friends, we can't leave you to face this on your own."

"Please, Leon, it's what I want." She looked to Kimber for support. "You can understand that, can't you?"

"Of course I do." He took hold of her hands and squeezed them gently. "Look, you know where we are staying . . ."

"Yes, you told me this afternoon."

"Then promise me you'll phone and let us know how Harvey is and if there's anything we can do?"

"Yes, Michael." She nodded. "Yes, I will."

At that particular moment, he knew that Halina would have promised him the moon and the stars just to get rid of them. Jarrell protested all the way to the door that they shouldn't leave her to face the crisis alone and was still protesting when Kimber shoved him into the Pontiac.

"You want to watch what you're doing, fella," he snarled. "No one pushes me around."

"Just shut up and drive."

"The hell you say."

Jarrell fired the engine into life, slammed the gear shift into first and let the clutch out. He took off in a shower of gravel, hit the brakes at the end of the drive and made a skid turn into Buchanan Street.

"Turn right on Pacific Avenue," Kimber told him, "then pull up, switch off and douse the lights."

"Jesus H Christ . . ."

"Harvey Yeo hasn't had an accident – I'd bet my life on it – but somebody has certainly put the fear of God into Halina. If I'm right, it won't be too long before she comes barrelling past us in that Chevrolet station wagon."

"That's if she comes this way."

"She has to," Kimber told him. "Part of the road's up and you can only go north on Buchanan."

Halina tossed the rest of the whisky down her throat and ran upstairs to the master bedroom. That agonised scream when the caller had put Harvey on the line was going to live along with her other nightmares for the rest of time. Kimber had sensed that something was terribly wrong, but he couldn't have heard it because she had kept the receiver pressed tight against her ear. Willing herself to stay calm, she unhooked the picture which concealed the wall safe and placed it on a chair. For a few panic-stricken moments she couldn't remember the combination, then it came to her – the month, the year of her birth and the date – and she spun the dial through the correct sequence.

She emptied the cash and jewellery into her handbag, then reached in and took out the small automatic which had been placed right at the back of the safe. A .25 calibre Bernadelli; Harvey had decided they would all sleep easier in their beds with a pistol in the house and had purchased a hand gun which could almost have fitted into his vest pocket.

The small box of .25 rounds had never been opened; ripping off the seal, Halina fed seven rounds into the magazine, then left the automatic on the bed while she fetched a camelhair jacket from the wardrobe and put it on. She tucked the pistol into the right-hand pocket where she could get at it in a hurry and went downstairs.

"Are you alone?" the caller had asked. "Answer yes or no." And when she had intimated that she had company, he had told her that she had exactly thirty minutes in which to wind up the party and get her ass down to Sosna Fashions on Sutter Street or he would make her a widow.

Luis met her in the hall with more questions than she had the patience to answer.

"Mr Harvey wants me to meet him downtown," she told the Filipino. "I don't know what time we'll be back."

The Chevrolet chose this moment to act up, the engine turning over sluggishly as if the battery were flat. There was a lot of humidity in the air and she supposed the leads were damp, a cry she had picked up from Harvey. But he had never told her what the cure was and she went on cranking the V8 until, in answer to her silent prayer, it finally caught and spluttered into life. Before the engine was firing on all eight cylinders, she shifted into drive and moved off.

Sixteen minutes left to reach the branch on Sutter Street; seventeen minutes and Harvey would be dead. What kind of man would kill another human being because a third party was one minute late for a phone call? A stupid question considering what had happened in Warsaw where some of the stormtroopers had had their cronies photograph them in the act of killing a hostage.

The Chevrolet breasted a steep incline and became airborne for a good ten feet before meeting the road again with a spine-jarring crunch and a loud metallic clang from the shock absorbers. "Slow down, the last thing you need right now is a ticket." Obeying her own advice, Halina caught a red light at the next three intersections. In a hurry to make up for lost time, she almost ran down a young woman alighting from a cable car at the Washington Street and

267

Leavenworth stop. The brakeman shouted something after her but the expletive was drowned by the exhaust. Two right turns and she was in Sutter Street looking for a parking space and getting more and more frustrated because it seemed the Fates were conspiring against her. Then, two hundred yards beyond Sosna Fashions, a Cadillac pulled away from the kerb and she slipped into the vacant slot.

Six minutes in hand; there was no need to run but the compulsion to do so was overwhelming. Halina grabbed her handbag, scrambled out of the car and slammed the door behind her. Heels clip-clopping on the sidewalk, she ran back to the shop and let herself in. She reached for the light switch, thought better of it and, groping her way through the showroom, went on up to the office on the second floor. Three minutes to go; she sank down in the swivel chair behind the desk and lit a cigarette to steady her nerves.

Inglis filled the glass and passed it to Witzleben who sat facing him on the floor behind the shop counter. Harvey Yeo was keeping them company but he was unable to move a muscle, much less ask for a drink. The bottle of Southern Comfort had been provided free of charge but without the knowledge of Per and Britta Uddenholm, owners of the General Store on Highway 121. They were both upstairs in their bedroom gagged with adhesive tape and trussed up like a couple of turkeys by their fifteen-year-old daughter, Kerstin. As soon as she had completed this task to his satisfaction, Inglis had taken the girl into the adjoining room and done the same to her.

The whole thing had gone like clockwork. They had driven up to the store a few minutes before closing time and he had held the family at gunpoint while Karl Heinz had parked both cars behind the building where they couldn't be seen from the road. No fuss, no problems and no last-minute shoppers either, but now the Herr Doktor had gotten chicken-hearted and needed to fortify himself with Dutch courage from a bottle.

"How much longer, Ray?"

"Give it a couple more minutes and then I'll phone her."

"That's not what I meant."

Witzleben spoke slowly and deliberately like a man who knew he'd had too much to drink and was trying to hide the fact.

"You've had enough," Inglis said and moved the bottle of Southern Comfort out of his reach.

"Oh, indeed I have." Witzleben placed a hand across his throat. "In fact, I've had it up to here."

The gutless old bastard wanted to call it off and walk away from the situation. Did he seriously believe that having kidnapped and tortured Harvey Yeo, he and the Sosna woman were going to forgive and forget? Were the Uddenholms going to tell them they had no hard feelings? Would they shit. The whole damned family would troop down to the Sheriff's office and file a list of complaints as long as your arm.

"It's too late for second thoughts, Karl Heinz," he said grimly. "Kidnapping, assault with a deadly weapon, demanding money with menaces; you're a party to all three felonies. The least you're looking at is thirty years in the slammer before you're eligible for parole. That's going to make you, what? Eighty-seven?"

"Eighty-eight," Witzleben said morosely.

"You think you're going to live that long, Karl Heinz?"

"No." The answer came in a faint, despairing whisper.

"Right." Inglis glanced at his wristwatch. "Time we made another phone call," he said, then froze, pointing like a gun dog.

A vehicle some distance off but definitely coming their way. It would be the first one since they had taken the place over, but the driver would have no reason to stop. Everything was as it should be. There were just the usual low wattage security lights showing in the store itself and the curtains were drawn in the upstairs rooms which faced the road. Furthermore, at seven forty in the evening, no one would expect the shop to be open.

The vehicle came on, the whine from the prop shaft suggesting it was a truck rather than a car. Witzleben had stuffed a knuckle into his mouth and was gnawing at it like a dog with a bone. Two small orbs of light appeared in the distance and rapidly became larger, then the beams played on the shop front, briefly illuminating the interior as the truck roared on by making a noise like a tank. The deep-throated snarl from the holed silencer got fainter and fainter until it finally died away altogether.

"You see, Karl Heinz – what did I tell you? There's nothing to worry about."

Inglis reached for the telephone which he had placed on the floor between them and dialled the number of Sosna Fashions on Sutter Street. The number rang only once before she answered his call.

"It's me again," he said gruffly.

"How's my husband?"

"He's okay."

"Let me speak to him."

"Later, after we've talked business."

"I've emptied the safe at home and brought everything with me."

"How much are we talking about?"

"The jewellery is insured for twenty thousand dollars and I've got about six hundred and fifty in bills."

"Your husband reckoned there was about nine hundred in the safe."

"He's mistaken."

"That's too bad." Inglis smiled to himself. The amount of hard cash and the value of the jewellery was unimportant; they were merely stage props which would set the police haring off in the wrong direction after the bodies had been found. But he enjoyed the mental torture he was inflicting on the Sosna woman and there was a definite purpose behind it. By the time he had finished with her, she would be as malleable as one of Pavlov's dogs.

"What about the safe in your office?" he asked.

"This is Sosna Fashions; when people buy from me, they either pay by cheque, credit card or charge it to their account. There is just the float in the safe and that amounts to exactly four hundred and fifty dollars in small bills and loose change."

"Bring it with you."

"Where to?"

Inglis frowned. Far from being malleable, the Sosna woman was becoming truculent. But he had an ace up his sleeve which would bring the bitch to heel. "Head north on 101," he told her, "then branch off on to Highway 37 beyond Ignacio. Switch to 121 at Sears Point and stay on it until you come to the General Store on the left-hand side of the road two miles beyond Schell Creek. You got all that?"

"Yes."

"So let's hear it from you."

Halina Sosna repeated everything he'd told her practically word for word, then said, "Now will you let me talk to my husband?"

"Sure." Inglis laid the phone down while he removed the gag from Yeo's mouth. "Say hello to your wife, Harvey," he said and motioned Witzleben to hold the receiver towards the younger man.

"Halina?" Yeo cleared his throat. "Halina, please do what the man asks."

Inglis grabbed the phone before he could say any more. "That is it; you heard him, he's still breathing but he won't be if you go to the police."

"I've no intention of doing so."

"You hadn't better because my partner is out there right now watching the shop and he'll be sitting on your tail all the way."

"I've already told you . . ."

"You've got fifty minutes to get here, lady. This should help speed you on your way." Inglis took out the scissors and this time jabbed the point into Yeo's left ear, producing a scream of agony that reached a note high enough to shatter a crystal goblet. "How's that for encouragement?" he said and hung up.

Witzleben looked as though he was about to throw up and Yeo was writhing on the floor, tossing his head from side to side while moaning like a soul in torment.

"Don't just sit there," Inglis said harshly. "Gag him."

Leaving Witzleben to get on with it, he picked up the shotgun and went on up to the living quarters above the store. Before looking in on Per and Britta Uddenholm, he leaned the Ithaca pump-action against the wall and took out the Colt Diamondback. Then he opened the door and walked into their bedroom.

Per Uddenholm happened to be lying on that side of the bed nearest to him but even if he hadn't been, Inglis would still have dealt with him first. A chair cushion served as a muffler for the revolver; pressing it against Uddenholm's face, he shot him in the head. One down, two to go. Ein, Zwei, Zufer – it was quite like old times.

CHAPTER 26

Kimber spotted Halina in the rear view mirror and immediately sank down in the seat until his head was below the level of the backrest. Presently he heard the sound of footsteps, then the kerbside door opened and she got into the Chevrolet.

"Hi," he said. "You left the car unlocked."

"Jesus, Michael." She flinched as if he'd struck her, then turned on him, her face contorted with fury. "You want to get out of this fucking car under your own steam or do I have to call a cop?"

"Why don't you drive on to wherever it is you've been told to go?" he said calmly.

"Are you deaf . . . ?"

"Of course, if I'm right and Harvey has been kidnapped, you really should call the cops, but I don't think you will."

"Don't bank on it."

Kimber ignored the latent threat. "This may look like a kidnapping," he continued, "but I've a hunch the person who phoned you has set a time limit that rules out any question of involving the police."

"Please, Michael, please get out of the car. He's got someone watching the shop."

"Has he set a rendezvous?"

"Yes."

"Then I'd stake my life he's bluffing about that."

"It's not your life that's at stake, Michael, but I can see it's a waste of time arguing with you."

Halina started the car, checked to make sure it was safe to pull across on to the right side of the road and drew away from the kerb.

"Where are we going?"

"The Sonoma Valley, to a General Store on Highway 121 two miles beyond Schell Creek."

"How far is that?" Kimber asked and looked back over his shoulder.

"I don't know – thirty-six to forty miles. Who's behind us? Leon?"

"Yes. Try not to lose him."

"Jesu. Every time they put Harvey on the phone, he's screaming in agony and you're worried Leon might not be there the next time you look round."

"We have to stop somewhere – a filling station on the outskirts of town . . ."

"No dammit, we're not stopping anywhere . . ."

"Leon has to know what's happening . . ."

"I'll tell you what's happening; that psychopath who's got Harvey is going to put a bullet in his head if I'm a minute late, and I believe him. Harvey may not mean a hell of a lot to you but he's all I've got."

Plain, quiet, colourless and ineffectual; that was how various colleagues had described Yeo. Listening to Halina, it seemed they didn't know him all that well. To Halina, he was something else. Harvey was the only man she had ever met who hadn't used her. Every one else had; Adam Nowotko, his father, Ladislaw, even Kimber to some extent. But Harvey had been the constant, uncomplaining, undemanding friend who had always been there when she needed him.

"Do you remember telling me in Paris that the hatred I felt for Witzleben was a cancer that would eat me up? Well, Harvey was the one who showed me how I could even the score. Bleeding Witzleben white was only part of it. I have a photograph at home which caught him in the act of passing an envelope to a Polish Intelligence officer in New York. Of course, we arranged things so that he was under the impression he was dealing with my lawyer back east."

It was, Kimber thought, a pretty neat way of compromising him. Having just provided Witzleben with a new identity, the CIA would not take kindly to the notion that he was in the pay of a Hostile Intelligence Service, and that was how the photograph would look to them.

"But now you've pushed him a shade too far."

"No, Michael, you're the one who did that. You told the Burns Agency there was no need for their man to be discreet. 'Be as open as you like,' you told them, 'I want my friends to know I'm looking for them.' When Witzleben heard that, he realised he could never reach an accommodation with you. You're the Mr Incorruptible who wants to put him behind bars, and even if it were only for a year or so, that would be an eternity at his time of life."

It was tantamount to an admission that she believed Witzleben

273

was behind the kidnapping. But this particular snatch had not been carried out for the usual reason.

"How much have you got in that handbag?" Kimber asked her.

"Twenty-one thousand." Halina slowed down and got into the lane as they approached the toll booths on the Golden Gate Bridge. Opening her purse, she passed a handful of coins to the attendant and sped on through. "Give or take a few cents," she added dryly.

"You think that will be enough?"

"I don't think money is part of the equation."

"No, Harvey is the bait to draw you into an ambush."

"You think I don't know that, Michael?"

"So what are you going to do about it?"

"I've got a .25 automatic in my handbag."

Halina back in control of herself, cool to the point of iciness, the way he had seen her in Warsaw. She had no idea what she might be walking into, but she had this itty-bitty .25 calibre piece and more courage than was good for anyone. But Halina couldn't go in there blind; at the very least, they had to work out some sort of drill for approaching the RV.

It took all Kimber's considerable powers of persuasion to make her see that but finally, one mile from Sear's Point, she agreed to pull off the road and stop long enough for him to walk back and brief Jarrell. When he returned to the Chevrolet, she merely started the engine and moved on. It was only after they had turned on to Highway 121 that suddenly, and for no apparent reason, she said, "About Maria . . ."

Inglis lit another cigarette from the stub of the one he had been smoking, then dropped the glowing ember on to the floor and stepped on it. The store was set back a hundred feet from the highway and, except for an oak tree right and forward of the building, he had an unrestricted field of fire. In war, the high ground was the dominating factor, no matter how small the battlefield or how few men were involved. The oak tree was the best fire position because the Sosna woman would be unable to use it for cover and he would have her cold. Unfortunately, that meant leaving Karl Heinz alone with Yeo and he couldn't afford to let him out of his sight.

The Herr Doktor was a liability; he had lost his nerve and could no longer be trusted. Left to his own devices for too long, he might do something stupid like cutting Yeo free, in the hope that he would be doing himself some good. There were three dead people upstairs and Witzleben had known what his intentions were when he'd

274

picked up the shotgun. But in his present state of mind, he was capable of deluding himself that he hadn't been an accessory to murder. And this was the man who had planned the theft of the Nowotko art collection, had recruited Walther Neurath and Oberführer Helmuth Morgen and had found a Swiss banker from Estavayer le Lac who could be trusted to collect the paintings and look after them once they had arrived at Dortmund in the boxcar.

Three years ago, this was the man who had come to him wanting to invest in his used-car business. If he had known then that the Sosna woman was bleeding him and that Karl Heinz was looking for a refuge to save what was left of his fortune, he wouldn't have touched his money with a barge-pole. It was that damned investment which had kept him tied to Karl Heinz and had led to this.

Inglis turned about and beckoned Witzleben to join him in the shop doorway where Yeo couldn't hear them. "She'll be here quite soon now," he said in a low voice.

"Gott sei Dank . . ."

"You're not in the Fatherland now, Karl Heinz, and keep your voice down."

"Ja – I mean yes."

Inglis stared at him, wondered if the cretin was capable of following even the simplest of instructions in his present state, then dismissed the question from his mind because there was no way he could spring the ambush unaided.

"All right, Karl Heinz," he said slowly, "here's what you do. When the Sosna woman arrives, I want you to open the door and push Harvey forward where she can see him. Keep the bitch talking as long as you can so that I can slip upstairs and line her up from one of the windows on the landing."

"What do I say to her?"

"You tell the Sosna woman she has to walk forward and put her jewellery on the ground before you'll let Yeo go. That's when I'll drop her."

"Good." Witzleben nodded. "Very good."

Inglis took out the Colt Diamondback and gave it to him. "I doubt you will need this," he said, "but you'd better have it just in case."

In reloading the revolver, he had deliberately left the chamber at the ten position empty as a precaution. There was no telling how Witzleben was going to behave and he didn't want him acting precipitately. If he did lose his head, the empty chamber would be the one which ended up under the hammer when he squeezed the trigger.

Kimber watched the odometer counting off the miles. According to the instructions Halina had been given, the General Store was two miles beyond Schell Creek and there was only eight tenths of a mile to go.

"Slow down," he said suddenly.

"What for?"

"Just do as I tell you." He reached behind him for the courtesy light in the roof, removed the plastic cover and took out the bulb. "Something I should have done before," he said. "Open the door and the light comes on, illuminating the interior. Makes you a perfect target for a sniper as you start to get out of the car."

"I hope you can shoot as straight as you can think," Halina told him. "That's my pistol you've got."

Three tenths of a mile to go, Jarrell somewhere behind them driving without lights. The ambushers would be expecting one vehicle, not two; when the dark shape of the Pontiac suddenly arrived on the scene, it might throw them for precious seconds. It wasn't much of a plan but it was the only one they had.

"The store should be around the bend ahead," Kimber said.

"Right." Halina nodded, gripped the steering wheel tighter.

The headlights on full beam swept straight across the road and picked out a wooden building which stood roughly one hundred feet back from the highway at an oblique angle.

"That's it," Kimber said loudly. "Get the oak tree between us and the store."

Halina put the wheel hard over, shot across the highway and raised a cloud of dust as she slewed to a halt on the baked earth. Before the Chevrolet stopped moving, Kimber went out the nearside door, hit the ground with his left shoulder and rolled over. He picked himself up and keeping low, scuttled round the front end of the car and moved up to the oak. Transferring the Bernadelli automatic to his left hand, he edged round the tree and took stock. Dimmed lighting in the store, two windows overlooking the yard on the floor above. Windows spaced well apart, could be at either end of a transverse landing which fronted the store.

Halina got out of the car and moved forward until she was level with Kimber on the other side of the tree. "Harvey?" She raised her voice. "Where are you, Harvey?"

"He's over here in the doorway with me, Mrs Yeo."

"Witzleben," she said quietly for Kimber's benefit, then raised her voice again. "Let me see him."

"Very well."

A figure emerged from the entrance to the store and moved a few paces forward into the moonlight.

"Now let's see the colour of your money. Come out and put it on the ground directly in front of your husband."

This is it, Kimber thought. The moment Halina shows herself, someone's going to blast her. But where from? And where the hell is Jarrell? He scanned the floor above the shop again; curtains drawn in the left-hand window, open in the right. Jesus Christ, that has to be where the sniper is. He raised the pistol, left arm extended as though fighting a duel, and squeezed off two shots in rapid succession. A shotgun boomed inside the building and blew the glass out of the window frame.

Jarrell saw the stab of flame from the shotgun as he felt his way round the curve. In one synchronised movement, he switched on the headlights, tripped them to full beam, flattened the accelerator and aimed the Pontiac straight at the Store. From the window above, the gunman pumped round after round at the car, shattering the radiator and windshield and blowing the nearside front wheel. Still doing close on thirty, the Pontiac ploughed through the plate-glass window, knocked over two freezer chests and came to a dead halt with three quarters of the chassis inside the building. Thrown forward by the impact, Jarrell fell across the steering wheel and set the horn blaring.

Witzleben raised the Colt to fire at the man standing beside the oak tree, found Harvey Yeo was in the way and decided to shoot him in the back first. Taking aim, he squeezed the trigger and couldn't understand it when the hammer went forward and there was just a sharp click. Untrained in the use of firearms, he was slow to react and was hit below the right collar bone before he thought to squeeze the trigger again. The punch from the .25 calibre bullet numbed the whole of his right side and the revolver slipped from his grasp. Inside the store, a dazed and bleeding Jarrell crawled out of the Pontiac and started looking for something he could use as a weapon.

Oblivious of the gunfire, Yeo was still on his feet, staggering towards the Chevrolet station wagon like a drunk. Halina broke cover and screamed at him to get down as she raced across the yard in her stockinged feet. With four rounds left, Kimber could only provide her with a minimal amount of covering fire, but he did the best he could, firing intermittently to keep the gunman upstairs in doubt. Out of the corner of his eye, he saw Halina deliberately collide with Yeo and knock him to the ground. The shotgun boomed for the fifth time and then she was up and running again straight at Witzleben.

Witzleben saw her coming and moved back inside the shop as fast as he could. He made no attempt to retrieve the Colt .32 revolver; the one thought uppermost in his mind was that he had to reach the Ford Thunderbird he had parked behind the store before she caught up with him.

Jarrell heard him blundering through the store and bobbed up from behind the counter, a tin of pineapple in each hand. He missed the target with the first one and smashed a display cabinet instead; the second can hit Witzleben behind the right ear and knocked him down. As he ducked below the counter to grab another two cans, he heard a shot.

Halina moved forward, pistol in hand. She had hit Witzleben in the left leg with his own gun, but he was still crawling frantically towards the door at the back of the shop which she guessed led to the stockroom. She called on him to stop and was glad when he didn't because it gave her the excuse she needed. Moving slightly to one flank, she took a deliberate aim and shot him in the head. Then she heard a movement behind her and spinning round, she fired again.

"Jesus H Christ," Jarrell yelled, "what are you trying to do? Kill me too?"

"Stay where you are, Leon."

"Don't worry, I'm not going to move an inch. I've seen you in action and you're a goddamned killer."

"Just shut up and listen." Halina placed a finger across her mouth, then mouthed the word again.

Inglis sat on the floor nursing his injured right hand. He had just blasted off the last shell at the Sosna bitch and her stupid husband when a freak shot had drilled a neat hole through the back of his wrist and made an even bigger but less tidy one when the soft-nosed bullet had exited from the palm. All fingers and thumbs, he set about reloading the pump-action shotgun with his left hand. One, two, three, four, five; he pressed the cartridges into the magazine and jacked a shell into the breech; then holding the shotgun in his left hand, he edged his way along the L-shaped landing towards the fire escape at the back. The ambush had gone off at half cock and there was no retrieving the situation. With no plan in mind beyond getting to the Dodge sedan at the back, he painfully raised the window with his injured hand and climbed out on to the fire escape.

He was halfway down the first flight of steps when a bullet struck the metal handrail and ricocheted. Kimber. The Englishman had read his mind and moved round to the back of the store and now there was only one way he could go. Turning about, Inglis ran back up the fire escape and scrambled through the open window; then hugging the butt to his left side and supporting the barrel in the crook of his right arm, he went on down the staircase to the store below.

One bullet left. Kimber didn't need to be reminded that this meant he had no margin for error. He had seen Halina run into the store and had heard three muffled shots, the last two in quick succession after a distinct pause. But just who had shot whom was the sixty-four-dollar question he couldn't answer. He moved forward, stopped at the bottom of the fire escape to kick off his shoes, then went on up in his socks.

The two pistol shots came from somewhere inside the building and were followed by a single deafening boom from the shotgun. Upstairs or downstairs? Kimber couldn't place the sound accurately and was undecided. Six years as an infantryman had, however, taught him that if you wanted to stay alive, taking short cuts was out.

He climbed in through the window and checked out the rooms off the landing. A young girl lying on the bed, a bloodstained pillow over her face; the parents in the adjoining room, gagged, bound, and staring up at the ceiling through sightless eyes. Three cold-blooded, vicious murders; Kimber thought he was going to be sick. Closing the door behind him, he moved back to the staircase and went on down to the store, uncertain what other horrors he would find.

The store was a small battlefield. A foot or so from the stockroom, Witzleben lay stomach-down on the floor, his head over on one side. What was left of his glasses was attached by one arm to his left ear. Beyond him, the second man was sitting down, shoulders resting against a freezer chest, head bowed as though inspecting the two bullet wounds in his heart. Some ten feet to the right of the dead gunman, Jarrell was crouching over Halina. He had removed his jacket and was using it as a pillow under her head. Her shoes were missing, both nylons were laddered and the satin blouse was more red than its original colour; Kimber noticed all the incongruous things as he drew nearer.

The 12-bore had all but severed her left arm above the elbow and had made a god-awful mess of her chest. Jarrell had applied a tourniquet to the stump but he couldn't stop the internal bleeding and her face already looked pinched and drawn.

"We'd better call an ambulance."

"I already have," Jarrell told him. "I rang for one while you were pussyfooting around upstairs."

"Are you okay, Leon?"

"Just a little shook up, that's all. I tell you . . . I've never seen anything like it . . . " He spoke jerkily, pausing frequently in the middle of a sentence. "This guy comes blundering into the store . . . shotgun cradled across his chest . . . and looking straight at me . . . and I know I'm looking at death. Only before he can squeeze the trigger . . . Halina calls out and says . . . 'Over here, Scharführer . . . and shoots him twice as he swings round to face her . . . then the shotgun goes off and Halina's on the floor."

"Maria." Kimber saw the name form on her lips.

"Where's Yeo?" he asked Jarrell loudly.

"Outside, I guess."

"You go and see to him. I'll take over here."

It wasn't that he could do a better job than Leon, but he was closer to Halina and he wanted her to know that he understood. Kneeling beside her, he took hold of her right hand, willing her to hold on. "It's all right," he murmured, "I'm here."

Her eyes searched his and he remembered what she had told him when they had stopped at Sears Point. 'About Maria – she had just delivered some routine papers to the Wehrmacht Headquarters and was leaving the Brühl Palace at the very same moment when Neurath and I were walking towards the radio truck. Later, when we came face to face at the Post Office in Napoleon Square, she told me she had seen me before but couldn't remember where. Maria was like a dog with a bone, she kept worrying at it, trying to extract the marrow. Finally, she made the connection the night we abandoned the Old Town.

'I kept waiting for her to denounce me as a collaborator and I was terrified because I was amongst strangers who'd never served with me before and there was no way I could prove the AK had used me as a go-between with Witzleben. I had to know what she intended to do but I didn't have an opportunity to speak to her alone.'

The opportunity had occurred in the sewers after the garrison had started to withdraw from the Old Town. Halina had just led a group from the Miodowa sector as far as the waterfall in the main channel and was returning to collect another when she spotted Maria on the opposite catwalk.

'I called to her, Michael, and as she spun round, she lost her footing on the slimy pathway and fell over. I heard her head strike the cobbles with a sickening thud and there was a loud splash as she toppled into the sewer. I couldn't find her, Michael, I ran up and down the catwalk shining my flashlight on the murky water but I couldn't find her.'

"It was an accident," Kimber said aloud.

"I know that."

He looked up and saw Jarrell standing there supporting Yeo with an arm around his waist.

"It was my fault for spooking her, she didn't mean to shoot at me."

They were talking at cross purposes but Kimber saw no reason to enlighten him. "How's Harvey?" he asked.

"None too good. But at least the Scharführer missed him with the shotgun and he's going to make it." Jarrell froze, head tilted on one side to catch the distant wail of a siren. "About time," he muttered.

"You hear that?" Kimber leaned over Halina. "You hear that?" he repeated. "Everything's going to be all right."

But they both knew it was too late.